M000284109

"A deeply reflective book about the resilience of the relationship between two women, which evolves from an innocent childhood friendship to a spiritual kinship that transcends the biology of blood relation. *Village Weavers* is a loving portrait of sisterhood, carefully and skillfully woven. A pleasure to read."

—CHERIE JONES,
author of *How the One-Armed Sister Sweeps Her House*

"Just beautiful! *Village Weavers* is a love story for our times and for all time. In Sisi and Gertie we recognise the timeless tale of a family torn apart by the forces of history but in Chancy's hands it feels new, fresh and uniquely their own. Spanning Haiti, the Dominican Republic, Paris, Florida, Arizona and back again, this is a true Diaspora story—frankly told and sharply contemporary—that speaks into the silences around race, class, colour and the myths of nationhood, while affirming that no matter how far we are drawn apart, it is the sea, the sea that holds us together."

—AYANNA LLOYD BANWO,
author of *When We Were Birds*

"Myriam J. A. Chancy follows up her illustrious novel *What Storm, What Thunder* with a story about two families caught between the histories that bind them. With *Village Weavers*, Chancy becomes a cartographer of the human experience as she navigates issues of race, colonialism, diaspora, and the ways we must redefine ourselves later in our lives. It is a testament to the capacity of the human heart, one that is capable of loving, of yearning and rage, and of living. Chancy pays homage to those estranged and passed as she brilliantly maps out a journey of reclamation. This is a defining work of impressive accomplishment. In the same way Jamaica Kincaid's *Annie John* or Toni Morrison's *Sula* announced before it, Chancy teaches us that it is never too late to reconnect with those we care about, to remember the power of love."

—XAVIER NAVARRO AQUINO,
author of *Velorio*

"Myriam J. A. Chancy's *Village Weavers* is a mesmerizing tale of two young girls, Gertie and Sisi, whose tender relationship is fractured by powerful forces around them—much like Hispaniola, the island they are from. As the young girls become women, we witness Chancy's radiant ability to wrestle with history, class, colorism, and racism, while telling a story that is deeply rooted in love. What the novel ultimately reaches toward, both on a personal and political level, is profoundly moving."

—CLEYVIS NATERA,
author of *Neruda on the Park*

VILLAGE
WEAVERS

ALSO BY MYRIAM J. A. CHANCY

FICTION

What Storm, What Thunder
The Loneliness of Angels
The Scorpion's Claw
Spirit of Haiti

NONFICTION

Harvesting Haiti
Autochthonomies
From Sugar to Revolution
Framing Silence
Searching for Safe Spaces

VILLAGE WEAVERS

✦ ✦ ✦ ✦

A NOVEL

✦ ✦ ✦ ✦

MYRIAM
J. A. CHANCY

TIN HOUSE / PORTLAND, OREGON

Copyright © 2024 by Myriam J. A. Chancy

First US Edition 2024
Printed in the United States of America

Manufacturing by Lake Book Manufacturing
Interior design by Beth Steidle

Library of Congress Cataloging-in-Publication Data

Names: Chancy, Myriam J. A., 1970– author.
Title: Village weavers : a novel / Myriam J.A. Chancy.
Description: Portland, Oregon : Tin House, 2024.
Identifiers: LCCN 2023046077 | ISBN 9781959030379 (hardcover) |
ISBN 9781959030522 (ebook)
Subjects: LCGFT: Novels.
Classification: LCC PR9260.9.C43 V55 2024 | DDC 813/.6—dc23/eng/20231002
LC record available at https://lccn.loc.gov/2023046077

Tin House
2617 NW Thurman Street, Portland, OR 97210
www.tinhouse.com

DISTRIBUTED BY W. W. NORTON & COMPANY

1 2 3 4 5 6 7 8 9 0

for Didine

for Gaby

Then I may tell you that the very next words I read were these—"Chloe liked Olivia . . ." Do not start. Do not blush. Let us admit in the privacy of our own society that these things sometimes happen. Sometimes women do like women.

—VIRGINIA WOOLF,
A Room of One's Own

And God blessed them, saying, "Be fruitful and multiply and fill the waters in the seas, and let birds multiply on the earth."

—GENESIS 1:22

VILLAGE
WEAVERS

SIMBI CALLS

Momo tells Sisi that her village is a place so small and insignificant that it cannot be mapped. If it were, it would not even be
a dot; it would be a speck, impossible to see with the naked eye.
It is a place one finds by following waters and springs that erupt
from the ground miraculously, teeming with unseen life.

They are both sitting on woven stools, low to the ground,
but Momo towers over Sisi. Momo is enveloped in a volumi-
nous white housedress. She reminds Sisi of a goose in one of the
books of fairy tales that her sister, Margie, reads to her from at
night. The white of the dress tucks around Momo's roundness
like a second skin. The paleness of the cloth sets off the mahogany brown of her protruding arms and neck in sharp contrast.
Momo's neck has many folds in it, as many folds as decades she
has lived on this earth.

Sisi pours a scoop of purplish kidney beans from a large burlap sack into a smaller bag, then hands it to Momo to close with
a piece of twine.

"Do you know what a riddle is, Sisi?" Momo asks.

"No," Sisi answers.

"It's a question that has an answer difficult to find."

"Like when Mami wants to know if she will get enough
orders for dresses in the spring to keep us here?"

Momo smiles. "Something like that, but harder. I think that my village is a riddle."

"Your village is a question?"

Momo laughs. "No, but many say that my village does not exist. Yet every year there are girls who come to us from the village, to stay with us. They are coming from somewhere, no? Not a nowhere place. My village is so small they say it does not exist, but it might be the most powerful place on earth."

Sisi frowns. Is Momo's story a riddle too? She watches as her grandmother's hands close the bags Sisi has filled with beans, swiftly turning the twine over and under their gaping openings and pulling it taut into a pucker of fabric, ready to be taken to market.

"We are people of the Simbi, Sisi, of the river gods. People will try to convince you either that they don't exist or that they are evil, but they do exist, and they are not evil. Do you want to hear more?"

Sisi sits awestruck. The best part of any day is this time, when she tries to help Momo as best she can before going to bed and Momo tells her a story. Sometimes the story is a memory; at others, a tale she heard and remembers from her village; and at others, like this time, it will be a story about the *mistè*, the mysteries, the *lwa*, the gods.

"Where I come from," Momo says, "deep, deep in the interior of Haiti, there are flat areas that give way to forests and rivers, gullies with springs, waterfalls. There is plenty for everyone but not a lot of work, which is why we leave that land and all its natural riches to come and toil in the city we find ourselves in now. If we had work, we would never leave, understand?"

Sisi nods, saying nothing, not wanting to interrupt Momo, because saying something can lead Momo to thinking about something else.

"Because of the rivers, the forests, there are also snakes. They are mostly harmless, but some are magical. The snakes are the Simbi coming onto dry land to see what we are up to up here, checking on us to guard us from foolishness, occasionally to warn us. The Simbi cried for a long time during the years that the invaders came from the land above to carve ours up, to tell us where we could and could not go. The snakes poured out of the earth and some of the riverbeds dried up until those men left, but nothing was the same after this. The Simbi warned us, but we did not listen.

"When I was a girl, not much older than you are now, I was the one who went to fetch water from the spring to bring back to the household. I did this every morning, early. I carried the water on my head like my mother taught me to, and I was told to be careful lest the Simbi come for me."

"Come for you? I thought they were protecting you."

Momo wags a finger in the air above them, the twine trailing down it like a wan flag. "The Simbi are capricious. They are hungry spirits that like little children, especially if, like you, they are *clair*, untouched by the sun. Luckily, I sunned myself every day, soaking up the rays and making my skin deep, dark brown like the earth, and the Simbi just let me go by every day, most days. Some other children were said to disappear, never to be recovered. Once, the Simbi took an old blind man, but they returned him, eventually, after restoring his sight."

"A blind man who could see?"

"Yes. When the Simbi take you, they return you with the ability to see, sometimes to see things no one else can, that you could not see before."

"I wish you had been taken. You could tell us about the unseen things."

"I don't know that we should wish for this: it is a lot of responsibility." Momo stops her activity to think.

Sisi waits. Momo takes up the twine and gestures to Sisi to continue filling the small bags between them from the burlap. She wants to take them to market in the morning. "There was a girl in my village who disappeared by the springs once. They said that the Simbi took her but gave her back because she was blessed by the sun. When she returned, she could read the people's dreams. She could heal the sick with her knowledge."

"How can you know if the Simbi come for you?" Sisi asks, filled, unexpectedly, with dread.

"You don't have to be afraid, Sisi."

"How do you know, Momo? How do you know they won't come for me?"

"Well, I cannot know, but what if I told you that that little sun-touched girl that the Simbi took and returned was me? What if I told you that the Simbi released me so that I could tell you that you have nothing to fear?"

"I don't believe you," Sisi says doubtfully. "You don't read dreams."

"Don't I?" Momo stops to think. "I don't, do I? But have you ever asked me to interpret your dreams?"

Sisi shakes her head, no. "What do they look like, the Simbi?"

"No one knows if Simbi are male or female. Some will tell you that Simbi are men, others will tell you Simbi are women. But there are many Simbi, and who knows which Simbi anyone thinks they might know? But I want to tell you about Simbi Andezo, Simbi Two Waters, because I think that she, he—well, maybe we should say 'they'—will be your destiny. Simbi Twin Souls."

Sisi's eyes widen even more.

Momo continues, "Simbi Andezo governs the waters, those of the sea before us and those of the rivers that course through the mountains behind us, forming the waterfalls and all the streams that travel through the land to nourish the rice and grain fields that feed us. Andezo watches over every creature that comes into contact with the waters, making sure that they do not drown or come to harm, unless a greater force wills it, a force greater than the Simbi. The Simbi are invisible and work in secret in the waters, but you can feel them doing their work of watching and protecting every time you step into the water—but watch out! If you come to *see* a Simbi, they might enchant you."

"Enchant me? How?"

"Do you think that a Simbi might want you?" Momo teases.

"I don't know," Sisi replies, "but maybe I don't want to find out!"

Momo laughs a deep, guttural laugh. Sisi loves Momo's stories about the *lwa*.

"Well," Momo continues, amused, "they have long hair like you, Sisi. They sing like the people do in church, like angels. But beware the siren's song. Simbi can save you or enchant you, but only rarely do they do both at the same time."

"Like the Simbi did to you?"

"Like they did to me. Because the Queen of Sheba is my invisible patron saint, a woman dark like me. But the important thing I want you to remember is that Simbi Andezo gains strength from the union of two forces, two sources of water, like twins. All the waters pour from the land into the ocean, but the ocean would be nothing without the rivers that feed it. And, like the Queen, you must not give yourself to the first person to come your way. You must ask them questions, find out who they are. Like the Simbi, you must test the waters, make sure that they are pure of heart."

"Pure of heart," Sisi murmurs.

"Yes, like you." Momo taps Sisi's chest. "You, in here. If you listen to the Simbi but do not fall under their spell, they can teach you how not to fall for the wrong people, the wrong friends, the wrong mate, you understand? You see me here, by myself?"

"You're not alone, Momo. You have Mami and me and Margie."

"Yes, that is true. But you see that I make my way without a *menaj*, is that not true? And your mother sees your papa maybe once a week, but he does not live here, is that not true? We are sources of water for each other. We are like the Simbi."

Sisi looks into Momo's face, hoping she can read the answers to the questions Momo's story stirs in her. But Momo's face closes like the setting sun. The night's darkness deepens.

"Enough storytelling for today," Momo says, all of a sudden looking tired. She pushes the finished bags together and closes the burlap against the remaining purplish beans. "I'll finish this in the morning. Thank you for helping, Sisi. You are a good little helper. Go find your mother, and then off to bed for you."

Sisi does as she is told, then climbs into her bed, where she listens to the murmurs of the house.

As she falls to sleep, the noises swaddling her—her sister's breathing, the shuffling of Momo in her room, her mother's pedaling of the sewing machine into the night—become like lapping waves beneath a pier. She imagines the Simbi swimming by, having made their way down from the gullies in the valleys, the streams in the forests, the waterfalls, the springs carved out by their snakes. She imagines the Simbi calling out to all of them in the house, to warn or to enchant them with their sirens' call.

PART I

BIRDS OF A FEATHER

SISI, PHOENIX, 2002

WHEN THE PHONE CALL THAT INTERRUPTS HER PLANS comes, Simone is missing her older sister, Margie, in a way that seems without proper measure, in the home she built for herself and for her daughter, Emma. Simone could have gone anywhere, as long as she was sure that Emma wasn't too far behind, and Margie could find her easily. She picked Phoenix for the name, for the sun, figured that it was a place where anyone could remake themselves. She planned to move farther north of the city, at some point, to find a place nestled somewhere in Sedona. She and Emma loved to get away to the copper-rust hues of the rock formations there, but the red of the soil reminded her of the island where both she and Margie were born but didn't return, because there was so little left there for either of them, so she stayed put in the condo. Ten years ago, she began to tell people, when asked, that she was native to Arizona, like a saguaro. She wanted to grow old in the desert and, like the saguaro, have her skeleton repurposed for shelter. When the three of them were together, Emma and Margie laughed when Simone told this lie to strangers. They reminded her that she was more raven or owl, making her nest in the hollow of a dried-out saguaro limb, or a fox, sucking its flesh for water, crossing the desert.

The phone rings, and for a moment, lost in thought, Simone imagines that it will be Margie on the line. As she looks outside, a yellow butterfly comes around the bushes on her walkout patio and advances toward the window that separates her studio from the outside. It taps itself lightly against the pane of glass, twice, and Simone's heart lights up: a message from Margie.

It is with this thought in mind that she picks up the phone, not expecting to hear the voice she does on the other end, looking at the yellow butterfly, thinking of home.

There is a pause Simone does not know how to fill, followed by Gertie's torrent of words about the distant past, the need to pass on information, to make sure that all concerned have all the pieces of the puzzle in hand, et cetera, et cetera. Simone listens to Gertie say that she is ill. She listens, but none of the information comes together. Her whole life is a struggle to reassemble strangely shaped episodes, pieces of a jigsaw turned out of their box, making little sense until each piece has found its place in the whole. She is tired of puzzles, of puzzling.

By now, Simone has weathered her own health scares. She always had an urgent sense of the need for vigilance, to look out for herself, for Emma especially, since Emma's adoption was closed and her daughter never showed any strong desire to know much about where she came from beyond Simone and Scott. For the most part, biology was not something that their family of three thought a lot about. Instead, Simone opted for what she called a "set of best practices." She took Emma in for her recommended milestone checkups as a toddler and took herself in for all the recommended exams throughout her life and ensured that Scott did the same, when she had influence, before things started to fall apart. The fragile state of her marriage kept her from returning to Haiti, which was in its own vulnerable state. She longs to go back to Port-au-Prince, to pilgrimage to the Rue Bonne Foi to see if the house in which she and her sister were raised is still standing. The last time she saw the house, it stood leaning forward into the shadowed street, boarded up, like so many houses were throughout the port area before their owners departed, as they had, for foreign shores. At that time, all she could think as the car barreled past was *Peyi la, li krasé*—the country is crumbling. Peasants who traveled from rural areas with all their hope in two hands came to make a go of settling in the bloated capital. Many had set up stalls to resell items made abroad or themselves fashioned artisanal objects to sell on the side of the road to tourists, a diminishing currency in the capital. The country was always on a slippery slope, descending, no peaks and valleys, no possibility of rising from the ashes.

Simone listens to Gertie tell her about her current health issues, the cancer that it is hoped was eradicated with a total hysterectomy. Simone imagines the pain, winces inwardly as she listens, though she doesn't utter a sound, no words of consolation. She can't muster them, she who is so used to cajoling and consoling. Maybe it is the surprise of hearing Gertie so many years since they last talked; maybe it is the shock of being spoken to about intimate things, as if they were still what they once were to each other.

Her thoughts stray from Gertie on the phone. She thinks about when she discovered, with Scott, that they wouldn't be having any children of their own; she'd wondered at the time why a total hysterectomy had not been an option. She'd wanted *everything* taken out. She'd wanted to become neutered, neutral, to be somehow beyond the stage of life in which the hope of conceiving, of birthing a child, resided. Then there was Emma, all curls and sunshine, gingerbread brown and carefree at two years of age. They fell in love with her and then fell back in love with each other; it had been that simple, and the anger at her empty womb evaporated. She took comfort in the fact that she didn't have to think too much about her period anymore, that there was no chance that she would fall pregnant accidentally. She went along, as most women did, with the exams every two years, and early, in her midforties, she went into perimenopause and that was that. She was relieved that the process was all over by the time she hit fifty, relieved that Emma's presence made her feel whole, though she knew she shouldn't have needed that. Emma's brown skin and her own almond tones made it plausible that she was her biological mother. She doesn't correct strangers when they assume.

Her mind returns to Gertie still talking on the other end of the line. Simone wants the conversation to be over, to get back to her work. It would be convenient if old age could be just that, unburdened with illness, operations, Simone thinks.

"Is Manuella with you?" Simone musters the effort to ask, to break her silence, to say something, anything, so she won't come across as cold as she feels.

"Yes, yes, she is," Gertie scrambles to respond. It is clear from the exhilaration in her voice as she answers that she hopes Simone has more questions, that her quiet reflects shock at the news. It doesn't seem to occur to Gertie that her voice alone, not the news that it carries, is shock enough.

Simone realizes that she is caught up in the stress and panic of the present moment. She thinks solely of how things were left after what, in the end, had been a disastrous trip back to the island—not to Haiti but to the Dominican Republic—a little more than twenty years prior. After that, they rarely spoke. Their river of conversation turned into the odd drip from a badly plumbed sink. She should never have gone on that trip. So many things had gone wrong.

It's too late, Simone is thinking, when Gertie cuts in. "Are you there, Sisi?"

"Yes," Simone responds, but she is, in fact, far away. "Can I call you back?"

Gertie pauses. "Yes, of course." She blunders apologetically. "It's been so long. I wasn't thinking. I just thought I should tell you what was happening with me, in case—"

"We're no longer children, Gertrude. You don't need to try to protect me. I'm taking care of myself."

"Yes, yes, that's true."

They both listen to the echoing chasm between them.

Simone breaks the silence. "I'm glad that Ella is there. I'll call her when I have more to say so as not to disturb you. She has my number, doesn't she?" She stalls. "Or she can text me with your results . . . if you want to share them."

"You won't be disturb—" Gertie says hurriedly, but Simone doesn't hear the end of her sentence though she can guess after it: she has already put the receiver down.

Simone wants to move on, to return to her drawings and paintings, simpler things. Gertie is not a simple thing, simple person, simple anything. There is, first of all, the matter of their mothers. Simone can't remember Gertie's mother speaking to her own at church, for instance, which was the place, outside of school, where most families met, if they did at all, although it is true that Gertie's mother was rarely in town. Once Simone saw the inside of Gertie's house, she suspected she knew one reason for the wedge between them. Unlike hers, Gertie's home was refined, modern. Gertie's had running water and toilets that flushed; they used rainwater barrels only in cases of emergency. Water wasn't brought in from a well. The reality of this difference struck Simone as a child like a slap in the face once Gertie stopped talking to her, seemingly overnight. Until then, they had been the best of friends, inseparable from the moment they met in first grade.

Despite their differences, their estrangement, and physical distance, Simone recognizes, reluctantly, that Gertie is her oldest friend. Maybe "friend" is pushing it since they haven't been in touch for decades. How can she reconcile having known Gertie most of her life with Gertie's call now? They are both old. What would be the point of renewing the connection?

Simone smolders with indecision. She is perplexed by the phone call, angered that it was not the voice she hoped to hear, will never hear again. Angry that, at the same time, even as she hung up the phone on Gertie, she had a desire to undo her action, pick the phone back up again, erase the years she has gone without hearing that voice she knows so well.

When she was a child, Gertie's voice made her feel safe, welcome. Simone came to resent it the moment it disappeared in what seemed an irrevocable betrayal of their friendship. She doesn't know if she has the trust in her to spare, to reopen this door.

PORT-AU-PRINCE, 1941

The first time Simone meets Gertie, she is drawing quietly at her desk when Gertie comes up behind her, breathes down her neck the way a child does, without self-consciousness. Simone flicks her ponytail across her neck and down her clavicle toward the warm breath cascading over her shoulder, as if to push Gertie away. She will forever be pushing Gertie back: it is instinct.

"*Sa w'ap fe la?* What are you doing?" Gertie demands. "*Se yon poul?* Are you drawing a hen?"

A hen? Simone is drawing a rooster, the one Momo keeps in the backyard and covets as if it were made of gold. There are hens, too, of course; they strut around the deep end of their yard in their golden plumage, with reddish combs and equally reddish, fleshy jowls flapping from their beaks as they hold their heads high toward the sky. Embarrassed, Simone covers her drawing with crossed arms—hoping that Gertie will go away. They are seven. It's as if she has been in school forever.

Simone is bored by the rituals of getting ready for school, walking there with her older sister, attending the classes, reciting, taking dictation, waiting for others to muster up the courage to answer the teacher, waiting for something to happen.

Nothing ever happens. But here is something—no, someone—who might disrupt the boredom, yet out of reflex, Simone wants her calm restored.

"*Ou ka we yon poul lakay mwen*," Gertie offers, undeterred. "I live not far." She points toward an imposing house across the avenue from the school, an old gingerbread house that was probably erected there in the days the island was a French colony. "You can see hens and a rooster there."

"OK," Simone mutters. She wonders if Gertie will really take her over to her house, and when.

She doesn't have to wait long. Gertie comes up to her during the lunch break, when everyone has eaten and is playing in the schoolyard, waiting for classes to start up again for the afternoon. "*On y va?*" she asks in a whisper, not waiting for an answer, motioning for Simone to follow her.

It is Simone's first year of school, and the thought of escape has not yet dawned on her, but perhaps she would feel differently if she lived across the street and could go home to see Mami and Momo, curl up to have a nap whenever she liked. Sitting in place for long hours isn't her idea of fun, and no one pays attention to her because it is known that she is a charity case. No one has to say a word. It is written on her clothes, the wear of them, the faded blue and red of the school colors and the restitched hems telltale signs that they are hand-me-downs, that her family cannot afford new school clothes for her every year. Some of the uniforms were her sister's, others offered by the nuns. Her mother lovingly repairs them so they look like new, but still, the other girls point out which were theirs whenever they can. *Look, she's wearing my skirt, my jumper, my dress*, they titter. Simone pretends not to hear. The other girls assume that she is at the school as the ward of a wealthy benefactor, but the reality is that her mother and grandmother make sure that all the school fees are paid, even if they have to work into the weekends to make extra money to send Margie and her to what are considered the best schools in this part of Port-au-Prince. It never bothered Simone before. As her mother always said, if you can get three generations of use out of a piece of clothing, you should, and there is no shame in making do with something that has been owned by someone else.

They too pass on to others what they can no longer use. When any one of them gets a new pair of shoes, Simone's mother makes sure that they look to see if they have a pair that they can give away. They make sure that the shoes they are giving are scrubbed and polished. After everyone goes to bed, the house boy—who is not a boy at all but a young man who guards the house, does odd jobs, and cleans the yard morning and night but doesn't go to school anymore—sets them in a row, as if on display in a store, against the brick of the outside wall at the front gate beyond the house. The next morning, they rush to the wall and find all the shoes gone as if angels have come and taken them back into the heavens to shoe the errant spirits that Momo says walk at night. Simone imagines the shoes making their way across the city, leading new lives. That's why she didn't think she would mind wearing the hand-me-down uniforms to school. But when the other girls point and whisper about the faded colors, she feels a shame she did not know she could possess.

Gertie leads Simone around the long porch that girds the entire first floor and into the concrete yard sloping away from the porch behind it. There, they find many hands at work preparing the evening meal. They watch as frowning women with wrapped hair and wide aprons tied around their waists move through the yard with baskets against their thighs or stand guard against large silver cauldrons set atop burning pits. Those cooking on the open hearths make requests of the others, who scurry to find the spice, herb, or vegetable requested, which is then placed into a gently simmering pot. Two of the women sit on a stoop below the porch and split open fresh bean pods, using their skirts to make bowls of cloth in which they catch the oval legumes before twisting the edge of each side of the fabric to gently tip out the contents into a wooden bowl. The beans are then gathered by a heavyset woman Simone assumes is the head cook, as she goes in and out of a kitchen below the house and seems to orchestrate the movements of the household workers as a conductor would a symphony. Simone has almost forgotten why she is there when Gertie points with her free hand across the yard. "There," she says, "there's Marguerite."

Simone startles at the mention of her older sister's full name. She follows the tip of Gertie's finger and sees a gathering of hens on the other side of the yard, pecking at a patch of yellowed grass. The hens are undisturbed by the human activity animating the yard as they gather their own meal.

"That one in the middle, the one with the golden throat." Gertie points once more. "That's Marguerite. She's mine. She came out of an egg, and I've had her ever since."

Simone is astounded. A hen all her own. She is impressed. It is funny to think of her sister as a hen, but Margie is often distracted, as hens are, busy at her own occupations all day long, dreaming about the day she will leave Haiti. The coincidence makes Simone feel closer to Gertie, as if the hen's name being the same as her sister's connects them somehow. Might they really become good friends?

"Let's get closer," Gertie says, dragging Simone around the circumference of the yard toward the brood of hens.

As they are about to reach the hens, Simone catches a blur of light blue flashing past them. The blue is a shirt and in it is a boy larger than them both and at the end of one of his arms is a cutlass. The blade glints from the glare of the midday sun. The boy swings the blade over their heads. Simone screams, and Gertie lets go of her hand. Simone holds up an arm above her head, to protect herself from the blade, then hears a sound like a gust of wind being cut through and a thwack as it meets flesh and bone not hers. She hears a screech, then a squawk, the flap of wings. The acrid smell of chicken droppings wafts up as the hens scatter, then a wet sprinkle falls onto her raised forearm like dew, like a rainfall announcing itself, drops falling from the sky tentatively, one by one, before a storm. Simone lowers her arm and sees the boy with the cutlass chasing down the headless chicken.

"*Poukisa ou pa te pwan li, timoun?* Why didn't you grab hold of it?" one of the women in the yard is yelling at the boy. "*Pral gen san toupatou, tou-pa-tou!* Blood everywhere!" she exclaims, as she continues shucking green beans into her bowled skirts. "*Ou pral netway sa, ou tandem, ti gason?* You'll be the one cleaning up, boy, not me." Then she spots Gertie and Simone. "*Ti moun, vin ici.* Girls, come here," she says, "*vin ici.* Here," gesticulating for them to get out of the fray, out of the way of the house boy, who is going about his work frantically, as if he has never done it before. Later, Gertie will explain that he is new to the household. He, of course, didn't know that one of the chickens was hers and was to be spared.

The boy is ignoring the woman, trying to catch the headless bird, which runs out of steam, falls over, shudders, and gives a last, futile kick of its feet into the air.

"He killed Marguerite," says Gertie matter-of-factly.

Simone is speechless, dazed. Marguerite is a chicken, not her sister. Gertie doesn't seem heartbroken over the loss. Simone draws a deep breath. Just a chicken. But doesn't naming a chicken mean that it has value, like family? Simone can't bear the thought of losing anything she holds dear.

"He could have taken another one." Gertie frowns, both hands fisted against her hips. "That was my chicken." The other chickens have flailed away from the scene and are hiding in the taller grasses along the back fence of the yard, as if they have seen all this before, know that one day, it will be their turn. Simone feels for them. Better not to be named, she thinks. Gertie shrugs. "I'll have to get another one," she says.

A woman approaches them from the top of the yard. She is wiping down her skirts so that they fall about her like rose petals in rough layers that contour her rounded hips. "*Kisa wap fè la?* What are you doing here?" she reproaches Gertie. "*E kiyès sa a ye?* And who is this girl? *Li gen san poul sou li.* She got blood splattered on her. *Vin isi pou'm ka ede'l.* Come here so I can help her with that."

Simone lets herself be stirred by Gertie and the woman to a spigot at the back of the yard. There, the woman shows her the blood splatter, little red flecks that fan across the arm she held up above her head. "*Sa pa fè anyen.* No worries," the woman says. "*Yon ti benediksyon.* It's just a little blessing." She smiles. She is missing her two front teeth, Simone notes, making her seem much younger than she is. The missing teeth comfort Simone. She smiles back, but she is ready for the afternoon to be over.

"Don't worry," Gertie says, patting Simone's free arm. "We're going right back. They won't even know we left." She turns to the woman. "*Nou pral tounen lekol to dwat.* We'll go right back to school."

The woman makes a noise as if she is sucking her teeth, but it comes out a whistle. "OK," she says, as if she is used to Gertie doing what she likes. "*Se pa mwen ki manman ou.* I'm not your mother."

Gertie laughs with her head back. Her laughter is high-pitched and throaty, Simone thinks, rising out from her diaphragm as if she were a red-throated tody, the little birds distinctive for their bright green heads and the long, fine beaks they use to retrieve small insects from flowers and leaves. Todies chatter in clumps close to their nests and make a lot of noise.

When they have nothing else to do, they clean their feathers in such a way that it sounds as if they are strumming the teeth of a hair comb.

Simone knows she will remember that first laugh emanating from Gertie's small body forever. She will remember Gertie smiling and laughing raucously, and later, much later, she will marvel at the discovery that emerald green is, indeed, Gertie's color, deepening the nutmeg brown of her skin to a warm, reddish-amber tone. Seven-year-old Simone is simultaneously awed and mortified: two feelings she will come to associate with Gertie always.

By the time they leave the yard, three more chickens have been slaughtered for dinner. Business associates of Gertie's father are coming to the house that evening, along with Gertie's mother, who is being driven in from Léogâne to stay into the weekend. Everything must be perfect now that the mistress of the house is descending. When she isn't in Port-au-Prince, Gertie explains, everything is much more relaxed, which is one of the reasons no one pays much attention to what Gertie does or doesn't do, except when her oldest sister, Andrée, comes around, as she always does, to check on things, though she has a family of her own now. Gertie is much younger than her other siblings, some of whom, like Andrée, are married and out of their parents' homes. Simone's home life, by contrast, is so much quieter, busy but quiet, money tight and dinners lean. There are rules to follow: Mami and Momo see after that. There are no luxuries like seaside or mountain homes, holidays away, or dinner parties for business associates.

Simone and Gertie return to the schoolyard in a hurry and slip into the games underway. As soon as they reappear, Gertie's friends act as if they have never truly seen Simone before when Gertie introduces her as "Sisi," a nickname that Simone is called only at home and that she hasn't shared with Gertie. It is a nickname she will carry all her life, in spaces in which no one knows of her connection to Haiti, even less of her connection to Gertie.

Sisi thinks about this as she changes out of her school clothes that night and spots a fleck of blood at the bottom of her skirt hem. It is almost imperceptible, a round droplet against a red thread. She goes to the bathroom basin and tries to rub it out, but the red outline of the droplet becomes more pronounced, clear against the blue of the surrounding madras. Only she will know that it is there: no one else will notice. She stuffs the dress into the dirty clothes bag that hangs on a peg by the side of the door of the bedroom she shares with her older sister: it will be cleaned and fade in time, but she will not forget.

That night, Sisi refuses her grandmother's grilled pork, a dish that takes three days to make and longer to plan for since meat is not cheap. She hates to refuse it but all she can think about as it is served is the spray of blood against her forearm that midday in Gertie's yard, how the droplets turned into pink rivulets against her skin as the cook in the yard wiped down her arms with a kitchen cloth until the hairs on her forearm glistened in the sun, the futility of the hen as it fought for a life already taken.

GERTIE, MIAMI, 2002

GERTRUDE IS DREAMING. SHE IS FLYING, HER ARMS extended into the air on both sides of her body, slicing through the warmth enveloping her like a chrysalis. But she is no butterfly: she is a blackbird in flight, able to make her body swoop, dive, turn at will with just a glance toward the direction in which she wants to go. She knows that it is night from the inky-blue shade of the sky before her, as she slices through billowing cloud formations. She maneuvers herself down, down, to see land, the island she knows is below. She courses through the air over the rivers tracing pathways through forest and plain, follows them to waterfalls and springs. She hears humming coming from the waters, a lullaby to put children to sleep. Other blackbirds are coming toward her from far away, and she experiences a surge of happiness at the sight of them, as they draw closer. She knows them, feels a familiarity that reminds her of childhood. Soon, they swoop together over rivers, following the movement out toward the ocean. But as the city flanked by the sea comes into view, Gertie falters. The other birds fall away, back toward the interior of the island. Gertie's wings fold and she plummets through the air. She is falling, a body among other celestial bodies, the stars, and soon she falls past mountaintops, trees, brush. Just as she fears the ground will break her fall, a softness gathers her up. She awakes with a jolt.

At first, Gertie thinks she is in her bed at home, but when she opens her eyes to look around her, she sees that she is in the hospital and Manuella, her daughter, named for Gertie's husband, Manuel, is hovering over her, nodding at her, with the satchel of clothes Gertie asked her to bring from home by her side. Discharge time. Gertie winces at the pain around her midsection. She cannot wait to get home, to regroup and recover, to put this ordeal behind her. Gertie's mind is on the phone call with Sisi.

"I don't understand," she says to Ella, perplexed. "I think it was the briefest call we've ever had. She didn't ask for details. Nothing. I found her cold. Very cold."

"But you haven't spoken in so long, Mom," Ella says. "That's to be expected. The important thing is that you reached out."

Gertie shrugs as Ella maneuvers her mother's arms into a loose blouse Gertie packed for the morning of her discharge. Though it will be hours before they are let go, Gertie wants to be ready as soon as possible, in case the doctors will let her leave the hospital early. She is fretting about everything she wasn't able to do before the surgery, from spring cleaning to setting up her cat stations to filing her taxes to making sure that Ella can find her will and other papers in case something goes wrong. Gertie has two cats, two rescues, that—next to her daughter, Ella—are her whole heart: Zuli, a calico, and Fredi, a black cat from head to toe, even the roof of his mouth.

"You have to think about yourself first," Ella continues, "but your mental health is also important. Calling Sisi is about healing that part of your life, so you're strong enough to face the rest of what you'll need to."

Two of Gertie's older sisters have died of cancer. She hasn't asked her brother if he has anything. Rico is more secretive or doesn't speak of such things. Uterine or breast cancer is seen as shameful, a sign of feminine deformity or weakness, though it is neither. Telling everyone means telling not just those in the family but Sisi, and others too. How many others, she isn't sure.

Ella eyes her mother with concern. She knows that Gertie has a habit of putting everyone else before herself, even if it causes her harm to do so, the evidence of which is the fact that she is in this hospital, coming out of a surgery that might have been avoided had she been paying more attention to the signs that something was going wrong, paying attention to that person closest to her: herself. Gertie ignored the cramping, the spotting, her belly growing rounder even as she ate less and less, for months, maybe years, until it was almost too late, and Ella urged her to make an appointment, get an ultrasound. The news was inevitable: cancer. It runs in the family like blood in the veins. When Gertie's OB-GYN delivered the news, Ella's eyes vacillated between being dewy with compassion and steely with anger: Gertie should have known better, those eyes said, given the family history. All Gertie's older sisters had had some form of cancer—breast, uterine, ovarian. Why Gertie had thought she would be any different, Ella didn't know and didn't care.

"Just think of what Papa would say," Ella continues, alluding to her father, Gertie's husband, who has been gone some fifteen years. "He would have wanted you to square things away with her, to have your conscience clear."

They fall silent. Manuel died unexpectedly, of a heart attack. There had been no time for planning, for goodbyes, none at all. He was there one minute and gone the next. Nearly thirty years of marriage ended, just like that, in the snap of a finger.

"But I'm always making the first step when it comes to Sisi. Sometimes that hasn't helped matters, just made things worse." She is thinking of the call she made when their daughters were teenagers, the call that reconnected them after years of living outside Haiti, estranged, the call that brought them back together for a reunion that ended in disaster.

Ella shrugs. "It's better than not trying."

Gertie's blouse slips over her aching belly. They will have to return for an outpatient procedure, to remove the staples holding together the seams where her stomach was opened. The rest of the stitches will dissolve over time, disintegrate into her flesh. Gertie pats Ella's arm. "You may be right. I don't know." She smiles up into her daughter's face. "But you'll be there to help along the way."

Gertie concedes that she needs the help for the time being, if only for taking care of Zuli and Fredi. She is not ready to admit that she needs care herself despite the fear that has grown since her OB-GYN told her that the intermittent spotting that started on a recent visit to Ella in New York was not a postmenopausal accident but a sign of uterine cancer. Since, she dreamed of dying in surgery, hovering above her body, never returning to it. There was so much left undone. So much to repair.

"Papa would have told you to make amends," Ella says, once the last nurse has been by to arrange her discharge, the operation that has taken what is left of her reproductive system away having been deemed successful, "that you'd live to regret it if you didn't." Gertie wonders if Manuel uttered those same words to Ella when she needed them most, when she needed to break away from her mother in order to live her own life, when Gertie refused to come around, accept her for who she was. And here is Ella doing what needs to be done, sitting quietly, standing when the doctors come in, all six feet of her, in contrast to her and Manuel, both of them small in stature, making up for their height in personality. They joked that they were cane-cutting stock, short, muscular, bound to the ground, but Gertie has a distinct memory of her father as a tall man, taller than most; and her only brother, Rico, who remains in the DR, is quite tall. Ella must have taken after her father's side of the family. Ella intervenes when needed, asks all the right questions like a dutiful daughter, though in the past Ella has been anything but dutiful. She is hardheaded, like Gertie herself. Like Sisi. Like all of them. She might not have grown up on the island, but she is of the land, like the rest of them.

Gertie knows without Ella having to tell her so that Manuel would have wanted her to make up with Sisi, the same way that he tried to make her see Sisi's point of view after that ill-fated trip they took to the DR, their daughters in tow. Nothing should have gone wrong. Yet it did. At the time, Gertie thought Sisi would get over it, that their differences of opinion about the island, about their families, would dilute over time, but Sisi didn't get over it, had too long a memory, and their differences, if Gertie could call them that, became stronger, pungent, like a black tea left too long to steep, embittered. Manuel understood before she reasoned it out for herself that the fight with Sisi had everything to do with a longer history, but Gertie was jealous of Sisi's ability to connect with Ella. After their fight, it was Manuel who said to her, "You're really angry at Ella, but it's easier to cast Sisi out, isn't it?" He sighed, adding, "You know you'll regret it, Gertie, you'll live to regret it."

The call to Sisi was briefer than she'd hoped. Sisi didn't ask questions to find out more about the situation, didn't ask Gertie if she needed anything or what she could do to help, didn't act as if the information could be of any vital nature to her at all. Sisi didn't seem to care. Gertie wants her to, even if they haven't spoken in decades. They were girls together, weren't they? The bitterness remained like effluent from an old trash heap, of which there were many accumulating by the sides of roadways in the capital they both used to call home. Old business can stink like that, have the smell of garbage.

Gertie stared at the receiver for some time after the call ended, listening to the deafening silence left in its wake. Now, she turns the conversation over and over like a stone in her mind, trying to understand if the door has been opened or permanently closed.

What they said, and did not say, lies there like a weight. Whether the door was opened or closed, she loved hearing Sisi's voice again. They have aged, but their voices are the same. The past seems far behind them yet not so far that Gertie can forget what it was like to be children together, what it was like to enter Sisi's house back then, in what seems now to have been an accident of fortune.

PORT-AU-PRINCE, 1941

Gertie knows that her older sisters, Yvonne and Fidélia, are having dresses made for a ball. There are balls for girls of the middle to upper classes, and every so often, dresses must be made. Sisi's mother has a reputation for being able to make dresses as fine as those coming out of France. She doesn't need a pattern to make them. She takes the client's measurements, shows them fabrics that will complement their coloring and figure, and the dress is delivered within weeks, made to measure and fitting perfectly. Gertie's father is going to check on the seamstress's progress when Gertie is left in his charge a few weeks after she and Sisi escaped from the schoolyard in search of a hen. Gertie's older sisters are in Léogâne by the sea, with their mother, and can't be bothered. Gertie's mother said she wanted an extended break, from everything, from Gertie. Gertie has a fever and has been left behind, to be tended by the house staff. Papa is used to having children, not taking care of them. Gertie knows that much by now, at seven years old; the youngest of six is often left behind. Papa has a funny way with children: he loves them, but he doesn't pay them much mind, especially the girls, until they reach a certain age and can be shown off or taken to balls, or betrothed, securing his legacy. Gertie's father has a will to multiply, and his children are there to ensure that he will never truly die.

Gertie's mother has told Papa to check on the dresses for Gertie's sisters, but he has somewhere else to be later this evening, and, not wanting to leave Gertie with the house help, though this is what her mother would have done, he takes Gertie along with him on the errand, stopping at Sisi's house before his final destination. Sisi and Margie are still at school.

There is an imposing portrait of a light-skinned man in the foyer of Sisi's house, a two-story made of wood, not as elaborate as their gingerbread. The man in the portrait wears a suit with a vest, a gold watch chain hanging from one of the vest pockets. He half smiles, as if he knows a secret that only he understands. Gertie assumes he is Sisi's father.

She is left alone in the vestibule as her father talks to Sisi's mother in the kitchen.

"What is she doing here?" she overhears Sisi's mother asking.

"It's just the one night," her father says. "I have another appointment."

"What kind of appointment, Frédéric? Like when you pass by here on Thursday evenings? Isn't it enough that I'm making the dresses for your daughters? Why do you want to humiliate me like this?"

"Why do you take everything so personally, Marie-Rose? This is not personal. And she's a child. Her mother isn't home, and you know how I am with children."

Sisi's mother guffaws. "Do I know how you are with children? Yes, I do. That's why you can't leave her here."

"Come on," her father says. "No one needs to know."

"But we'll know, me and my mother. And the children, what about them? The girl: *she'll* know." Gertie knows that "the girl" is her. She feels the room spinning around her.

"It's the one night. You'll take better care of her than the house servants, who already think I'm a no-account."

"What do you care what they think, Rico? It's your house."

Papa sighs. "You know well that it's *her* house, and she knows about everything that goes on there. This is why I need to get away."

"You could try to take care of the girl yourself this once."

Gertie imagines her father gesticulating the way he always does when a situation is beyond him. The gesture is usually followed by his picking up his hat, his jacket, and his keys and leaving the house.

"I need to go," he says. "I told you I have an appointment. She'll be better by morning. They're always better by morning. I'll get her on my way home, in the afternoon." He pauses. "Someone will get her." He vacillates. "And I'll owe you something. Whatever you want."

There is a long silence. Marie-Rose responds but Gertie doesn't hear more because, in the next moment, the whole room sways before her eyes and she is falling from a great height. She closes her eyes, and seconds later, her body thuds against the planks of the polished wood floor. Everything swirls around her. She hears footsteps running toward her; then hands are carrying her away, stripping her of her dress, rubbing her with something that makes her skin prickle, makes her skin feel cool while something within her burns slowly, like smoldering coal. It is her father. She feels his strong hands on her back.

"She needs to stay here," he says decisively, seemingly to no one at all; then his hands disappear from her body and she is left there, beneath layers of covers, on a thin mattress, feeling hot and cold all at once, a fire inside, refusing to go out.

When she awakes, later, she is tucked into a foreign but comfortable bed and Sisi is looking down on her with a damp, cool cloth in her hand. Sisi smiles at her in a way that vaguely reminds her of Papa at the breakfast table earlier that day. She cannot quite put her finger on it except that they both have a dimple in their right cheek, in the same place.

"*Ça va?*" Sisi asks, concern in her hazel eyes. "Are you feeling better?"

Gertie nods. "*M'pa pi mal.* I'm not so bad." Then: "What happened?"

"You fainted," Sisi says. "I didn't see you faint. That's what we were told. You had a fever when you came here and Mami put you to bed in our room"—she gestures across the bed—"Marguerite's and mine. Margie, my sister," she clarifies, but Gertie doesn't make the connection. Gertie stares at Sisi, who continues, "I found you here after school. You've been sleeping for hours. You missed dinner, but there's some left if you're hungry." Sisi looks expectantly into Gertie's face.

"And Papa?" Gertie asks, propping herself up in the bed. She remembers why they came. "The dresses for my sisters?"

Sisi shrugs. "No one was here but you when we got back from school. Mami says they'll come get you later in the day tomorrow. It's Saturday, so they'll take their time." She adds, "If you feel better by morning, we'll take you on our walk, OK?"

Gertie nods, though she doesn't know what walk Sisi is talking about. Anything sounds better than the pounding in her head.

Sisi senses Gertie's disarray and plunges the cloth she is holding back into a chipped enamel bowl filled with lukewarm water. She squeezes the cloth over the bowl and brings it to Gertie's face as she saw Mami do earlier that night. "There, there," she coos, imitating her mother.

Gertie feels like crying. She can't remember the last time she was cared for in this way.

"I'll tell Mami that you're awake. You can have broth if you feel better." Sisi smiles from ear to ear, without guile, without fear, her true self shining through, the dimple in her right cheek deepening like an impression left by fingers deflating a freshly risen dough. Their friendship is in the first stages of bloom.

Even though she is tired, Gertie rises with the rest of the household the next morning. Sisi has explained that Saturday is the one day of the week when her family is all in the same place, together, and Gertie, who doesn't have a family that likes to spend time together, doesn't want to miss a minute of what family life could be like.

"Should we wake your grandmother?" she asks Sisi, spotting Sisi's grandmother still asleep in the adjoining room.

"No," Sisi whispers back as her sister, Margie, signals them to be quiet and shut the door to Momo's room. "She sleeps in on Saturday. It's the one day she has off all week."

Sisi explains that Momo rarely joins the family on their Saturday morning rituals, tired from a long week of going to market. She rests and prepares for the new week on Sunday afternoon, after the family returns from Mass, which Momo doesn't attend. Gertie's eyes betray her incredulity: Doesn't attend church? She has never heard of such a thing. She can't wait to be all grown up so she can skip church too and sleep in on Saturday mornings. Gertie and Sisi giggle as they hear the grandmother snoring lightly.

After Margie shushes them past Momo's door, they brush their teeth and perform a quick birdbath, as Sisi calls it, pouring clean well water from a jug into a basin installed in a wooden frame that serves as a sink in the absence of plumbing. Like birds, they spill all around the basin, staining the floorboards, which are beginning to warp from the exposure to damp, their arms flailing like wings straining for flight.

"*Allons-y!*" Margie exclaims as the girls scramble to get dressed and follow her to the ground floor of the house. "Let's go!"

"*Vous êtes prêtes?* Ready?" Sisi's mother asks. "*Wap bon pou ou.* It will be good for you," she says to Gertie. "*Ou bizwin respire le lanme.* You need sea air."

"*Wi*," says Sisi, nodding.

"Oui," says Gertie, feeling the anticipation of the morning growing large within her.

"Na we ou pita, Mami. We'll see you later," Margie responds. *"Pa enkyete'w. Mpral fe menm jan nou toujou fe.* I'll do the same as usual. Don't worry."

"OK, Margie," Sisi's mother says, already preoccupied with other things in the kitchen. *"Nou pral we you pou manje maten a.* See you at breakfast. I'll get everything ready." She turns her back, signaling her complete confidence in Margie, and then they are off, out of the yard and into the streets.

The group walks down to the port to watch the sun rise over the docks. The streets are empty, save for the occasional vendor peddling cut melons, freshly picked yellow-fleshed avocados, morning porridges, and large sheets of manioc crackers that have been made into sandwiches, slathered with spicy peanut butter. Margie holds each girl by the hand, and they watch her exchange pleasantries with the peddlers. Gertie marvels at the warmth Sisi's sister emanates, the way she protects them and keeps them close. Gertie looks up into Margie's face, the sides of her cheeks resembling the wide curve of the banana leaf, the hue of her skin the deep brown of mahogany. Margie seems genuinely happy, and Gertie is in awe of the teen's unvarnished pleasantness. How different she seems from Gertie's sisters!

When they reach the docks, they sit in a row at the far end of one of the piers, feet dangling between the edge of the wooden platform and the space above the roiling waves bringing the salt water to the edge of their world. They can see the sweep of the ocean unfurling itself into a horizon beyond which it is impossible to imagine themselves, beyond which they cannot yet imagine venturing. After a moment of looking out, Margie tells them to sit tight while she goes to walk below the dock, close to the water lapping upon the broken rocks that collect beneath the mooring posts.

"Hey," they hear her yelling out to fishermen who look to be about Margie's age, cleaning their nets. "*Koman pwason yo e?* Are the fish biting?"

Gertie and Sisi watch Margie walk toward the young men. She holds her sandals in one hand and with the other gathers up her skirt in a clutch of cloth by her knees. The fishermen are clad in cutoff shorts and salt water–faded T-shirts. They hear Margie ask the fishermen if they are returning or just heading out. The responses of the young men are swept away by the winds and the swishing sound of the waves coming up onto the shore beneath. Gertie and Sisi hear snatches of words here and there, then robust male laughter, raucous and sharp like marbles falling when thrown against one another in a yard game. They hear Margie's quieter laugh bouncing up occasionally. Margie seems afraid of nothing. Soon, they see her bounding back toward them while some of the young men continue the work of pulling in their catch and others repair holes in the netting.

Margie is breathing heavily, happily, as she sits with Gertie on one side and Sisi on the other. "*Gade*," she says, "*gade*." She points to the horizon. Ribbons of red and orange streak the sky vertically as the sun rises. They sit quietly together for a good quarter hour before breaking the magic spell of the dawn.

"I never tire of this," Margie says to neither girl in particular. "Girls, you have to remember this, all right? One day, you might leave here and never come back, so remember every detail as if you won't ever see it again." She looks to both sides of her, at Sisi, then at Gertie. "I'm very serious about this."

Gertie glances at Sisi and Sisi back at her, past Margie, whose hands are folded against her chest as if holding a rosary. Margie is ten years older than they are, twice as tall, and all the older boys at the high school seek her favor while she ignores them.

"*Kiyes li panse li ye?*" Gertie has heard her older sisters say about Margie. "Who does she think she is?" "*Li panse li se yon renne.* She thinks she's a queen," Andrée, the oldest, said to the next oldest, Altagracia. "*Larenn Sheba.* The Queen of Sheba." Altagracia laughed. "*Larenn en-ba-lakou is more like it.* Queen of the back alleys." "*Se koule li.* It's her color," Andrée said. "It's why they hang on her every word. Those boys like dark girls to fool around with; that's how it is." Gertie's older sisters often complain that Margie takes on airs, that she thinks she is better than everyone. How can she believe this, they say, as dark as she is?

Margie is the deep color of glistening pine tree bark after a summer rain. Gertie's color is somewhere between Margie's and her eldest sisters', "sun-kissed" as her mother likes to say, the caramel tone of a peach pit, while Gertie's mother looks like the orangey fruit of the peach, her skin reddening when she allows herself to color on rare forays down to the beaches outside the capital. Gertie wonders why her sisters feel this way about Margie's color: it makes her think of the top heights of the mountains during school trips, the coolness of the air as it descends upon the peaks at night, the air laden with a moistness for which they bring undershirts and light sweaters to keep warm. Yet Gertie knows that her sisters sometimes think the same thing of her, that they wish her ill, although color can't be all there is to it. Despite their ill-natured gossip, Gertie knows that behind it resides a desire, an aspiration the sisters' tongues cannot shape.

Gertie huddles closer to Margie while Sisi does the same on her other side. Margie is as close as the two of them can get, at this point, to a priestess interpreting the grand world beyond them. They sit at her side, watching the horizon and its changing colors, disciples at her altar, though altar girls are not allowed at church, girl priestesses not at all. This is not true in the other religion most everyone practices in Haiti. *That* religion allows girls and women to be goddesses. Looking across at Sisi, Gertie can see that they both feel the same way toward Margie: that she is some kind of goddess incarnate. This is what the older girls and Gertie's sisters must already know, Gertie thinks.

"Close your eyes," Margie intones. "Feel, smell the sea air." Without opening her own eyes, which are lightly closed, she adds, "Mami is right. There's nothing like the sea air to cure."

Gertie closes her eyes, takes a deep breath, and brings the salt air into her lungs, along with the briny smell of the catch remaining in the nets below.

"Isn't this amazing?" Margie continues. "Isn't this lovely?" She points to the young fishermen below. "One of those guys tried to convince me that he was a Simbi come from the interior to join with the sea." She laughs. "Incredible, but who's to say he isn't?" She squints.

"What do you mean?" Sisi asks. "Momo told me about the Simbi when I was helping her with the beans. I thought no one could see the Simbi."

"Usually, no," Margie responds, "but sometimes the Simbi can inhabit a person. That's how they can get from the water to land, from river to ocean bed to shore."

Sisi frowns. "Why did he tell you he was a Simbi?"

Margie laughs again. "He was trying to take me away, in his *chaloupe*, said he could take me far away for days into the ocean and to other lands." She looks down at the girls on either side of her. "Don't worry. He was joking. He's not a Simbi. He can't be."

"How do you know?" Gertie asks. She's never heard of the Simbi. Such stories are not told in her house.

"You don't know the story, then," Margie says, looking at Gertie. "They are the spirit of the waters, of rivers and ocean. They bring the two together. They watch over those who have been blessed or given over to the waters at birth but also those who come to them later, in humility, holding all of nature's beings sacred. They keep their children from drowning, if they can help it, but they drown those who violate the rules of nature. Do you know what that means?"

Gertie shakes her head, no.

Margie puts a hand on Gertie's shoulder. "I know it's not easy to be an Alcindor. I've known your older sisters forever and I wish I didn't. Andrée and Altagracia terrorized us when I was your age and they were still in high school. Yvonne and Fidélia, who are around my age, aren't any nicer. That family." Her voice trails off as she looks into Gertie's face with undisguised pity. "But you know that yourself. You can be sure that if your sisters came in contact with the Simbi, they would drown and never be brought back to the surface!"

Sisi gasps.

As if to punctuate Margie's pronouncement, a large wave rolls in, crashing and breaking into frothy spume beneath them. Gertie stares at Margie. How does she know about her sisters' meanness? Gertie wants to ask Margie more questions, but she remains silent, trying to understand what Margie is saying about the Simbi.

"The Simbi will show you who to love, who to leave alone."

"That's what Momo said," Sisi interjects.

"But how?" Gertie ventures. "How will we know?" Her sisters are fond of telling her that anything to do with the spirits, the *mistè*, is false. She wants to know if her sisters are wrong, if the spirits can bring her friendship, love; bring her to a better world than the place of struggle and loneliness she knows at home.

Margie shrugs. "When the Simbi appear, you'll know. They will come to you in dreams. You might see them beneath the surface, but watch out!"

The girls jump.

Margie whispers, "If you come face-to-face with a Simbi— they might charm you."

Sisi giggles. Gertie can see written on Sisi's face that she loves these stories about the *lwa*; she shows no fear of them.

"Well," Margie continues, amused, "they might look like mermaids, or they might look like little girls with long hair like the both of you, or they might be angels that haunt the eaves at church. Be prepared to feel overwhelmed, to tap into a power greater than yourself. You might be afraid, but you have to fight for that greater thing and let no one convince you otherwise."

"But how will I know what to fight for?" Gertie asks.

Margie thinks for a moment. "My guess is that you'll know because if you don't fight, what you lose will be greater than what you had before. You'll lose more than you had." Then she closes her eyes again, and the three sit together, silently, listening to the lapping water beneath them, imagining the Simbi as water snakes or mermaids, swimming by, calling out.

Gertie doesn't know what to make of Margie's pronouncements, with the warmth of her charm like the sun rising into the sky at midmorning; none of her older sisters speak like her. Gertie's older sisters are always in a hurry, leaving or arriving into Léogâne, leaving or arriving into Port-au-Prince, leaving or arriving at a beach on the far outskirts of the city. They would never walk down to the port area, which they claim is unsafe and filled with transients. They wouldn't stop to sniff the morning air or get up early to watch a sunrise. It isn't that they are busy like Sisi's mother or grandmother: they can't be bothered with such things. But neither are they goddesses. Margie looks and acts like one, the depth of the ebony brown of her skin like so many polished votives to be offered to the *lwa*. Though Gertie has never seen a vodou ceremony herself, she can imagine Margie in the white dress of an initiate, her hair turbaned, her skirts fanning around her like white-hot flames surrounding the wick of a candle. If Margie is fire, then they are moths, attracted to the heat. Gertie makes a mental note, as her entire body is awash in crests of sea air, not to tell her sisters any detail of where she has been. It will be a treasure she will hold tightly to her chest.

The three sit together sniffing the air as dolphins might, as if they have been underwater a long time and have just come up for air. Margie breaks the spell: opens her eyes, slaps her thighs, then puts an arm around each of them.

"Let's go back, all right, girls?" she asks without waiting for an answer. "I'm sure Mami has everything ready for us by now." She smiles down at them, radiating light and love into their upturned faces. They are sunflowers.

Margie jumps to her feet and pulls them up with her. She helps them to swat the dust from the dock off their skirts, then runs ahead of them but slows down after half a block. Gertie and Sisi run after her, giggling all the way.

When they reach the house, they find Sisi's mother by the gate, purchasing hot *akasan*, a porridge made from corn flour, whole and evaporated milk, and all kinds of warming spice, from a street vendor, a very thin older woman, Sisi's grandmother's age, who doesn't seem strong enough to be pushing the cart holding her large metal kettle of porridge, her ladles and containers. Sisi's mother hands the vendor a household container into which to pour the porridge, so the woman doesn't have to lose one of her own at the beginning of her day. Sisi's mother purchases ten ladlefuls, one for each person in the household, including the house servants, most of whom turn out to be related to Sisi's grandmother and have been sent to the household from the countryside with the hope that being in the city will bring good fortune.

Sisi's mother sits all of them down at a wooden table covered with a wax cloth printed with blue flowers and gives them each a bowl and a big spoon and then an overflowing ladle of the steaming *akasan*. The scent of star anise, nutmeg, cinnamon, and the golden sweetness of cane syrup intoxicates the dawn. It is a holiday, or a new year, or someone's birthday. Gertie takes up her spoon and eats the porridge so quickly that she can see clear to the white bottom of the ceramic bowl in minutes. She is completely cured of whatever ailed her the day before.

After breakfast the family disperses, each one returning to her own preoccupations—Margie to study for an exam, the house cook starting to gather items for the later meals in the day, Sisi's mother sewing in her atelier, her grandmother stirring above them, dragging her bags of beans into a storage space. Gertie and Sisi are left to wait for someone from Gertie's house to pick her up. But her father doesn't come. He sends a driver instead.

The driver honks the car horn to call Gertie out of the house. She jumps up, embarrassed, thanks Sisi's mother, and kisses Sisi on both cheeks.

Sisi runs after her, asking, "Is that your . . . ?"

But Gertie motions her away, saying she'll see Sisi in school. Let her think that the man in the car is her father. She is too ashamed to say that her father hasn't bothered to pick her up himself, though she was sick and, Gertie reasons, this is what a father should have done.

When Gertie gets home, no one is there to greet her, no father, no mother, no siblings, just the servants. She goes to her room, shuts the door, and cries at the realization that she has been happier for half a day at Sisi's than any other day in her short life. She realizes what felt like a holiday to her is just a Saturday for Sisi.

SISI, PHOENIX, 2002

WAS IT THE SHORTEST CALL THEY EVER HAD?

Simone wonders after hanging up on the call with Gertie. There was a time when she and Gertie talked endlessly, when Simone jumped out of bed as the sun rose because of the anticipation of seeing Gertie's face in the schoolyard. Gertie's face, when Simone arrived hand in hand with Margie, would light up like the florets of a sunflower turning toward the sun. Gertie's wonder appeared to intensify as she slipped her hand into Sisi's, taking Margie's place. Was that it? Was that what Margie had always been trying to warn her about, that Gertie longed to take Margie's place in Sisi's life?

It takes Simone most of the day to recover from Gertie's unexpected phone call. Before Gertie called, she'd been sitting in her studio, caught up in thoughts of missing Margie instead of continuing work on an illustration for a children's book and a commissioned painting of a weaver bird. The book is about the relationship between a child and an injured dove. Painting a brown dove against a pale background was proving a challenge, like trying to differentiate the eggshell of a white egg against the tooth of watercolor paper. Simone had consulted Audubon's *Birds of America*, the one gift she kept from Scott after the divorce despite all she'd learned about Audubon's cruelty to the birds he painted, remembering that his pigeons were almost blue. She was trying to avoid having the dove confused with the brown of a muddy puddle in the scene, the site of the first encounter between the child and the bird, when the child bent down to pick the bird up. The child was also brown—a fact that otherwise delighted Simone. She was trying to make the most of the splash of color in the present scene while mustering all her skill to find washes that could set off the pinafore from the child, from the water, from the dove, making grays and blues for the bird's feathers and head, suggested by Audubon's rendering, finding muted reds and oranges to highlight the warmth of the child's complexion. Frustrated with her lack of progress, she was alternating between the two projects, turning to the commissioned painting of the village weaver for relief, but a relief that brought with it homesickness.

In Haiti, the village weaver is known as a *madan sara* because it talks all day long as market women are said to, hovering over their wares under the sweltering Caribbean sun. Since her grandmother was taciturn, someone who didn't believe in idle talk, and who was stern in the home she kept, where Sisi, Margie, and their mother lived with her, Simone doesn't really think of market women in this way, as loose and free with their banter, though it is true that some of the women talk a lot and pass gossip back and forth between their stalls when the workday grows long and the heat so stifling that it is difficult to breathe. It is true that the male birds' black-hooded heads extend to their chests like the kerchiefs the women wear to shelter themselves, knotted behind their necks, above the shoulders, while the female birds, all of yellow, make her think of Ochún, the maternal sea goddess. The birds never bothered Sisi. They were beautiful creatures that wove striking nests from grassy strips that hung gourd-like from the fronts of palms. They were social, gathering to make colonies that filled the air with cacophony. The males made as many nests as they could in a season, moving to a new nest as soon as a mate started to incubate her eggs so that they could have multiple nests at one time. Eventually, after the weavers had had their broods, the nests dried out, leaving the palm trees on which they hung looking, wistfully, like abandoned tropical Christmas trees. Simone often wondered if the birds were called *madan sara* not just because of their constant chirping but because of the dexterity of their weaving. She observed, when she accompanied her grandmother to the Marché de Fer, the Iron Market, in the heart of Port-au-Prince, that some of the market women busied themselves making baskets for sale from dried, stripped fronds, as dexterous as the birds, their banter back and forth across the winding paths through the market punctuating the air with song.

She usually took pleasure in finding and fine-tuning such details for her illustrations, but that morning, she was filled with frustration and dread, the source of which she could not locate, until her thoughts turned to Margie's final days. She yearned to see Margie in any form, even as a small yellow bird.

"How will I know it's you?" Simone asked Margie before she passed away a few years ago. "What sign will you use?" She grasped Margie's hand. "Just don't do anything spooky."

Their entwined fingers had the look of tree branches made knotty and wiry by the elements, by time. Veins strained against papery skin. Still, they giggled the way they used to when they were girls.

"Like what?" Margie squeezed her hand back, the words coming forth slowly, as if there was cotton in her mouth.

"Don't flicker the lights or walk around the house making floorboards creak."

Margie half laughed, her chest moving up and down in a stutter, swallowing any sound she might have made to lighten the moment. "You don't have floorboards," she said, sweeping her free hand over the covers. "What do they call that stuff?"

Simone chuckled. "Laminate. One wonders what they will think of next, right?"

"Do you remember Momo's house?"

Simone nodded, wiped a tear from her eye. "We didn't have running water back then."

"And now we have toilets that spray, wash, and buff your behind!"

"All I'm saying is that, however you return, we have to agree on something I can recognize and that won't scare the crap out of me."

Margie sighed. "Agreed, Sis. Agreed." Her eyelids fluttered for a moment, closed and opened like wings; then she smiled, and her eyes opened to reveal the dark brown irises that reminded Simone of the deep basins of freshwater ponds. "However I return, I'll come back dressed in yellow, always yellow."

"Yellow?"

"Yes." Margie grasped Simone's hand more firmly, shook it. "Yes. Like Ochún. I'll come to you whenever you need the reminder that your fortune is yourself."

"Oh." Simone scoffed, not unkindly. "So you think I need the reminder." She shook her head.

"We all need the reminder, from time to time, especially us, coming from where we come from . . ." Margie's voice gave out, trailed off.

Simone continued to hold Margie's hand, to stroke her thumb. The details of what Margie was going through had been explained to her by the hospice nurses: loss of lucidity, pain, fogginess, lack of appetite, loss of control over her bodily functions. Simone had been ready for it but not, somehow, for the long stretches of quiet between them once she'd installed Margie in Emma's room, the room that faced the lake in the backyard. It was a man-made lake but that hadn't mattered to Simone when she'd found the town house, the only one she could afford with the money from the divorce settlement. What mattered to her was to be near a body of water, any water, so she could feel somewhat at home. Emma, now in her thirties, hadn't lived there as a child, only visited when she needed a break from her own life in California, which was what had brought Simone out west in the first place, but she'd made it so that Emma could feel it was like home for her as well. Arizona was the next state over, not all that far, as distances went, not as far as Haiti. "You flew the coop," Margie liked to say of Simone of her movements in the US. Something she said about her son. "You all do, sooner or later." Emma's move west for college was the perfect exit; Emma didn't find it odd to be sharing her first apartment with her mother, and Simone didn't have to fight with Scott, who liked the idea that Emma wouldn't be alone far from home. The truth was that Simone couldn't fathom remaining in the same midwestern city as her soon-to-be ex-husband, a city that repelled her like a seed from an apple split open. She became the cool mom, the one who welcomed her daughter's friends when they needed a place to stay, made them food when they studied. Then, slowly, wanting more space for herself and her work as a children's book illustrator, something she'd ventured into clandestinely in her free time as her marriage faltered and later failed, she'd begun to think of where she could live on her own, without appendages, and settled on Arizona after an artists' retreat. She'd stationed Margie in the room that held her daughter's collection of stuffed toys and the brown-girl dolls Simone never had the heart to liquidate. Margie looked small in the middle of the simple bed in the room, like a girl herself.

"Do you know, Margie," Simone said, holding the hand that felt cool to the touch, "do you remember the *ti seren*?"

Margie's eyes flickered, opened, then closed.

"We would see them when we went high into the mountains for summer vacations. Do you remember? Jumping from tree to tree, making little staccato chirps to signal between them. Yellow-bodied birds with black crowns?"

"Hmm," Margie intoned, nodding slightly.

"Maybe you can come back as one of those, a flying mermaid?" Simone chortled though Margie's impending passing was nothing to laugh about. She would miss her sister as if a part of her had been removed, would feel her presence in her life forever, a phantom limb.

"Finches," Margie said. "They call them finches here."

"Yes," Simone said, "I know."

"Do they exist in Arizona?"

"Yes. Goldfinches. There are red ones too. They're here year-round, some of them."

"How will you know when it's me?" Margie swallowed with difficulty.

Simone let go of Margie's hand to get her water from the nightstand, bringing the glass to her lips and tipping it forward slowly until Margie could feel the coolness of the water touch her parched lips and take a sip at her own rate. She indicated that she was done by closing her lips and pushing against the edge of the glass with her bottom lip. The movement reminded Simone of herself as a child, when it was Margie who often was left to care for her while their mother and grandmother, Momo, were running their businesses out of the house. They were ten years apart, which should have been enough to create a gulf between them, but instead, they had grown up closer than close. At times, Margie was a substitute mother, not just her older sister. At others, it was Simone who took the lead, as she was doing now, taking care of Margie as her body continued to fail.

"You'll have to make it clear it's you, but not in a creepy way. That's why I don't want any flickering lights or any of that kind of stuff."

Margie nodded. "You always hated those vampire flicks."

Simone pointed at the stack of books on Margie's nightstand, which she hadn't touched for weeks now. "No horror for me." Emma had mailed several mystery novels for her aunt a few months earlier, knowing they were Margie's favorite. It was an area the sisters disagreed on, Simone opting for light and historical reads, Margie always with any kind of mystery underway.

"They make me believe in humanity," Margie said, in reference to the stack, at which they both laughed.

"But seriously," Margie started again, smacking her lips against renewed dryness, reaching for the water glass. Simone intervened, fetched the glass for her, repeated the ritual. "Seriously, I'll do that. I'll come back. Dressed in yellow, a bird, a flower, something. And you'll know it's me. I'll make sure that you know. The same way we always know when Momo is around, or Mami."

Momo had told them, when they were children, that whenever they saw small brown birds around, they should look up and say hello, because it was an ancestor that came to visit them. When Momo passed, Sisi had observed a small brown bird hopping about beneath the casket. When she told Margie, who had been out of Haiti at the time of the funeral, Margie burst into tears. Then it was Mami who reminded them to talk to the birds as if they were family, in case they were being visited, and when she, too, passed, Simone was certain that visits from *nègès wanga*, green-bellied hummingbirds said to be embodied goddesses that could charm anyone, were Mami saying hello when there was no other way to talk across the divide of time and space. Any small bird she came to think of in this way: messengers from other worlds.

"You'll be able to talk to me whenever you want," Margie said. "I don't want you going to the graveyard, whispering like an old lady to the wind."

When Margie passed, Emma came from California to help Simone with the final arrangements, the cremation. Simone saw to it that a Mass was given. There was no question of sending her body back to the island, of trying to have her buried in the family plot, what plot there was of it left. Margie's son, Ti'Mo, came and went, quick as lightning, taking the ashes back with him to Miami.

Simone misses their conversations on sundry subjects, from their children to the weather. It didn't matter what they talked about, there was always something to be said. When they talked about the past, their history, about Haiti, there was always another stone to turn up toward the light. The morning of Gertie's call, she was attempting to focus on her work, but her mind turned from the muted tones of the common city dove to the commissioned painting, the village weaver with its bright yellow plumage, black head, and red-ringed eye, the wings demarcated with black. The thought of the brilliant plumage of the birds, their high-pitched, comforting chatter, their nests when first made, bursting with green promise, cocooning offspring, all of this made for a strange nostalgia as she tried to settle down to the mundane strokes of her work. It made her think of Margie, and it was then that the yellow butterfly came into view, at eye level, across the pane of glass of the picture window separating her studio from the burgeoning bushes hemming in her patio.

The butterfly appeared, like a wink, and Simone knew that it was Margie because the butterfly spent too much time hovering in front of her, as if to attract her attention. Her heart surged with hope, and then the phone rang, interrupting her dreamlike state. Simone went to answer the phone. If there was someone whose voice she would have liked to hear, it was Margie's. Lord, she misses her older sister. She misses her like she misses fresh-squeezed passion fruit juice poured over ice on a hot day, or rice and *sos pwa*. She misses annoyances like the way Margie would never quite come out and say that she disagreed with her—sucked her teeth instead, the smack of tongue and teeth loud and clear over the telephone line.

Simone would normally have ignored the phone altogether, letting it remind her of the outside world without bringing her away from her desk, but she was hungering for interruption, anything to move away from the ache of loss that is, in some way, the cost of living. She picked up the ringing phone and it was Gertie, unexpectedly, on the other end of the line. Gertie, of all people. It had been years—*years*—since she had heard the low timbre of Gertie's voice. There was a time when Simone avoided answering her phone in order not to have to hear that voice, until the calls stopped coming, and Simone could relegate the time of their adult friendship to the dust bin, as she had the memory of the years they had been friends as children, before they knew who they were or should have been to each other. How strange it was, then, that the yellow butterfly appeared at the moment of Gertie's call. Was Margie's spirit bringing her a message, a warning?

Simone did not ask a lot of questions, just listened. She did say she would wait for Ella to send her an update. She doesn't know if promises made to Gertie mean anything at this point, if either Gertie or Ella will feel that they can call upon her to keep them. The past, their deep, deep history, infects everything like an undetected cancer pervading a living body. Was it that past now making itself known, proliferating in Gertie? Simone shook her head, wishing that she'd hung up when she recognized the voice on the other end of line as belonging to the one person who managed to make her feel simultaneously angry and elated: Gertie had the power to make or unmake her.

When she put down the phone, Simone felt a swirl of undigested emotions. She almost wished that phone technology had not been invented, that they were in the age of telegrams sent over long distances, such that when the news reached its recipient, whatever was being communicated no longer mattered, or mattered less, since nothing could be done about it, the event being relayed long out of date. But now there are endless ways of being in touch, and she resists them.

When Margie was the first among them to leave Haiti, it could take months for their letters to reach her, weeks for Margie to answer. She left to discover the world, she said, to lose herself, their mother said. "*Laissez-li pati*," Momo said. "*Lap we kijan mond la ye.* Let her go. She'll see how the world is." Momo thought the world had a thing or two to teach Margie, and it seemed that might be true since at first all Margie talked about in her letters was how much she missed them, the house, the island. Later, she wrote them about other things, of the land she had gone to, all the possibilities that lay beyond Haiti too. She promised to expand Momo's business. "Tourist dollars," Margie wrote, "that is the future!" "*Ti fi lap reve nan couleu*," Momo would say. "The girl dreams in color," shaking her head as their mother read Margie's letters aloud on the day they arrived, after dinner, when the house and street beyond would grow quiet. After the letter was read, their mother would compose a group answer to Margie's letter, to which Sisi would add a list of questions that always began, "When are you coming home?" which was all Sisi ever wanted to know, though, out of politeness, she would add others, like, "How is the weather there?" "What are you eating?" "Do they have mangoes?" "Have you met anyone nice?" "I just want to know when she'll be coming back," Sisi sighed to her mother, who would nod and choke back tears that she would never let Sisi see fall, though at the beginning Sisi would cry herself to sleep in the room she had shared with her sister, she missed her that much. When Momo died, they sent Margie the news by letter and photograph, all stuffed into a large manila envelope from which Margie had to extract a black-and-white glossy photograph showing Momo at rest in a simple coffin, the lines of her face eased of their tension in a way that Simone had never seen in life. Margie did not have to get herself down to church in a black dress, nor did she have to shake hands in a long procession and look into faces that bore faint resemblances to one another, accepting condolences.

The distance, Simone thinks now, was good for something. It offered a cushion of sorts, a space in which to sort through emotions when there was nothing else to do.

In Margie's absence, Sisi's world expanded while Margie's light faded in importance. But Margie was all-important in what turned out, in retrospect, to be the last days of Sisi's childhood friendship with Gertie.

PORT-AU-PRINCE, 1942

Sisi and Gertie are inseparable. The glimpses they got of each other's lives at the beginning of the school year make them more enchanted with each other, and they attend school after the holiday break with newfound zeal. Though to others it seems that they are invested in their studies, Sisi knows that they are invested only to the extent that studying affords them more time together.

It turns out they are both new in the school, and though Gertie has the advantage of being a known quantity among the families with names, she is relatively new to the capital, having lived until recently with her mother in Léogâne, coming to the city only a handful of times when her mother visits with friends, sometimes taking Gertie with her when she made her rounds. Making rounds, Gertie explains to Sisi, means sitting in strangers' living rooms for hours on end, waiting for sweets to be passed around while the mothers engage in endless chitchat, gossip, and exchanges of information that could be helpful to their husbands or to the grown children they hope to marry off. The visits bore Gertie to death, she says, but through them, she knows a few of the girls at school. Some are the same girls giving Sisi a hard time about her faded uniforms, but Gertie tells her to ignore them. Some in this set Gertie likes well enough, like a girl named Louise Lombardo, the daughter of Italian immigrants whom Gertie knows both from Léogâne and from school. Gertie tells Sisi that Lou can be counted on and so Lou joins them from time to time at recess and, because she is not as studious as they are, hangs around them in the hope that Sisi and Gertie's studiousness will rub off on her.

The three enter an art contest together. Sisi takes first place with a masterful drawing of a rooster strutting through a yard that resembles the space behind Gertie's house. Gertie manages third place with a drawing of a green-chested tody since Sisi told her that her boisterous disposition resembles the bird's and Gertie likes green. Another girl places second between them, an unassuming, quiet girl named Odette. Odette drew a beach scene, a family of peasants gathered on a shore, next to an *ajoupa*, a simple structure with a thatched roof common in rural areas. Odette wears hand-me-down uniforms given her by the nuns at school, and they are threadbare, not restitched like Sisi's. She is smart and kind but often left out of the schoolyard games by the popular girls, who scorn her appearance. Sisi is surprised that Odette's picture has not won first place and tells her so, and just like that, Odette becomes part of their group.

A few of the older, popular girls are resentful of how easily Gertie has fallen into a friendship with Sisi, of how Lou takes to them and how they include Odette, singled out for exclusion. What are younger girls for, if not to provide a following for the older ones? Gertie and Lou lead their group into devil-may-care antics and throw caution to the wind. Sisi finds this out soon enough when a routine recess period devolves into name-calling.

That afternoon, months after their foursome jells, the girls have a game of *osselets*, or jacks, in the schoolyard, and one of the stuck-up, older rich girls accuses Odette of hiding one of the game pieces in order to win. Odette opens her hands wide to the other girls to show that she isn't holding anything, but the taunting continues. The accusing girl, Julie, with plaited brownish hair curled around the wide circumference of her head and freckles interspersed like a constellation across the bridge of her nose, a coloring that means she is a *grifòn*, insists on searching Odette's pockets, on making her turn them inside out. One of the pockets has a hole and Julie pounces on this as if it were an admission of guilt.

She points at the hole. "See?" she says to the other girls. "She took it and put it there and it fell out."

"Odette wouldn't do that," Gertie says, aghast. Odette is so very quiet, Sisi thinks, not the kind of girl to cheat or steal or make stories up about other girls.

Sisi's brow furrows. She takes courage from Gertie's defense of their friend. "Why are you accusing her?" Sisi asks. "Did *you* take it?"

"*Sa kaka poul la di?*" Julie says to the others, her voice rising. "What did the chicken shit say?" The cluster of girls gasps collectively, then laughs behind cupped hands.

"What did you call her?" Lou advances threateningly with both hands folded into fists by her sides. The group takes a hop back. A few peel off, not wanting to be a part of what will come next.

Julie turns to face Gertie, ignoring Lou's fisted hands. Everyone knows that Lou will do whatever she wants. Gertie is a lesser-known quantity. Julie places both her hands on her hips and squares off. "*Ou tande'm.* You heard me." She exaggerates each word coming out of her mouth. "*Mwen te mande ki sa kaka poul la di.* I want to know what the girl the color of chicken shit has to say. *E pou kisa l'ap defend pin griye boule la?* And why is she defending that piece of burned toast?" She flicks an open, dismissive hand in Odette's direction.

"You're going to swallow those words!" Gertie bellows at Julie. Lou advances toward Julie with fists up, ready to fight. Julie doesn't budge. She smirks at Lou tauntingly.

"What are you and your little tribe going to do?" Julie says. "With all your little baubles." She points to Gertie's necklace. "Whose locket is that, Gertie? Why do you wear it every day at school?"

Gertie blushes. "My papa gave it to me."

"Your papa? Why would he give you such a thing? A little baby like you?" The other girls laugh: their days of being in first grade are over. It is these girls' turn to be picked on.

In the meantime, Sisi's thoughts meander away from the gaggle of girls tittering as if from a distance. She spots a bird swooping in the breadth above them, a blackbird with spotted red epaulets, and wishes she could join it up above. She spreads her arms out wide and throws her head back as if to lift off the ground, as she finds herself doing in her dreams at night.

"What is she doing?" one of the older girls says, pointing to Sisi.

"What did I tell you?" Julie scoffs. "These girls are worthless. They aren't worth our time." She steps forward so that she stands chest to chest with Gertie, then extends an arm, her hand reaching, reaching, until her index finger taps the surface of the silver locket. Gertie steps back, and Julie's fingers catch in the silver chain on which the locket hangs. They hear a snap as the chain breaks. Gertie's hands move to her neck as the locket falls. She catches it in midair.

For a moment, Julie seems indecisive, worried, but when she sees that, though the chain has broken, its pieces are in Gertie's hands, she shrugs.

"*Sak pase la?*" Two nuns come trotting from opposite edges of the yard toward the girls. "What is going on here? You older girls should know better than to pick on the little ones."

Julie drops her arms, turns on her heel, lifting up dust from the yard as she does so, gathers her troop and stalks off before the nuns arrive. When they do, there is nothing left to see except for the *osselets* and red rubber ball left on the ground. "Whose are these?" asks the older nun.

Lou inspects the remains of the game. "There's not a one missing here," she says, crouching down close to the ground, her skirts gathered between her thighs. "Julie was losing so she made something up."

"What happened?" says the other nun, pulling on the edges of her habit.

"Nothing much, Sister," Lou says. "*Pa anyen.*" Lou picks up one of the *osselets*, then throws it down onto the ground. It bounces off another piece.

Sisi gathers all the pieces together with the rubber ball they were using to play. Gertie is clutching the broken pieces of her chain and the locket in her hands.

"Do you know whose these are?" the older nun repeats. The younger nun pulls at her habit again, mumbling under her breath that there is nothing important for them to attend to. The two nuns drift away, as the popular girls did, back to the fringes of the yard, waiting for recess to end and classes to resume.

"We don't know but Odette should have them after all that," Lou says. "Take them."

Sisi nods and hands the pieces to Odette.

"I don't want them," Odette says, pushing back against Sisi's hands.

Lou takes the pieces from Sisi's hands and places them in Odette's. "There," she says, "they're yours."

Gertie turns to them. "I want to go back to my house to drop off the locket. I'll have to ask my papa to fix it. I hope he won't be angry with me for wearing it to school."

"We can't leave," Odette says.

"Of course we can," Lou replies. "We can do whatever we want."

"You can," Odette says, "but I can't."

"You're with us," Gertie replies. "We'll protect you."

"No," Odette says firmly. "I can't."

"It's OK," Lou exhales. "I'll stay here with you and they can go. Anyway, Julie has no right to call us those things."

Odette shrugs. Evidently, *she* has heard such things before. Sisi doesn't know what to say. Gertie and she exchange glances.

"Well, first of all," Lou continues, "*kaka poul* is nutritious. My mother saves it when she can and adds it to the herb beds in our backyard. I mean, you can't get any better plant food than that." Lou is always funny even when events aren't. "And what's wrong with burned toast, anyway?" She flings her arms open, her hands and long fingers outstretched on either side of her. "It's great! You know it's morning when you catch a whiff of burned toast coming into your room from the kitchen to tickle your nostrils!"

Sisi has an image of Lou from earlier fixed in her mind, with those same hands drawn into fists alongside her body, ready to fight Julie tooth and nail in the schoolyard. The thought of it makes her laugh, and soon all four of them are laughing together.

"Not kidding now, though," Lou says. "She was wrong. Where did she get off talking to us like that? I'd say, Sisi, you're a white bird of paradise: a beautiful tropical plant offering food to all the birds from the cups of your flowers." She turns to Odette.

"And you, Odette, you are the rarest of ebony woods that people look for when creating the center posts for their homes: strong, unbreakable." She is holding both their arms now, as she turns to Gertie. "As for you, I have no idea."

They all laugh again.

"Come on," Gertie says, taking Sisi by the hand. "We'll be back in no time if we leave now."

They leave Lou and Odette behind in the schoolyard and go to Gertie's.

Gertie's house, pretty as a picture, painted in pastel pinks and greens, with carved eaves and cutout trims framing each of the shuttered windows, is steps away. Although Sisi visited Gertie's yard a few short months ago, she has never been inside. Yet she has heard about how the gingerbreads feel cool any time of year, the wide windows and doors opening for cross ventilation in a way that the small, squat clapboard houses with corrugated rooftops that collect heat cannot. She admires the long second-floor windows whose wooden shutters open to the outside while the first floor, bedecked with the same long windows, some double in width, features a wraparound wide veranda painted the same color as the shutters, both a gray blue that resembles the shade of storm clouds. Wicker rocking chairs stand on the porches in an inviting way, but Sisi wonders if they are merely ornamental: she has never seen anyone sitting in them as she walks to and from school, and she wonders if she, Gertie, Lou, and Odette might sit there one day, lazing the afternoon away, as if they were not little girls but old *taties* who had lived long, hard lives, deserving of rest and a mug of tea to cool the body in their wiry hands.

As soon as Sisi follows Gertie into the house, entering from the yard, she realizes she has never set foot in a house so grand. The yard is much quieter this afternoon than the first time she was here, with the hens pecking away at their patch of earth.

Sisi shudders a bit as they walk past them, thinking back to the slaughter, the small point of the hen's blood that still stains the hem of her uniform, hidden from view. Their house boy who is not a boy waves to them. He is whittling something from a piece of wood. One of the cooks is fanning herself with the turned-up edge of her skirts. Sisi says hello timidly to her; the woman nods. Then, the two of them walk past the work kitchen in the yard, the one that is hidden from visitors. They walk into the formal kitchen in the house with its pink and green, black-speckled tiles, its large silver and copper polished pots hung by nails along the walls while others bubble from a wood-fed stove. Sisi loses all will to think through whether she should be here in the middle of a school day. There are decorative bowls filled with fruit. These are covered up with serviettes to keep the flies swarming above them from landing.

After the kitchen, to the right, there is a formal dining area, and to the left, a living room with heavy ebony furnishings and doilies sitting prettily under carvings, china plates, and framed sepia photographs of individuals Sisi assumes are long-dead relatives, as it is customary to honor the dead by framing their pictures so they will not feel too lonely. As Sisi takes in the fancy surroundings, Gertie flounces by an older kerchiefed woman who was in the kitchen when they entered. Sisi guesses she is an auntie or grandmother until Gertie moves past her without offering her a kiss hello, signaling that the woman is a household servant, though in Sisi's home, the children say hello to all the adults, whether they are family or working in the house. Sisi gives the woman a hesitant smile as she, in turn, looks quizzically at the thin girl. She rakes her eyes critically over Sisi as if assessing her worth as one would a sack of beans at market.

"That's Yéyène," Gertie says with a wave of the hand. "She's the main cook."

Yéyène gives a suck of her teeth. "*Lekol fini?* School over?" she asks suspiciously, her eyes narrowing to slits. Yéyène is thick but sinewy, clearly a woman who works hard at all her tasks, whether in the kitchen or elsewhere. Her skin is a smooth polished brown resembling the heavy furnishings in the living room.

"Just a break." Gertie shrugs. "We have to get back in a few minutes." She doesn't want to show Yéyène the broken necklace. It is a precious thing she should never have taken to school. Instead, she tells Yéyène that they are hungry. "*Nou gayen gran gou!* We're hungry from all the studying. *Ou pa gayen yon ti bagay pou nou?* Don't you have something for us?"

"*M'gayen, m'gayen.* Of course I have. *Chita non.*" She says, indicating the kitchen pointedly. "Just sit yourselves down."

"I'll be right back, Yéyène. I have to put something in my room," Gertie says, leaving Sisi alone.

Yéyène hustles Sisi back to the formal kitchen and into a chair at the table. Sisi hears Gertie clamber up some stairs, then hears the hushed tones of a conversation between Gertie and another woman. Sisi watches as Yéyène moves around the kitchen, then sets in front of Sisi two plates and a decorated cookie tin from which protrudes wax paper that has been used and reused many times, as Sisi can tell from the whitened folds that run across it. Yéyène places two glasses of *korosól*, soursop juice, on the table. Sisi then hears another girl's voice rise from upstairs and Gertie making excuses in response, then quiet, then Gertie's steps retreating, coming back down toward the kitchen. Gertie says nothing when she returns. Instead, she busies herself with revealing what the wax paper enfolds: dark round balls covered in shredded coconut.

"Are those rum balls?" Sisi asks, as Gertie passes the box to her.

"No, silly," Gertie laughs. "We're too little for that." She turns to Yéyène. "She thought they were rum balls."

Yéyène smiles and turns her back to them. She has other things to do.

"My dad brought these back from one of his trips to the other side of the mountains. They're coconut-and-honey sweets."

"Oh." Sisi sighs in relief. "I bet they're good."

"Try one," Gertie says, pushing the tin closer to Sisi.

As Sisi bites into the sweet, she senses a vague familiarity, as if the coconut balls are something she has been given to taste before. She doesn't especially like coconut, but the sweetness of the honey is addictive and she doesn't want to disappoint her new friend by saying something disagreeable. "What are they called?" she asks.

"*Jalao*," Gertie responds. "*Je sais*. I know. *Pas facile à dire*. Not easy to say."

"*Vraiment, non*," Sisi laughs. "Not at all."

"You can just say you had coconut-and-honey balls. My dad brings them so he can have what he calls a taste of home, though he never lived that long in the DR."

"Your dad's Dominican?" Sisi asks shyly. "I think mine is too."

"Well . . ." Gertie thinks about it. "I guess. He was born there, but his parents are from both sides. They moved back to Haiti when he was six, and he goes back for business and to see family. We take vacations there sometimes or go for special occasions. What about you?"

"No. I've never been on the other side. I don't know if my papa is from there. My grandmother calls him a *pagnol*. I think that just means that he's white. What is it like over there?" Sisi asks.

Gertie is thoughtful. "It's like here." She shrugs. "Except everyone speaks Spanish. They also pay a lot of attention to what people look like."

Gertie seems to speak with reticence, but Sisi can't help but ask more questions. "What is your father like?"

"He's really nice," she responds. "He gave me the locket that Julie broke."

"Is it really broken?" Sisi asks.

"No," Gertie says, "just the chain. I can get that fixed. I'm glad that it wasn't the actual locket. I shouldn't have been wearing it." Gertie frowns, then shakes off her disarray. "What about your father? What is he like?"

"He comes to the house once a week to hang out with my mother. I don't think he likes me."

"You must be wrong, Sisi," Gertie says. "Maybe he's just shy, you know? Some boys are like that."

"I don't know," Sisi replies. "He's just not around that much." She searches for a way to change the subject and comes to focus on the sweets. "These are so good."

Gertie smiles and eats another. "Help yourself," she says, pushing the tin back in Sisi's direction.

Sisi forgets about sitting on the front porch and acting like old ladies after a long day's work as the two busy themselves with eating the sweets and washing them down with the juice. Will she tell anyone about this later? Her sister, maybe, as they walk home, or maybe not, as she will inevitably hear Margie's stomach rumble from hunger after the long afternoon and the seemingly endless walk home toward the port. She thinks to ask for a wrapped treat for Margie because it wouldn't be fair to let her walk home hungry. She has tasted the fruit of privilege and it is like a plum, tart on the tongue, bitter in aftertaste, and yet she wonders when she will taste it again.

After they eat the snacks, Yéyène shoos them out of the kitchen, saying she has to get dinner underway. Gertie proceeds to give Sisi a tour of the rooms of the main floor. She doesn't take her up to her room, as Sisi would have done in her own home, but shows her all the other open spaces downstairs, from the formal living room with its heavy wooden furniture, where everything looks untouched and polished, as if in a museum, to a wood-paneled office dominated by a large, club-footed desk.

When they reach the study, Gertie motions for Sisi to follow. Sisi does, but as soon as she enters, there is a strange familiarity in the room. It smells of shoe polish, the stubs of cigars, and the aroma of cologne that men of a certain class wear.

"This is Papa's study," Gertie says, installing herself in the leather-clad, wooden swivel chair behind the desk. "He does all the accounting for the house here." Gertie looks quizzically at the pile of papers on her father's desk and fans them with her fingers. "And for other things."

Sisi nods though she isn't sure what those "other things" might be. The room smells eerily of Thursday nights, when her father comes to call at the house. They eat together with Mami at the dining room table as if a special guest has come, but it is father and mother, Sisi and Margie sitting around the table, Momo upstairs because she says she doesn't "approve of that man," and that is that. He spends the night sometimes and is gone by morning, leaving behind a stale odor of cigar.

Sisi is about to comment to Gertie about the similarity of fathers, about how Gertie's father's study reminds her of her father, when a boy about Margie's age pokes his head into the study. He hisses at them, "You two better get out of here. You-know-who is upstairs, and she'll have a cow if she sees her!" He coughs, then shakes a hand in Sisi's direction, as if she were a stray. "*Degaje!*"

Sisi's blood rises up her neck with embarrassment. She reverts to the girl Gertie found, hunched over her drawing paper in class, hiding from everyone in her imaginings, wanting to remain invisible. She recognizes Gertie's brother, Rico, from the boys' school. He is at home sick with a cold but why is he shooing her like a dog? Is it because she is a girl, or something else? She doesn't have time to find out because as soon as Gertie hears the phrase "you-know-who," she jumps from her father's swivel chair, grasps Sisi's hand, and flees with her back through the formal rooms, the kitchen, back to the yard, and out, into the street.

"'Scuse'm," she splutters as they reach the side of the road. "It's my older sister. I swear, it's like having one of the evil stepsisters in 'Cendrillon' as your real-to-God sister. She's awful. She would just chew you up and spit you out in a second: a second!" Gertie snaps her fingers dramatically. "Like that, you'd be gone," she adds for emphasis.

Sisi's hands fly up to her mouth.

"My sisters are nothing like yours," Gertie continues.

"It must be terrible!" Sisi says. But she doesn't really know what to say. Margie protects her, helps their grandmother get her things to market, walks Sisi to school, and tells her stories at night. She can feel Gertie's fear and trepidation. Better to leave right away than to endure "you-know-who's" wrath, whoever she is.

But as they make their way back toward the school, it dawns on Sisi that she has been identified as the cause of the problem. Why her? She did as Gertie wished and followed her home. She didn't ask to be taken over there. They are running back as fast as they can, like a *lougarou*, a werewolf, might be on their heels, though werewolves only come out at night, everyone knows.

Sisi doesn't look back toward Gertie's house, but she can hear someone calling out behind them, "*Pa tounin ici*. Don't come back!" The spell of being in the house, with all its marvelous things, is broken, just like Gertie's silver chain. All the promising fine things in ruin.

They run all the way to the edge of the schoolyard. All the other girls have long gone inside. But Margie is there with an angry look on her face that stops them dead in their tracks. Sisi has never seen Margie looking so angry.

"Where have you been?" Margie asks as soon as they are within reach. "And why is that woman yelling at you?" Margie is looking out above their heads, squinting, holding one hand above her eyes to block the sun. "Who is that, Gertie, one of your sisters? Your mother?"

Gertie gulps audibly, out of breath. "It's Andrée, my older sister. She's visiting from out of town. And my brother, Rico." She adds, as if it could make a difference, "He has a cold."

"Why did you leave school?" Margie turns to Sisi, ignoring Gertie's explanations. "What were you doing off school grounds? The nuns came to get me over at the high school because they didn't see you return from recess. They had no idea where you'd gone."

Sisi doesn't answer.

"We've done it before," Gertie replies instead, but that answer does not make Margie any happier.

"What!" she exclaims. "You've what? What's gotten into you, Sisi?" But the tone of her voice betrays her thought, that it is Gertie and her family infecting Sisi with mischief and irresponsibility, that no good can come out of their escapades to the stately Alcindor house that dwarfs the homes around it. "And you," she says, turning her wrath on Gertie. "It's one thing for you to go home: your house is steps away, but you know very well how your sisters are. Everyone knows. How could you take Sisi over there to meet them!"

"I—I," Gertie stutters, "I didn't know that anyone other than Rico was home. It's the middle of the day. We just needed to get away from the other girls." She tries to explain what had transpired earlier in the afternoon, but Margie holds up a shushing hand. Andrée is strutting down the street toward them. Rico is a distance behind, watching.

"Here comes your sister. You should get into the school. I'm going to have a word with her."

Sisi takes Gertie's hand and the two walk hurriedly toward the school building. A nun waits by an open door to escort them back in but not before they overhear Andrée and Margie's conversation. They speak as if they know each other.

"Why are you yelling after my sister?" Margie asks.

"Your sister?" Andrée responds as she arrives in the yard. "What was she doing in my parents' house? What was she looking to get?"

"She's not a dog looking for a bone," Margie says, hand on her hip. "There's nothing at your house that she can't find in ours."

Andrée snorts. "I'm pretty sure that there are plenty of things up there," she says, pointing back to the imposing house, "that a girl that age would want."

"Not Sisi," Margie emphasizes. "She doesn't need anything from you."

"Are you sure? What's her name?"

"What do you mean?"

"Doesn't she go by Val, your mother's maiden name? Aren't you a Bontemps?"

"Yes, I am," Margie says with a note of pride.

"Then why don't you have the same last name?"

"You know why," Margie replies. She folds her arms against her chest. Rico lingers in the background.

"I do. Do you want everyone else to know?" Andrée sweeps a hand toward the school. Sisi and Gertie are nearing the back door, held open by the nun, whose face is turning beet red. "And why is your sister running around without escort into our home like a *restavek*, as if she has no home of her own? I took her for a vagrant."

Margie scoffs. "For a vagrant, a *restavek*? Come on, Andrée. She's wearing the school uniform. The uniform you wore once. You know very well who she is. You're just afraid that your mother will find out she was there."

"Nothing of the sort," Andrée replies. "Mother stayed back in Léogâne and I'm just checking in to make sure all is well here since she can't and my father does whatever he wants. She'll never know, but that's not what matters. Appearances count. We haven't seen much of you at the parties since your father died. He was a fine man."

"I don't see what that has to do with anything," Margie says, arms still folded. "And why don't you just stick to your husband's family. Aren't you married now, with kids? What does it matter to you what your father does or doesn't do, and with whom?"

By now, Andrée is almost nose to nose with Margie, who stands her ground. "I make it my business. Reputation means everything, doesn't it? The lot of you are just a bunch of women living together without any men in the house, no one to give you status."

"My God, Andrée. In what century are you living? Marriage hasn't changed you one bit. You're just like you were when I was in grade school, full of spite." Margie unfolds her arms and leans forward into Andrée, pushing the older girl back. "We don't need men to give us women value."

Andrée regains her footing, brushes lint from Margie's shoulder. Margie takes a step back from Andrée. "Do we not?" Andrée asks shrilly. "Do we not?"

"Keep your hands off me," Margie says.

"Well," Andrée replies, smiling, "tell your sister to keep her mitts off us, off Gertie."

"They're just kids," Margie responds. "Just let them be. What harm can their friendship cause?"

Andrée demurs. "You don't want to find out." With that pronouncement, she turns on her heel and walks back to the Alcindor house. There, she speaks to her brother, who has retreated to the porch. He scratches his head as she speaks. They have words for a few minutes, then both disappear into the house.

Sisi watches. What is wrong with the Alcindors, with being friends with Gertie? Margie walks them back into the school and leaves for her own without any further explanation.

Sisi tries to ignore Gertie for the remaining class periods though Gertie keeps showing her drawings and spelling homework. Sisi is wound up inside, not understanding why the older popular girls turned on them at recess, why the oldest Alcindor sister ran after them as if Sisi were a robber. Gertie tries to make things up to her, insisting that there will be more escapades in the future.

"You'll have to come back," Gertie says, "another time. When you-know-who isn't there."

But Sisi isn't sure she wants to return.

When it comes time to leave school, Sisi waves goodbye to Gertie half-heartedly. She feels something waning, like a cut flower wilting. She walks silently with Margie in the direction of the port.

Halfway home, Sisi remembers the coconut ball wrapped in wax paper she had asked for, then shoved to the bottom of the left pocket of her uniform skirt when they fled from the Alcindor home. She was keeping it for Margie but forgot about it during the altercation with Andrée outside the school. She pulls it out of her pocket and hands it to Margie quietly.

"What's this?" Margie says as she opens the paper to reveal the ball. "Where did you get this?" She takes a bite and grimaces.

"At Gertie's," Sisi says, almost in a whisper.

"Too much coconut, too sweet for me," Margie replies. She shoves the rest back into the wrapper and hands it to Sisi without missing a beat of their walk. Sisi's heart continues to drop. She eats what remains of the sweet greedily, as if eating it could bring back the earlier magic of the afternoon. Margie looks at her with disappointment written all over her face. "Sisi, you don't want to want anything from those people, not even the sweet things."

"Why not?" Sisi asks. The coconut sweet is sticking to her teeth. She passes a finger around her teeth to dislodge the bits sticking there and swallows.

Margie offers no explanation.

They keep walking in silence. When their modest two-level house comes into view, Sisi's steps quicken. She wants to tell Momo about the day and seek her counsel, but Margie seems to read her thoughts, catches her by the shoulder as Sisi begins to outstep her. "Sisi, don't tell Momo or Mami about today."

Sisi looks over her shoulder, up into Margie's face. She wants to tell them everything. "Why not?"

Margie's face clouds over. "It will make them sad." She stops in her tracks, her hand on Sisi's shoulder softening. "You don't want to make Momo and Mami sad, do you?"

Sisi shakes her head no, but who can she tell? Who can explain to her what is happening?

"Let's keep this between us," Margie says. "For now, just be careful around Gertie and don't go over to her house. It's not worth it with that family, trust me."

Sisi's pace falters, slows, and they walk up to the house together.

Sisi avoids Mami's workshop and turns away from Momo's door. She sits at the desk in her room and pulls out a sheet of paper. She draws the red-shouldered blackbird she saw in the sky at recess. She is no longer certain whether it was real, but drawing it tethers her to a possibility that soothes her, that resides somewhere beyond the here and now, the too-real confines of the house and whatever it was that Gertie's older sister thought Sisi had no right to want. The sweets were good but nothing sweet ever lasts.

Even later, Sisi finds that she has eaten too many of them: her stomach aches and she cannot eat her dinner. Margie says nothing at the dinner table, and neither does Sisi when her mother wonders what is wrong and sends her to her room with a cup of *tibonm* tea.

Sisi never sets foot again in Gertie's house.

Soon, all their lives will change.

GERTIE, MIAMI, 2002

THEY ARE BACK HOME. GERTIE HAS CHECKED ON ZULI and Fredi, who are making themselves cozy on the blankets at the foot of the bed, securing her periphery. She learned long ago that cats regard humans as big versions of themselves: once you are accepted as part of their colony, they do for you what they do for one another, acting as lookouts when you eat, keeping you warm when you feel sick, and rubbing themselves against you for comfort.

"So you say that she didn't ask you many questions," Ella restates to Gertie, returning them to the question of the phone call with Sisi.

Gertie nods.

"Will she be coming to see you? What else did she say?" Ella continues peppering her with questions.

"She didn't have much to say," Gertie replies. "Can you help me get comfortable?" A pang of pain ripples through her midsection, a reminder of the recent operation. She reaches for the vial of painkillers.

"Let me get that," Ella says, lifting the vial out of Gertie's reach. "Is it hurting a lot?"

Gertie nods. Like a cat, she is trying to hide how bad she feels, not just because of the post-op pain but because of the call with Sisi. It did not go at all as she had expected. But what, truly, had she expected? That Sisi would forget everything about the past? That she would have, somehow, gotten over twenty years of near silence wedged between them like a vacuum? In a strange way, Sisi's apparent rejection is familiar, like the reactions she might have received from members of her own family had she reached out to them, those that remained.

"I just need to stop thinking for a while," Gertie says to her daughter. "She said something about you sending her the results; I think she means for the biopsy."

Ella pauses as she hands Gertie a glass of water to wash down the pills.

"I didn't say that you would—just that you could," Gertie adds hastily, peering at her daughter. "I think she just didn't want to reach out to me. You're a safer bet, I guess."

"Maybe. I don't know. I won't be in touch with her unless you ask me to."

"I told you it wouldn't be easy. That's why I didn't want to call her in the first place."

"I'm pretty sure that if she had heard what the doctor told us, she would want to be here, patch things up—you know," Ella stresses, "before it's too late."

"I don't know." Gertie swallows the pills, closes her eyes. "You get older, and nothing seems that easy. I don't know if it's worth it."

"Of course it is," Ella responds stubbornly. "You two have got to patch things up."

The way Ella pinches her face as she used to do as a child concentrating on a task, as if her life depended on getting an equation right or a piece of paper glued in the right place in an art project, suggests to Gertie that she has been in touch with Emma over the years. Gertie has just not known. Ella keeps things to herself, as she kept so many things close to her chest throughout her adolescence, a time when it seemed that Sisi understood her daughter better than she did herself.

"All right, all right." Gertie shoos Ella away as she sinks into the bank of pillows the two of them piled up on her bed. Gertie drifts, thinking about her older sisters. Sometime later, she thinks she hears someone come back into the room, but she is already descending into a drugged lull. She tries to call out her daughter's name but instead calls out, "Manuel," as she used to when ill and needing comforting in the middle of the night. He came to be her whole world even if he was not there in the beginning and left too soon. Gertie cannot remember crying out for her mother to cradle her back to sleep for the simple reason that she never had a mother who would come, out of nowhere, to soothe the dark away. Always, other arms did the gathering up, none belonging to a mother or, in the end, to a father.

Zuli and Fredi stir and flop closer to her, abutting their backs to her as if their warm, purring bodies can bear witness to her pain, take it away. Gertie groans, on the brink of sleep. If only it were that simple: to purr things away. She keeps her eyes closed, knowing that it will be a matter of minutes before the painkillers send her off floating into a cottony numbness that she both seeks and resists.

PORT-AU-PRINCE, 1942

For Gertie, Sisi is the prime focus of her time at the new school in Port-au-Prince. She and Sisi continue to be inseparable despite their older sisters' altercation in the schoolyard. They compare notes about their classmates, class trips, homework, books, church, the next holiday. They plot the next art contest entry, prepare for the next recitation. They start planning out their lives away from their respective families. But nothing, no planning, no plotting, can prepare them for the day both are called out of their classroom without warning, first Gertie by her recently married older sister, Altagracia, then Sisi by Margie.

At first, neither knows why they are called out of the classroom. Altagracia takes Gertie away to the far side of the corridor, where Fidélia and Yvonne are waiting for them. Sisi is taken by Margie to the other side. Neither can hear what the other is being told by her sister. Gertie hears Sisi begin to cry softly, and then she sees Margie put her arms around Sisi. Gertie is watching Sisi and Margie locked in an embrace that Gertie recognizes as sadness when she hears Altagracia speaking about Papa.

Altagracia says, "Papa is ill and asked us to get you to him."

"Where is he?" Gertie asks, alarmed.

"In the hospital," Fidélia says matter-of-factly.

Gertie tries to make sense of her sisters' words. She looks at Sisi and Margie across the corridor. She feels sad for Sisi, who has likely received similar news. Is it their mother, or the grandmother, Momo? She remembers the elderly woman's soft snoring in the early light of morning that Saturday she awoke at Sisi's after a fretful, feverish night. Her heart goes out to Sisi in the same way that it swells as she thinks of Papa, helpless, in a hospital, waiting for her and her sisters to get there.

"What happened?" Gertie asks.

None of the sisters answer.

She cannot remember Papa having been ill lately, but she has not seen him for several evenings and it is true that the week before, he seldom ate his dinner. He seems preoccupied, but Gertie is used to his many moods. He can be jovial one day, full of mirth, then his mood darkens, and he disappears, evening after evening, and she is left with Yéyène, or Fidélia, who is always locked away in her room, with her books. Gertie looks at Fidélia. Her face is grave. She, too, is looking over at Margie and Sisi with a worried air. What is it about grief, that it enters a space a fog and leaves it burdened?

Going on eight, Gertie and Sisi see life extending itself in front of them like an unending hair ribbon that they can lay flat or bend in new directions, giving their lives new shapes and chancing into unexpected encounters. But it is one thing to imagine that you can take that ribbon into your hands and bend it at will and another to discover that there is another ribbon, an invisible one, over which you have little control. Gertie nods to her sisters and follows them out of the school. She didn't have a chance to wave goodbye to Sisi, who has left with Margie. Gertie makes a note to find out what is going on with Sisi when they return to school the next day.

Gertie sits between her sisters in a car driven by the same man who retrieved her from Sisi's house in the fall. They do not speak to one another. A feeling of dread spreads over Gertie, a thickness, a weight, under which she has difficulty breathing, a caul from which she might never be loosened. Gertie searches for the oval of the locket that Papa gave her. Yéyène helped her get the chain repaired and she continues to wear it whenever she thinks it is safe to do so, hidden beneath her clothes. It brings her comfort, a secret that no one can wrest from her.

They arrive at the hospital and Gertie follows her sisters through the shadowy corridors and then into a bright room where Papa lies, looking thin and gaunt, propped up by many pillows. There are many others assembled around the room. All Gertie's siblings are there, including Rico and Andrée. But there are others she doesn't know, a few young men as tall as Rico, towering next to him like trees in a forest. When they turn to look at her, they are of different hues but carry an air of eerie familiarity, as if Gertie should know them. There are a couple of girls Fidélia's age, teenagers holding on to each other as if readying themselves for a strong gale to come through the room, though there are no windows open, no storm announced. Gertie does not know where to stand. She catches Andrée's eye, but all

Andrée does is glower at her as if Gertie is herself out of place, not these other young people with strangely familiar faces, who look at her sadly or with indifference. Gertie shrinks beneath her invisible caul, hiding beneath it, its weight. There is no one to turn to. Among the assembled, an older, tall man in a white smock stands on the other side of Papa. He faces Andrée. "He doesn't have much time," the man says, as if he is ending a long-winded explanation. Andrée nods.

"Are all of my children here?" Papa asks. "Is Gertrude here?"

"Yes, yes," Andrée replies impatiently. She beckons Gertie to stand closer to their sisters and brother, away from the strangers among them. "She's here, and all the others. That we know of," she adds with a tone of irritation.

Despite his weakened state, Papa dismisses her irritation with an authoritative sweep of his hand.

Gertie stumbles through the assembled bodies crowding around the bed. "I'm here, Papa," she says. "I'm here."

But as she emerges at the foot of the bed, she sees that there is another girl her age there. A girl she does know, who is not one of her sisters. "What are you doing here?" she asks.

"That's my papa," Sisi says, pointing to the man in the bed. "That's him," she repeats, stupefied, as if she, too, cannot believe the sight of Gertie, of all the others crowded around the room.

"All of my children," Papa murmurs from the bed.

"Your papa?" Gertie asks Sisi. "I thought you said your papa was a come-and-go father. How can he be yours too?" Gertie looks about the room, and it seems that no one else but her and Sisi are surprised. She notes that Margie is nowhere in sight.

"Where's Margie?" she asks Sisi.

"Outside, waiting for me," Sisi answers. "He isn't her papa," she adds by way of explanation.

"My Lord," Andrée snorts. "At least Mother isn't here to see this."

This is why Margie hugged Sisi in the hallway, Gertie thinks. Papa is her papa.

Papa places a hand on Andrée's arm. "I asked for all my children, so that you would know that I see my legacy in each of you, and you should too."

But then Papa's breath becomes labored, and he sinks farther into his pillows. The man in white, the doctor, takes Papa's pulse, then pulls the older siblings aside.

The older sisters eye Sisi with suspicion as they leave the bedside. Gertie watches as they brush their skirts against Sisi, refusing to bend down and embrace her. The caul engulfing her turns into a heavy anchor girding her midsection. Gertie looks over at Sisi and it dawns on her that Sisi is not just her best friend but her *sister*. Sisi, with whom she pinky-swears and holds hands at recess, who believes every word that comes out of her mouth—their father's mouth—is not just her best friend. Her sister! Gertie gasps audibly while Papa's breath grows more strained.

"We're half sisters?" Gertie asks.

"Something like that," Sisi mutters, seemingly in shock herself.

A priest enters the room to provide last rites. He absolves Papa of his sins and the strangers with familiar faces, including Sisi, of theirs—the fact of being born out of wedlock.

It is the beginning and end of all Gertie thought she understood of the world. The threads that tie her to Papa, to the world of Léogâne, to her school friends in Port-au-Prince, to her mother, whom Papa did not call to the hospital, have been cut loose. Everything she understands unravels.

Gertie bursts into tears.

Sisters? Like Andrée and all the others? Sisters? It is a calamity worse than Papa's impending death. Worse than anything that Gertie can imagine, then, at seven going on eight years of age.

SISI, PORT-AU-PRINCE, 1942

MARGIE IS RESPONSIBLE FOR GETTING SISI TO AND from school, which is a good forty-five-minute walk away from their house, located in a neighborhood sprawling southwest of the port, alongside the edges of the city. The walks to school feel to Sisi like a rewarding adventure because of the potential for stops at the roadside stalls with Margie. If it were anyone else taking her, they would rush her along, make her keep up with their long strides despite her short ones. When she returned from Gertie's house after the bullying in the schoolyard and after Margie exploded at Gertie's sister Andrée in the street, Sisi was comforted by the fact that she had a sister like Margie who would come to her defense, comforted by the knowledge that she had her friends, Lou, Odette, and Gertie, most of all Gertie.

The house Sisi lives in has no running water, electricity. They haul water up the stairs to the second-floor bathroom, use oil lamps to do homework after dark or, in her mother and Momo's case, to square up their ledgers after a long week of work. Their live-in help receive room and board in exchange for household chores, cleaning, and cooking. As one departs, to marry, to travel, or simply to find a better, paying position, another takes her place: the household is always full of girls and women, humming. Life is lean but they have plenty, more than enough, Sisi thinks.

She remembers when Gertie spent the morning at her house after an evening bout of sickness the prior school year, left there by a father who had business to attend to and business with Mami who made dresses for Gertie's older sisters. They had a beautiful, luminous morning with Margie by the sea, the whole of their futures spread out before them. It isn't common to visit the houses of people unrelated to oneself, and Sisi remembers Gertie's visit distinctly, partly because it happened only that once but also because, once she was inside Gertie's house a few months later, she came to realize that they were from markedly different worlds.

Everything changes even more the day that Margie comes to fetch Sisi, not after school but in the middle of class, the nun teaching the class telling Sisi to step out to meet Margie in the corridor. Minutes later, she sees Gertie meeting other girls about Margie's age, on the other side of the same hallway. Margie tells her that Papa is ill and asking for her. She is to take her at that instant to the hospital where he is.

"Is he going to die?" she asks Margie.

"I don't know," Margie says, hugging her tightly. "All I know is that he asked for you and that we must hurry."

Sisi nods into Margie's shoulder and catches sight of Gertie peering at her from the other side of the hall. Sisi wonders what is going on with Gertie but doesn't have time to ask; Margie whisks her away, to Papa.

Once they arrive at the hospital, Margie explains to Sisi that Papa has been admitted for a ruptured appendix and that an infection has set in; the doctors are doing all they can, but it seems that he has been admitted too late. All they can do is keep him comfortable and execute his last wishes.

"One of them is to see you one last time," Margie says, gently pushing her into the room to find Papa.

"Aren't you coming with me?" Sisi pleads.

"He's not my papa," Margie says. "He asked for his children. You'll be all right," she prods. "Go on."

Sisi holds back when Margie says "children." Isn't she the only one? As she turns her back on Margie, she thinks about the imposing photograph of a man in a vest in their home, Margie's father, long dead before she was born, a man she never met and who Margie hardly remembers. She feels the suffocating heat of the hospital, poorly ventilated, closing in on her.

Sisi tries to be courageous as she walks into Papa's room. She finds him ashen, lying in one of the hospital beds, beads of sweat across his forehead, moaning softly as he holds his stomach, as if it might just burst. It is frightening to see him this way. There are so many people crowded into the room, so many taller than her. She makes her way to the foot of the bed, where she can close her eyes a moment, take a breath. She does just this, but as soon as she opens them, it is Gertie she finds standing next to her, looking at her with wide eyes, mouth agape. What is Gertie doing here, of all places, at the foot of Papa's bed, not in school where she belongs?

Standing next to Gertie at the foot of her father's hospital bed, Sisi feels her world waver and collapse as she comes to understand something about her connection to Gertie, and all those tall people in the room. She and Gertie are different in a number of ways: Sisi likes to draw and Gertie likes to play; Gertie is popular while Sisi is a hand-me-down friend; Sisi likes spending time with her mother while Gertie's mother is nowhere to be found, not even in church; Gertie spends more time with the help in her house than with her family, while Sisi sits enraptured listening to Margie or Momo tell her stories about the Simbi and the *mistè*, or listening to Momo recounting tall tales she hears at market. But they are alike in one way.

"*C'est ton papa aussi?* Is he your dad too?"

Gertie's childish question bounces through Sisi's mind, a button falling out of the blue from a tailor-made garment before a special occasion, clattering noisily against floor tiles with no time for repair.

Sisi nods in affirmation, not knowing what to say. If Margie were in her place, she would have laughed, taken things lightly; she knows what it is to have a ghost for a father.

Sisi looks past Gertie to the other tall people in the room. She recognizes Gertie's older sister, Andrée, and others who have the same facial features. She recognizes Gertie's brother, Rico, who, along with Andrée, chased her out of the gingerbread house by the school. The others assembled, all very tall too, she does not know. There are no mothers in the room, only Papa's children, all thirteen of them. Gertie's older sisters are looming over her and Gertie like egrets, svelte and long-beaked, elegant but ready, it seems, to peck at them should either of them say or do the wrong thing. Under the hot gaze of the elder sisters, Sisi endures the weight of their blame, as if she chose Papa for herself. Sisi watches as her father's mouth gapes open like a carp's, watches as the whole of Gertie's mouth, so much like their father's, opens and closes, cries out against the injustice of the news. Their father. Her father. She watches Gertie cry fat tears.

Sisi does not shed a tear because, by now, she has learned that tears are a waste of time. The thing to do is to swallow whatever it is that might cause their flow, not to bury the pain but to cross it as a school of fish or pod of dolphins do waves.

She absorbs the new information, which she should have suspected, because Gertie's mouth always reminded her of her father's. It is cavernous and always telling stories, endless stories that loop together like an ouroboros, without tail or beginning. Her half sister. But Gertie is legitimate. All the Alcindors around the bed are, with their different heights and sizes, anointed heirs to whatever Papa might bequeath. But Momo always said that her papa was without a penny to his name, which is why he did not live with them, so this must be true of their papa too.

Gertie's older sisters flounce by Sisi at the foot of their father's deathbed, and Sisi realizes, all at once, the meaning of a phrase she has heard the nuns at school pronounce while talking among themselves about a few of the students: "outside child," as if that phrase explained everything, why a child is slow, unruly, or has difficulty in the classroom or at home. She realizes, then, as Gertie's older sisters (her sisters?) glare at her as she stands by her father's hospital bed, that she is that child, although she is neither slow nor unruly and comes from a happy home.

Sisi always thinks of her father as the outside child, outside person, the one who comes in from out there to be fed and stroked and cajoled, like a cat without a proper home. It dawns on her at the foot of the hospital bed that the reality is that it is she and her mother who are the strays that he comes to pet and play with, while Gertie and her siblings are the inside cats, the reason that Momo insists Sisi attend the school a forty-five-minute walk away, though there is a perfectly good school run by the same order of nuns closer to home. That school is good enough for the outside children, the less wealthy, the working class, while the faraway school is for *legitimate* children, in other words for inside children, the ones with wealth to show, who can purchase new uniforms every year. Sisi understands then that Momo has made her pass for something that she is not.

Sisi goes home from the hospital with Margie. Her father is dead. She says nothing to Mami or to Momo, who understand when she takes nothing for dinner. Mami retires to her room and does not come out for a few days.

Later that same night, Margie finds Sisi crying in her room despite herself, puts a hand on her back to calm her. "At least you knew him for a time," Margie says. "The rest doesn't matter so much."

Does Margie know? Has she always known? Sisi thinks again of the fight with Gertie's sister, Andrée. Their different last names. This makes Sisi cry all the harder.

"But Sisi," Margie goes on, "you know you'll always have me and Mami and Momo. All those other people don't matter. You have us."

"There were so many kids there, Margie," Sisi splutters. "Gertie was there. Gertie was one of them. She and I are sisters too. Like you and me."

Margie shakes her head. "No, not like us. Never like us. We have different fathers, true, but we've grown up here, together, with Mami and Momo, who love us both. Nothing can change that."

Sisi turns to embrace her sister tightly. She can't say everything that is on her mind and heart: that she feels betrayed by Gertie; that she can't understand why no one told her about the other children, that Gertie is one of them; that her heart breaks in two for Mami. She holds on to Margie.

"*Pa jan'm kite'm,*" she cries. "Don't ever leave me."

Margie hugs Sisi back. "I'll always be in your heart. We all will."

For Sisi, it is the beginning of a dying season.

From that day forward, everything changes: Gertie stops speaking to Sisi and one day disappears from the school altogether. Margie graduates high school a few months later and leaves Haiti. Then Momo dies, leaving behind her penciled accounts and bags of unmeasured beans of all colors, maroon, purple, off-white, navy, brown, littering the ground of her storeroom on the second floor. Nothing is ever the same again.

SISI, PHOENIX, 2002

HAD THEIR FRIENDSHIP BEEN GIRLISH INFATUATION, or something more, blood calling blood? Simone ponders the question over and over and never comes to a conclusion. She wonders if it was the marked difference in their households that prompted Gertie to cut off their friendship after the deathbed meeting, as if they were never friends. Was it the lack of running water at her house, the simplicity? Was she told, by her mother, sisters, that Sisi was simply not worth her time? Then there was Andrée's obituary, many years later, after they'd all left the island, naming Simone as a surviving family member; the woman had passed away, from a cancer, and reached out of the grave to claim Simone. Simone did not want to be claimed. She had moved on with her life long ago. Why do *they*, the Alcindors, not move on—they who have everything: the name, the titles, the land, the riches? Why do they keep returning?

Instead of being called to the deathbed, Sisi would have preferred, back then, to receive a photograph of her father in a large manila envelope announcing his death. Gertie's tall sisters could have sent a portrait of their father, taken in his younger years, when he wore a thin mustache that made him look somewhat like Zorro, had he worn a mask about his eyes, a wide-brimmed hat, and a cape. A *dignified* image of their father at his smartest, wearing a suit and a vest from which hung a chain that led to a watch tucked away in a pocket, out of sight, like the portrait of Margie's father that hung in their entryway. It wasn't until that moment at the foot of the hospital bed, watching her father struggle for breath, that Sisi realized that she was like that watch to her father, tucked away, out of sight. Maybe her father returned every Thursday to their house because her mother was to her father the chain, something that kept him tethered.

Yes. She would have preferred that Gertie's family mail them a nice portrait of him and spare them the deathbed pageantry. This way, she would never have found out what she did, that inside and outside meant different things, that she was an outside child without a proper name, that outside fathers had other families that took up most of their time, that they gave lavish gifts to at holidays and birthdays and took for rides in fancy cars into the mountains on the weekends. Most of all, she would not have found out about the other siblings, the half siblings, half-in and half-out. She would never have found out that Gertie, her best friend, was, in fact, her half sister, the loss of her as quick as she had been found.

Simone exhales heavily and turns away from the phone placed back on its carrier. Gertie's voice remains in her ear. She can still feel in herself that warmth she always felt as a child, when Gertie would turn to face her to tell her a secret, the product of her latest adventures. There is no one, not even her daughter, who affects her in quite this way.

After all these years, Gertie's voice, a palpable connection that Simone can feel in the spaces between their words, makes something in her vibrate. Gertie is her tuning fork. As angry as she is after receiving the latest call, something else in Simone is peaceful, recalibrated.

This makes her angry too.

PART II

SISI
WHITE BIRD OF PARADISE

OHIO, 1978

THE MOMENT SIMONE HEARS ABOUT THE STARLINGS falling out of the sky—the common blackbirds speckled with golden flecks that descend onto their snowy patio by the dozens after the start of each new year, startling everyone with their liveliness, foraging seeds from bushes and grass—she knows that she has to save herself before she, too, falls out of the vast world.

Weeks into the new year, instead of welcoming back the starlings, Simone watches as a blizzard dumps feet of snow across the region. They stay indoors for several days, waiting for the city's two snowplows, Scott jokes, to circle the outer rings of the urban center where they live. Scott makes a game of shoveling out their front walk with Emma: first they build a fort, then a snowman, then Scott carves out a path on the walkway for the mailman from the street to the house. Simone doesn't join them. She watches. On the radio, she hears that the storm killed more than fifty people across Ohio and though she is warm at home, she withers inside, a seed too long kept underground, wonders if she will be next.

Simone has been feeling unsettled for some time, teetering against her will into what seems like a vast, bottomless pit that nothing and no one can save her from, she knows, except herself—has she the will to do so. When the starlings fail to show, when she hears that they have fallen—by the hundreds, dead, straight out of the sky and onto the frozen ground like large pieces of buckshot—and the winter grips the earth and will not let go, Simone takes this as a sign, realizes that she has to pull herself up, away from the edge of everything she thinks she knows, back into the land of the living. She has been floating aimlessly for so long within the confines of her marriage, of motherhood, that she has forgotten what it is like to be who she was before, when life would come to her as an expanse, like the ocean that lay feet away from the house in which she grew up.

She noticed all kinds of birds shortly after she and Scott moved into their town house off the beltway that connects the outer reaches of the city to its center, each neighborhood bounded by invisible lines that determine who can live within a particular space and who cannot, some of that related to ancestry but mostly based on the color of one's skin. Where they settle is a kind of no-man's-land: this is how Simone describes it when asked. It is desolate and everyday birds are brown like the dirt that covers the roads each winter, turning the beauty of fresh-fallen snow into a mucky curtain of slick mud. The winters are long, gray, and each early spring, as the days grow longer and warmer, she has the distinct sensation that a caul is being removed from around her head, or that she has been keeping herself underwater and has suddenly come up for air. Every time, a fog lifts that she has been unaware of carrying. Each time, she is reborn. It is a condition that affects a larger number of people than she imagines. There is no name for it other than the winter blues. At the same time, she doesn't see how anyone can be cheerful under such conditions—with the steady draining of light between late fall and the onset of winter around the end-of-year holidays and the reemergence of light six months later. It could be worse, of course; they could be living in one of those places where it rains all winter and fog shrouds the city most of the year. Nothing could be more depressing, but this no-man's-land is a contender.

They live in a city of about a quarter million on the border between Ohio and Kentucky, surrounded by wheat and mustard fields, many of which are being sold off by farming families that have been there for generations to developers promising to bring vitality back to the city. Those developers construct new structures for incoming transplants and there they landed, in a duplex of which only one wall is shared with an adjacent couple who are elderly and mostly quiet. New developments are usually filled with internationals and so they are asked few questions and Simone passes though she isn't quite sure as what. She doesn't have to answer questions about whose people she belongs to and since she doesn't belong to anyone around, there is nothing to deny. She can tread the color line quietly and Scott makes it more plausible that she is somewhat whiter than she is because, so goes the thinking, why would a doctor—even if he is just a veterinarian—marry a colored girl if he could have had his pick? When they try to place her, at a barbecue or a dinner party with Scott's colleagues from the university, where she has a part-time job as a technician in one of the labs, Simone can laugh off the questions presented to her under the guise of flattery because isn't that what Southern belles and beauty queens, which is what they think she could be, do? Laugh, bare their pearly-white teeth, grin and bear it?

She is tired of it all—the grinning, the bearing—she wants, some days, to tear into translucent throats through which she can see the threading of veins, pulses beating. Why are any of them pursuing this idea of blue bloods when they were an invention of colonization? Not again, Scott says, his head in his hands, when she starts a diatribe against the neighbors or their colleagues, expounding on the history of the Americas. Can't I have one night without a history lesson on settler colonialism? Can't we live in the present? But the present is the past, she says, bewildered, because Scott was not like this when they first met, in France, where he was spending a year studying abroad.

It has taken years for her to understand that Scott never gave history much thought, married her because it was a whim, something he could do to break out of the expected, the hum-drum life spreading out before him like the blueprint his father and grandfather had laid out: high school, going to college, spending a year abroad because that was what rich kids did while the poor ones backpacked on a gap year, before returning home to take over working in the family vet hospital, marriage, kids. Marrying her was part of the plan but marrying *her* her, a foreigner, was a way to spice things up a little, disturb the peace, before following up with the plan and settling down, though with a slight browning of the family tree, if they believed, being Southerners, albeit from Florida, that the tree hadn't been browned before. Simone highly doubts it; she doesn't believe in such things as pure bloods and bloodlines: home has taught her better.

Even though she left Haiti twenty years ago, she misses almost everything about it: the rooster's cry in the yard at the break of dawn; the brightness of sunrise; the brilliant green todies hopping in and out of trees; the majestic trogons; the light blue swallows with their gray-tipped wings; the high-pitched warblers; the way the light dappled through the wooden shutters in the living room where her grandmother used to take her naps when they were all in school; translucent pink- or green-bellied lizards skittering across the tiled floors in pursuit of flies; the steady rat-a-tat of her mother's sewing machine, the needle piercing up and down through fabric as her mother made the next debutante girl's coming-out dress or graduation frock. Her mother made her and her sister simple print dresses for everyday wear that cinched, belted, at the waist and cascaded slightly, in pleats, to mid-calf. Her mother found prints that were in fashion so that she and Margie always looked smart alongside the other girls at school, when it became more common for dresses to be store-bought than tailored. She repaired the hand-me-down uniforms Margie passed down to Sisi and made sure they looked new, though the fading blue and red fabric gave away that they had been restored or refreshed. The sound of her mother's industry wafting up to the second floor of the house was a familiar, comforting sound from her childhood, like rain drops falling in a light pitter-patter across the uneven surface of undulating corrugated roofs. It was a sound she never imagined never hearing again, never waking to, so many years later, now in her own home, with Scott and her ten-year-old, Emma, a sound neither Scott nor Emma can claim as their own.

The starlings were a comforting sight, the first new year they spent in the town house when they arrived years ago, when Emma was a toddler. The birds came by the dozens, searching for grains in the underbelly of the snowdrifts covering their porch and sidewalk, the speckled golden flecks in their plumage a promise of better things to come, a hidden treasure beneath the surface of things. Simone waits for them every winter, at the start of each new year. They are her sign that she will emerge from the dormancy, that the caul will begin to loosen, and that the feeling of being submerged beneath the surface of a placid lake, with something or someone keeping her head down, perhaps a Simbi seeking to lure her to unknown depths, will soon subside.

This year, however, the starlings never come, and Simone remains weighted down, foggy. She reads in the paper that the starlings fell dead from the sky, by the hundreds. A dread fills her as she scans the news item, right next to an entertainment headline about a film director fleeing to Europe to escape prosecution for assaulting a minor (story continued on page six), because she knows that whatever the reason for their falling, it is the beginning of calamity. She feels this same vertiginous fall in herself, the coming of an end, of whatever it is she calls her life, the life she has with Scott and Emma. With Scott. Always Emma.

Something is over, has been over for quite some time, but she doesn't know how she knows, can recognize signs: the dead birds; Scott's habit of turning away from her at night without a kiss goodnight; the way Scott forgets to call to tell her he is eating dinner out with coworkers; his failure to introduce her at work gatherings, leaving her off by herself next to the beverage table, mistaken for the waitress; the way they no longer make plans for the weekends; the way Emma looks to one and the other worriedly when they eat dinner all together, and asks them about their respective days the way they used to ask her about kindergarten, the child become the parent.

She packed the gaps in their relationship with art classes. She enrolled in painting, pottery, photography, and illustration classes at the local art museum, and that filled the time for a while, especially when Emma started school. She renewed her love for nature with "plein air" classes, laughing to herself when the instructor couldn't pronounce the French, and kept to herself when the other students seemed to be trying to figure out who was single. She doesn't make friends, doesn't feel the need to: she has Scott, Emma. But as the end, proclaimed by the falling birds, careens toward her, she has become aware that there is no longer a clear grouping, a family unit. They are individual cells coexisting. She cleans, cooks, and organizes things. She is fulfilling a role, one that she expects of herself but that gives her little satisfaction, so that when the illustration teacher tells her, over her shoulder, "You're good at this. You could illustrate children's books," she feels a thrill she hasn't felt in a while.

She begins to dream of Gertie, of their first encounter, Gertie looking over her shoulder at her crudely drawn chicken that might as well have been a giraffe for all the skill she had back then. Gertie's curiosity; Gertie's affirmation. That feeling of being seen. In the dream, Gertie's face turns into that of the teacher from the art museum and disappointment sears her, even as she hears the same words in the classroom: "You could turn this into something." It is Gertie's voice she longs to hear. She startles awake, sweating. Scott is snoring lightly with his back turned to her, oblivious. It is the beginning of a kind of ending, the first step on the unfurling road to another elsewhere.

But there is no going home. Home is no longer a destination. She hasn't been in touch with Gertie since she left Haiti. In fact, from the day they discovered their sisterhood, she saw Gertie less and less as if Gertie had been a mirage or a ghost rattling about in an abandoned house. Before Margie left, she kept Sisi up-to-date on the goings-on of the Alcindors as if she was afraid that if Sisi heard the news from anyone else, she might make a fatal mistake: renew her friendship with Gertie. She learned from Margie that the Alcindors went by their mother's name because their father's name was Spanish and the mother had inherited the family money. They were always opening and closing businesses: a Dominican-style bakery (it closed—not enough people were interested in what was being sold); a hardware store (it stayed open—everyone always needed a bolt or a tool or a handyman); a candy store (who didn't like candy?); a hotel (it was in the gingerbread house across from the school and only *moun lot bo*, foreigners, stayed there); and then, then, Margie said, hands gesticulating, Rico, the not-yet-grown boy who, with Andrée, the eldest sister, had come chasing Sisi out of their house, opened a bank, the biggest on either side of the border and, Margie underscored, they didn't offer microloans to women or to beggars: they were in the business of being in business, that is, of making money, not in the business of making the world a better place. Margie was bitter about them, the

Alcindors, the way they flaunted their wealth and looked down on everyone else, especially Sisi. She had not forgiven the way Sisi had been treated by Gertie's older siblings or how she had been dropped entirely by Gertie after the meeting at the hospital. Margie thought that the more she told Sisi negative stories about the Alcindors, the more she would be convinced that she had lost nothing.

Sisi listened to Margie's stories about the Alcindors and laughed along with her, hiding her longing for Gertie's friendship until it crept up onto her shoulder like a fog rolling over a hill or the voice of the instructor at the museum, his honey tones opening up a door within her: "You should seriously try your hand at this. You could be making a living."

A living. A life. Doesn't she have both?

PORT-AU-PRINCE, 1943–46

A weight descends upon Sisi's household after Papa's death. It is not just the fact of his passing but the message that Mami receives in a hand-delivered note shortly after Sisi's visit to the hospital. The note confirms Papa's death and says that none of them, not even Sisi, may come to the funeral. The Alcindors claim that they observed Papa's wishes while he was alive, but the dead can have no ears or eyes.

"Who sent you this note?" Momo demands to know, rapping the top of the dinner table with her knuckles.

"Who do you think?" Mami says sharply, aggravated at her mother. "Isn't it obvious?"

"I know it's from the Alcindors," Momo replies, "but I want to know: In whose hand is it written? Is it the wife who dared send you this, or one of the children?"

"She would never," Mami states confidently. "I know what it is to be shamed. To write to me would mean acknowledging our existence. She would never do that. I would never do it."

Margie takes the letter from Mami's hand and examines the lettering. "It looks like how the nuns teach cursive at the school. It was one of the sisters—Andrée or Altagracia. It might have been Yvonne, though she's not mean like the rest of them."

Mami grasps the letter. "What does it matter? What it says is plain. They don't want us showing up at the funeral. They don't want us to make demands." She crumples up the letter. "As if we ever did! Have they no shame? Do they think we have no shame?"

Momo slaps the surface of the table with an open palm but says nothing more. Her disgust is plain, but all Sisi can think about is the fact that she will never see Papa again. She isn't sure she said goodbye to him at the hospital or, if she did, if she understood that it would be for the last time.

"Is Gertie going?" she asks quietly.

Mami, Momo, and Margie all turn to her. They seem to have forgotten that she is there.

"Am I the only one that they aren't letting go?"

"There are others, I'm sure," Momo says wryly.

"I saw the other children at the hospital," Sisi responds.

Margie looks to Mami and then to Momo.

"Are the others going?" Sisi persists. "Why is it only me who's not going?"

Margie puts a protective arm around Sisi. "It's not just you, Sisi. It's all of the outside children who aren't going, but they just want to make it clear to us that we're not to go to the viewing or the service or the burial. Do you understand?"

"I can't say a final goodbye to Papa?"

"No," Mami says. "I'm afraid not, Sisi. We must do it in our own way. In our own time."

Sisi is kept out of school for three weeks. Mami and Momo claim that this will be enough time to let things blow over. Just the Alcindors and the families of Papa's other children know who was gathered in that hospital room, and why. The nuns, if they realize, will say nothing in order not to lose revenue. Family secrets come with the territory in private schools of their kind. It is always better to look the other way.

The whole time, Sisi frets about Gertie and what she must be going through, losing her everyday papa, not just the once-a-week papa she knew. Gertie has only the mean older sisters, including the one who yelled at Margie in the street. Who could be consoling her now? Sisi doesn't dare ask. The mood in her house is heavy enough.

Despite her previous complaints about Papa, even Momo misses his weekly visits. She replaces them with a cleaning ritual, asking the live-ins to sweep and mop the floors of the house with her from top to bottom. Sisi joins the women as if the effort could somehow sweep away the weight pushing down upon them like thunderclouds, as if, with the tile floors gleaming in the sun, a momentary spark of life will return. Then, her mother exhales heavily from behind the closed door of her atelier, and instead of the rat-a-tat of her sewing machine comes the soft stutter of her weeping. She sounds to Sisi like a stream gurgling over river rocks, such as she saw during a school expedition deep into the mountains where a cascade fell from the gap of a cliff into a river below. It makes Sisi's heart sink to hear her mother crying like this, to hear love's loss manifested. After the crying stops, a framed photograph of her father is placed next to the one of Margie's father in the foyer; to this is added a green candle they light every Thursday, around the time Papa would have come to dinner, next to a bouquet of yellow or orange flowers. They blow out the candle when it is time to go to sleep.

Green, Momo tells Sisi one night, is the color of a god who loves women too much, a powerful god who had many children and too little time to tend to them all. With this, Sisi understands that Papa could have been a son of Ogou Feray, a warring god who likes flowers. She prays to the god to keep Papa safe, even if he walked in shadows when alive. Slowly, the inky cloud that descended on the house starts to lift and Sisi's thoughts turn to Gertie, to what she can do to make up for her absence. Sweets, she thinks. She can bring Gertie a sweet from home.

"Can you help me?" she asks Margie, avoiding explaining that she wants to do something special for Gertie. "I've been gone so long I want to bring something to school for my friends, for Odette and Lou."

Margie looks at her thoughtfully, and for a moment Sisi thinks Margie can see right into her thoughts. Sisi frowns, trying to push out Margie's penetrating gaze, but Margie speaks her thoughts aloud. "Don't do anything for that Alcindor girl, Sisi. I told you before that it will just get you in trouble. It's not worth it. You'll get hurt."

"But it's not for her," Sisi protests, "just for my friends."

"Ask Momo," Margie says, ignoring the protest, "but don't tell her it's for Gertie."

"I'm telling you that it's not for her," Sisi insists, as she runs off to ask Momo for her help. Momo gives her a pensive look but doesn't refuse her request. She tells Sisi to ask the cook for a big pot, for condensed milk, star anise, cinnamon, limes, sugar, coconut milk.

"I'm ready," Sisi yells when everything is gathered in the kitchen. "Ready!" she yells again when she doesn't see Momo coming down the stairs.

"Hold your horses," she hears Momo say after a few minutes. "The old are not getting any younger." Soon, they are melting butter, sugar, adding the anise, the cinnamon, the milks, bringing everything to a boil.

"Do you know what the secret to *dous* is, Sisi?" Momo asks. It is the first time that they have made the sweets together. "It's the beating of the ingredients together on the stove," Momo says as she demonstrates with a large wooden spoon, "beating air into the sweet until the texture changes and it begins to get a pale caramel color and crystallizes. When it starts to crumble on the sides of the pan, you just keep going until the mixture begins to stiffen, and then you pour it out into a flat pan before the whole thing seizes up. But first, squeeze the lime juice in. Can you do that?"

"Yes, ma'am." Sisi squeezes the limes that the cook has cut in half for them. She watches as Momo beats in the juice. The color of the mixture pales and, bit by bit, becomes just as Momo said, caramel-colored, and the liquid stiffens and crumbles against the sides of the pan as Momo continues beating vigorously.

"Do you have the pan ready?"

"Yes, Momo," Sisi says, placing a large tin pan across the stovetop.

"Step back now." Momo pours out the steaming contents in one stroke of the spoon, smoothing over the surface until the stiffening mix reaches all sides of the sheet pan. "It doesn't have to be perfect," Momo says, "it just has to be flattened a bit. We'll just let it cool and then we can cut it up and put it in some tins." Thin dots of perspiration run across Momo's top lip. Momo wipes her mouth with a napkin. "Your friends will thank you for this."

Sisi smiles. Later, they cut the sweet together and wrap the pieces up in wax paper before placing them in a tin for Sisi to take to school. Sisi is sure that this will make Gertie smile.

"Don't expect too much," Margie says before Sisi goes to sleep, but Momo shushes Margie with a hand on her arm.

"Let the girl have hope, Margie," Sisi hears Momo say as they close the door to her room. "Those girls may have a deeper connection than we'd like but it is there, like rivers that flow way onto way, like the Simbi. We can do nothing about it."

Sisi goes to sleep with Momo's words on her mind and dreams of the Simbi calling out to her and to Gertie from the depths of ponds, wells, riverbeds. Could the Simbi truly snatch any girl they wanted and bury her with their water songs?

At school the next day, Sisi is greeted by Lou and Odette. They both give her a big hug to welcome her back. As she opens the tin of sweets, she asks, "Where's Gertie?" Odette looks over to Lou.

"She didn't come back after you both were taken to the hospital," Lou says.

"The nuns said that her father died," Odette adds. "Didn't your father die too?"

Sisi nods but doesn't clarify that Gertie and she share a papa.

"That's strange, isn't it?" Lou states, her hand fishing into Sisi's tin. "That both your dads would die the same day." Lou brings a square of *dous* to her mouth and pops it in.

"But isn't she coming back?" Sisi asks, ignoring Lou's last statement.

Lou shakes her head.

"Can I have one too?" Odette points to the tin.

"Of course." Sisi hands it to her.

"These are so good," Lou says, "better than the ones my mom sells at the store. Did your mother make these? She's a seamstress and a sweet maker too?"

"No," Sisi replies, "my grandma made these. She doesn't make things like this often. She doesn't have the time."

"She should." Lou's hand fishes again after Odette takes a piece. "These are great."

"When do you think Gertie will come back?" Sisi tries again to find out about Gertie.

Lou shrugs. "I don't think she's coming back. The school year's almost finished, so her family sent her back to her mother's."

"Where's that?" Sisi asks.

"Léogâne. It's not far but far enough." Lou's hand plunges back into the tin. "Can I have more?"

"Help yourself," Sisi replies, discouraged. Gertie is not coming back? Léogâne is too far to walk. It might as well be the other side of the earth.

"My family has a house over there. I'll probably see her over the summer if you want me to take a message to her," Lou offers.

"I'll think about it," Sisi says, wilting inside. Gertie left without leaving her a word, without saying anything. Can she believe that Gertie's sisters have a power so great that they could keep Gertie from writing a note, from saying goodbye?

"OK," Lou says nonchalantly. "Glad to have you back. I'll bring you cookies next week if my mom can spare a few from the store."

Sisi nods but her heart is cold. There will be no shared grief, no shared loss. She won't find out all the things there are to know about Papa that he didn't have the time to share himself. Is it a Simbi that is keeping Gertie from her? Has Gertie walked too close to the edge of a pond or been beguiled by a river's song? Has Gertie been asked to fetch water and been pulled into a well, never to be heard from again? There will be no easy answers.

Sisi never sees Gertie at the school again. Despite her growing friendships with Lou and Odette, Sisi misses Gertie's tumbling laughter, her propensity for wearing bright green, both traits reminding her of the little todies that hop from tree to tree up in the *mornes*. She misses the companionship, the trading of sweets at recess, of whispered secrets, studying together and pushing each other to get the best grades in the class. When Sisi thinks about their exchanges now, it doesn't seem like such a shock that they should find out that they are sisters: they fit together like puzzle pieces, completing each other in ways that are effortless, without sharp edges.

Though Lou and Odette remain steadfast, the other girls at school, Sisi observes, go back to treating her like the outsider she is, the one who receives the hand-me-downs, who doesn't have extra coins to buy sweets from the vendors installed outside the gates of the school, within reach of the students, the one whose lunch meals are brought in all the way from the house by the port by the live-in girls because, although doing so is time-consuming, it costs less than paying the nuns for meals at the school. What does it matter if both her mother and grandmother are working women and have to pay others to make sure she has food to eat? The food is always piping hot and savory, usually rice and beans, sometimes stewed chicken. At recess, Sisi sees the older girls who bullied her, Gertie, Lou, and Odette, whispering among themselves. What do they know? Simone wonders.

When Margie finds out that Gertie has not returned to the school, she says, "Maybe it's all for the better." Sisi is shocked. Doesn't Margie remember that Gertie is her best friend? "You have other friends now, anyway."

Sisi is silent. They walk in the port area one early Saturday morning, watching the sunrise and fishermen coming back from the early morning catch, as they did with Gertie. So much has changed in so brief a time. "You need to focus on your studies because I'll be leaving soon."

"Leaving?" Sisi asks, a sinking feeling overtaking her. They watch a great blue heron inching its way from where the ocean meets the sand. It holds its head high as if contemplating the sunrise as they are. The heron's long head curves forward and the yellow beak darts into the water to reemerge with a silvery fish clamped firmly in its grip, flashing and squirming. The heron tosses the fish quickly into the air, then swallows it in two, three gulps, before resuming its resolute stance of aloofness. Sisi turns her gaze from the heron to Margie's lithe form and notes a slight resemblance between her sister and the heron: both are tall, elegant, seemingly insouciant. She shakes the observation away to ask, "Where will you go?" She follows her question with another question, on the edge of exasperation: "What will you do?"

Margie laughs and sweeps Sisi up in an embrace, then they sit next to each other on the pier overlooking the ocean. She holds Sisi with one arm and with the other she points toward the horizon, where they can barely make out a landmass—it is probably LaGonav, the island sitting like a fleeing fish in the open mouth of the curved bay. "Out there, Sisi," she says. "I'm going out there."

But what can be out there worth going toward? Sisi thinks. The nuns told them in history class about a war raging in Europe, schools like theirs decimated by bombs, people losing their lives, their families, children like her orphaned. What does Margie want with this outside world? "Isn't it dangerous out there?" she asks her instead.

"Don't worry," Margie replies, looking out onto the ocean, shading her eyes from the sun. "I'm not going overseas, not just yet. It's going to be some time before that part of the world is normal again."

Sisi squints. "But where, Margie? Where?" She is aware that she sounds like a beggar. She thinks of the beggars that stand outside the church after Sunday service, their heads down and their palms held up level with their foreheads for a dropped coin. Sometimes they are on their knees, mendicants. Sometimes, Momo gives Sisi a few coins or a folded *goud* bill to leave in their hands. She feels the warmth of the beggars' hands touch her own as she leaves the offerings, whispers of thanks wisp up from their downturned heads toward her ears, and she shivers, wonders if the beggars are angels, envoys sent to test them.

"Jamaica, Cuba, Guadeloupe, la Martinique," Margie is saying, counting off island names on the fingers of her outstretched hands.

Sisi's eyes open wide. "You're going to go to Jamaica in a *chaloupe*?" A *chaloupe* is no bigger than a fisherman's boat, maybe half the size. They are the traditional vessels of the Taino and Arawak, their predecessors. A few of the tradeswomen who are not afraid of the sea use them to travel between villages, using the riverways like roads, the coastlines like a compass. They like the narrowness of the vessels, less to lose, they say, easier to navigate, but Sisi imagines Margie tossed overboard by a roiling wave. The sea can be tumultuous, a vengeful, hungry mother calling back her kin, that underground place where so many of their ancestors perished during the crossings from beyond, some crawling back to the shore on the back of salty foam to make the earthbound aware that they remained, that not all had been lost. Sisi doesn't want this to be Margie's fate.

"No, silly. I'm not going to do that."

"Shouldn't someone go with you?" Sisi wonders. Though Margie loves to talk to the fishermen, Sisi has never seen her roll up her sleeves and pull in a net teeming with silver-scaled sardines with black underbellies. No, Margie is not a fisherman.

Margie stands and wipes the dust from the pier from the back of her skirt. Then she pulls Sisi up and does the same to the back of Sisi's clothes. "Don't worry." She looks her in the eye. "I won't be going alone. It will be a group of us. Members of a cooperative. Like a delegation. I'll be safe." She stops. "Just make sure you get your work done and don't cause any trouble for Momo and Mami. Pay attention to who your friends are and don't do everything they do because you want to be part of the crowd."

It is true that they have been insulated from the war going on across the ocean, but its effects have been felt through shortages.

Momo's business has been hit by it, as well as the Lombardos'. Lou often talks at school about what can no longer be gotten in the store, soaps and fancy toiletries, imported sweets. It is one of the reasons her mother is interested in buying local. Sisi falls silent and they walk home from the port absorbed, only to start the conversation again at the kitchen table that evening.

"But you'll come back, right?" Sisi asks. "You wouldn't just leave us behind, would you?"

"Of course not," Margie says. "But everyone has to leave someday. Momo left her village, and when my father died, that left Mami on her own until your papa came along." She bites her lip. Papa's passing is so new.

Mami and Momo shake their heads.

Margie leaves Haiti the next year. She does so against Momo and Mami's wishes. Margie claims she is leaving for them, to improve their businesses and to learn about the markets. She is going with other young people who have formed a cooperative together to open up markets for Haitians in neighboring islands. Momo and Mami want Margie to stay longer in school, get a certificate from the Institut Français of Port-au-Prince, which grants business and administration degrees that are recognized in the metropole: a guarantee of work. Margie promises that if things don't work out, she will enroll, and they leave it at that.

The whole family, including the cousins and live-in girls, accompany Margie and the other young people in her cooperative—three boys from good families and two other girls from modest families—to the ship in the port set to sail for Guadeloupe. From there, they will go to Martinique, and maybe even, later, on the way back, to Cuba and to Jamaica. Sisi wonders why they don't just go across the mountains to the DR, why they are going so far away, but doesn't ask. She knows that it is just her desire to keep Margie close that makes her wonder.

Everyone stands on a pier and waves so much Sisi thinks her arm might fall off, but she doesn't want to stop. She wants Margie to see her waving until they can't see each other any longer. She wants Margie to know she is loved.

When Margie and her group disappear from sight, Sisi drops her arm. It feels leaden. Inside, a balloon swells up, choking her from the top of her belly to the bottom of her throat, preventing her from responding when spoken to. When asked how she feels, she just nods and keeps her head down, walking home a few paces behind the others. When they reach the house, she runs to her bedroom, shuts the door behind her quietly, climbs into bed, and opens her mouth to let the balloon deflate, but all that come out are tears. First Papa, then Gertie, now Margie.

Two years pass and eventually they have a stack of Margie's letters, written in the unmistakable cursive the nuns taught at the school, full of loops and elongated letters that curve prettily from left to right in straight lines. Margie writes to them about the upheavals taking place on the other islands, about a man who writes about revolution, freedom for populations that have been colonized by the French, the English, and so many more, but who have been unable to free themselves the way Haiti has. She writes about how the people of these places also have languages and spiritualities that mix the European with the African like they do, how schoolteachers want to teach students in their own languages. Margie wonders if teachers in Haiti will one day teach in Kreyòl. She begins to write about returning, excited by the prospect of what will come to Haiti, what she is discovering is happening elsewhere. "Much of what others dream about,"

she writes, "we already have." She begins to wonder what she has been seeking, out of the island, that cannot be found there.

Then Momo passes away, abruptly. Margie has not yet returned. They send her a photo of Momo in her casket with letters explaining what has happened: a heart attack while she was doing her inventory. She fell over onto a large bag of dry kidney beans. When they found her, she looked, simply, like she had fallen asleep. All Margie can do in response is write back; she too feels the loss, keenly; she will come home—soon. She intends to take over Momo's business. She has made headway with her group, she writes, met many people, found new markets for their wares. Even with Momo gone, the business could continue. Sisi thinks that this is a cold response, but she cannot blame Margie: two years is an eternity.

Odette and Lou come to Momo's funeral, surprising Sisi. They dress in black from head to toe and stand on either side of her, each holding a hand. Feeling their palms against hers, Sisi doesn't feel like crying. It helps her to miss Margie less, to forget the hole that Gertie has left. She sees again the blackbird with the red epaulets that she thought she saw flying overhead that day in the schoolyard when they stood firm against the bevy of bullying girls. She knows now that the three of them are the bird, she the body, Lou and Odette, on either side of her, the red-tinged wings. For the first time in a while, despite Momo's sudden departure, Margie's absence, Papa's death, and Gertie's disappearance, Sisi thinks that she could fly somewhere beyond the horizon.

OHIO, 1978

SIMONE FINDS MARGIE BY TELEPHONE TO TELL HER ABOUT
the starlings falling dead out of the sky, but all Margie wants to
talk about, at first, is the director who has fled to Europe.

"Do you think he did it?" she asks Sisi. "I think he did it."

"I don't know," Sisi muses. She didn't pay that much attention to the item.

"Is Emma still talking about wanting you all to move out
West? It seems like such a dangerous place," Margie continues. There are reports in the paper of missing women, warnings
against hitchhiking.

Emma does talk a lot about moving to California, ever since
she discovered that Disneyland was there and begged them to
take her there on a family vacation. They didn't, but the lure of
the West remained. Who can blame her, thinks Sisi, growing
up in a gray place, so unlike the island where she herself grew
up and that she talks incessantly about? But Haiti is no longer
the place where she walked with Margie on the port, looked out
onto the ocean and wondered about the lure of the Simbi. The
innocence of the place has been lost to dangers no one could
have imagined. She can't, now, take Emma back there. In contrast, the American Midwest is calm; it is safe. She has no real
cause for complaint.

"The birds," she says, changing the subject.

"What about them?" Margie asks, distracted. Sisi can tell
that Margie is poring over the entertainment pages.

"Didn't you read the story about the blackbirds, the starlings, falling out of the sky?"

"No. I don't think so. I'm not sure we have those out here in Florida."

"Don't you remember I sent you a watercolor of the ones that came last year, right in front of the house? Every time they come, it's like a family reunion."

"The birds," Margie says, pondering. "I remember you telling me about them." Her attention shifts to Sisi. "What about them?"

"They didn't come this year and I think—" She takes a deep breath. "I think it's about the ending of something, for me, of my time here."

"With Scott?"

"Yes," Sisi says. "With Scott. I don't belong here."

"You always said it was a gray place. I can't say that I'm surprised."

"I think I need to leave Scott and find another way to make a world," Sisi says. "I think it's a sign." She doesn't know how but she knows she has to leave, not just for herself but for Emma.

Margie makes a suction noise on the other end. "Well," she says resolutely, "nature always knows before we do."

Sisi nods to herself. She isn't sure if Margie is speaking about the global warming that they have been hearing about in the news lately, or about the state of Sisi's life. She begins to explain how and why she has come to feel trapped in her life in a bleak region that she cannot come to call home.

"If nothing changes," she says, "I'll have to find the strength to change it for myself."

"What about Emma?" Margie asks pointedly. "How do you think she'll take it?"

Sisi can't find the words to form an answer. She attempts to collect her thoughts as they skip ahead, stones on the surface of a pond disturbing algae and lily pads in their wake. If Odette and

Lou once formed the wings of Sisi's imaginary red-shouldered blackbird, one that didn't exist in Haiti, and Sisi the heart, then Margie is like the blue heron Sisi remembers watching that morning long ago when her sister told her she would be leaving: elegant, steady. Margie always studies all the possible options opening or closing before her. She skims over the surface of things because she can fathom the depths below, knows instinctively how to find the essential in things and when it is time to plunge into the deep to bring up a catch, or to spring up, to spread her wings, fly. Margie goes toward things rather than flees. It is a rare quality that Sisi believes she does not have. If it had been Margie in her place, in this turgid, gray place that offered her not a grain of welcome, where no one seems ever to have left a five-mile radius, well, Margie would have left long ago.

"I'll do it in my own time," Sisi replies, finally, not knowing if that means weeks, months, or years. She is afraid it might mean the latter, that she will not have the strength to just up and leave, start over again after these many years with Scott, this cocoon they've created together, keeping her insulated from the world.

"I'm sure that you will," Margie responds in measured tones. "I'm here if you need me."

Lou was right to call Sisi a white bird of paradise when they were children. She is an anomaly, a plant that grows hardy in tropical ground. This gray place is not for her. Why did she think she would continue to bloom here? Having Emma is not enough now that Emma is in grade school, off doing her own things, conspiratorially hoarding the secrets of nascent friendships with little girls Sisi has never met. Was she this way with Gertie, she wonders?

They end the call with Sisi feeling lighter but no surer of herself. Margie is at the end of the continent, on the tip of it, as close to the Caribbean as she can be, in Miami. Margie is fond of saying that at least the state has its feet in Caribbean waters.

Sisi doesn't feel she could belong in Florida. Besides, Gertie is there, and after more then thirty years, she doesn't want to run into her as Margie occasionally does. There are so many stores in Miami in which you can get the latest book out of Haiti that everyone is talking about, or get *mango france* fresh off the boat, or buy a bottle of five-star rum arrived straight from the distillery in Port-au-Prince. Simone feels lighter because she understands now that there will be no end to her winter if she stays. Relearning how to draw is not enough to repair the unraveling net of her marriage.

After the call with Margie, Simone decides to play hooky from work, to head to Safari John's, a sprawling international food store on the outskirts of town. When Emma was smaller, she took her there, despite the store's problematic name, because the displays kept her entertained: plastic green dinosaurs and a purple full-sized elephant at the entrance, blow-up cars above the cheeses, wheelbarrows of pumpkins in the fall, a huge honeycomb display with a panting dog below it, and a tram jutting over the parking lot as if one could jump onto it and take a ride to Chicago. Emma loved getting lost in the aisles as they searched for new things to cook, but Scott didn't have an adventurous palate, and after a few years, as Emma outgrew the novelty of the garish displays, and Simone of a place calling itself a "safari," she stopped making the hour-long trip. She retreated to their side of town, where a smaller, quieter market offered a few novelties—plantains, wild rice, fresh fruits, the occasional mango, sometimes flown in all the way from Haiti or the DR, which could be as expensive as five dollars apiece. A rare treat but neither Scott nor Emma liked mango, the sour-sweet taste of it. Emma said it made her tongue tingle, so Sisi let go of the flavors of her childhood and swapped them for all things American: sliced cheese, cereal with cold milk in the mornings, hot dogs, ground beef, sliced white bread, apples. Like the gray days of winter, the plates she served for dinner lost their color. Every time Scott complimented her on a dish of mashed potatoes, gravy, steak, asparagus spears, her heart sank a little, just as it did when Emma declared that she was no longer going to eat *bananes pesées*, the smashed and fried plantain wheels that Sisi occasionally but rarely made to accompany Sunday dinner.

This morning, she goes directly to the Caribbean aisle. There is an inflated palm tree tied to the rafters above the shelves crammed with manioc flour, different types of cornmeal—fine-grain, medium, coarse—and packets of preprepared *bouilli*, some, if they come from the DR, with caricatures of brown-skinned people similar to those that appear on American brands of rice and syrup: smiling dark faces that are supposed to have cultivated whatever it is that is being sold, their good humor evidence that their history of exploitation is long past, or reconciled. Simone bristles at the illustrations, thinks of how she could do better, will do better, once she lands more accounts. For now, her focus is on purchasing staples from home, if she can find them, and serving a different kind of plate tonight, maybe sweets to win over Emma. She can make *dous*, the confection made from condensed and coconut milks and a touch of lime juice Momo taught her, or *tablet*, a peanut brittle fragrant with nutmeg, ginger, cinnamon, and anise, often sold in open racks in the streets of Port-au-Prince. Maybe she can go *toward* something, the way Margie always does, rather than depart, reaching for all those things lost, forgotten, misplaced, and find her way as one does in the dark, avoiding the sharp edges of things in order to find one's footing, not fall.

By the time Scott returns home from the clinic that day, Simone has made a dinner of stewed chicken with cashews in the sauce, and *riz collé*, rice cooked down with kidney beans, onions, garlic. To go along with it, she made a generic salad, sprinkled with shredded cheese, in case neither Scott nor Emma likes it, but both surprise her and eat with gusto.

"Why don't you cook like this more often?" Scott exclaims, as if he never told her that he prefers American fare to her island dishes.

Could it be this easy to return to all that was dismissed and put aside?

For a moment, Simone imagines that she could rekindle the light in her marriage, bring it back, but when she tries to reach for Scott in the night, he turns away, as he usually does, half-asleep, muttering about how tired he is and something about an unsolvable case at work, a cat or dog that keeps losing weight at the university pet clinic, and what he is going to do about it. She considers telling Scott about the starlings fallen out of the sky but thinks better of it. Instead, she plots how she might introduce Emma to corn porridge like her family used to have on bright Saturday mornings after a walk on the port, or maybe the sweet coconut balls that Gertie introduced her to the second time she went over to her house, giving her a taste of what children ate on the other side of the island, of maybe what *their* father ate as a child. She muses about that. What does she know about her father? This, too, has been lost. She falls asleep trying to remember, uncovering a vague memory of sweetness lodged in her mind.

PORT-AU-PRINCE, 1949–50

The World Expo is about to open at the edge of the city, on a stretch of land just above where they used to live close to the port. The city thrums with expectation. They moved from the house without running water toward the center of the city after Momo's passing, to be closer to the school and closer to Mami's clients, many of whom don't like to come to the port area which they claim is becoming a little seedy with so many fishermen and marines from who knows where. The new house is tucked away at the end of a long lot occupied by two other families. It has two floors, like the old one, but it is more elegant and has running water. By this time, Sisi is about to embark on her years at the high school, where she used to see Margie on the other side of the fence from the elementary school. Odette and Lou are her best friends and the three, now fifteen, can be found everywhere together, though Lou is the more adventurous of the three and often does things on her own.

Louise cut her hair short by the time she was thirteen and wears jean pants rolled up at the bottom to the edge of her calves when she isn't in school. She smokes and drinks at the gatherings she goes to on the weekends. She runs with an older, faster crowd of artists and freethinkers but always returns to report what she did or saw to Odette and Sisi, whose families won't let them go unattended to the kinds of parties that Lou raves to them about.

"I'm the wild seed," Lou often says to Odette and Sisi mysteriously, but neither knows what she means, exactly. They know that Lou has gone as far as to attend vodou ceremonies with her boyfriend, Philomène, whom everyone knows as Lolo, a tall, gangly, doe-eyed boy from one of the wealthiest families in town, who graduated ahead of them by a few years. The two have gone to ceremonies in Gonaïves and Léogâne. Whenever Sisi hears Lou speaking of Léogâne, she knows Lou will mention Gertie, who lives there. They saw Gertie at the last biennial inter-private school recitation contest, the year before last. Lou claims that Gertie wanted to speak to Sisi, but Sisi was consumed by the competition. Money at home is tight with Momo gone, and she needed the scholarship promised to the winner.

They faced each other just before the competition, but Sisi was too nervous to say much.

"Whatever happened between the two of you?" Lou asks, as the three of them talk about going to the Expo. "We all used to be so tight in grade school."

Sisi shrugs, not wanting to admit the truth. "Things change, Lou. You know that."

Lou gives Sisi an enigmatic smile. "True. Things do change. Anyway. Gertie's a bit of a bore. I tried to get her to come to a *rara* band practice and she wouldn't come. Her family told her that everything folkloric was below them and that she had their family name to protect. Can you believe that?"

"I can," Sisi says, thinking about the day that Gertie's siblings Rico and Andrée chased her out into the street. "They think they're too good for anyone." Was it true, then, in the end, that the issue is their class difference? That Gertie didn't want anything to do with her because she has no money, no status? A Simbi didn't enchant her after all.

"Well, forget about her. Her loss. What about the Expo? Do you two want to come? Please, you have to come! Everyone is going to be there," Lou pleads. "I have tickets for all of us and for Lolo. My parents won't let me go with just Lolo and they'll be there too."

Odette lives outside the city limits on her family farm while both Lou's family and Sisi's have moved farther into town. "My parents will never let me," she says. "We're too young, anyway."

"Too young!" Lou exclaims, lighting up a small, thin cigar. "How about you, Sisi? I bet we can convince your mother to let you come with us. All the big stars will be there: Miles Davis, Celia Cruz, Martha Jean-Claude. I mean e-ve-ry-one will be there! I have tickets to the Jean-Claude concert."

Sisi is curious, especially because Martha Jean-Claude will be singing. Jean-Claude is a rising star with a series of concerts at the Rex, on the brink of international stardom. It is said that she dabbles in vodou. She sings the old vodou chants in her repertoire, in Kreyòl. She has no qualms about being associated with the religion scorned by the church and that no one with money admits to taking part in. "I want to come," Sisi says finally, "but I don't know if Mami'll let me. She'll want to know about a chaperone."

"Look," Lou says, "my parents have a section in the Italy pavilion. We can just vouch that we'll hang out there most of the time. My mother can be the chaperone. She'll agree." She winks at Sisi.

"OK," Sisi replies enthusiastically, even as Odette's face falls at the realization that her friends are planning a major event without her, "I'll ask them and let you know."

In the end, Lou's suggestion works and Sisi's mother agrees to let her go on the condition that they check in with the Lombardos at least once an hour.

When the day of the concert comes, Lolo disappears, lured by friends to lay bets at the cock-fighting tent, leaving Lou and Sisi by themselves at Simbie, the nightclub where Jean-Claude is to perform. He says he will be back to pick them up in plenty of time to catch the second act. Lou shrugs as he lopes away. They have agreed on a time to meet as well as a meeting point, the foot of the Luminous Statue close to the Italian pavilion, where Lou's parents have a stand.

"Want a drag, kiddo?" Lou asks, her eyes twinkling. Lou is laughing at her discreetly, Sisi knows. She bristles at being called "kiddo." They are the same age, after all.

"Sure," she says. "I'm game." She has never smoked before and chokes back tears on the first try.

"Not as easy as it looks," Lou says jovially, patting Sisi on the back until she regains her breath. "It's a dirty habit, anyway. I wouldn't recommend it. Look, look," and she points up toward the stage. "There she comes."

Oh, what a sight it is! Sisi has never seen anything like it, anyone like *her*, as resplendent as Martha Jean-Claude, who comes onto the stage with arms wide, smiling from ear to ear in such a way that it makes clear to the audience that she knows she is luminous. The copper skin of her bare arms and shoulders glows from within, and her two-tiered necklace made from carved abalone shells sparkles and gives off a blue hue under the stage lights, which produce a halo effect around her form as if she were a heavenly apparition. She is a peacock with all of her plumage out, with her hair piled high underneath a head wrap that has been swirled around large curls to form a crest atop her head. She wears a light yellow cocktail dress with a form-fitting satin bodice held up by thin spaghetti straps and a billowing taffeta skirt sashed with a multicolored, checkered madras cloth. Jean-Claude struts across the stage in heels two inches high that make her appear to levitate, and as she moves the cord of the microphone across her body expertly so as not to trip over it while making her way toward the waiting crowd, raising the microphone to her lips, the drummers seated on the stage behind her start to beat out a fast syncopation that brings everyone in the audience up on their feet. She begins to sing a *rasin*, a roots love song. The lyrics speak of seizing a young man's love, holding on to him until the singer's heart bursts. Jean-Claude makes enticing, circling gestures with her free hand, alongside her hip bone. Everyone in the crowd grabs whoever is closest to them, whether woman or man, and dances. Lou reaches for Sisi and they jump up and down to the rhythm of the drums. The crowd presses from all sides. There is no room to move but it feels like heaven, a true gathering of joy.

They are slick with sweat, excited. The air is electric as Jean-Claude continues to sing and the crowd chants with her. She kicks off her heels as a guitar player strums the melody to "Ezuli Malad-o," an invocation to Metres Ezuli, goddess of the oceans, and they watch, dancing together, as the crowd spills back onto the dance floor to become a wave of torsos and limbs. Jean-Claude's voice deepens as she addresses the goddess. Arms rise up in unison as if the crowd is united in an entreaty, an offering, pleading for a child in need of curing that only Ezuli can heal, as the lyrics speak of a woman lamenting the loss of her child to the ocean, of the child descending beneath the surface of the waters never to be seen again. The song makes Sisi think of Momo's story about the Simbi. She wonders about the missing child, whether the child is truly missing or if it has heard the Simbi's song and followed it into another world. *I don't have any luck*, the singer sings, *my luck's run out.* The crowd dances slowly. Everyone gathered seems to share the pain of the loss of the child, the same grief. The beat slows and Jean-Claude shifts to a ballad about the poor *moun inosan*, the innocent ones, and the dancing crowd disperses, many singing along approvingly while others move away to light up smokes on the fringes of the dance floor. Lou grabs Sisi's arm and drags her to the edge of the tent to do the same.

From where they stand, looking back, Sisi moves her hips to the rhythm of the crowd, following the movement of the arms back and forth as the spectators swing them above their heads like congregants in a church. Lou is moving against her, following the rhythm, the drums, as if she herself is a syncopated surface, the taut skin of a drumhead. Her back is turned to Sisi as she smokes and as Jean-Claude moves on to her big hit, her rendition of Oswald Durand's poem "Choucoune," an allegory for the beauty of Haitian women. The crowd goes into a frenzy, jumps back on their feet, and Lou's head falls back onto Sisi's shoulder.

"Come on, Lou," Sisi says into Lou's ear, which is against her mouth. "Let's go! We're going to miss the finale and the encores."

Lou turns so that her mouth is against Sisi's neck and kisses her on her nape. Sisi can feel Lou's entire body turn toward her, into her. Has Lou been drinking? Lou's body is slack. Sisi grabs her by both arms to keep her from falling. Lou, instead, swiftly shifts her body so that they are chest to chest and kisses Sisi on the mouth. Sisi is surprised. She has never been kissed before, not like this, not by anyone. Lou's mouth is soft, moist, searching. A flutter rises across Sisi's stomach, butterflies. Her pulse quickens. A flush of heat moves over her. She has the urge to wipe away the sweat pouring down her temples as if Lou weren't there, pressing up against her. Lou's eyes are closed. Her tongue darts urgently, softly, across the channel of Sisi's parted lips. A stream of smoke passes from Lou's mouth into her own. Sisi starts to choke, pulls away abruptly, coughing. She looks around. Has anyone seen them?

The drummers beat the taut goatskins forming the tops of their mamas and papas tied with lanyards bound across the length of the hollowed oblong drums carved out from white cedar logs. They hold on to the wooden bodies by curling their feet over the cords at the bottom of the drums, pulling on them to ring from the depths of their instruments the deepest reverberation of the echoes from the loins of their common ancestors. They embrace the drums firmly within the circle of their thighs, as if clinging to the belly of lovers. Their palms move smoothly yet firmly across the goat skins, caressing the surfaces to coax from them the most subtle and resonant of laments to match the delighted fever of the crowd.

Lou laughs, wipes her mouth, and pulls Sisi back under the tent, into the agitated crowd as if nothing has happened, as if she hasn't just kissed Sisi. Maybe Sisi has misunderstood. Maybe Lou simply lost her balance. Sisi looks up at Jean-Claude on the stage, resplendent, skin glowing under the lights, as she dances conspiratorially in unison with the crowd's undulating brown swell. The music stops abruptly, the drummers holding up their hands inches above their drums. Martha beams a smile across the room, kisses them goodbye. "*Mesi, mesi,*" she yells into the microphone, and in one smooth motion she exits, sweeping up her discarded heels from the stage floor with one hand as she disappears.

The crowd slowly disperses, murmuring their appreciation for what they have just witnessed. Lolo returns from the cockfight, later than expected, clutching a fistful of bills in one hand, a faint spray of scarlet across what was once a clean, light-blue linen shirt. Sisi's head spins. She sits down to steady herself, to feel the ground beneath her.

"My God," Lou cries out, running up to Lolo and leaving Sisi behind, what is left of her cigar dangling between two fingers as she brings her palms to his cheeks, "what happened to you?"

"I won!" Lolo exclaims as he bends over Lou, tips her back, and kisses her emphatically on the mouth. Sisi feels a sudden pang of jealousy. It surprises her. She bats away the feeling. "I made a bet, and my rooster pecked the other one to death." Lolo sweeps a hand dramatically across his shirt as he rights Lou next to him and clutches her beneath a long arm as if she herself were a hen, he, a rooster. "Here's the proof!" Sisi makes a show of admiring the splatter on Lolo's shirt, the drops of blood a reminder of things that cannot be undone, changed, reshaped. Many things are that way, Sisi thinks.

"My hunter," Lou laughs, as she pecks Lolo on the cheek playfully. She winks at Sisi. "Men will be men, what can be done about it?"

The lyrics of Jean-Claude's first song upon the stage come back to Sisi. To seize love when it presents itself. But how to know when to love, whom to love? How does one know when the Simbi are calling, whom to follow and whom not? Does one want the heart to burst? Is love, in the end, heartbreak after heartbreak?

❖

After the concert, Sisi and Lou go back to see the exhibits at the Expo, especially the international ones—Italy, Argentina, Guatemala, Palestine, Puerto Rico, the newly formed state of Lebanon—which make them dream of the faraway places beyond the islands to which they might one day travel. They make Sisi wonder about Margie, where she might be and how she is getting on. Margie's letters are growing fewer and farther between. Mami keeps a running letter to her to which she adds a paragraph or two every week until she estimates that the news is substantial enough to send. Often, Sisi adds a line or two, just to fill things out, but after the concert, she feels she can say nothing about her world, her inner life, which is all in turmoil. She describes, instead, the pavilions of the Expo, how the boulevard has new trees, and a new name, after the American president, Truman, who sent a message that the president of the Republic read on the Expo's opening day. She tells her about the concerts that she hears about from Lou secondhand, about the American jazz trumpeter Miles Davis bringing down the house and the Cuban songstress Celia Cruz, who entranced concertgoers with *son* and led a conga line out of the main performance tent into the wide avenue leading to Place Bolívar. There was a rumor that Dizzy Gillespie and Miles Davis were taken out to Gonaïves one night because they wanted to see a vodou ceremony and that Gillespie fell into a trance in which he played the trumpet with his eyes closed. A feast was organized for them with a pig roasted in a pit, an effort to duplicate the revels that took place in Bois Caïman on the eve of the Revolution. Sisi writes all this to Margie, what she hears from Lou and what is rumored, but she doesn't say anything about what she experienced with Lou outside the Simbie the night of the Jean-Claude concert, listening to the drummers, listening to her own heart thumping from within her rib cage as Lou leaned against her, Lou's breath laden with the scent of tobacco, her hair smoky.

For months after, they don't talk about it. They avoid the subject until Sisi can't stand it any longer. She wants to know if Lou felt the electric current that ran through her as Lou kissed her. She wants to know if the fluttering in her belly comes with the territory, if she will ever experience that again, that feeling of suspension and wonder.

"About that night, at the concert . . ." She lets her question trail off into the wind, following the wisps of Lou's cigarette smoke as they walk home from school one day.

"Yes?" Lou asks in return, brow furrowed. "What about it?"

"Do you do that often?"

"Do what?"

"You know."

"Know what?"

Sisi is exasperated. "Kiss girls!"

"Oh, that!" Lou flicks away the question along with the ash from her cigarette. "You're worried about that? I was just letting off steam, feeling good, you know? Music will do that to you. And I was doing a shotgun so you could experience smoking without choking to death." She laughs.

"A shotgun?"

"When I blew into your mouth. That's how some people get high, but we weren't doing anything serious. It was just smoke. Don't worry, Sisi. You didn't do anything wrong or anything to feel bad about. We were feeling great and I . . . well, I . . . I just got a little carried away. Just forget about it, OK? That's the thing to do."

With those words, Lou hugs Sisi to her fiercely, the cigarette held tightly between her lips. "Besides," Lou says as she lets go and throws the stub of her cigarette onto the pavement, where she puts out what is left of the embers under the sole of her shoe, "I won't be here much longer. None of us will."

There was a coup a few months after the start of the Expo, despite its success. A military general took over and declared himself president to the dismay of the elites while the rest of them watched the change in government with arms crossed: What could anyone do, what could anyone say? The future seems both desirable and uncertain because, on the one hand, the Expo has put Port-au-Prince on the map and, on the other, a coup is not a sign of stability. It is then that Margie returns, in the middle of 1950, with the Expo on. They did not expect her, and she doesn't return alone.

Mami opens the door one night, saying over her shoulder, "Who would come knocking so late . . . ?" Her voice trails off when she sees who is standing at the gate. It is not just Margie but, as Sisi can see over her mother's shoulder, a child in Margie's arms. Sisi at sixteen registers that despite all the letters written and sent, she is not the only one concealing.

They go out to the gate to help Margie with her luggage and what turns out to be a small boy sleeping in her arms. Mami holds Margie close. "Is this why you didn't come home?"

Margie doesn't answer. Sisi scrutinizes the boy, who is two or three years old. He must have been born around the time that Momo died. Margie seems, all at once, like a much older, removed, person. She has kept a child secret for years.

"What's his name?" Sisi asks in a hush.

Margie smiles at her and says, "Simon. After Momo, like you. We call him Ti'Mo."

Sisi nods, not wanting to pry and ask about the "we" of Margie's sentence. She wonders if Margie was enchanted, finally, by a Simbi fisherman who left her a child. The boy is Sisi's color, not Margie's deep brown. He has Margie's eyes and nose, but his lips are another's. Sisi doesn't dare ask questions because she is happy that Margie has returned, though nothing will be as it was before because Sisi is getting older and Margie's dreams have shifted, not away from Haiti but toward her son.

"I hear that great things are happening in Port-au-Prince," Margie continues as she is brought over the threshold of the house.

"Oh, yes." Sisi begins enthusiastically to tell her about everything, but Mami places a hand on her shoulder to quiet her.

"Let's let Margie catch her breath and rest, shall we?"

Sisi wants to tell Margie that despite the coup, the city palpitates with energy. The eyes of the world are on Port-au-Prince. Every day is filled with anticipation. The plumage of the birds is more brilliant, their songs sharper, more exuberant. Sisi has a sense that she might take flight, grow wings, but she understands that the fact that she and Margie have kept the truth about their lives to themselves, withheld vital information from each other, means that, as sisters, they have become estranged. She wonders if there will be a time when they will renew their sisterhood or if, just as she lost her connection with Gertie, they will drift away from each other until all that is left of their bond is a memory, a longing for something, once experienced, that can never be fully recovered.

OHIO, 1978

SIMONE RIFFLES THROUGH A STACK OF ILLUSTRATIONS she has been working on for drawing class. She is in an agitated state. Could it be that what she'd thought was a better life was just, in the end, compromise, settling? Was Lou, with her bohemian lifestyle, her constant smoking, her arrests, and an apartment that probably needed airing out from all its books and papers from years of organizing protests and allowing strangers to sleep on the floor by the half dozen, happier than she was, all this time, hidden away in the middle of nowhere, in a vast, swath of gray that was a muddy brown half the year, buried under snow the other half? There is the spring, the burgeoning of new things, the explosion of flowers garlanding the trees and sidewalks as if a parade were about to take place, and the fall leaves, which, for a moment, make all the trees resplendent with copper hues as if Midas had suddenly awakened from a long slumber to blanket the world in gold. Scott lives here well enough, acclimated to the seasons, but Simone longs for that life she could have had, the imagined life she never lived. She doesn't know how she is to branch out, start anew.

Her hands fall on the image she is looking for, a peacock she saw at the zoo strutting freely across a walkway leading to the hippo enclosure to which Emma, at six, led her with determination. She saw the peacock out of the corner of her eye, registered the crown, the long train of feathers. The peacock reminds her of Martha Jean-Claude upon the stage, the way Lou swayed against her, the kiss, the movement of the crowd, all of it so alive. She wonders if she will ever feel that way again.

Back then, Simone didn't really want to be free. She wanted everything to stay the same, simple, as things were when she was a child. She wanted Gertie, Odette, Lou, all of them. But each was lost, in turn. In the end, against the backdrop of the politics of the day, she wanted everyone to be safe. She wanted everyone to stay close to her. She didn't think of things like happiness for herself, but she wanted it for everyone else; she just didn't want them all to go.

She wanted Margie to be happy when she returned. She remembers that.

In the end, it was Margie's return that helped her to understand the true meaning of sisterhood, helped her to let go of the hold that the memory of Gertie had on her—an encounter so electric, so visceral, that she has since measured all her encounters, whether with friends or with suitors, against it, in spite of herself. Sometimes, she does so to determine whether she wants to take the risk of being scalded again, at others, to determine if a connection has the same underlying feeling of recognition. When the kiss happened with Lou, she could not make sense of its meaning. She knew that she didn't want to lose Lou the way she had lost Gertie, to something she couldn't help, or be the cause of the loss herself. She became careful with Lou, in order to preserve the connection that had been, from the start, almost as vital as that with Gertie.

Lou was right, of course; they all did leave, eventually, some to the foreign shores exhibited in the pavilions of the Expo, others to places they had never heard of before.

※

PORT-AU-PRINCE, 1957

Less than a decade after the Expo, the country is on the edge of a precipice and Margie is knee-deep in the politics of the day. She tries to convince Sisi to leave with her and Ti'Mo but Sisi doesn't know which way to turn at that point. It has been just the two of them, and Ti'Mo, with their mother for years. Sisi likes it that way; she doesn't see why anything has to change. Mami's work dwindles as the country's affairs sink, but she has just enough to keep the household going with Sisi's additional income from the office positions she has found at local businesses since completing her business administration degree and Margie managing Mami's business along with what was left of their grandmother's market ventures. Sisi gets along well with her nephew, and Margie is as magnetic as she has always been, perhaps more so since she found her calling in activism.

Their house has become an unofficial headquarters of sorts for young activists and socialist artists who began to dabble in communism, feminism, after the labor organizer Daniel Fignolé served a one-month term as president in '57, just before the elections that brought Duvalier into power. During that month, Fignolé managed only to make a claim for the rocky island of Navassa, inhabited mostly by marine birds, gannets, herons, seagulls, which cover it with so much white excrement that the rocky reefs appear, at a distance, to be permanently blanketed in what is elsewhere called snow. Fignolé was derided as a fool for wrestling with their northern neighbors for such a small piece of land, an outcropping of lava rock left over from a distant subterranean eruption of the kind that formed all the islands at one time or another. The mandate that brought him to the attention of the electorate was not this claim but his role in the Mouvement Ouvrier Paysan (MOP), the peasant workers' movement.

What most of them didn't understand at the time was that Navassa had been in dispute since the late 1800s, when US Navy ships started to navigate the Caribbean Sea, on the lookout for adversaries, they said, to defend their shores from invasion, particularly from the Germans and the French with investments in the area. According to Fignolé's claim, Navassa had belonged to Haiti since the Treaty of Ryswick of 1697, when it was established as a French possession, along with surrounding islands, of which Navassa is one. It had been in dispute ever since. Margie explains, to everyone's wonder, that bird excrement is almost as valuable as gold, that there once was a lucrative if small colony on the rocky island, with its own blacksmith and a church. The colony, made up mostly of laboring Black men managed by white overseers, pickaxed and dynamited their way through bird droppings so thick they had become a phosphate called guano, a fertilizer prized by the Americans who use it to feed their lush, blond corn and wheat fields. *That* was why Navassa was crucial, emphasizes Margie as she explains Fignolé's bid. Such claims make for lively if sometimes confusing conversation at the dinner table since neither Sisi nor Mami is involved in politics as deeply as Margie. Sisi pares Ti'Mo's fruit while Margie talks.

Gone are the days of the Expo, when they had hope of the country flourishing. Despite the coup that happened in its midst, President Magloire ousting and taking credit for Estimé's brainchild, there remained a feeling of goodwill, a tentative veneer of possibility as tourism grew and the country was no longer treated like the outcast that it had always been since the days of the Revolution. Haiti became a favored child of the US despite the years of occupation just after which Sisi was born. A reconciliation had begun with the nation occupying the leeward side of the island. Drinks like *morir soñando*, a concoction of evaporated milk, sugar, and orange juice poured over ice, proliferated.

The drink had been created there, a year before the Expo, and became popular in Santo Domingo, while those who had heard of it in Port-au-Prince scorned it. It resembled a drink that Momo used to make as a tonic when anyone was ill, milk mixed with pressed carrot juice. The DR had not been invited to take part in the Expo because there was bad feeling after it was found out that their president, Trujillo, had ordered mass deportations of cane cutters from the border zone in '37. Later, it came out that the deportations were a euphemism for extermination, with thousands of Haitians killed, along with dark-skinned, working-class Dominicans who were seen by their government as expendable. For this reason, even as it was later found out that the Vincent government in power in Haiti at the time was complicit in covering up the massacre, Estimé had expressly let the Trujillo government know in no uncertain terms that they were not welcome. It might have been this that led to Estimé's downfall, Sisi conjectures, as he had no firsthand evidence that killings occurred. The only concrete proof that existed was the absence of returning cane-cutting peasants to their fields after *zafra* season. Their plots were small squares of land that went back to the redistribution of land after the Revolution, when Saint-Domingue ceased to be a French colony. The military men on both sides of the island were closer than anyone could have guessed and shared the common outlook of rule with an iron hand. There was also the problem of the rise of Black consciousness, Sisi is beginning to understand: the Dominicans were not inspired to join in the movement. But wealthier Haitians, similarly disinclined, drank *morir soñando* as a sign of détente between the two nations. The drink became all the rage, at least at parties and in the households of the rich, who crossed the border liberally, without differentiating between the two sides, as if they were of the same coin. For some, life could be sweet like that, easy, the political mood changing in the span of a few years toward the sweet or the bitter with no essential difference in their quality of life.

Ultimately, Fignolé was exiled to New York as a new president-to-be made his way into the center of things. It was not the first or the last time a presidential hopeful would have to leave Haiti, along with his followers. They all knew that Martha Jean-Claude had to leave under Magloire, for advocating, along with her Cuban husband, for the rights of the poor and the homeless. Jean-Claude's husband, a journalist, was arrested for trying to redistribute money to the destitute while Jean-Claude herself was imprisoned two years after the Expo. After, she followed her husband into exile, first to Venezuela, then to Havana. Jean-Claude didn't seem to have suffered from the change in life and continued giving her concerts all over the world in her seamless gowns, her hair gathered atop her head. She recorded a duet with Celia Cruz, the Cuban songstress who had come to the Expo, the same year of her exile. Lou bought the record and she and Sisi played it incessantly on their turntables until their parents got tired of hearing the same song over and over again. That didn't seem so long ago. At the time, she and Lou had dreamed of following in Jean-Claude's footsteps, marrying a dissident, being exiled, starting over elsewhere. It had all seemed so romantic but now Sisi was beginning to understand the instability of the world in which they lived, that nothing about it should be idealized. Activists who supported the MOP and other candidates for the new elections were running scared: many scattered to the four winds, scrambling to emigrate wherever they had some kind of tie, as Jean-Claude had. A new president was elected, though "elected" might be too strong a word for the process.

Voting day, Margie comes home ashen-faced, visibly shaken. She steps into the house, closes the door precipitously behind her so that all in the house run to see what has happened. Ti'Mo bursts into tears the moment he sees his mother, and she gathers him to her in an empty gesture of consolation she needs as much for herself.

"They took my ballot at the box," says Margie, and she adds, "at gunpoint!"

"*Kisa?*" Mami exclaims, incredulous.

"The army is everywhere," Margie says. "They ask you to open your ballot before putting it in the box and then when they don't see *his* name there, they tear it up or change it, and send you away." She extends her left hand. "But they still cut the nail of your little finger and make you dip it in ink to show you've voted even if you haven't been able to vote the way you wanted." Her little finger is stained a deep indigo blue-black color.

"I suppose it could have been worse," Mami says. "They could have beaten you."

"But people *are* being beaten," Margie replies. Then tears stream from the far corners of her eyes as she buries her fingers in Ti'Mo's short curls. "Some people aren't going to come out of this day alive." She pauses. "I was a coward. I let them take my ballot. When they saw that I didn't vote for *him*, they threw my ballot away." She laughs hollowly. "But I knew I had to come home to all of you"—her grip tightens on Ti'Mo, who, sensing that something tragic is transpiring, stops squirming under his mother's touch—"so I walked away instead of fighting them."

"That isn't being a coward," Mami says, looking at Ti'Mo, who is staring up at them, following the conversation with wide eyes. "You have responsibilities. You had no choice."

"Soon they'll figure out who's who," Margie says unequivocally. "There'll be hell to pay."

Mami shrugs. "Maybe it won't be so bad. Maybe these are strong-arm tactics to deliver what he claims for the country." Sisi doesn't believe Mami's words: Who would need to get an army to make sure that they are elected if the people believe in them?

What will it mean for the rest of them if they don't go along with his "promises"?

"*Je ne sais pas,*" Margie says. "We'll have to wait and see, then decide what to do. They say that both Jumelle and Déjoie are leaving the country straight away. Jumelle may already be gone. Chiara Lombardo told me so."

Sisi looks up at the mention of the Lombardos and wonders if Lou is also involved in the fomenting dissent. Since her return, Margie has spent a great deal of time at the Lombardos' shop. She has become close to Chiara, Lou's older sister, who is also an activist.

Lou still wears her hair short, eschews dresses and wears pants even for more formal occasions, and smokes her thin cigars, but she is more serious, focused as the politics of the day grow more strained and consequential. Sisi doesn't have the courage to follow suit but watches Lou with admiration, the same admiration she reserved once for Margie.

A few evenings later, it is Lou who comes bursting into their house, crying, saying that Chiara has been taken in.

"Taken in where?" Margie says, holding Lou by the shoulders at arm's length to better hear her.

Lou wipes away tears. "We don't know. My parents are beside themselves. Army men came and took her away."

Mami retires to her atelier. They listen to the rat-a-tat of the sewing machine, understanding that she needs to distract herself. Ti'Mo is reading a comic book on the floor, between his mother's feet. "It's going to be all right," Margie says, determined. "We'll get her back."

Later that night, a young man from the youth activist group shows up at the door and reports, "They're arresting journalists, especially women journalists. Anyone they suspect of having organized against the new president."

This is how they talk about the new government, without names. They are afraid of who might be listening. Eventually, they will call him other things, not even the president, because the danger is everywhere: walls and ceilings have ears, doors never close or lock entirely. They begin to live like a people under glass, as if everything can be seen.

A week or two later, Chiara is freed. How, Sisi doesn't know, but when she emerges, she isn't the same woman they knew before. When Sisi sees her again, she can hardly recognize her. Her face is swollen from beatings; her hair, which, unlike her sister, she has kept flowing, dark as a raven's, is shorn short; her eyes are bloodshot. She will not speak of her ordeal. The Lombardos liquidate their assets and offer to take Margie and Ti'Mo abroad with them, back to Italy. Margie agrees to go alone, without Ti'Mo.

"Can you trust them?" Mami asks, overwhelmed by the prospect of losing Margie again to an unknown world, though they are all swimming now into unknown waters as the new government surrounds itself with military men and forms a secret police for the protection of the masses, they say, for the fortification of the president, it seems.

"Yes, Mami," Margie says, consoling Mami, then Ti'Mo, going to one, then to the other, as she announces her decision. She comes to Sisi last, resting a hand on her shoulder.

Sisi can feel her deflation. They are all defeated by the succession of events of the last few years.

"I'll go to Italy first, then I'll try to make my way to France; then maybe Sisi can bring you and Ti'Mo over." Sisi can't respond. They all nod as Margie speaks. Sisi is stupefied. Lou will leave with her family. Life will never be the same.

Margie's departure comes soon enough. They prepare as quietly as possible. After taking care of her paperwork to leave the country with the Lombardos as their housekeeper—this is what they put in the paperwork: housekeeper/manager—Margie reports that the older sisters in the Alcindor clan, Gertie's older sisters, all have positions at the French and Italian consulates. One of them gave her a hard time, knowing that Margie has never kept a house, but the Lombardos were firm: they would not leave Margie behind. In the end, they got the paperwork done, but Margie will never forgive the Alcindor sisters. Margie can't but add, "It was a good riddance to you that Gertie disappeared from your life."

Sisi nods in response but she isn't so sure. Now, again, she will be left alone, with Mami and Ti'Mo, no one to talk to, confide in, no one who can serve as a compass when Sisi isn't sure which way to turn.

PORT-AU-PRINCE / PARIS, 1961

No one can imagine what is to come. No one can imagine it because no one has seen anything like it: journalists disappear; men in blue carry guns throughout the city and countryside; gunshots ring out early in the morning, late at night; a soccer team is shot dead the morning of a big game; cadavers are left to rot in the streets, some opponents of the regime, others not; a fort is reputed to be a torture chamber: if you are taken there, chances are you never come out.

All these things seem not to be happening. What can be reported and what cannot be openly reported changes from week to week, month to month, grows heavier from year to year. The *teledjòl* carries the news from household to household through half-said things, whispers floating slowly aboveground like bread dough not allowed to proof and failing to rise in the heat of the oven. These are days when you have to look up at the sky rather than at the road ahead because of the corpses lying there, unlikely fruit ripening under the hot rays of the sun. Life is neither dream nor nightmare but hallucination. You go to work or to school and then you come home; go to market, then home; no divergences allowed. You do not attend parties or political gatherings unless summoned. You do not go out of your way to check on anyone, unless they are family, and even then . . . If you are disappeared, then God bless you for leaving no trace of yourself to pain those needing to forge ahead.

Orders for gowns continue to come in for Mami, who was worried about the work drying up as the regime installed itself. New elites have been created, supporters of the one-who-cannot-be-named, while the old elites remain cocooned in the removed realities they made for themselves long ago. Most did not know what they conspired to create until it was too late, but rather than abandon their new standing, they simply hide behind the heavy doors of their houses, outfitted with all the personnel they can want and protected by men with guns, trained by the foreigners who never really left though the occupation ended more than twenty years before. These men know how to put down a man as one would put down a dog and they outmatch the untrained section chiefs who are simply *pye nu*, barefoot and desperate men with guns allowed to run amok among the population with orders to spread fear and terror. The new elites put on children's birthday parties with five flavors of ice cream, including crushed peanut cream and chocolate mint. They hold debutante balls and graduations and have gowns made for their daughters and suits tailored for their sons.

Ti'Mo is sent to school in a clean uniform they now can afford to purchase each school year, with a leather *cartable* for his schoolbooks, pencils, and paper. Sisi walks him as she was walked by Margie, even though the school is not so far away.

The morning air is always calm, sometimes too calm. If they see a dead man on the road, flies buzzing over his nose and mouth, they look away and hope he will not be there on the way back home from school. If the cadaver is gone, then they say to themselves that it was never there, and if a neighbor asks about her missing husband, everyone who saw him lying in the road lies to her and says that he probably ran away with his mistress.

What changes everything are the disappearances of innocents, of people they know, among them, Odette, who wasn't involved in politics yet somehow vanishes into thin air. No one knows where she has gone, not her parents, not the school they attended where she is now a teacher. Then schoolchildren disappear as well. Sisi and Mami grow afraid, even if they get along with the neighbors, mind their business, and don't go to political gatherings of any kind. It doesn't matter anymore what you do or don't do. The hand of death can befall you at any time, by order of the palace or by the whim of a disgruntled section chief targeting whoever is unfortunate enough to cross his path on a given day when he (because, though there are notorious women section chiefs, some who are said to be involved in the torture of political prisoners, most of them are men) needs a body, any body, on which to let out the buildup of frustration that comes with terror's territory. Yes, they grow afraid, and they start to think of how much money they need in order to leave everything behind. By the time they are close to being ready, Mami is a thinning reed; the anxiety of the preparations has made her lose weight and she has deep circles under her eyes.

One morning, after taking Ti'Mo to school, Sisi finds Mami slumped over her sewing machine the way they found Momo keeled over her sacks of beans. There is a spot of blood on the fabric she was pushing through the throat plate when she collapsed. Her finger must have gotten caught, briefly, in the needle bar, glancing off the feed dog to move with the fabric, leaving a small dot of scarlet on a sheer pink muslin that she was readying to attach to the underside of a skirt. For Sisi, there is no choice but to move forward. She dials the undertaker with trembling hands and makes the arrangements to have Mami embalmed, then buried. She wants to have the body removed before Ti'Mo returns from school. The undertaker understands and takes everything in hand, places announcements in the church circular, arranges the service. This comes at a price, of course, but business is thriving, in fact, so the undertaker, who knew Mami and Momo, makes Sisi a fair price, fair, as things go, for the dead.

The service and burial are swift. Sisi is touched at how many people come to remember her mother. Sisi will take Ti'Mo to Margie in Italy, as planned. The Lombardos found Margie a position as a manager with friends of the family, people they knew long ago and assume to be trustworthy, even though they insist on paying Margie under the table at the beginning because, the friends say, it will take forever to get through Italian red tape. They don't think much about it at the time since things are often like this in Haiti. Things will regularize and then Margie can apply for papers, and all will be well. Margie and Sisi pool their resources, enough for passage for Sisi and Ti'Mo to Italy by plane, and then, once Ti'Mo is delivered, Sisi will go on to Paris, to Lou, by train.

Lou is overjoyed at the prospect of hosting Sisi. She sends directions for how to navigate Gare du Nord in Paris upon arrival. She meets Sisi there, and at first sight, on the station platform, the girls run to each other, Sisi with her hand luggage thumping against her thigh. Lou throws her arms around Sisi, causing Sisi to drop her luggage on the ground. Oh, how Sisi has longed for such an embrace after these months of fear and terror. Lou squeezes her tightly and for the first time in a long while, Sisi can breathe.

"*C'est mauvais, n'est-ce pas?* It's bad, isn't it?" Lou whispers into her ear in French rather than in Kreyòl as she continues to hold on to Sisi.

Sisi nods into Lou's shoulder and begins to cry.

"*Pas ici.* Not here," Lou says as she encircles her friend in one arm and takes her luggage in the other. "*Allons chez nous.* Let me get you home and we can talk about Odette, about your mom, about everything. There's so much for us to catch up on. *Tu as besoin de repos*—rest. Rest, and then we'll talk."

Sisi lets herself be led away, feels for the first time in months that she can surrender herself, fall apart. Ti'Mo was happy to regain his mother, and Margie seemed well enough. The Lombardos are keeping an eye on her. She and Ti'Mo go over to their house for Sunday dinners. Things would be all right, Sisi thought, when she had to leave them to reach Paris. But it was on seeing Lou that Sisi realized how tense she was, how the years of living under siege, in fear, have weighed on her. Sisi lets herself ease into a state of *relâchement,* of letting go, and soon they are as they were as children, talking conspiratorially as they make their way from the train station to the metro, to Lou's apartment, as if no time has passed. Yet Sisi can feel the ghosts hovering around them, those who should have been there but are not—Momo, Mami, Gertie, Odette, and many more dispersed, like them, across many countries, far away from the island.

Lou lives in the 18th Arrondissement. It doesn't take long to get there from the central train station. If they didn't have the luggage with them, they could have walked through the streets and gotten to the walk-up apartment in less than thirty minutes. The area is known for its artist quarter, but farther north it turns into an enclave for African immigrants—from Algeria, Morocco, Benin.

"I'll show you the neighborhood tomorrow. They call it La Goutte d'Or," Lou says as they pass a halal butcher and then a bakery advertising melted chocolate and hazelnut spread covered lugaimat and harissa, sweet squares made of semolina and almond flour, with whole almonds pressed into their centers.

Sisi wonders if the brightness of the baked goods is the reason they call the area the Golden Drop. "*Repos*: you need rest," she hears Lou say as she continues to peer at the wonders in the shop windows. She nods absent-mindedly. The exhaustion of the travel begins to creep up within her.

Lou's apartment is a riot of color and textures, as Sisi could well have expected. Nonetheless, she finds herself overwhelmed by its cacophony. More surprising is that Lou doesn't live alone. Sisi finds women's undergarments—laced, frilly things—hanging from the shower rod. Sisi wonders whom they belong to as she brushes her teeth.

As if guessing at her curiosity, Lou speaks through the bathroom door. "*T'inquiètes*—never mind the mess. *C'est à Samiah.* Most of that is Samiah's." She halts herself, then resumes. "*On vie ensemble.* We live together. You'll meet her soon enough. *Elle travaille.* She's at work." Lou inhales audibly and Sisi hears her steps receding behind the bathroom door.

So. Lou lives with a woman. Sisi isn't too surprised. She is curious, in fact, as to who this woman could be. The weight of the last months drains from her. No sooner has she emerged from the bathroom and changed out of her traveling clothes into a cotton nightshirt that Lou left out for her on the daybed of the guest room than she finds herself falling into a deep, cottony slumber. She doesn't wake from it for an entire day.

※

When Sisi finally wakes, it is to the sound of whispers. She hears the scraping of a knife against toast. She smells the butter being spread, melting into the pores of the bread. She hears Lou and a woman speaking French in low tones in the kitchen. She assumes it is Samiah. There is a third voice with them, a male voice. She can smell coffee, too, and imagines it being poured out from a glass *cafetière*.

It is early spring and there is a crispness in the air. The window above the bed is open, and Sisi can smell the redolent blooms beyond the apartment building—lilacs, roses—and the scent of pine trees. She closes her eyes to take it all in. There is a faraway hum of cars and bicycles going by, the chattering of pedestrians down below, the rapid, chirping whistle of red-bellied robins hiding in the brush of tall trees, but it all seems quiet compared with the hustle and bustle of Port-au-Prince. There are no street hawkers, and Sisi does not hear the distant short pops of gunfire, a sound that can be mistaken for a car backfiring or firecrackers being lit and thrown up into the air to burst. It all seems too quiet, so peaceful.

She is in Paris, liberated, free to become whatever she chooses to be. She can find work with her business administration degree, which is a French degree.

"*Tu crois qu'elle voudra venir?* Do you think she'll want to come?" Sisi hears the woman she assumes is Samiah say.

Lou's answer is indecipherable.

"OK. OK. *Je te laisse expliquer.* I'll let you explain everything," Samiah says, answering Lou.

The male voice chimes in, but Sisi can't make out what it is saying.

Sisi readies herself to emerge from the guest room, slipping into the bathroom to take a shower first. When she steps out, the three are at opposite ends of the apartment, two poring over papers at a desk in the living room and Lou sitting at the kitchen table, where a breakfast setting has been left waiting for Sisi.

Samiah smiles, redirecting her attention from the papers on the desk to Sisi. Next to her is a slim man with sandy hair. He is dressed simply, in jeans and a white T-shirt. He stands up first, extends a hand to her. His gray eyes search hers as he introduces himself. "*Je m'appelle* Scott," he says. "*Je suis un ami de Lou et de Samiah.*" His handshake is firm, his palm moist. Sisi notes that his skin is smooth, soft, unlike her mother's and grandmother's hands, or the hands of the women who worked in the household where she was raised.

"*Je suis un étudiant.* I'm a student," he says, as if guessing her thoughts.

"*Vous êtes Américain?*" Sisi musters. "*Votre français est impecca-ble.* Your French is good." Confused, she turns to Samiah, who has risen to her feet and is now bending across the desk to grasp Sisi's shoulders to kiss her on both cheeks. The gesture is famil-iar, comforting.

"*J'essaye,*" Scott answers. "When in Rome and all that. . . . I'm here on my study abroad year, and I met Samiah through her brother at a seminar at one of the universities. I offered to help their efforts."

"Efforts?" Sisi asks, kissing Samiah back on both cheeks. "*Enchanté,*" she says to her, returning her smile. They part and grasp each other's hands across the desk in a further gesture of welcome. Meeting Samiah is like meeting another childhood friend. Sisi is reminded vaguely of Odette, of Gertie.

Lou comes out of the kitchen to embrace her. "*Ah bon: vous vous êtes tous rencontrés.* I see you've all met," she says.

"Oui. Yes," Scott starts, then stops himself. He shoves his hands in his back pockets while Samiah sits back in her chair, starts to move the papers around.

"I suppose I should explain what we're doing here," says Lou. "Sit, Sisi. I'll bring your breakfast out here and we can explain everything to you."

For the next hour or so, Sisi listens as Samiah, Lou, and Scott describe in rapid-fire French how Algerians and other people on the African continent are fighting for their freedom. There is a left-leaning movement to articulate the possibilities of a future where former colonies can be free to govern themselves. Samiah and her brother are French Algerians, born to a middle-class family of mixed French and Algerian descent, in occupied territory. Scott, who comes from a well-to-do family in the States (French classes in prep school, he adds, to explain his facility with the language) and eagerly seeks out ways that he can rebel while not having to risk much himself, bankrolls their ventures, paying for the printing of posters, renting spaces for rallies, and providing bail money when things go south. Freedom is not without risks.

"Scott is just a dilettante," Samiah says, waggling a pencil at him.

Scott blushes. "But I put my money where my mouth is."

"You sure do," Lou says. "And we thank you for it."

"*Sérieusement*. Seriously, Scott provides what we need," Samiah continues.

Scott gesticulates as if airing his hands dry. "*Passe-partout*."

They laugh. "Oh, *être un homme*—to be a man," Lou says. She lights up a cigarette.

"A wealthy white American," Samiah adds, pointedly.

"Oh," Sisi says, bringing her coffee cup from her lips to the desk. She isn't sure if this was said as a joke or an insult. She looks over at Scott.

"*Coupable!* Guilty!" he exclaims.

"That's why we love this guy," Lou says, swishing her smoke over the desk. Sisi is wondering if she and Scott are together when Samiah gets up from her chair to hug Scott from behind, resting her chin on his tousled hair. He reaches an arm behind her and closes his eyes. Samiah and Scott? A threesome? Sisi has heard of such things. With Lou, she thinks, anything is possible.

Lou bends toward her, frowning. "Now that you're here, we want to know if you'll join the cause. These two are organizing a rally taking place later this week, and we need all the help we can get."

"Of course," Sisi says without thinking about what she might be getting into. "Of course, you can count on me." She nods vigorously.

Samiah smiles at her from above Scott's head. Scott lets go of Samiah. He seems to discern Sisi's discomfort. "Your friend just got here, though. Maybe she needs time to understand what we're up to before she jumps in. And she needs to see the city!"

Samiah steps back from Scott, sits back down in her chair. A glance passes between her and Lou. Lou smirks. "Let me guess. You'd like to be her tour guide."

Scott smiles. "You have to admit that I'm good at it."

The two women laugh and give each other a knowing look Sisi cannot decipher. Has someone finally tamed Lou? Sisi finishes her toast and coffee.

"Ready to see something?" Scott asks.

"Now?" Sisi says. "I just got up."

"Well, no time like the present. Decide what you're wearing, and I'll take you out. We can leave these lovebirds to themselves."

"Scott!" Lou interjects sharply. "*Je ne lui ai encore rien dit.* I haven't told her yet."

Scott looks confused. "Oh, no? I thought you two went way back."

"Yes," Lou says, running the fingers of her free hand through her thick, short hair, wisps of which are jutting out in different directions coquettishly. "But I haven't told her." She looks up at

Scott, who is standing, ready to head out into the streets. "You know how things are."

Abashed, Scott nods. "Sorry, I just thought you two were tight and . . ." His voice trails off. "Maybe another time, then, Simone. I'll take you out on the town without these two and acquaint you with this old bawdy city."

Scott picks up his things. As he kisses Samiah goodbye, he whispers to her, "Don't worry. I'll be back to finish things up with you tomorrow. We're organized, and this will make a difference. I'll make sure everyone knows about it."

Samiah hugs Scott tightly, then Scott waves at Lou, squeezes Sisi's hand in goodbye, and leaves the three behind.

"Well, now you know," Lou says.

"Know what?" Sisi asks, wanting Lou to spell things out for her.

"Hmm," Samiah says. "Maybe I'll hang out with Scott for a while." She opens the apartment door and yells out to Scott to wait for her. He is on the stairs, descending, and yells back that he will wait for her on the landing. Samiah puts on her coat and is about to leave when she turns back, hugs Sisi, then goes to Lou and plants a kiss on her mouth, tousles Lou's hair.

Lou kisses Samiah back, then pushes her away toward the door. "Go, go. We'll see you later."

Lou brings out a pitcher of lemonade from the kitchen and gestures Sisi back toward the living room.

"Samiah made this for you yesterday," she says. "Let me get ice cubes for us." She leaves for the kitchen and returns with two glasses half-filled with ice. "She found limes in the market that reminded her of home. She thought you would like this."

Sisi reaches for the glasses and sets them on the low table in front of the couch. "That was kind of her. I love lemonade," she says as she thinks of the days of studying together with *jus korosól* or bitter passion fruit juice made sweet with cane juice or sugar. "I feel at home already," she adds. But Sisi is somewhat bewildered. What is she to make of this gesture of Samiah's? Is she to accept it as a welcome or as a kind of warning, that she is in Samiah's home, not hers? It is a kind gesture, she tells herself, nothing that should make her feel threatened, and yet there is something of that feeling flowing through her as Lou pours the lemonade from the pitcher into the glasses, with a distant look in her eye as if the filling of the tumblers is ceremonial, a testament to something between her and Samiah that is deeper than what might linger between them, her and Sisi, after all this time.

They sit on cushions strewn on the floor, their backs against the bottom of the couch. They are suddenly quiet. Despite the many letters they've exchanged over the last few years, picking up in person leaves Sisi tongue-tied.

Lou restarts the conversation. "I think about Odette a lot, that it could have been any of us disappeared like that."

Sisi takes a sip of her lemonade and ponders Lou's statement. "I don't know, Lou. I think about it all the time. Why her? Why not any of us? And what did she do? She was so unassuming."

"Didn't you hear?"

"What?"

"It was because she refused the advances of a new section chief in the area where her parents' farm was."

"Really? I didn't hear this. But we didn't stay as close as we were in school after Margie came back."

"I heard it from Gertie."

"From Gertie?" Sisi is surprised.

Lou continues, "Her parents refused the man, and he burned down part of their farm. That was apparently a warning, but they didn't think much of it and kept on with their work. Next thing they knew, Odette was gone, disappeared."

"I hadn't heard all that, just that the parents never found her body, or never got it back. I hadn't heard all those details."

"Yes," Lou says. "Things are that bad."

"It's hard to imagine, isn't it?" Sisi steps around the mention of Gertie. "That just a few years ago the whole world was coming to us, to see the Expo, and now we're all dispersed, all over that same world."

"It's a shame, is what it is." Lou declares. "We'll never see those days again."

"It was such a great time. Things were never the same after." Sisi pauses. Should she tell Lou the truth of it now, should she wait? She decides against telling the whole truth. "After the Expo, I mean. But there's hope, somewhere, if not for us, for others."

"Is there?"

"Isn't there? Isn't it why you're doing this work with Samiah? Because you have a hope for better?"

Lou shrugs, takes a sip of her lemonade. "You know what would make this better?"

"Rum!" they both say at the same time and explode into laughter.

Lou gets up to find the bottle she keeps stored away in one of the kitchen cabinets. "The real stuff," she says. "Haitian rum." She taps the bottle with a forefinger, then hands it over to Sisi. "Help yourself. But don't tell Samiah we desecrated her offering!"

Sisi laughs and pours herself a couple of ounces of the amber liquid. "I won't. But tell me, is Scott your boyfriend? Or is it the two of them . . ." Sisi's voice trails off. She doesn't feel equipped to ask about Samiah directly.

"Scott?" Lou scoffs. "Scott doesn't have a revolutionary bone in his body. And you know I need fire in my life." She takes the bottle of rum from the table and pours herself a finger into her lemonade. "Scott was attached to Samiah when I met her. They were kind of a package. You know how that goes." She rolls her eyes.

"You mean," Sisi says, "the two of them are . . ."

"Oh, no. God no." Lou thinks for a moment. "Well, to tell the truth, I think Scott has a huge crush on her, but they're just friends." She takes another swig of her drink, then lights another cigarette. "OK if I light up?"

"You've already done it."

"I have, haven't I," Lou says. "Sorry, force of old habit. Samiah hates it. I'm trying to quit. We can go in the kitchen and I can sit next to an open window."

They move back into the kitchen with their drinks in hand and sit at the table. Sisi is grateful for the hard back of the chair holding her up. She needs the feeling of something tangible.

"*Samiah est ma femme*," Lou says firmly, with a light edge to her voice as if to push Sisi back before she puts up any resistance. "She's my girlfriend," she repeats, more resolutely, taking another puff from her cigarette, letting out the smoke, and looking straight into Sisi's eyes across the haze.

Sisi feels a tug in her belly. She isn't sure if it is fear or desire. Lou, though older, looks the same to her as she always did, cool, self-assured, the kind of woman she wants to be and might never become. Curiously, knowing the nature of Lou and Samiah's relationship appeases her. Instead of feeling jealousy, she is happy for Lou.

"How did the two of you meet?" Sisi asks.

"My sister, Chiara. She came here after we moved back to Italy. I followed her. She can practice law here. She works for a private firm but she also volunteers, helping people who need it with consulting services, immigrants mostly. She married this really wealthy guy, in politics. Sometimes he helps her out with harder cases. Samiah's brother was jailed for—" She temporizes, choosing her words carefully. "Sedition."

"For what?"

"Sedition. Against the French state."

Lou puts out the stub of her cigarette and shakes another out of the pack.

"You don't smoke cigars anymore?" Sisi asks, pointing to the pack.

Lou shrugs, smiles. "You remember everything, don't you?"

Sisi blushes, looks away.

"You have to move with the times," Lou responds, lighting up the second cigarette, "but I do need to quit. Cigars were the first to go." She takes a drag, pulls a saucer toward her to use as an ashtray, and Sisi has to admit to herself that Lou looks elegant doing it. "Do you want one?"

"No. I never took it up."

"Not even after I showed you how to do a train?" Lou asks coyly, smirking.

"Not even after that."

They are flirting, the drinks going to their heads. Sisi enjoys the banter, but she is conscious that this is Lou and Lou does a lot of things without meaning them while Samiah is real, too real. She reasons that, for Lou, everything aside from Samiah is lighthearted fun. She has become, or has always been, inconsequential.

Lou opens the kitchen window and stations herself next to it, flicking her ash out onto the sill. "Dirty habit but I haven't kicked it yet. They say that her brother, Amir, organized to overthrow the French occupation of Algeria." She takes another drag of the cigarette. "And he probably did. He and Sam are half French, half Algerian, but they fight for the freedom of their country. I love them for that. I mean, I love her, but I also love her because she fights for her country." Lou looks over at Sisi. "There's a war going on there, you know, a civil war. If they fight back, they're accused of being terrorists. If they don't fight, they lose their country. The French think that being dominated by them is a gift, you know? If I can't fight for my own country, at least I can fight for hers." She shrugs. "The French don't under-stand that the civilizing mission failed long ago. People want to be free on their own terms. Anyone who comes from a country like ours understands that. Freedom is something you take. It's yours. It's not something anyone can give you."

Sisi thinks of what they have left behind in Port-au-Prince, of Odette's disappearance, of how difficult it is there, now, for anyone to organize dissent. Too risky.

"That's what the demonstration is for?" Sisi asks, referring to the flyers scattered over the desk that Samiah and Scott were discussing.

"Stay here long enough, Sam and Scott will have you paint-ing posters for her events." Lou laughs. "And you'll probably fall in love with her a little too," she adds quizzically, smiling behind the smoke of her cigarette.

Sisi grins. "I wouldn't mind. Helping to organize," she adds quickly, not wanting to be misunderstood.

Lou continues good-humoredly, "You can stay here as long as you like. We're happy to have you. We can figure out your next steps. There's no rush."

"Are you sure Samiah won't mind? Do you have the space?"

"We've talked about it, and she absolutely doesn't mind. Half the time there are people over here night and day, you'll see, one more isn't going to break the bank. If it does, we'll just ask Scott for a loan."

They laugh.

"Well," Lou says, putting out the cigarette, "now you know everything."

"I know nothing, and you know it."

Lou goes back into the living room and puts on a jazz LP: Sisi recognizes Miles Davis. She follows Lou into the living room, drink in hand. Does Lou ever think about their time at the Expo, or was it, as she said then, just nothing, just the kind of thing that Lou did to pass the time, because she was bored or had nothing else to do? Sisi shakes off the questions in her head: she is here, now, in the same room as Lou, and they have so much catching up to do. Sisi tells Lou in more detail about finding Mami passed away at her sewing desk, the haste to make arrangements to bury her, how everything changed so quickly in the last few years, since the Expo.

"Remember Lolo?" Lou asks. "Whatever became of him?"

"You would know better than me," Sisi answers.

"He was a skinny guy, wasn't he? And he loved those cockfights!"

"It's just amazing how much is gone," Sisi muses. "We—Margie and I—were explaining this to your parents when I brought Ti'Mo over, and it felt like we were all in mourning. Everyone is leaving. Everyone who can."

"That's the truth," Lou says. "Everyone who can, and that's few people in the end. I guess we're the lucky ones." They fall silent for a moment, thinking of all they've left behind.

"It's funny, you look a little like Samiah's little sister, you know," Lou says teasingly. "You have the same coloring and shape of face."

Sisi shrugs. "You'll have to show me a photograph, but I'll take that as a compliment: *Samiah est éblouissante*."

Lou looks away. "Don't I know it."

Sisi feels as if she has put her foot in her mouth. "I mean," she says, struggling for other words, "you make a stunning pair."

Lou flicks Sisi's words away by fluffing up her short hair from behind and to the side of her face. "We make a stunning something, that's for sure. But let's talk about other things. How did you find Margie? How is her son? Are my parents looking all right? It's been a while since I've seen everyone, and Chiara tells me nothing. We're always so busy here, what with the demonstrations and everything."

"Margie is doing fine," Sisi says, "happy to be reunited with her son. And your parents are looking great, doing great. It's been an adjustment to return to Italy after so much time away, and I guess it's not heartening to be leaving the home they made elsewhere for the same reasons they left Italy in the first place, because of fascism."

"Fascism," Lou murmurs. "Call it by any other name."

"It's what it is even if what's happening on the island doesn't have a doctrine yet. The repression is the same. The fear, terror, the same, or similar." She cycles back to their previous conversation about their childhood. The alcohol has made her feel bolder. "But whatever happened to Gertie? Is your family still in touch with the Alcindors? When did you speak to her about Odette?"

"Oh, we speak from time to time. The conversation about Odette happened over a phone call sometime. But you never told me why the two of you stopped speaking to each other. What was it? A boy? Something between your parents?"

"You might say that," Sisi responds, "but I wasn't the one who stopped talking."

"That's what she says. That when she tried to, you didn't give her the time of day."

"What did she mean by that? We've seen each other a handful of times through the years but never talked after the funeral."

"What funeral? Momo's? The one Odette and I came to?"

Sisi shakes her head. "No, my father's funeral. Not long before Momo died. She didn't come to Momo's funeral. I remember that. It was just you and Odette. And I didn't go to my father's funeral."

Lou frowns, puzzled. "But she couldn't have gone to Momo's funeral. She wasn't living in Port-au-Prince by then." Then Sisi sees everything fall into place in a look of clairvoyance on Lou's face. "You mean to say that that time you two were pulled out of class when we were kids, you were going to the same place, the same hospital rooms?"

"Hospital room, singular. We had—have—the same father."

"My God, Sisi, I never put it together. You two are sisters?"

"Yes, half sisters," Sisi says. "That was the day we found out. Gertie stopped speaking to me after that and I could never figure out why, so I let go. I let her go. It was too painful to try to hold on."

"I don't think she stopped talking to you on purpose. There had to be more going on."

Sisi stiffens at the thought of reopening the door to Gertie. "I don't know if it's worth it at this point."

"You're sisters," Lou says, finishing her drink. "It's got to be worth it. I don't know what I would do without Chiara. We need our sisters!"

"But I have Margie," Sisi responds categorically.

They hear a key turn in the front door lock. It is Samiah returning to the flat.

"*Vous allez bien?* All good?" Samiah peers in from the door.

"In here, honey," Lou calls out to her from the living room. "We've turned your lemonade—no offense—into drinks. Do you want one?"

Samiah takes off her coat. She blushes as she does so. "I'll join. I brought you food because I know that Lou hardly cooks." She winks at Sisi. "And you probably talked all afternoon."

"Perfect!" Lou exclaims. "You're a lifesaver. We've been drinking the whole time and haven't had anything to eat since you and Scott left."

"That's my Lou," Samiah says, taking out packages of food and leaving them out on the kitchen table.

"Oh, and I told her about us, Sam, and she doesn't mind, do you, Sisi?"

Samiah looks over at Sisi questioningly, as she puts out plates for each of them.

"No. Of course not," Sisi hurries to reassure Samiah. As they look at each other over the kitchen table, Sisi wonders what

Lou shared with her about their childhood in Port-au-Prince, if Samiah knows about the kiss. "I mean, I only care that you're both happy, that my best friend is happy."

Lou returns with a glass for Samiah. "Let's drink to that!"

They make a toast and start to eat what Samiah has brought, pita with hummus, stuffed grape leaves, chicken shawarma, and salad.

Sisi observes Samiah giving Lou a side glance as they eat. "What is it?" she asks. She doesn't want to do anything to mar her reunion with Lou. She has missed her and Margie so much since they left the country, missed Odette.

"It's just that—" She smiles at Lou. Lou nods back. "You look a lot like one of my younger sisters."

"Oh," Sisi says, blushing, "Lou told me that earlier, but I didn't believe it."

"Ah," Samiah replies, putting a hand on Lou's thigh next to her. "What I mean isn't just that you look like her but that you could be one of my sisters."

"Honey," Lou says, "believe me, Sisi has enough sisters as it is."

Sisi laughs, knowing that Lou will fill Samiah in about Gertie later on.

What Samiah says is a compliment, to be sure, because Samiah herself is a stunning woman with long, raven-black hair framing a chiseled face with long eyelashes contouring large, rounded eyes. Her eyes are a light gray color. The hoods above the eyelids are full, almost puffy, while her eyebrows are shapely, resembling winged blackbirds in flight, Sisi thinks. Her lower lip is the shape of an out-turned rose petal, the upper lip resting against it a smaller imitation of the eyebrows, curving around the lower as if to protect it. Sisi flushes, looks away. She imagines Lou kissing Samiah with meaning, a meaning that has escaped her.

"I'll leave you two alone," Samiah says after they eat.

Sisi wonders if Samiah noticed her reddening. "Please don't leave on my account."

"Oh, no. It's not you. I have to help organize a demonstration in the morning," Samiah says, gathering up the papers left behind on the desk. She hands Sisi a flyer from the stack.

Sisi looks down at the paper. It reads, "*Lutte pour la libération d'Algérie*" ("Fight for the liberation of Algeria") and features a woman with a fist in the air. An address is printed below the woman, what Sisi assumes to be the meeting point, and then a phone number to reach the organizers.

Samiah places a hand on Sisi's forearm "I hope you'll join us." She adds, "*Scott sera la*. Scott will be there. Any friend of Lou's is a friend of ours."

Lou's eyebrows arch. "I know what that means. Beware, Sisi, you might just be seduced by a Yankee."

The three of them laugh. Samiah retreats to the main bedroom and leaves Lou and Sisi to clean up and catch up deep into the night.

That is how easily they renew their friendship, how easily Sisi slips into her friend's life and becomes part of a coterie of artists, activists, insurgents. She has never felt more alive, more free, more capable, or useful, even. She does help Sam with her organizing, goes to a few marches, runs with the others when they see too many cops approaching, regroup as needed. Scott helps to find her work in a stationery company that has no idea that she uses her employee discount to print flyers and posters designed to foment dissent, bring down the empire. Life takes on a flow and a possibility Sisi has not felt for a long time.

She is amazed at how Lou has re-created family with Sam, at how involved their friend Scott appears to be, generous with both his time and his money, though he disappears at times as well, saying that he needs to separate his life as an activist from his life as a flaneur. He likes to wander the streets of Paris at night, frequent the cafés and read in his spare time. He reminds them that he is a student and needs to fulfill his credits for his baccalaureate, though they can't tell exactly what he studies. He has an interest in animals, that they know, and, to Sisi's delight, often points out birds flying overhead in the middle of demonstrations, comparing their plumage with the pictures in a book he keeps in his back pocket, taking notes for a list that becomes longer week by week. Whenever things get a little heated in the streets, he offers to take Sisi out to discover the city, and this is how they get to know each other, how Sisi begins to acquire a taste for leisure, a respite from a life belea-guered by politics.

"How do you do it?" she asks Scott once, over cups of strong coffee that remind her of home.

"Do what?"

"The activism and then remove yourself from the scene, do this." She picks up the espresso cup before her gingerly and motions it in Scott's direction.

"Well." Scott purses his lips. "I want to think of myself as a good guy, you know? So I do what I can, but it's not my world. It's theirs. All I can do is support it, but it's not my life."

"But don't you think that you should be there when things get tough?" Sisi says, thinking of Odette, of all that she has left behind. She is trying to measure Scott.

Scott shrugs. "I'm there as much as I can be, but if I were there more, it would damage me."

"Damage you how?" Sisi asks, inquisitive, feeling her whole body lean forward despite herself.

Scott flushes. "I guess I can tell you."

"What's the secret?" Sisi smiles.

"It started with Samiah," Scott says. "I took a class on Marxist ideology and the professor brought her brother in as a guest speaker and she sat in on the class. I thought: My God, what a beautiful woman! I've got to get to her. But there's no getting to Samiah without being involved in her causes, so I got involved, and then I met Lou. And you know, Lou. Wow! As soon as I met her, I thought, I'm in over my head, and it turned out that they were in love with one another so I was out of luck, or in luck, I don't know. I just couldn't get away from them. But sometimes I have to step back, for my own sanity, you know what I mean?"

Sisi laughs. "Do I?"

"You're in love with them, with Lou, right?" Scott studies her.

"I might have been, once, with Lou," Sisi says, thinking as she answers. "But I think of Lou, and Samiah now, as sisters. I just love that they are who they are and what they are. I mean, who wouldn't want to be like them? But I'm not that brave, I don't think."

"Neither am I," Scott says and pays the bill with a few loose coins. "Shall we move on to something stronger?"

"Why not?" Sisi allows herself to be swept away to the next port of call, a bar in the Moulin Rouge district, where anything goes and no one cares where you're from or what you do.

She spends months like this, staying at Lou and Sam's apartment, organizing the demonstrations, printing up the flyers, hanging out with Scott in the cafés and bars, getting to know him, but then two incidents bring the whole magic of it crashing down around her.

First, there is the matter of hiding two Haitians in the apartment who came to dinner after landing at the airport—siblings, a priest and his sister, a nun. The two organized against the government and fled into hiding. Chiara had given them

Lou's address. They were to stay there for a weekend before moving on to the South of France, to a bucolic village where they could assume new identities. But before they get to dessert, their first night in the apartment, there comes a pounding at the door, and they hear the deep voices of two men demanding that they open.

Quickly, quickly, Lou has the man hide in the bottom of an armoire, a piece of furniture in which it is possible to conceal things, and she tells the sister to get beneath Sisi's daybed, behind the luggage they store there, and has Sisi sit on top, reading a magazine. She shushes Sisi as Samiah moves to open the door and inquires as to what the men want. They flash IDs at her and stalk into the apartment forcefully. They are dressed in dark, tailored suits; their hair is cut short, down to the scalp; and they wear sunglasses, as if ashamed to show the whites of their eyes.

"What are you looking for?" Samiah dares ask.

The men push her out of the way.

"We'll call the police," Lou says, arms crossed, a cigarette dangling between two fingers. She brings the cigarette up to her lips and takes a drag from it. Sisi notices that her hand is shaking.

"*Ouap cheche polis?*" one of the men laughs. "And tell them what? That you and your woman are going to bring down the French government?"

"Yes, we know who and what you are," the other man says. "Just hand them over to us and we'll be on our way."

"With what authority?" Samiah says coolly. "We'll call our lawyer."

"Chiara Lombardo?" Lou offers, naming her sister. "She works for a firm here. She'll know what to do."

The men look at each other. They take a step back. Chiara may have been a pariah in Port-au-Prince, but they can't touch her here. She has regained her Italian citizenship and acquired

French citizenship. She is married now, to a French politician, who protects her all he can.

Pronouncing Chiara's name has the desired effect: the men retreat. "We'll be watching," they say, leaving. "We'll get them somehow."

They do, in fact, have to call Chiara, and then Scott, who helps them to smuggle out the brother and sister in the dead of night. They have to abort the plan to send them to the South of France and instead send them deeper into another country where they can't be so easily found. Scott helps with first-class train tickets, pays for a hotel room at their destination, makes sure that Sisi, Lou, and Sam make it back to their flat unscathed, then goes on his way. It all happens so fast that there is no time to think, but Sisi watches and absorbs it all: she sat on the day-bed with a woman she hardly knew trembling beneath it. She could feel, no, smell the fear dripping off the woman as they listened to the conversation between the men, Samiah, and Lou. She helped to prepare the two for the transfer to a car sent by Chiara's husband; then she stood watch in front of the apart-ment in case the two men in suits returned.

This is how she learns that the secret police of the one-who-cannot-be-named reaches far outside the island. Leaving is sometimes not enough. You could be killed in your sleep while on vacation, or that first night when you thought you could breathe again, or in a lover's embrace. If they want to find you, they can; if they want to liquidate you, they will.

Sisi remembers the singer Martha Jean-Claude, her flight to Cuba for having expressed herself artistically in a way that the then president thought was a criticism of his rule. She thinks of Odette, sweet Odette, who, like so many others without an agenda or political aspirations, was killed to make a simple point: that no matter who you are, or what you care about, you could be eliminated from the face of the earth, never to be found again. That is all He wants everyone to know: that He can, and will, again and again, until everyone falls in line, and He will just have to lift a little finger for the whole population to quake and do his bidding. A cruel form of power.

"Does this happen a lot?" she asks Lou, after the siblings are dispatched.

Lou flicks away her cigarette and pushes her fists into her pants pockets. "Enough," she says, nodding. "Enough."

Sisi isn't sure if Lou is speaking of the number of times such things have taken place or if she means that she wants an end to it, to the persecutions, the being chased, the terror exceeding national borders.

What protects Lou and Samiah is money, plain and simple. Money and status—her sister and brother-in-law, and Scott. By association, this protects Sisi, but it just makes her feel more vulnerable since she has neither money nor status of her own, only what grace they extend to her. She feels the unease she lived with in Haiti creep back into her, slip under her skin, needling her. She is less at home in Lou and Samiah's apartment, remembers the woman beneath the bed, trembling, and herself sitting above, wondering what would happen next, if they too would be disappeared. In short, she begins to look for ways out, though she says nothing to Lou and Sam, hoping they will not notice her distress. She is afraid of disappointing them. It is Scott who notices first that something has changed. A few days later, he takes her to dinner rather than out to coffee or for drinks.

"Is this a date?" she asks as they amble through the cobblestone roads.

Scott smiles. "If you want it to be." He finds her hand and holds it as they walk. She does not pull away, allows herself to feel the comfort of his grip, the square knuckles enfolding hers.

"Where to?" she says, breathing in the fresh air, relieved to be out of the cramped apartment.

"*Par ici.* This way," Scott says, and they walk side by side toward the Champ de Mars in the middle of the city.

It makes Sisi think of the Champ de Mars back home, with a statue of a maroon sounding the conch for the call to arms. The founding fathers were also there, all represented, from Dessalines to Louverture. Here in Paris, the Champ de Mars is a rolling green, with benches where children play, an area for *pétanque*, a game of rolling balls, and, of course, at the end, with its back to the Seine, the imposing Eiffel Tower. She feels safe walking with Scott by her side as he leads them to an old standby, a traditional restaurant on Rue du Commerce where they can get *steak frites* and an aperitif without it costing them an arm and a leg, though cost is no object for Scott. The dinner is planned to make Sisi feel more at ease, and they talk about Scott's studies, which have been advancing slowly since he got involved in Sam's work. Scott changes the subject as he sees Sisi stiffen the more they talk about the demonstrations and what has just transpired with the smuggling out of the Haitians. He asks about Sisi's work, about her family.

"Lou tells me that you have a sister? What does she do? Is she also here?"

Sisi recounts how Margie, like Lou and Chiara, was involved in politics at home and how she left for Italy first, then had Sisi take her son to her, which was how Sisi ended up in Paris at Lou's invitation. "But I have two sisters," she volunteers spontaneously, not knowing why she is telling Scott so much about herself except for a desire to be known, to have a net beyond those with whom she grew up.

"Oh," Scott says, between bites of food. "This is really good." He grins across the table at Sisi. "How's your food? Let's get a digestif, yes?" He calls the waiter over, saying "*Garçon, garçon,*" in his heavily accented French that nonetheless continues to impress Sisi. "But you were saying about this other sister? Is she here also?"

"No," Sisi starts. How to explain Gertie? Does she need to? "I have a half sister. She's not here. I think she's in the States or the DR. I'm not sure."

Scott's fork stops in midair. "Not sure how?"

"She's my half sister, on my dad's side. He was a Dominican Haitian."

"Meaning?"

"Haitian but of Dominican descent."

"Ah." Scott continues eating. "And why don't you know where she is?"

"Oh, we were friends when we were kids, before we knew that we were sisters, and then it all stopped when my father died."

Scott chews his food, musing. "That's a shame," he finally says. "I have brothers, but none of them have come here. France, Paris, doesn't interest them. They like it where they are." He laughs.

"So, you're the adventurous one in your family."

"I'd say so. And I'm not that adventurous. I like good things." His hand sweeps over the table. "Like this. And good company." The drinks come and Scott makes a toast: "To you. To us. Let's enjoy life while we have it."

With those words, Sisi allows herself to be swept off her feet.

"I have a proposition for you," Scott says, as they share a dessert of a *mille-feuille* oozing with yellow custard and streaked with chocolate sauce.

"Proposition?" Sisi repeats.

Scott nods, dabs at his lips with the cloth napkin. "I noticed that you were pretty scared after the incident the other night.

Do you think, maybe, that you've worn out your welcome at the apartment?"

"I don't think so," Sisi protests. "Have they said something?" She panics inwardly. Has her cowardice cost her Lou and Sam's friendship?

Scott demures. "No, no, nothing like that. What I mean is that maybe you need to cultivate a bit of distance. That could be done by moving to your own place."

"But where would I go? I haven't thought about it."

"That's just it. Where I live, which is not far from here, I could show you—" He halts. "There are chambermaid rooms for rent at the top of the building. They used to be for help working for each apartment below, but now they're rented out to students. I live in one of the apartments. The place is owned by one of my roommates' uncles. I haven't seen the chambermaid rooms, but there's one available for rent in the building. It's not too expensive. If it is, I could help you with it. I could show it to you after dinner and you could think about it?"

Sisi hasn't given any thought to moving out of Lou and Sam's but, presented with it, likes the idea of having more freedom, a space of her own. All the time spent with Scott has shown her that there are other ways to live that can be hers. "All right," she says. "I'm game."

"Good." Scott is delighted. "We'll go there after dinner. But before we do that, I have something for you."

"Really." Sisi smiles. "What is it?"

Scott fishes out a slim book from the pocket of his trench coat, slung over the back of his chair. It is a paperback copy of John James Audubon's *Birds of America*.

"For you," he says, presenting it to her. "Audubon was from Haiti," he continues, as Sisi holds the book in her hands. She opens it and caresses each page as she looks over the birds pictured there, one after the other. "Née Jean-Jacques Rabin in

Les Cayes. The story is that he was born in Saint-Domingue, then his father brought him to France when the Haitian Revolution started. The father changed his name, had his wife adopt him, and gave him a new start." Scott smiles and he really does have a winning smile, a smile Sisi can lose herself in, she thinks.

"Thank you," she whispers to him. "I've heard of him, but I didn't know he was Haitian."

"I don't think he thought of himself as Haitian. He lied all his life about where he was born, his heritage, but he had such an eye for color, didn't he?" Scott puts a finger on one of the pages to stop her on a plate depicting a passenger pigeon. "Even his pigeons look like they're tropical, don't you think?"

Sisi laughs. It's true. Audubon's pigeons seem ready for life in the tropics. Maybe being from the island, from Haiti, seeing the world in a different way, with more layers of color, a different quality of light, was what made Audubon such an attuned depicter of birds. Sisi feels better. Between the dinner and the book, Scott has revealed himself to be thoughtful, maybe a catch. She flips through the pages of the book; the paintings of the birds, with their bright plumage and dramatic poses, remind her of her childhood world, of the desire she has to draw birds and everything else in sight. They remind her of simpler times when she and Margie and anyone else around would walk to the port on Saturday mornings to take in the sunrise. Scott instantly is this to her: the possibility of an opening, the emergence of something new, like a new day. Maybe like Audubon, she too can elude her past.

"Did you know that you have a bird reserve off the coast of Haiti?" Scott interrupts her thoughts. They were now drinking from small cordial glasses filled with Grand Marnier. Scott knows the finer things in life. "An island called Navassa. The US has preserved it for the future. We should go there sometime."

Sisi nods but doesn't explain about Navassa, about anything. She is content to be swept up in Scott's vision of the island, of her. She wants nothing more than quiet in her own mind and Scott's chatter creates this, a white noise against the anxiety within her.

After dinner, they walk over to Scott's building to check out the maid's room for rent. They have to walk up several flights, and, as they go up, others come down, mostly young people who make clattering noises on the steps and say, "*Salut*, hello," as they rush by. Though the neighborhood is elegant, the maid's quarters is several floors up from the street and all it contains is a room where the kitchen doubles as the bathroom, the sole privacy possible a shower curtain strung on an oval guide rail that can be pulled to surround the bathtub and toilet.

"How quaint," Scott says, when he sees the kitchen/toilet area, somewhat disappointed that the space is not nicer.

"*C'est Paris!*" Sisi quips, not at all put off by the arrangement. They had much less in the house on Bonne Foi, no running water or sewage, despite the house being large. "Yes," she says. "I think I'll take it."

"*Superbe!*" Scott says cheerfully. "I thought you would! I've already made a deposit for you because I didn't want you to lose it. These go fast."

"I'll pay you back every penny," Sisi says.

"You don't have to," Scott says, waving her off.

"But I want to. I need to," Sisi says, remembering Momo's story about the Simbi, the necessity of finding support beyond a helpmate, a spouse. "I have to stand on my own two feet."

"OK, OK." Scott holds up his hands in surrender. "We can make an installment plan."

Sisi nods. "That's it. I'll just have to find a way to break it to Lou and Sam."

"I may have started to prepare the ground for your departure." Scott runs a hand through his hair.

"Oh?"

"I just dropped hints about your needing space and they theirs, you know, that kind of thing."

"You think of everything!"

Scott looks overjoyed. Sisi feels so many doors opening when just days before, the world had seemed to tighten around her, the politics of the island inescapable; but there are other options, other ways of being. In a few weeks, she has moved in.

Sisi hears the noises of unknown people running through the hallways, hears the pipes rattling, but there is a quiet in the space that allows her breathing room. Occasionally, there are break-ins and thefts since the doors downstairs aren't always pulled completely shut by those who come and go. Sometimes, those rushing through the halls and stairs aren't residents but petty thieves. Sisi simply doesn't open her door unless someone knocks on it, and she has few reasons to open it since she isn't one to welcome just anyone into her apartment. Sometimes, she goes down to hang out with Scott and his roommates in their apartment. They become good friends. They become occasional lovers and this is how Sisi begins to learn English, a language she never thought she would learn, or need. Lou and Samiah have yet to visit.

Then, in the fall, a few months later, the second incident takes place that changes the course of Sisi's life. Sisi takes part in a demonstration for Algerian rights. At first, it is exhilarating: so many people turn out to march along the Seine, in the heart of Paris, to call for an end to the Algerian War, a war many of the demonstrators, French and Algerian alike, consider illegal, and for the French, a stain on their good name. But it all unravels when the police descend upon them in droves, with instructions to move the protesters out of the city streets. The confrontation ends with blood being spilled, Algerian activists slain, bodies thrown into the Seine.

Again, Sisi watches, takes everything in, helps where she can. But she is traumatized by the sight of the batons falling onto the backs of people she considers friends, the sound of bones cracking, the sight of blood seeping out of wounds. Samiah is one of them, not killed, but her face split open by a police baton falling upon her cheekbone. Lou, Sisi, and Scott drag her away from the demonstration as she insists that she is fine, the blood trickling down her jawbone and onto the collar of her shirt.

"No, you're not," Lou says firmly, then, to Sisi and Scott, "Help me get her away from here."

Sisi does as she is asked, for Samiah and Lou as much as for herself. But it is Scott who does the legwork. Sisi wants to flee. The City of Light is not the tranquil haven she imagined that first morning in Lou's apartment, the two women and Scott murmuring to one another in French quietly so as not to wake her.

With Scott's help, they get Samiah to the hospital, where she is stitched up and given an injection for the pain. Lou is handed painkillers to take home and dressings for the wound, to be changed every six hours. She will be all right, they say. She just needs to rest and then return to get the stitches taken out in a few weeks. No more demonstrations, they add. No more.

The doctors want to keep Samiah overnight, for observation, in case she has a concussion, but Lou says no, that she will stay up all night to watch her if she has to, and they take Samiah home. Sisi can see that it is taking everything in Lou for her not to cry as they settle Samiah in their bedroom, but she holds everything inside. Sisi helps to put Samiah to bed. When she lived here, Sisi never looked closely at the contents of the room, a perfect blend of both women, Lou's sharp edges and Samiah's softness. There are pictures of the two of them on the walls, on the beach at Cannes, sitting at a café, in the courtyard of a mosque. Sisi leaves Lou by Samiah's side, knowing there is nothing more she can do. She stays overnight in the guest room while Scott goes back to his apartment.

There is nothing in the news the next morning about what happened the night before. The police deny that any of the protesters have been harmed or thrown into the Seine. The families of the slain cannot retrieve their bodies, since they are said not to exist, and have been fished out and vanished from the waters. The city resumes its quick pace, and it is as if nothing happened, except for those who have been harmed or disappeared. When Sisi looks upon Samiah's bandaged face, the dark circles under Lou's eyes, she sees the inescapable imprint of damage. Sisi wants, dearly, to escape.

Everywhere it is the same: certain people can be disposed of, never heard from again. It doesn't matter, Sisi thinks, if the people in power are elected or take their posts by force. It doesn't matter. She feels small, insignificant. She doesn't know if she has any fight left. She pours the coffee for everyone and makes the toast, spreads the butter on the slices, looks for jam in the refrigerator, hopes that there will be a way out. Then she goes back to her maid's room, grateful to have somewhere, anywhere, to be.

PARIS, 1962

After the incident on the Seine, Sisi takes distance from the organizing, sees Scott more, Lou and Sam less. Sisi's apartment, if she can call it that, in the 7th Arrondissement, is closer to her place of work, farther from the areas routinely used for demonstrations. She wants to be as far away from any agitation as possible. She hasn't come all the way from Port-au-Prince to Paris to remain unsettled. She doesn't help organize anything anymore and doesn't volunteer when someone needs to be hidden in a closet or under a bed. Samiah heals with a jagged scar tracing the contour of her left cheekbone, betraying her involvement in the Seine incident. When they do see each other, they don't talk about the demonstration or the nocturnal visit of the Haitians they helped flee to another country. They don't even celebrate the holidays together. Sisi wants all that to be behind her, a calm, quiet life before her. But that life never comes.

The following spring, there is an insistent knocking, a muffled baritone voice asking, "*Ça va?* Are you all right?"

Sisi is sleeping and it takes her a moment to realize that the banging is at her door, so accustomed is she by then to all the noises of the building, the people coming and going in the hallway and up and down the stairs. She stumbles out of bed, ties a wraparound to her waist, and opens the door to find Scott there, looking weary and concerned, a pile of excrement strewn across her door, dripping onto the pink-tiled entryway.

"*La vache,*" she exclaims, looking at the oozing shit. "No peace anywhere."

She didn't hear anyone come up the stairs, not even Scott, doesn't know when the door was vandalized.

"Who could have done this?" Scott laments. "I'm so sorry. But you're all right?"

"Yes, yes," she says, assessing the situation. "Anyone could have. The doors downstairs never stay shut or locked."

"But why you?"

Sisi shrugs. "Why anyone?"

But she knows why. Try as she might to blend in, to look and act like everyone else, Sisi, with her jet-black, thick hair and olive skin, is often mistaken for Algerian. Even Samiah had said, when Sisi first arrived, that she could have been mistaken for one of her sisters. As Algerian independence took shape, many French took umbrage against it. Sisi hears conversations in the street: some Parisians perceive the impending independence as a humiliating loss, arguing that the Africans are still in need of tutelage, even if the Africans in question often cannot be differentiated from the French, which is, partly, how the Algerians are winning their war. When she walks alone, sometimes she is yelled at, people telling her, "*Retourne chez toi!* Go home!" And they don't mean back to the island, they mean back to Algeria, or wherever they think she's from, if not Algeria then usually Morocco or Ethiopia, back to a continent on which Sisi has never set foot. When she is with Scott, she blends in; it is assumed that she is white or, if not quite white, at least French. How could he realize that without him, she looks like a different person to everyone else?

"Look," Scott says, "you get changed and I'll go get supplies from my apartment and help you to clean this up. Sound good?"

Sisi nods wearily. She is tired of Paris. Tired of cleaning up. Tired of the politics.

She gets changed, fills a bucket with soapy water, and waits for Scott to return with the gloves and scrub brushes. When Scott comes back, he rolls up his sleeves without hesitation. Sisi notes that, though Scott likes fine things, he is not afraid of honest work. They talk as they work to quickly wipe up the mess, holding their breath as they go, pretending that what they are cleaning up isn't what it is until Scott finally exclaims, "This is truly disgusting!" There is a long, startled silence from Sisi, after which they both burst out laughing. Their friendship is cemented.

Once they are done, they pour the dirty water down the toilet, gather everything else—the scrubs, the gloves—into a bag to throw out, wash up, and put on their coats. They've decided to go out to dinner, to the same place that Scott took her a few months back when he proposed the maid's chambers.

"It will air out by the time we're back," Sisi says, hopeful, after opening the slanted attic windows.

Scott nods, holding the bag of refuse away from himself, and leads the way out. He puts the bag down the garbage chute at the end of the hall and they saunter down the steps to the landing.

"I have another proposal," Scott says over dinner. "Why don't you move into the apartment with me? You'll save your money, and then you can decide what you do next. I'll be going back to the States next year. I've stayed here far longer than I expected. My year abroad has turned into a gap year and then some. Everyone is wondering when I'm coming back. Seems like the right time, and that might be an option for you too, yes? I can keep helping you with your English."

Sisi nods. What is there to lose? Scott has proved himself a good friend, an ally, and they are already lovers.

She moves out of the maid's room and into the apartment, signs up for a formal English course, and they end up married within a few months.

She travels to the US to be with Scott. Scott promises that there can be a future there, a possibility of a place to call home. She calls Margie, still in Italy, to tell her to think about following her there with Ti'Mo. Sisi wants the future Scott promises, the open arms of a wide-eyed America, a place she has heard so much about but never reaches.

OHIO, 1978

SIMONE DOESN'T REGRET THE DECISION SHE MADE TO marry Scott, even though she's keenly aware that she lacks Lou and Sam's courage. She admires Lou for being able to lead an unconventional life; not everyone has that in them. But she has come to realize that she married an idea more than she did a person. But she knows that she doesn't have it in her to stare down society. What she saw and lived through both in Port-au-Prince and in the streets of Paris, demonstrating with Lou and Sam, terrified her. There is shame in this realization but not regret. Scott is a measure of her limits.

A few months ago, the rainbow flag was introduced and flown in San Francisco during a Gay Freedom Day Parade, and Simone watched the coverage with awe. Times are changing. She admires the men and women who marched, could imagine that if Lou and Sam were there, they would have walked proudly. But she would not have been among them. A month ago, Harvey Milk, an out gay man and an elected official, was killed in broad daylight by another official, just twenty days after Californians had defeated a bill that would have made it possible for schools to discriminate against gay teachers. The feeling of inescapable terror Sisi has known since young adulthood descends upon her when she reads the news, and her plans to leave her marriage dwindle. Sisi's conversation with Margie about the starlings falling out of the sky took place almost a year ago, at the start of the year. It is the beginning of winter. A new year is around the corner.

Sisi is about to make *akasan*. She pours the cornmeal into boiling water mixed with evaporated milk, stirring in vanilla essence, sugar, a pinch of salt, and cinnamon with a wooden spoon. She is thinking about how the starlings will probably not come again in the new year when the phone rings. It is Margie. They talk at least once a week but have not spoken again about Sisi's decision to end her marriage, and every time the phone rings, Sisi wonders if Margie will bring her back to the subject, but she never does. This time, something else entirely has prompted Margie's call.

"Are you sitting?" Margie asks.

Sisi laughs. "Should I be? I was making *akasan*."

"*Akasan?*" Margie wonders. "I haven't had that in a while. You need to take everything off the stove and sit down."

Simone can tell from the tone of Margie's voice that something is serious. "Is Ti'Mo all right?" she asks instinctively while she does as told, moving boiling mush off the stovetop and turning off the range. She sits down at the kitchen table.

"He's fine."

"Is it Lou, Chiara?"

"They're fine," Margie says. "It's about something else, but I wanted you to hear this from me first. Remember the Alcindors?"

Sisi's mind flits. Gertie. What has happened? But she doesn't come right out and ask.

"Of course," Sisi says, holding her breath.

"One of them has died."

"Gertie?" she blurts, her chest closing in on itself.

"No."

Sisi exhales. "Who then?"

"Remember when I went to the Italian consulate before leaving and I told you that the Alcindor sisters, the older ones, the ones I had gone to school with, were working there, and at the French one?"

"Yes, I remember," Sisi says. "One of them processed me for France. She couldn't help herself and said something like 'Good riddance' when she stamped my visa."

"Well, one of them has died, and your name is in her obituary."

Sisi can't process the information. "There must be a mistake."

"No," Margie says. "They went and listed you as next of kin!"

"That's crazy," Sisi says. "Why would they want to do that after all this time?"

"Gertie said it was in this sister's will. Your sister, I guess. You were listed by your maiden name: Simone Val."

"You spoke to Gertie?"

"We bumped into each other at the Publix. Well, I think she planned it since she knows I go there, but she wanted you to know about the obituary because it's in all the major papers, here and on the island. She wants to talk to you and explain. She says she has nothing to do with it."

Gertie. Wanting to talk to her? They haven't seen or talked to each other in well over a decade.

"Well, that could be anyone's name. No one will know it's me, I suppose. I'm just glad Mami and Momo aren't here to see this. Momo would have had a fit."

"Mami also. It's her name too. There's a reason you don't have your father's name and it isn't just that he didn't give it to you. Mami wouldn't have it!"

"Exactly. Who are they to do this after all this time?"

Sisi did see Gertie once, as an adult, at the consulate, just after the older sister stamped her visa and shoved it back to her across the desk. Sisi took the visa, feeling hot in the face, and was about to leave when someone touched her elbow. She turned around and a young woman about her age peered at her. "Sisi?" the woman asked. "It's me, Gertie."

Sisi looked at the woman claiming to be Gertie and recognized their father's lips, those thin lips that kissed so many women, made so many children. The rest of her looked nothing like who she would have imagined Gertie to be, grown up. Everything about her was coiffed, reeked of money and status. Sisi didn't smile, didn't say hello. She shrugged off Gertie's hand, stung by Gertie's older sister's words, "Good riddance," and she, too, wanted to be rid of them, of the Alcindors, of their pretentiousness, their money, their satisfied air reflected in Gertie's countenance, her clothes, the scent of the perfume she wore, Chanel or Givenchy, something expensive, Sisi knew. She turned and walked out the door and didn't look back.

"What should I tell her?" Margie asks.

"Am I going to have to see her?" Simone hates that she sounds like a child. She is a mother, a wife. The Alcindors—Gertie—still have some power over her.

"I don't know. I don't think so. Not if you don't want to. You can just talk to her on the phone and go from there. It might be good . . . I don't know, a form of closure, *ou pa panse?*"

Sisi nods. Maybe. Just maybe. "OK. I'll talk to her. But this is strange."

"Yes," Margie agrees. "Strange, indeed. *Me ou bizwin finmin pot sa a*, close the door, finish with this."

"You're right," Sisi says. "Finish with this business. Bring an end to it."

But is it possible to bring things to an end with someone tied to you by blood? Is it like the rivers and springs tied together in a subterranean circuitry, impossible to see from the surface, invisible to the naked eye? Are they, like the Simbi, looking to rejoin each other the way oceans pull the waters across the mountains and valleys of the island, seeking connection, conduits one to the other that shift by the pull and push of the moon? Or is it that Gertie's pull is the call of the Simbi itself, asking Sisi to return to the source? It is a call Sisi cannot *not* answer. It is a call tied to destiny, an unalterable fact of being from the island,

tethered at once to it, as to the ancestors, as to the spirits binding them all together. It makes them one across time and space,
unable to deny that to be human is to be powerless to the forces
of nature, powerless to the wind and waves gartering them on
the island, guiding them in ceaseless motion beyond it, wherever
they might wander.

PART III

GERTIE
TODUS TODUS

MIAMI TO ORLANDO, 1978

FIDÉLIA CALLS TO SUMMON HER TO ANDRÉE'S HOUSE IN
Orlando. By then, Andrée is on the losing end of a valiant
fight against the recurrence of a cancer. Gertie has avoided
visiting Andrée during this time by using her caseload as an
overworked social worker in urban Miami and her daughter,
Manuella, now fourteen years of age and more difficult to use
as an excuse. For the Alcindors, not seeing one another reg-
ularly is normal, even under such circumstances, yet Gertie
manufactures excuses. When Fidélia calls, however, it is clear
by her tone that the sisters are giving her no choice in the matter: Gertie must come, not to help in the decision-making but
to hear what decision has been made. As usual, Gertie is simply to do whatever they ordain, or do nothing if she doesn't like
what has been decided. They are informing her so she does not
stand in their way.

Gertie prepares for the worst but could not have imagined
what the sisters have come up with this time. She leaves Manuella with her husband, who is relieved to have a reason to avoid
the sisters himself. The Alcindors and Pueyos are well known to
one another, going back generations on both sides of the island,
meeting over and over in its small ecosystem of elites, but marriage has brought them together too narrowly. Manuel endeavors
to avoid them, which was not easy before Manuella arrived, but
since she has, they do everything they can to protect her from
the many worlds they think could harm her. Gertie embarks on

the drive up the I-95 from Miami to Orlando solo, relieved that she is alone but dreading what is to come.

The sisters have had their share of health problems. Gertie has a vague notion about a contraceptive trial run by the US Department of Health in Port-au-Prince in the late fifties, trials that began in Puerto Rico, then somehow wound their way to their island. She does not know if her older sisters were part of the trial, but she suspects so. The US occupants left long ago, around the time Gertie was born, but left traces of themselves. Though genetic presdisposition may have played a factor, along with environmental degradation, it seemed plausible to assume that the trial, in which large doses of estrogen were meted out, might have contributed to the sisters' declining health as they aged, not gracefully, off the island. Gertie is always amazed that her nieces and nephews are so welcoming to their mothers as she suspects that her sisters have been no kinder to their own children than they have been to her. Somehow, the children have overcome what she thinks of as the Alcindor curse: a congenital inability to love without hidden motives. The sisters were never warm, even toward their own, yet family loyalty—or was it tradition?—overcame the absence of nurture.

Gertie squints at the road, her thoughts unfurling within her at the same time as she keeps a close eye on the painted dividers on the asphalt before her. There are aspects of family life that one cannot shed as lizards do their skins. Rather, Gertie thinks, every flagellation scars over, creates a carapace, a thickness that constricts so that every family encounter becomes more difficult to negotiate, dreaded. She sighs and the sound of her own lassitude surprises her, the weightiness of it. What is she getting herself into?

The drive gives her time to think about her relationship to her sisters. She thinks about how the sisters have always treated her—all of them, Andrée, Altagracia, Yvonne, Fidélia—from the time that she was little. She was the *rejeton*, the one that hadn't been expected, born many years after Fidélia, who was supposed to be the last of the five Alcindor children, an uneven number to keep the gods appeased. Gertie's siblings, including her brother, Rico, had come in quick succession when their mother was in her twenties, and then there was Gertrude, all eighteen inches of her, and a few shades darker than the rest. The sisters always made a point of telling her not to sit out too long in the sun when she was playing in the front yard of the house in Léogâne, which was filled with trees good for climbing. She would stick out her tongue at them in response, eliciting cries of disgust. "You'll never marry," the sisters would say.

Ever since she was old enough to walk and to hold a plate, the sisters, especially Andrée and Altagracia, would make Gertie fetch things for them, make their beds, carry their dirty clothes down to the yard for cleaning. At first, their mother laughed along with them, at Gertie, struggling beneath the weights they would put on her small frame, but as Gertie became friendly with the staff and with their children, she tried, too late, to rein in the older daughters. "She likes it, Mother," they would say.

When she was five, the older sisters had the grand idea to dress her up as a maid for Carnival, complete with a kerchief over her hair and a smock with two pockets in the front. Gertie hadn't thought anything of it. She liked having her hair wrapped up, as they all did at night, to keep the oils in, their mother said, to keep the undulations in their hair flat, said the sisters, and she could carry her dolls in the pockets. The sisters gave her a tiny broom made of sisal and then rouged her up garishly so that she looked like a tart, a baby tart. Her mother didn't recognize her when the sisters brought Gertie into the living room to show her off.

"She'll think she can only be a handmaiden," their mother protested. "She'll get the wrong idea."

But behind their mother's back, the sisters giggled and conspired among themselves. "A maid, or a concubine, what else is our Gertie going to be?"

When did Gertie realize that they, the sisters, would be her undoing if she listened to any of them?

LÉOGÂNE, 1940

Despite the sisters, Gertie's early childhood seems idyllic, up until the time it is decided that she will be transferred from her mother's home, in Léogâne, a small but lively town an hour or two out from the capital toward the ocean, to school in the big city. Her father stays in the city most of the time and they see him on the weekends.

Gertie looks forward to spending time with him in the city, the way her older siblings do, always returning from the capital with lots of tales about what they have seen and done, what their father has bought them and with what money. Wads and wads of cash, Rico tells Gertie, while the sisters just laugh things off and say that talking about money is crude. It is enough to know that their father has plenty of it, but only because it was given to him by their mother, who has it from her father before her. Their father smirks when the older girls make these assertions. He shoos them away. "You don't know what you're talking about. There's enough money on both sides of the family to keep the lot of you clothed and well married into eternity." Everyone laughs at this. Gertie too, though she isn't sure what anyone is laughing about. Is money a laughing matter? She doesn't think so. It's the thing everyone seems to be lacking, in search of, or putting away for a rainy day. So say the cooks and the women who keep both houses, and care for Gertie, as part of their duties.

Gertie listens. She is the youngest of all her mother's children. She overhears the cook and the housekeeper in Léogâne talk about her when her mother has one of her dizzy spells and remains lying down in her room, in total darkness, so that her head won't ache. When Maman has her dizzy spells, you must stay very quiet; everything must be whispered, and everyone must walk on tiptoe. Gertie takes off her slippers, the ones made of smoothed leather with colored bands on top to keep her feet in place, and gets round the house as quiet as a cat. She soon discovers that this is an easy way to eavesdrop. She is already small so being silent too can make her nearly invisible, though invisibility isn't an attribute that her siblings would assign her. No, not that.

She walks on tiptoe, without slippers, through her mother's house, taking care not to make a noise, and finds herself just outside the kitchen door. There, the housekeeper is explaining to the cook about Gertie. "I think they had her to keep the peace, poor child."

The other woman sucks her teeth. "They didn't think about it, did they?"

"They can afford another mouth."

"Rich people don't think about such things, do they?"

"The girl has nothing to do here. She walks around completely lost."

Gertie is startled. Does she walk around aimlessly, without anything to do? Isn't sleuthing an activity she's read about in books? She thinks she would make a good investigator. Gertie wrinkles her nose and continues listening at the open door.

"They don't pay her much attention," the housekeeper continues. "*Madanm la se yon ka et msieu la, li toujou deyò.*"

"*M'konin sa. Yo di ke li gayen lot ti moun.*"

Gertie is unsettled. Other children? What does she mean, Papa has other children?

"*Lot ti moun?* Hey!" The housekeeper snaps two fingers together in the air. "*Se pa etonan madanm la li toujou nan kabann li konsa. Sa pa etonm ditou.*"

Not surprising, they are saying. Not surprising that Maman stays in her house all the time, humiliated.

The cook tsk-tsks. "Has he tried anything with you?" she asks.

"Let him try!" the housekeeper cries out. She brandishes her broom with two hands like a sword and acts like a musketeer.

Gertie laughs out loud from her hiding place at the sight of her and stumbles into the kitchen. Both women become completely silent.

"What did you hear?" cries the cook.

"Nothing," Gertie exclaims. "Nothing," she insists as the housekeeper squints at her curiously.

The housekeeper gives the cook a hard look. "Like I said, nothing to do."

"*C'étaient des plaisanteries,*" the cook says to Gertie, just jokes. "We're just silly women. Don't mind us, all right?"

Gertie stops laughing long enough to nod in response, but she is old enough to know that the gossip of the house is often true, as when she heard the cook say that Andrée, her oldest sister, was married to a neighbor because they'd done something that made her huge as a watermelon, then flat as a pancake months later when a baby came out. Gertie is an auntie twice over already.

Later that night, she asks her mother about what the cook and housekeeper said.

"Where did you hear this?" Maman asks, then laughs one of her hollow laughs, the kind she reserves for Papa's business partners when they come around the house for unannounced dinners. "Your father! With other children? Put that right out of your mind. I don't know who could be spreading such lies! Don't listen to them! People who say such things are just spreading evil. They're evil." She cups Gertie's face in her hands and asks in a strained whisper, "What else did you hear, darling?"

Gertie tells her what she overheard about why she is the youngest child in the house, with no one to play with, and sees her mother's face harden. She lets go of Gertie's face and smiles wanly, all the while trailing an index finger down Gertie's cheek.

"You'll be pretty one day, Gertrude," she says, as if she hasn't heard what Gertie said. "You're darker than my other girls, but you're the prettiest by far." She seems faraway in her mind and sends Gertie to bed on that thought.

By end of week, a new cook and a new housekeeper have been hired, the others let go. They don't gossip in front of Gertie, so she finds out little, creeping around the house without her slippers on. In fact, the new cook, who is also Gertie's minder, tells her to put them on, always, even when her mother is sleeping, or else she'll catch her death of a cold and she hasn't come to the house to take care of ill little ones: she has three at home.

"Why don't you bring them here?" Gertie asks, innocently.

"I'll see if I can bring the youngest," Céleste says, after a pause. "He's not in school yet and you would probably get along."

Gertie claps her hands. A new friend!

Céleste does bring her youngest child for a time. Gertie's mother takes no notice. She is too often in her bed, sick, taking her meals in her bedroom and asking for Gertie to be brought to her before bedtime. Gertie thinks it prudent to tell her nothing since it seems that anytime she speaks to her about anything that goes on in the house, people she likes disappear.

Now, if she was able to make her older sisters disappear, Gertie would have been perfectly happy. Most of the time, they aren't around, the oldest married with a husband and two children, and the second in line always out and about with a different suitor each week. The younger two are preoccupied with school and their coterie of friends. They go back and forth between the houses in Léogane and in Port-au-Prince. Her brother does whatever boys do and it is mostly just her at home, along with Céleste, Céleste's son Brig, and the new housekeeper who is too old to have children Gertie's age, too old to have any interest in wagging tongues. Gertie's father comes for the weekends, and everything seems harmonious for a time until the month before Gertie is to start school in the capital.

That July, Gertie's second-oldest sister, Altagracia, is to be married in neighboring Santo Domingo. They are to go by car across the chains of mountains to the other side of the island. They form a caravan of several cars, actually, one behind the other, packed to the gills with newly made dresses, suits, presents for the new in-laws and newlyweds. It is the most exciting adventure that Gertie has been on in her young life. She is to be a flower girl at the wedding, one of several but the sole girl from the bride's side.

Everyone is excited. Gertie can see that the planning has breathed new life into her mother, and it is a wonder to see her flitting about gaily. Gertie has never seen Maman so enthusiastic about anything. When she comes across Gertie, she grasps her by the shoulders, kneels in front of her, and exclaims, "A wedding, Gertie! It's been ages!" Then she darts away to the next person she needs to speak to about flower arrangements, place settings, dresses, and boutonnieres for the men's suits.

The trip takes a few days and they stop at inns along the way. Céleste comes with them on the trip, along with her son Brig, which Gertie finds wonderful because she has someone to keep her occupied when the wedding plans become dreary. There are the late-night crying fits between her sister and her mother, with her father walking out into the night to drink with the other men in the party, including her older brother, who is now old enough for this kind of thing. Why her sister and mother are crying most every night Gertie doesn't know, but it seems to her that Altagracia, the one getting married, had other plans for herself. She doesn't want to get married! Gertie's mother is crying over this fact because she loves a good wedding and what comes afterward: the gifts, the dancing, the cutting of the cake, the setting up house, the children! Who wouldn't want to get married? she asks Altagracia night after night.

Gertie tries not to listen, but she can hear the conversation from the other side of the wall in the room where she is staying with Céleste and Brig. The answer seems clear: to avoid becoming their mother and father, who live, for all intents and purposes, in separate houses, far away from each other, despite having made several children together over the course of a twenty-five-year marriage.

Gertie assumes the sleeping arrangements will remain the same when they reach the Hotel Condado in the capital, where the wedding is to take place. It is the oldest, most ornate building that Gertie has ever stepped into. She follows Céleste and Brig into the hotel lobby, only for all three of them to be pushed back out, down the front steps, while the rest of the traveling party is shown through the lobby and to their respective rooms, one after the other.

Gertie does as she is told. She has been mistaken for the cook's daughter, but it doesn't bother her. Better to be the cook's child than to go hungry at night, she thinks, but then she hears her mother's curdling scream ring out across the lobby.

"What have you done with my daughter!?" her mother is yelling at the hotel concierge, whose waxed mustache curls are beginning to droop a little from the heat of the day.

Gertie stops in her tracks.

"Isn't your daughter here, *señora?*" the concierge stutters, pointing to Altagracia.

"The little one," her mother says, her right hand held flat down and at mid-thigh to indicate Gertie's height. "The little, darker one," she says, then pauses for effect before adding, "*La niña negrita.*"

Gertie is following the cook out of the entrance, but she hears her older siblings snigger and repeat the Spanish word her mother has pronounced. *Negrita, negrita.* Over and over again, swallowed between mouthfuls of laughter. She doesn't understand what is so funny about this. She is small, and she is darker. What can be wrong with that?

Then, swiftly, as the laughter and chatter grow in strength, with all the travelers in the lobby wondering what the fuss is about, why Gertie's mother is asking about the cook's daughter, Gertie sees Céleste swivel, take a quick breath, and push Gertie back into the lobby with one hand while tugging with the other at her own son to take him in the opposite direction into the darkening night, toward the maids' quarters behind the building.

"There she is." Gertie hears her father's booming voice as she stumbles back inside the hotel. The lobby is all polished brick and potted palms, a worn red carpet unfurled across the middle of the walkway to indicate where guests are to step and where the help are to stand to the side. Papa grasps her quickly by both shoulders and squeezes her into him while crouching down. "She's fine," he says to her mother, who stands at the far end of the lobby, toward the inner sanctum of the hotel. "*La perla* is here all in one piece!" He beams at the concierge and everyone else standing around. He has never called her "*perla*" before.

Her mother turns away, exasperated, and stalks off toward her assigned room, leaving Gertie behind with her father. The older siblings look at the two of them, not knowing what to do next: go after their mother or console Gertie, who appears completely unscathed.

"Are you all right, *niñita*?" Gertie's father asks her, kneeling by her side. She is nearly sitting on his knee.

She nods that yes, she is OK, then whispers to Papa, "I didn't know that Maman spoke Spanish. Did you?"

Papa bursts into laughter, whispers back, "She would have to, to keep up with me! You'll see, one day you'll be speaking Spanish too. It's in your blood."

Gertie wishes that the moment could last forever, sitting there on Papa's knee, receiving advice about a future for herself she cannot yet imagine.

"Well then," Papa says, standing up abruptly, letting Gertie off his lap. "All is well! Let's get on with things. We have a wedding to put on." He holds out a hand for Altagracia, in the lobby, gestures to the young man who is her intended, and the three of them walk away into the courtyard where the wedding is to take place in a few days' time.

With that proclamation, Gertie is forgotten again as each one in the party looks for their luggage and asks for the keys to their room. Eventually, Papa follows Maman down the long corridor that leads away from the lobby to the rooms, and the about-to-be-newlyweds are left to whisper under the palms with no chaperone but Gertie, who sits on the stairs between the lobby and the courtyard, waiting for someone to remember her.

In the end, the person sent out to fetch Gertie is Fidélia, a sullen and severe fifteen year old.

"Maman sent me to get you," Fidélia says. "Do you know how much trouble you're in?"

Gertie shakes her head no, she doesn't know. She follows her sister silently to dinner, to her bath, and then to bed, wishing that it had been Céleste who came to find and take care of her, as she usually does when they are at home. All the while, Fidélia complains about every task. "You're so slow." "Why did they ever have you?" "You really aren't good at anything, are you, Gertie?" "Why did I get saddled with you?"

Gertie doesn't answer. She is used to her siblings' umbrage when they are around, even if she doesn't entirely understand its source. What she does understand is that her mother has other worries, bigger worries than her, but that Gertie is in the way, an added worry. Gertie doesn't have time to think about how unnatural this is, how it should have been her mother who came to find her. In fact, it was a surprise to hear her mother shout for her earlier. There are so many other things to be excited about that she doesn't fret too much about it. She is tired and the journey has been long. At least she has a place to sleep and she has been fed, despite Fidélia's insistence that Gertie curl up far away from her on the bed and face the wall. And they are in Santo Domingo, the city her brother says is paved in gold! In days, she is to be a flower girl in her sister's wedding! She will do a great job and then the sisters will see that she is good at something. She will prove them all wrong: they will finally see her.

Gertie remains in Fidélia's room for the duration of their stay in Santo Domingo. Every night it is the same: Fidélia makes her brush her teeth. Fidélia makes her bathe. Fidélia tells her to say her prayers and go to sleep facing the wall. They don't play or exchange thoughts or anything of the sort. Gertie feels the loneliness of the time before Céleste and her son's arrival creep back, but she goes to find them during the days, if she is not needed at rehearsal, and experiences relief away from her family. She sees that her father is keeping an eye on her, so she doesn't worry about what her siblings are saying, how she is becoming a disgrace because she appears to prefer the cook's son to them. She does, it is true. She won't deny it and since her father says nothing, she stays away from her siblings and close to Céleste and Brig whenever she can. When she must interact with her family, she remains as quiet as a mouse, as quiet as possible.

The morning of the wedding itself, even Fidélia forgets about looking after Gertie, but Gertie is confident that she knows what to do: she brushes her teeth, takes a toilette, finds her dress hanging in the closet of the hotel bedroom, and pulls it on. She will find a grown-up to help her with the yellow sash that is to be tied around her waist. She is proud as she gazes at herself in the full-length mirror she found on the inside of the closet door.

The dress is a miniature version of her sisters', with lace lining the short sleeves and hem, the whole garment a creamy white the color of whipped cream. Gertie feels beautiful in the dress, which is likely the most luxurious item she has ever worn in her short life. The one thing she doesn't know how to do is her hair. It should have been pressed when they first arrived, but Fidélia has been so mad at Gertie trailing her wherever she goes that when it was Gertie's turn at the hairdresser's, when they called out, "Next?" Fidélia didn't say anything. Fidélia just glared at her, daring Gertie to stand up for herself. This had the effect of making her feel minute, smaller than small, and she couldn't utter a peep. Gertie figures that she can ask Céleste for help, or, just maybe, her mother? She doesn't know but she will figure it out. Fidélia left the room hours before, to get ready with the bridal group, leaving Gertie to herself, so Gertie finds her hairbrush and comb and goes to search for Céleste in the maids' quarters at the back of the hotel. But Céleste is nowhere to be found. Gertie wanders for some time.

"Gertie," someone yells out to her as she walks through the lobby. It is Fidélia. "Where did you go? I've been looking for you for hours!" Behind her is their mother, looking shocked and breathless.

"You weren't looking for me," Gertie says, standing her ground. "I've been looking for . . . for . . . for someone to do my hair!" She shows them her brush and comb in hand.

"She looks dreadful," their mother says. "Why didn't you get her hair done at the same time as you, Fidélia? I trusted you to get her ready!"

"She doesn't listen, Maman" Fidélia says. "I told you! Gertie's impossible!"

"No, I'm not," Gertie says. "I'm nearly seven and I'll be going to school soon. You left me behind and you wouldn't let me get my hair done!"

"Is this true?" Maman turns to face Fidélia, who shrinks under her mother's anger.

Gertie doesn't hear Fidélia's mumbled response and as the two try to sort themselves out, Papa comes striding through the lobby.

"Here you all are!" he exclaims, smiling, bringing his hands together in a gesture of mock gratitude, as if he is about to pray, right there, in front of all the strangers.

Gertie giggles.

"And why is this one's hair all over the place?" Papa says. "We must take care of this!" He grasps Gertie by the hand and walks her away from Fidélia and their mother's bickering. They hardly notice Papa and Gertie walking away.

Together, they find Céleste, who does her best to gather Gertie's tight curls atop her head in a large puff that she garlands with flowers that were set in the courtyard for the wedding.

"You look like a princess," Brig says.

"Just beautiful," Papa agrees while Céleste looks back and forth between them.

But when Gertie comes traipsing down the aisle in front of the bridal party with the flower petals, instead of the gasps she hoped to hear, of wedding attendees stunned by her beauty, she is aware of whispers and laughter.

"What is the cook's daughter doing in the wedding party?" someone asks, a little too shrilly.

That person is promptly elbowed by another attendee. "That's the last daughter," comes the correction. "The little sister."

"Oh. She doesn't quite fit in, does she?"

Gertie looks up and catches her father's eyes. She wants to cry. What can be so wrong about how she looks? Hadn't he and Céleste and Brig thought her beautiful? She looks at her mother and sees a mask covering her anger. Gertie wants to fly away. Instead, she carries on throwing the flower petals, but her happiness has withered just as the petals she flings will soon. She wanted to be visible to everyone but all she wants now is to be swallowed whole into the ground.

Once her role is over, Gertie flees beneath one of the cloths thrown over a table at the reception. There, unfortunately, she hears every remark about the darker hue of her skin, how her curly hair disturbed and shocked the older women who attended the wedding and expected more from an Alcindor. She disappointed everyone. Gertie cries silently under the table and falls asleep curled up on herself, like a cat with nothing else to do.

Gertie has no idea how long she has been sleeping under the table when a hand reaches under to pull her into the light. It is her father. He doesn't say anything but raises her to her feet before walking her over to a far corner of the courtyard, away from everyone else.

"I have something for you, Gertie, something that I hope will help."

They sit together on a bench in front of a brick wall on which a bougainvillea flowers pink buds. The walk in front of them is filled with the bush's papery petals.

"Here," her father says, pulling from his vest pocket a thin silver chain on which hangs a locket. "I want you to have this."

"Me?" Gertie asks, as she accepts the trinket into her small hands. "Don't you want to give it to someone bigger?"

"No, Gertrude." Her father strokes his chin. "I don't think anyone else will appreciate it like you will. Here, let me show you."

He reaches into her hands and opens the locket to reveal the face of an older woman. It is an old photograph, or maybe it is a drawing. Gertie isn't sure.

"Who is this?" she asks.

"That, Gertrude," her father says, "is my great-grandmother. They say it's a fair likeness and I thought you would like it."

Gertie nods. Indeed, the woman looks regal, beautiful, her skin a deep and rich color Gertie can only guess at, like her own.

"You see," he continues, "when people make fun of you, say that you're too dark, or not dark enough, or call you 'la negrita'— all those things—you must remember that this color comes from somewhere, somewhere we all come from, that matters. This woman is the first woman we know of from my side of the island. She was the great-grandchild of Africans, those who came here from the other side of the ocean, way back in the early 1700s. She made a life for herself here. She had to. She had no choice in the matter. She had children, with a Spaniard, a land-owner. I don't know if they loved one another. I hope so. Either way, her first name was Freda. Her blood is in my veins and in the veins of all my children, from the oldest to the youngest. That means you too, Gertie."

Gertie is skeptical. "Then why am I the one getting picked on?" she asks. "If we're all the same."

"Well," Papa says, "it's not easy to explain this world, this island, Gertie. It's something you'll have to figure out as you get older. I just want you to know that there's nothing wrong with having a little color. It just means that Freda is coming through and that you, and anyone like you in the family, are making her visible so that the others can remember her, but sometimes they're afraid of what that means."

"Why would they be afraid?"

Papa's face pinches, as if he all at once feels a pain in his side. He appears to be thinking. "Freda was a very courageous woman," he says. "We don't know much about her. What we do know is that she left the DR, crossed the mountains on her own to settle in Haiti, in the North, and for many years she made the crossing, back and forth."

"What did she do?" Gertie asks, fingering the locket and examining the sable face in the portrait that she sees she resembles. The woman looks stern. She is not smiling. Gertie looks up expectantly into Papa's honeyed face.

"She was a businesswoman," Papa says proudly. "She bought goods on one side and then sold them on the other. Whatever was needed." Papa waggles his hands as he describes Freda's business acumen. "She was an uncommon woman in those times. She was afraid of nothing. One has to imagine that she saw a lot, lived through a lot. Heard the kinds of things you hear, felt the scorn and disapproval for a darker-skinned woman making her way in business at a time when only men did such things, and certainly not women who looked like her."

"Like me?" Gertie whispers.

"Not exactly like you. You have the privilege of being an Alcindor and what that means today. You have me and your mother and your siblings. You have class standing on both sides, but in those days, a woman like Freda was alone, on the margins of society."

"How did she survive?"

Papa points to his head, then to his chest. "By smarts and by heart, Gertrude. This is how you must be like her. You will resemble her not just by the depth of your complexion but by the depths of your heart. Now, when you start school, I want you to seek out the smart girls and learn everything you can. I don't want you wasting time with girls who care solely about their dresses and ironing their hair, you understand?"

Gertie is confused. Her older sisters focus only on their hair, their dresses, and which ball they will attend and with whom, with an eye toward achieving the right kind of marriages. They don't speak of love. They don't speak of knowledge. They speak of which one of them will first get a motor-driven car and which of them will have houses perched on the hillsides in Berthe or Pacot, overlooking the city, which of them will have second homes on the Spanish-speaking side of the island.

Papa seems to read her thoughts. "Your sisters are doing as your mother . . . as we"—he wavers—"taught them. But for you, it can be different. You can make choices that suit you."

Gertie wonders why anything should be any different for her than it has been for her sisters. It is true that her complexion is a little darker than the others', but hasn't Maman told her that she is the prettiest of them; didn't Papa *just* tell her that she has the biggest heart? Why shouldn't she want dresses and balls and a good marriage?

"If you choose to marry," Papa says, "do it for love, nothing else. You will be happier for it."

"Is that what Freda did?"

Papa takes the locket from her for a moment and admires the fading picture. "I want to believe so, Gertie. They had many children and, eventually, lots of land, mostly on this side of the island, but she never forgot her early struggles. When she talked and talked about them, we came to understand that we belonged to the whole island, that there was no division to be made between east or west, light or dark, rich or poor. Do you understand?"

Gertie nods as he hands her back the locket, letting the chain curl like a small serpent into a coil in her palm.

"Keep this safe, Gertie. Don't be like us, like me. Be like Freda. Be who you are. Don't worry about what people say. These people who want to make you feel bad for what you are, are just soulless, aimless people, even your siblings." He whispers. "I love all of you, but don't be like them. Don't be like I've been to so many."

"Like you too?"

Papa rubs at his eyes as if he is all at once growing tired. "Not like me, Gertie. It took me many years to understand that there is more to life than money and politics. I'm understanding this day by day, watching the way you appreciate everything in front of you, everyone. I see you with the cook and her son, how you treat them. You make me very proud, Gertie." He kisses her on the forehead. "I just want you to have this." He closes her hands over the locket. "For now, just remember that this is nothing to be ashamed of: you are beautiful, *mijíta*. Don't let anyone take that away from you, *comprendes?*"

Gertie nods but she doesn't fully understand. Papa takes the locket from her hands and strings it around her neck. The locket slips beneath the bodice of her dress, where it is hidden from sight.

"Ask Céleste to keep it for you, later," he counsels her, but later, when she is back in the room with Fidélia, changing, being chastised for having disappeared and, according to Fidélia, nearly ruining the wedding, she realizes she forgot to ask.

She is in her underwear when Fidélia's eyes fall on the locket. "What is *that?* Where did you get that? Gertie! Did you take this from someone? Did you steal it at the wedding?"

Gertie's hand flies up to her neck. "Papa gave it to me," she says, too quickly.

"Really?" Fidélia says, dumbfounded. "I don't believe you. You're too little for anything like this."

Gertie is about to put up a fight, but Fidélia, sensing her resistance, relents and puts out her hand. "Give it here. I'll give it back to you when we get home."

"OK," Gertie says reluctantly, "but don't forget. He'll be mad if I lose it. I'm sure he will be."

"I won't," Fidélia says sweetly, and the sweetness makes Gertie's stomach lurch because such sweetness in her sisters always hides something else, a sticky, sour resentment that never yields to softness. She waits until Fidélia falls asleep to go digging into the drawer where she saw Fidélia put the locket away, then puts it in a sock. She feigns sleep when, the next morning, Fidélia searches high and low and doesn't find the locket. She feels Fidélia's gaze boring into her but doesn't move a muscle. She is facing the wall, as she has every night, the way she's been told. When Fidélia finally leaves the room, Gertie dresses and goes to search for Céleste in the maids' quarters. She tells her what her father said about Freda and that he told her to give Céleste the locket for safekeeping. Céleste nods as if she understands everything, including the fact that Gertie's sisters can't be trusted.

On the way back across the mountains, it seems that everything around her, the company, the nature beyond the cars, is quiet. They have left behind the newlyweds as well as the older siblings, who are going to stay on at the resort for a week or more, doing whatever it is that young people do.

When they make it to Léogâne, Gertie's mother asks that she continue to the capital with her father, to ready herself for school, she says, which is a month away. Papa asks that Céleste and her son come too, but her mother does not allow it. "Those children are getting too close," Gertie hears her mother say to Papa, to which he responds, "They're just children."

"Children who will one day be adults," Gertie's mother says. "We have to nip this in the bud. Case closed."

Gertie hears Papa sigh the way he does when he can't get his way, which is much of the time, at least at home, Maman's home.

Before she leaves for the capital with Papa, Céleste comes to say goodbye, presses the locket into her hands, and whispers in her ear, "Don't forget this. Don't forget where you come from," to which Gertie nods, knowing that she has been entrusted twice over.

ORLANDO, 1978

CANCERS: CERVICAL, BREAST, UTERINE. THE SISTERS have had them all, or one or the other, as the years have passed. Gertie wonders if she will be the next afflicted. But the Alcindors remain unlucky in this way: they age but their cancers are often masked, manifesting or misdiagnosed as something else— weight gain, menopause, ministrokes, age, you name it, they are told everything under the sun, until whatever mass is growing from within, hidden beneath layers of skin, decides that it wants to graduate from a peanut-sized growth to one the size of a walnut, from a walnut to one the size of a tightly fisted orange. In the case of Andrée, who has come up with the idea of the obituary, a small tumor graduated to the massive size of a plump grapefruit before it was found, or that of a baseball, the old kind, the hard ones that used to be hand-stitched by Haitian women grown myopic from feverish sewing in inadequate light, some blinded by a slip of a needle held too close to the eyes while they were told to work without bathroom breaks.

Aging, though, gives the sisters a distinct advantage, Gertie always thinks. It gives them the time to ponder their relationships to others. This is the way that Gertie can wrap her mind around why the sisters would want to name Sisi in Andrée's obituary. The sisters don't know Sisi any longer, and she does not know them. Gertie knows that Sisi married an American, has a daughter. Nothing more. She imagines Sisi happy, happy as Gertie is herself, though she remains plagued with a tugging feeling of regret that tells her that they might have been happier had they remained in each other's lives. Gertie thinks that the sisters might want to make up for past contempt.

When the sisters started talking about the obituary, Gertie doesn't know, but there is no mistaking the tone of resolution with which they address Gertie after calling her to Andrée's bedside. Andrée, in her early sixties, has been felled, finally, by a third bout of cancer. She survived breast and ovarian cancer only to be diagnosed, in the end, with a cervical cancer that might have come from one of the first two, it isn't clear. But this one was called late, after it spread, and after yet another surgery and rounds of chemo, her doctors don't think she will survive—though no one knows the strength of resolve that resides in an Alcindor, especially a female one. Altagracia, the second-born sister, always jokes that the Alcindor women have survived blights, hurricanes, unfaithful fathers and husbands, dictators—on both sides of the island. Among such things, cancer is yet another storm to ride out. But, this time, Andrée, the oldest, has reached the end of the line. When she and Altagracia called Yvonne, Fidélia, and Gertie to Andrée's bedside, it was to share Andrée's final wishes so that they would be well known in advance.

"I've written my obituary," Andrée says, thrusting a piece of paper into her younger sisters' cupped hands. "To spare you the trouble."

There is a faint whiff of dread wafting through the room, as when the shells of broken eggs are left to dry in a waste bin. They all know that Andrée enjoys having the last word, no matter how she gets it.

"She insists," Altagracia states. "I told her we could have taken care of it."

Yvonne and Fidélia nod. Yes. Yes. They could have written a wonderful homage to their eldest sister, something dignified, that would erase all the ignominy of the past, erase the betrayals of their father, the sting of the unfaithful husbands long gone, the false friends, the slippery road of politics under dictatorship. Elites were needed in such times, to provide a veneer of normalcy, families with names and with money to paper over harms.

Andrée pushes the paper along toward Gertie.

"You read it out loud, Gertie. You have the best voice."

It is a trick, of course, to reveal the contents of the obituary. She falls for it, reading in her best boarding-school voice, until the moment she reads, at the end of the list of surviving siblings, "Simone Val," the name echoing in her head as she hears herself utter Sisi's name before she registers what she is reading. She stops.

"Simone Val? Really? What right do you have to claim her now?" Gertie looks around the room, bewildered. "Why?" she asks the sisters. It is they who told her, so long ago, to stay clear of Sisi, they who disrupted the connection that had brought her joy in such a lonely childhood, convinced her that, as a sister, Sisi would turn out to be just like them, shallow, cruel. They who made her distrust the definitions of simple words, like "home," "family," "sisterhood."

"Gertie," Andrée mocks, then coughs, a long racking that sets her whole frame, slight as it is, to heaving. Altagracia and Yvonne crowd around her, hold her by the elbows as if they could somehow put her back together again. Humpty-Dumpty fallen on her head. Cracked. She looks like a puppet whose strings have abruptly been dropped, though Gertie knows that in this family, it is most often Andrée who pulls everyone else's strings. What is she about to pull off, this time, as her last breath draws near? "It's the right thing to do. Don't you think it's about time?" She laughs an empty, shallow laugh. Her next words come out almost as a whisper: "Especially after you dropped her like a wet rag."

"But it was you," Gertie corrects. "All of you." She looks from face to face. Each is closed against her, lips pursed, eyes looking away. "Don't you remember? All of you convinced me that being friends with her would bring us dishonor. You were ashamed that Papa's last wish was to recognize her by having you bring her—and the others—to the deathbed, without telling her mother. You convinced me that the friendship would be harmful to you, to me. I believed you." She looks around the room. "You didn't let me go to the funeral in case the Vals would show up. You cared that much about not being associated with them then."

"Well," Altagracia starts, in defense of Andrée, but of herself too, "after that scene in the hospital, which was a disgrace, with Papa calling her, all the outside children he had, to the deathbed alongside all of us. We were trying to protect you. We couldn't have held our heads high. We kept you clear of the scandal. Thank God that was all Papa did, call her to the deathbed, and nothing more. No one had to know." She lays a weak hand on Gertie's shoulder. "But things are different now."

Gertie looks down at the thin membrane of skin covering the blue veins of her sister's hand, papery thin. She shrugs it off. "What is different now, I'd like to know. And since when did you ever try to protect me from anything? You were all trying to protect your marriages." She turns back to Andrée, who seems to recede into the sheets and pillows surrounding her, becoming smaller and smaller by the minute. Is she shrinking from guilt, from shame? Gertie wonders. She shakes the sheet of paper at Andrée. "What are you trying to do? Why can't you tell the truth, even now?"

Andrée coughs from the pillows, sending flakes of dust into the air as she stirs against them, resolute. "You can't refuse a dying woman's wish."

"But this, Andrée? This?" Gertie shakes the paper in the air, looks into the faces of her sisters gathered around the bed. They avoid her eyes. "You are all mad."

"I'm setting things right," Andrée insists. "Recognizing her. Legitimizing her. Giving her a right to Papa's name."

"Did it ever occur to you," Gertie articulates slowly, "that she doesn't want his name—hasn't had it and doesn't want it? Has it occurred to you that she hasn't needed us all this time and doesn't need us now? I mean look at us in this room. Look at how old you've all become."

"I'm sure she'll be grateful to be acknowledged. It's never too late to do right."

"How is this doing right? You're not listening to yourself. Grateful? That's the kind of language people use to talk about their underpaid domestics, you know? You haven't tried reaching out to her, or asking for her forgiveness for what you did long ago, making sure that no one knew that she was Papa's, ours. That he loved her, like us."

"Hah!" Altagracia scoffs. "That's rich, don't you think? Loved her as much as us? I wouldn't go that far. He loved the mother. What was her name?" She snaps her fingers in the air.

"Marie-Rose," Gertie says. She doesn't know how she remembers.

"Papa was just a man," Fidélia states flatly.

"Perhaps, but he was also a father," Gertie counters.

"You are so sentimental." Andrée moves an arm limply above the bedclothes. "Why, after all this time? It's a simple declaration. Not of love, obviously. Take it for what it is."

"And what is it, exactly?" Gertie asks.

"It's armistice, capitulation, letting the world know that we accept that Papa was not a perfect man, that we, the Alcindors, are not a perfect family. Or," she says, "think of it as an act of contrition. Asking for forgiveness for what I did to you, to her, before I pass. Isn't that worth something?"

"The problem is that you don't want that forgiveness. What you want is to claim her, own her. You think she'll come crawling to you, asking for the family name, the family jewels, when there aren't any to claim. We all know Papa didn't have any fortune to his name. All the money was Maman's. That's why he married her, isn't it? Theirs wasn't a marriage bed made from love."

Altagracia groans. "You are exhausting."

"So much," Fidélia agrees.

Yvonne is drinking juice and brings her glass up to her lips to avoid having to say anything.

"This is absurd," Gertie exclaims. "It will be an insult to Sisi after all this time." It is strange to say Simone's nickname in their presence. Sisi's name puckers her mouth like an unripe crescent of orange. Her training as a social worker kicks in. She thinks of what is just. Desires don't repair torn family dynamics. What is required is work, a true apology, reaching out. Not this.

"Her name shouldn't be in this obituary. None of us should be trying to claim her like this, without consulting her or getting her permission. You're going to publish this, right? It will be everywhere. She'll be blindsided. No one knows she's Papa's except for us and whoever she's chosen to tell. Why would you tell the whole world just for your selfish ends? It's not making things right. It's not right."

"Well," Yvonne, usually silent, intones. "It's not your choice. This is Andrée's wish."

Andrée nods weakly from the pillows. "My wish. Dying wish."

"You're dying and you still can't help yourself," Gertie yells out, throwing the piece of paper onto the floor as if it were alight in flames. "You'll regret this."

Andrée cackles. "I might," she says. "But I'll be dead, so . . ." Her arms rise above the sheets and part in a gesture of futility, swanlike, before dropping back into the messy folds of the unkempt bed.

Altagracia suspires. "Gertie, you've always been confused about these things, haven't you? You just never figured out how things worked on the island, for this family, how we negotiate who we are."

Gertie wants to slap Altagracia silly but restrains herself, glances across the pitying faces of her elder sisters. "Well," she says, slowly, knowing them better than they know themselves, "you made sure that I was, didn't you? Do what you want but just know that I think it's wrong. You're all a bunch of cowards for doing this. She doesn't want and, more importantly, doesn't *need* your recognition. You're just so full of yourselves." With those words, Gertie leaves the sisters to themselves.

She hears Altagracia, Yvonne, and Fidélia fussing around Andrée behind her, cooing at her as if they are feeding a newborn chick, but Andrée is returning to the source, to whatever came before. Gertie hopes that somehow, that return will be to something kinder than what she was in life.

As she leaves, feeling lost, Gertie thinks that part of herself was set adrift at the foot of her father's deathbed. At times, she imagines that it is Sisi she lost there, or that Sisi has taken the lost part with her. At others, she simply wonders if what was lost there can ever be regained. Thinking about Papa and Sisi now, as she drives away from the sisters down the wide Florida highway, Gertie regrets that she didn't have enough time with Papa, not enough time to learn much about him, his side of the family, what he was really like beyond his penchant for loving women too much, not enough time to find out what of Papa Sisi inherited.

LÉOGÂNE, 1945

GERTIE IS OFTEN LONELY IN THE FAMILY. THE LONELI-
ness becomes acute after Papa dies and she is sent back to
Léogâne. There, there is no Sisi, no one with whom to share
secrets, just those she left behind—like Céleste and Brig—
before being sent to the city for school. She senses that there is
a feeling of shame attached to returning, a sticky feeling, like
morning mist that takes time to dissipate, leaving traces of salt
upon the skin.

Gertie longs for a return to the gingerbread house by the
school, to run down the street and into the playground, to meet
the new friends she made there, Odette, Sisi, even Lou, whom she
knows from social gatherings because Lou's father and her own
have some business together, in the capital, and the well-to-do
families always become intertwined. Those connections made it
easy for her to find her place in the school in Port-au-Prince,
but those friends she chose on her own are all the more special
because they are just that, chosen. Should it matter now that Sisi
is more than this, more than a chosen friend, more than a friend?
Andrée made it clear that it would be *dangerous* to become more
invested in a friendship with Sisi. Why, Gertie isn't exactly sure,
but she knows that their link through Papa threatens the sisters
and their place in the fishbowl in which the upper echelons swim.
But if Sisi is, indeed, her sister, doesn't she have a duty to stand
by her, the way Andrée, Fidélia, and the others are always telling
her that *they* come first? Isn't she family too?

Gertie thinks the sisters have a funny way of showing alle-
giance. Once they return her to Léogâne, the sisters claim that
they will come see her as often as possible but just Fidélia still
lives at home and returns with her to Léogâne. Fidélia is often
shut up in her room, preparing for exams she will never pass.
Maman is preoccupied but Gertie sees her leave the house more
often.

After Papa's death, Maman is invited to other women's
houses for afternoon coffee, and sometimes Gertie goes along if
there is another child there for her to play with, but she dreads
going as it returns her to that time, before she met Sisi, when
playdates were part of a pantomime. She is dressed to fit the
part of a young lady, though she wants to run in the dirt, chase
after the chickens, and prefers playing tag with Brig to keeping
her skirts clean, sitting uncomfortably on an overstuffed divan,
eating cookies and drinking milk with another girl sitting in a
fancy dress, pretending they are ladies-in-waiting when all they
are waiting for is an end to the heat of a sweltering afternoon,
an end to their mothers' gossip sessions, conducted in hushed
tones over strong cups of coffee while the cooks keep up with the
demands of cleaning up the remains of lunch while preparing
whole meals from scratch for dinner.

Once, the girl at the house Maman and she go to asks Gertie
if she wants to see her room, and Gertie nods against her will.
She wants to run away, cry, throw a tantrum, but she knows
none of those options is of any use.

"OK," she says, heart sinking, and follows the girl up mahogany steps to a second-floor landing. The steps creak.

"*Allo? Allo.*" The girl's mother's voice echoes through the
house from the living room below. "*Constance, ou vas-tu?* Where
are you going?"

They are supposed to sit like marionettes in a room off the
kitchen, dolls, miniature versions of their mothers.

"I'm showing Gertrude my room," Constance yells back.

Gertrude. That is who she is here. A name that closes her off from everything, that encapsulates her in an upper-class chamber with no play, no soil in her hair from falling on the ground as a chicken escapes her grasp and she lies there, laughing up into the sky, Sisi looking down at her with an air of bemusement, and the house boy laughing at them for being so clumsy, so untutored in simple things, simple things that, for others, make the difference between feeding themselves and going hungry.

Here, in Constance's room, everything is in order. Not a brush or comb out of place. Constance holds up each item on her dresser toward Gertie for examination, pointing out its refinement and where it was bought.

"This one my grandmother purchased in Santo Domingo. This came from Mexico. Someone brought this from Paris." And on and on. It is nauseating.

Gertie is bored to death. "But what do you do for fun?" she bursts out. "We should just go back downstairs."

"Sure," Constance says brightly. "We can try to overhear what our mothers are saying and find out the gossip. It can be useful at school."

Gertie nods though she doesn't have much interest in accruing social points, points that can be garnered by learning something unsavory about another girl and using it against her. She knows how this game is played from overhearing her sisters, and Papa telling them to leave well enough alone, that he doesn't want one of his businesses to go sour because of women's tales. She follows Constance down the stairs, back to the room off the kitchen, where they pretend to play a card game while secretly listening to their mothers talk. But the talk is not about another girl; Gertie's mother is telling Constance's that she is worried about Gertie. A girl without a father will be looked down upon, and she knows that Constance is in the same boat. She thanks

Constance's mother for having them over. Gertie's face flushes as a flame of shame runs up her spine to the edges of her jaw. She clears her throat. "Is there more milk?" She holds up the glass in Constance's direction, asking to be served.

When Gertie returns home that day with her mother, they find Fidélia at the kitchen table, deep in conversation with Andrée who is visiting them from the capital. Gertie's heart leaps. Is she returning to Port-au-Prince? Have they changed their minds? But neither Fidélia nor Andrée talks to Gertie. They talk to Maman about her.

"How did things go?" Fidélia asks.

"Fine," Maman says. "Mme Antoine understands the situation. I spoke to her as one widow to another, and she agrees that it will be good for her girl as well to have the two of them associate. They can help each other navigate the other girls. They won't be alone."

Andrée nods. "It's the perfect match, then."

"Yes," Maman says. "I think so." Then, looking over at Gertie, who stands in the entryway to the kitchen, not knowing whether to enter or retreat, she adds, "If she behaves herself."

"Will you?" Andrée turns to address Gertie.

Gertie nods.

"She will," Fidélia answers in her stead. "She has no choice if she doesn't want to end up an old maid like me."

They all laugh at this, but Gertie doesn't know why this is funny. Maman employs what she understands to be old maids in the house, and they are hardworking, coming from far away to stay at the house four days a week, returning home on the weekends to be with their families, if they have them. What is wrong with being an old maid? The question churns in Gertie's head along with the events of the afternoon, slides in next to the loneliness girding her heart. If she plays this role long enough, will they let her go back to the capital, find Sisi again? Or should she forget about her life in that other place that made sense with Papa in it, laughing at the dinner table and making fun of all the pomposity of the ruling classes, while being one of them, running around town making his deals, having his dinners in and out of the house, making grown-up life seem enviable?

"Are you staying for dinner?" she asks, with a tinge of hope in her voice she wishes she could keep silent. What does she want from Andrée, from any of them? Every day that passes, she is made to realize how little they care about her happiness.

Andrée turns amber eyes toward her. "No," she says, icily, "I have my own family to return to. I just came to check on the status of things." She turns back to the table. "And on Mother's state. It's not easy to lose a husband."

Or a father, Gertie thinks, or a best friend. Or to find out that your best friend is your sister on the same day that your father dies.

Gertie runs to her room. If only Papa were here to talk to. She closes the door to her room and searches for the locket Papa gave her. It remains well hidden in the book that opens to reveal a secret chamber in its middle, where she keeps other treasures like a stone she found on a walk into the mountains, shells from a trip to the beach, a handful of beans from Sisi's house that Momo, the grandmother, gave her at breakfast the one time she was there, telling her they were seeds of hope. There, along with these treasures, she keeps Papa's locket. She takes it out now and decides that she will wear it, in plain view. She can play at being like them and hold a few things back for herself, preserving them, she thinks, for some time in the future when things will be different, when she can be in the world the way Papa was, not caring what others think, living for life itself. She is becoming used to the idea that family means waiting, and silence, absence. You are supposed to count on something invisible, unreachable. Sisterhood is like a loose net in which fishermen catch fish that never see the hands of their captors, a net full of holes and empty promises that doesn't let you go, but doesn't hold you close either. Maybe when she sees Sisi again, she can explain this theory to her and they can try to make sense of it together, untangle the netting.

Gertie listens to the beat of faraway drums in the night. Papa told her once that Léogâne has another, invisible world hidden inside it, a spirituality her foremother, the one in her locket, practiced. He told her to listen to the drums as to a beating heart. Gertie tries to do so by shutting her eyes and holding on to the locket in one hand, but she isn't sure she can feel anything. Rather, she feels her heart breaking into a thousand little pieces as she lets the locket lie coolly against her chest, the silver of it a shiny oval against the brown of her skin. It occurs to her that the grandmother in the locket is also Sisi's, a thread between them perhaps stronger than Papa, but Gertie doesn't know how to access it or if she will ever see Sisi again to tell her about Freda. Does it matter less or more that Sisi is her sister than that, for a brief time, they were the best of friends? Gertie chooses to believe that their friendship might outlast their distance, that the invisible threads that bind them might just bring them back into each other's orbit. When or how that might happen she cannot guess, but it makes her heart ache a little less to believe that this could be so.

MIAMI TO ORLANDO, 1978

GERTIE FRETS ABOUT THE DAY THE OBITUARY WILL appear in the Miami newspapers. Her surviving older sisters will make sure that it is sent out to all the siblings, aunts and uncles, cousins. It will be spread far and wide from continent to continent, clipped, photocopied, mailed, passed from hand to hand. How can she keep it from falling under Sisi's eyes, Sisi, on whom she herself has not laid eyes for thirty-plus years?

Andrée passes away with fanfare a few months after they gathered about the obituary. The sisters organize a several days' wake, as she wished, as might have been done in Port-au-Prince, though it has been a long time since any one of them has had a home there. Rico remains, though in the DR, running his lucrative businesses with one foot in Miami or Montreal. The sisters have not been able to maintain the same level of wealth, have had poor marriages or ones that did not offer the luxury of controlling interests in their husbands' affairs. The sisters' power has faded over time yet looms over her, an omnipresent weight that, try as she might, Gertie cannot shake off. It has become integral to her, a phantom limb that she carries with her from place to place, decade upon decade, and she feels its weight as she drives up again from Miami to Orlando to attend the wake, which will, as Andrée wished, be followed rather than preceded by the burial, the latter to be attended by close family and friends only.

Does Andrée have any friends? Gertie wonders as she drives north up the Florida Turnpike. She imagines how Sisi will feel if and when she comes across the announcement of Andrée's passing containing her name. How will she feel about being recognized by the Alcindors at last? She can't imagine that it will be something that Sisi would want and though they have been out of touch since childhood, crossing paths fleetingly before leaving the island and hearing about each other through their siblings occasionally, she is certain that the obituary will be just one more cruel joke played by the sisters, designed to drive them further apart, never to reconcile.

LÉOGÂNE, 1947

Gertie's chance to return to Port-au-Prince comes in the form of a competition among private schools, a poetry recitation contest. She is staring out the window of her school in Léogâne at wisps of clouds slicing the blue of the sky when the French literature teacher announces at the beginning of class that the winners from each middle school will go on to a larger competition in the capital. Gertie doesn't listen to anything else the teacher says, doesn't care what the ultimate prize might be. All she hears is "voyage to Port-au-Prince" and she is in. If she wins for her class, then for her school, her sisters, her mother, can't say no to her going. They will have to let her go or allow a school official to take her. Gertie straightens herself up at her desk, smooths out the lined paper before her, licks the tip of her sharpened pencil, and focuses on that day's *dictée*, the exercise of every school-aged person learning French, wherein a paragraph is read aloud with every punctuation mark named and the student replicates the passage, in writing, getting every *virgule*, every accent, every syllable right, down to the final *point-barre*.

She is going to get herself to the capital somehow, even if she has to sit down and learn the entire contents of the Larousse her brother bought her years ago.

During Easter recess, Lou comes over to study, they tell the adults, but in reality, Lou is more interested in killing time. She sits on Gertie's bed with Gertie's poetry books in her lap—the ones from which Gertie has to choose her poem for the contest—and teases the thin sheets out from their binding as if plucking petals from a flower.

"What are you reading these for?"

"The contest," Gertie says.

"What contest?"

Gertie's jaw drops. "Aren't you going to try for it? The recitation contest?"

"Oh that," Lou says nonchalantly. "I already live in Port-au-Prince, so why try? It's all of you out here"—she gestures her slim hands in the air—"you country bumpkins, who have to break your heads to try to get to us. I don't have time for these kinds of things, and anyway, I don't believe in competition. It's capitalist, exploitative, primitive, you know? That's what I keep telling Odette and Sisi. They're also trying for this, for whatever big prize they've promised. I bet it's just one of these books with a pretty cover."

"Did you say Odette and Sisi were practicing?"

Lou nods, shrugs. "It's all they talk about. I mean, it is so boring to hang out with you three. All you talk about is school, school, school. There's more to life than books. For instance, have you heard about the Communist Party? All the literary types are talking about it. Those people just *write*, they don't study *words*, they emote, they bring ideas to life."

"You need words to do that," Gertie counters, bristling at Lou's summation of her study as a waste of time. But she is secretly pleased that Odette and Sisi are striving for the contest:

she might see them before long. Hopefully, Sisi hasn't forgotten all about her.

"It's easy to forget about you all the way out here," Lou intones, as if reading Gertie's mind. "It's as if you've fallen off the face of the earth, though you're not that far away, by car, anyway, when the road is clear."

Gertie's blood rises to her head. She wants to know if everyone feels that way, if Sisi ever asks about her, if all her friends at school have forgotten about her.

The distance between Léogâne and Port-au-Prince feels as far as going to the DR. It isn't as if she can just drive herself or go on foot, or do any of those things that boys can, or fully adult people like her siblings, who come and go, appear like *coup de vent*, a swirl of wind, when you least expect them. Her siblings remind her every chance they get how lucky she is to be so protected from the outside world. How lucky she is to be so secluded, unburdened by real responsibilities. How would they know? she thinks, but keeps the thought to herself, having learned long ago that it is no use contradicting them.

Gone are the days when she hoped for Andrée to return and spend time at the house, or when she hoped for Rico, who moved to the DR a few years past and made his fortune, to come home for a visit, laden with sweets and stories of the other side of the island, where everything is supposed to be more beautiful, more abundant.

She has gotten used to the sleepy seaside town, to the way the houses all resemble one another. She is used to the tam-tam of the drums in the evenings, which she is told to ignore, has become oblivious to their meaning though she senses the pull to a community that is there, invisible, perhaps accessible, but to which she has no entry: as far as she is told, it is forbidden. She cultivates, instead, friends introduced to her by her mother, the daughters of other widows like Mme Antoine, whose daughter, Constance, has also entered the contest, and rebuilds her understanding of herself in the world, as an Alcindor, which doesn't mean much to her but means so much to everyone else. Gertie focuses, instead, on her studies, and where these might take her. Anywhere but here, she thinks. Her goal is to attend a postsecondary school in the capital and, eventually, to leave the island. If she has something in common with Lou, it is a realization that there is more to life than tea parties and a good marriage.

"Oh," Lou says, swatting at Gertie's forearms, "forget I said all that. We haven't *really* forgotten you. I'm just saying that there's nothing out here, so it's easy to forget that you're all the way here too. And there's always so much going on, the parties, secret meetings, everything." Lou throws up her hands. "It's busy."

Gertie has heard a version of Lou's talk every time she visits; she always has stories to tell about communists, socialists (what is the difference?), new trends in the capital, new music. Lou is interested in the fringes of life though she comes from one of the wealthiest merchant families in the capital. Lou slams the book she is holding brusquely, making a few of the loose sheets fall to the ground. Gertie jumps.

"Come on," Lou says. "There's more to life than studying! Do you want to see a *rara* band get ready for their finale this weekend? I know where the best ones are."

"How do you always know this stuff, Lou?"

Lou shrugs. "I know things. Do you want to see?"

Gertie does but knows that her family will be against it. "I really have to stay in and study."

Lou pleads. "They make costumes too. Sometimes of Papa Legba and of other *lwas* but mostly they play their instruments." Lou strikes an imaginary metal horn in the air. *Rara* players make their instruments from found objects, bamboo, or steel, striking them with wooden sticks that resemble drumsticks but are made to bring out the tonalities of the *kone*, the cones or horns, the players blow, like saxophonists. They improvise.

"I hear them from here," Gertie says. "It's just a lot of noise," she adds, repeating something she heard her mother say.

"It's not the same as being in the crowd, in the street. I bet it sounds like noise from in here because you can't see the performance, what it's all about."

"I don't know, Lou. My sisters and my mother are against it."

"You can't always do what they want you to do. It's like you're a nun."

Gertie doesn't know what to say. "Maybe another time?"

"That's what you always say but OK, I'll leave you to your musty old poems. Oh, by the way," Lou adds, "I forgot to tell you that Sisi's grandmother died, you know the old lady who sold beans at the Iron Market? Odette and I went to the funeral."

"What?" Gertie exclaims, letting the book she picked up from where Lou left it on the bed slip from her hands and onto the floor. "I could have. I could have tried if I'd known."

"No, you couldn't have. It all happened so fast, and anyway, by the time we could have gotten word to you, it would have been over." She places a hand on Gertie's shoulder. "Don't worry about Sisi. She'll be fine. We're looking out for her."

Gertie nods.

"You never did tell me what happened between the two of you." Lou prods, "Do you want to say?"

Gertie shakes her head, no. She has understood enough from Andrée and her other sisters about the status of outside children to know that it would be a horrible thing to betray Sisi like this, to let everyone know who her father is, or was. "It's no big deal," she says instead. "I just hope we can be friends again."

"OK," Lou says, exasperated. "Suit yourself. You know where to find me later if you want to hang out—without the books, though. Come to the beach this weekend, all right, after

Mass? Papa is doing a *boucan*. You'll like it. He promised conch and red fish. You can see a few of the rest of the girls who came down for the holidays. It will be like old times." She pauses. "Kind of. I mean, girls like Julie will be there." Lou smirks at Gertie, evoking the schoolyard fight from long ago. "But you'll have me to protect you." She flounces out of the room, leaving Gertie to her books, wondering what she is missing down below, in the streets.

Lou doesn't care about being on the podium. Lou's future is assured: she doesn't study, doesn't feel the need to, is not like them. But Gertie has a goal, and that is to reach the capital on her own steam, maybe to reconnect with Sisi. The competition will get her to the capital and then she can see what her next steps might be. She hopes that what Lou said about Sisi and Odette is true and that she will find herself in the finals with them, like when they were much younger, competing for the same accolades, three musketeers, side by side against the world.

The day of the recitation contest, the sun shines brightly overhead. Gertie wears Papa's locket for good luck. She has chosen a poem by Alphonse de Lamartine, about a pressed flower found in a book, which expresses everything she remembers about the morning she walked on the port with Sisi and Margie, the beauty of the horizon, the freedom of the shore, "an unspoiled sky free of storms." She savors the moment she can recite the final sentences: "Your perfume is in the clouds, / and I find, in turning the page, / the mournful vestige of that beautiful day!" If these words cannot reach Sisi, nothing can.

Gertie and Constance, accompanied by Fidélia, are driven to the capital by the family driver. Despite potholes, the road feels smooth underneath, like nothing can go wrong. In her mind, Gertie sees the poem she has been studying for the past weeks march in neat lines, every word a little soldier parading its meaning, signaling to her, while Constance hums absent-mindedly to herself next to her; they have never become true friends. Fidélia reads a book and ignores the girls. None of them speaks to the driver. Gertie understood long ago that this is forbidden. Nonetheless, she is giddy with excitement.

She somehow convinced her mother to buy her a new frock for the occasion; the dress is green with many folds in the skirt. It makes her feel buoyant, like she is floating on a cloud. Maman stayed back in Léogâne, saying that she didn't want to run into any of the society ladies at the school. Her widowhood has drawn a new border around her, a moat, and she uses its parameters to move in and out of society as she pleases. Maman, Gertie understands, is not so much alienated as in seclusion, negotiating her every step, every move, as if the future depended on which tea she attends or does not attend, on when she uses her presence to signal whether an event has relevance.

As Léogâne recedes from view behind them, so do thoughts of Maman and her machinations. Gertie looks forward, hoping against hope that when she takes the stage with the other finalists, Sisi and Odette will be there, as in the old days, that something can be repaired.

They fly toward the capital, the distance that she thinks of as unbreachable dissipating with every kilometer.

"*Nou preske la*," the driver says as the gingerbread house they used to call home comes into view. Altagracia lives there now with her family, but they do not see her. The driver just parks the car on the property while Fidélia hustles Gertie and Constance over to the school, steps away. Other girls and boys dressed in pretty frocks and suits are tumbling out of cars or walking up to the school from the roadway. Most are wearing clothes they wore to Easter service.

Gertie is pleased that her frock is entirely new, sewn for this occasion. She wonders, briefly, if Maman had Sisi's mother make it the way Papa used to have the older sisters' dresses made. Did the sisters know he did this? Did they care? Gertie's hands become clammy with dread, a sign that her feelings of anticipation are being swept away by a wave of anxiety. What if everything she dreamed about goes wrong? What if no one remembers her after these years of having been removed to the coast?

"You're here!" A voice rings out toward her as Gertie, Constance, and Fidélia approach the school gymnasium. It is Lou.

Gertie breathes relief, remembers their exchange just before Easter in Léogâne. She nods.

"You made it through! So did the others," Lou says, hugging Gertie. She lets go of Gertie, then grabs her hand, pulling her forward through the crowd and toward the stage.

"Wait," Gertie hears Fidélia say, "wait." But she is being led away from both Constance and Fidélia, the crowd muffling what she supposes to be Fidélia's warning. Maman let them go on the agreement that she wouldn't speak to Sisi, wouldn't try to engage her in any way. It looks good for them for Gertie to go, but the sisters don't want any more entanglements with the Vals.

Gertie lets herself be led. Fidélia frowns at her from the third row of the auditorium. She can feel the wave of disapprobation flowing out from Fidélia and over the heads of the attendees in front, washing over her, stifling her. She tries to pull back on Lou's hand. Lou looks back over her shoulder, oblivious to Gertie's discomfort, and in another minute, Gertie is standing toe to toe with Sisi, with Odette just behind her, both in church dresses that are flattering, pale blue and gray respectively. Gertie feels like a screaming parrot in front of them in her bright green dress with the billowing skirt. She tries to push down the folds, flatten them, make herself somewhat smaller.

"Here we are, then," Lou says, satisfied, crossing her arms against her narrow chest. "You all made it to the finals! You can show off how smart you all are to everyone." She laughs and looks back and forth between Gertie, Odette, Sisi. "One of you is definitely going to win. Gertie has her heart set on it."

But what Gertie has her heart set on is something else, an encouraging glance from Sisi, a smile even. But Sisi will not meet her eyes, says to Lou, "It's not just winning that matters."

Odette nods, agreeing; she is looking uncomfortable, her gaze moving furtively across the other girls' faces as if she is afraid to pause too long on anyone. "I'm going to go," she says nervously. "See you up there." She waves goodbye to the other girls and disappears backstage.

Sisi has grown, Gertie observes. She is almost taller than Gertie now; she is pretty, too, in a casual way. She resembles someone, but Gertie can't exactly say who. A family resemblance, like her other sisters. What could she say, to be forgiven for her disappearance, for allowing her sisters to take her back to Léogâne and commit her to a silence not of her own making? She wants to reach out and hug Sisi in the same impulsive way she used to when they first met, tugging her along the way Lou just did Gertie. She wants time to evaporate, searches for the right words to say how sorry she is. "Look," she says to Sisi finally, "I want to say . . ."

But Sisi doesn't let her speak. She puts up a hand between them. It becomes a wall. Gertie remembers the wave of disapproval flowing to her from Fidélia as she crossed the auditorium floor. The disapproval solidifies in Sisi's gesture as if Sisi were now one of the Alcindor sisters, objecting to Gertie. Sisi's hand, palm out, hovers in front of Gertie's chest. Gertie's hand flies to cover Papa's locket protectively. She is wearing it, hidden beneath the top layer of the dress.

"Sisi," Gertie tries again. She wants to tell Sisi how much she has missed her. She wants to apologize for not knowing about Momo's passing, for not having been there. Her fingers rest against the curves of the locket. Should she tell Sisi that other things bind them together? "I'm sorry about Momo," she says ultimately. "I'm—"

"No," Sisi interrupts her.

"Gertrude." Gertie hears Fidélia calling out to her from behind, but she does not turn back.

"I need to focus on this," Sisi continues. "You don't need this. Why are you here? It's my scholarship on the line." Sisi turns away, without a backward glance, dismisses her.

"Gertrude." Fidélia is coming closer, arriving, then has a hand on her, pulling her back. "Remember what you agreed to," she says, reminding Gertie of Andrée's words after Papa's funeral. *Stay clear of the Vals.*

"Scholarship?" Gertie asks, turning to Lou, who is standing between her and the space Sisi vacated, while Fidélia pulls her in the opposite direction.

Lou shrugs. "Yes. That's the ultimate prize. Not new books. You don't need it, but other people do."

Gertie allows Fidélia to pull her away. How has she been so obtuse? Of course both Odette and Sisi have made it to finals, not just because they were the first and second in class but because they need the prize purse. Gertie hasn't bothered to look at the prize list. She just wanted to get to the capital by any means necessary, to be accepted back into the fold, to move beyond her mother's moat where she is drowning alive. Sisi is right. What *is* she doing here? But there is no going back now, none. Fidélia is tugging. "Know your place," she hisses. Know your place. That's all they tell her since Papa's death.

Gertie climbs up the wooden stairs to the stage, where chairs have been set out in rows. On each one is a piece of paper with a student's name, arranged in alphabetical order. She is in the front row for Alcindor, Sisi at the back for Val. Odette is somewhere in the middle. Each of the girls on stage takes a turn reciting her poem. The more dramatic reciters are kept on stage while the others are eliminated in four rounds. After each elimination, the best reciters are asked to repeat their poems until only three are left to be ranked by the judges from first to third. The first place winner takes all while the others get ribbons and certificates. As she waits, Gertie thinks about Sisi's last words to her before Fidélia caught up with them. Sisi needs the scholarship. Then what Lou said: that Gertie does not. Should she relent, throw the contest? What can be gained now from winning? Then they are four, then three: Odette, Sisi, and Gertie. Gertie doesn't *need* to win. She doesn't feel her usual desire to show off. Alcindors, though, *do not lose.*

Odette forgets a line in her poem and is dismissed. It is just the two of them left, Sisi and her. Her and Sisi. What should she do?

Sisi is called to recite her poem again. She has chosen a poem by Victor Hugo, about a little girl reduced to eating stale, dry bread in an unjust world. She delivers the lines impeccably, pausing dramatically when describing the girl's tender eyes. She ignores Gertie at the front of the stage. Then it is Gertie's final turn.

Gertie touches the locket for courage, then takes a page from Odette's performance: she skips two lines in her Lamartine poem, the ones about carrying the flower on her chest to breathe in its perfume, in order to live. The judges gasp at the omission. She is as sad as the lines themselves, as if she is losing everything in that moment, not just the contest but the hope of resuscitating her friendship with Sisi.

The school's administration emerges on stage to give Sisi her prize: a new dictionary, the renewal of her scholarship. There is muted applause. Lou and Odette rush back to the stage to congratulate Sisi, but Gertie slips away, Fidélia towing her and Constance to the gingerbread house. They will stay overnight, then head back to Léogâne in the morning.

Gertie doesn't eat that night; she stays locked in her room, crying, wondering if anything will ever change. To everyone on the outside, it seems like she has everything: multiple homes, her mother, her siblings. But since Papa died, all has been lost.

As a result of the run-in with Sisi at the recitation, the sisters decide she will have to attend high school elsewhere and send her to a French-language boarding school in the DR.

MIAMI TO ORLANDO, 1978

GERTIE REMEMBERS THE DRIVE FROM THE CAPITAL back to Léogâne the morning after she threw away her chance to win the middle school recitation contest. The journey then seemed quite long, much longer than when she had been on her way, buoyed by the hope that returning triumphantly to the capital would repair her relationship with Sisi. Instead, she returned to Léogâne weighed down by the reality that she was regaining the loneliness of days filled with study and social obligations and nothing more. She has that same feeling in her center as she continues up the highway from Miami to Orlando, the same feeling of dread. Andrée has passed and now there are duties to fulfill, all the things she has been taught to do for the sake of the family, for the sake of appearances, despite having broken away from them all through marriage, despite having made her own way in the world. Some chains can't be broken, she thinks, as she drives with single-minded purpose.

It is with this thought that she comes to sit in Altagracia's overstuffed living room, trying desperately to make sense of the words that her sisters' friends are lobbing toward her, about Andrée's generosity of spirit, her ability to make everyone feel welcome, her friendship. They describe no one she recognizes as her sister. She copes by thinking about the stack of files waiting for her at home, files about children in foster care, women fleeing abusive husbands, husbands working on getting various addictions under control to be reunited with wives or children, the occasional misfit kid who has been turned out of doors by careless parents and is now homeless. These files represent the real world in all its harsh clarity. Who is this Andrée that the sisters' friends are jabbering about? Generous? Welcoming? A friend to all? Gertie has never met her. She looks about the room, at all the bejeweled women in all shades of brown, doused in scents that remind her of a Parisian perfumery. The fruity sweetness of various brands of eau de cologne mixed with the smells of the cheeses and cold cuts laid out on a long table in front of Altagracia's bay window overlooking the greens of the golf course in the condominium she shares with Yvonne ever since Yvonne left her husband high and dry with his mistress in Santo Domingo, causes Gertie's stomach to churn. It may have been that and downing a third rum and Coke. Drinks are being liberally dispensed at the open bar on the patio. Gertie decides to return there, to the patio, glass in hand, to clear her head and regain her senses.

By the bar, she finds Fidélia nursing a martini. The sisters are nothing if not predictable. Fidélia smiles wanly and Gertie surmises that she, too, is drowning her sorrows, whatever they may be.

"It wasn't my idea, in case you're wondering," she says to Gertie. "I had nothing to do with it."

"Excuse me?" Gertie asks.

Fidélia waves her glass in the direction of the assembled guests. "The obituary. It wasn't my idea."

"Oh," Gertie says, "OK." She shrugs. "I didn't think it was."

"But you did," Fidélia says, reengaging. "You don't think much of me, do you?"

Gertie wants to tell Fidélia that she doesn't think of her in particular. The sisters are a block, a malevolent force that has always torn through her life to derail things that seemed stable apart. They are the swiping winds of a hurricane.

"It was mostly them. Most of the time. I just went along with things."

Gertie nods slowly. She has learned in all her years as a social worker that people reveal themselves most when they are not prodded, that it is important to listen, not just to the words they say but to their silences between words, their gestures, body language. She reads in Fidélia's posture, her arms folded against her lithe frame, one hand holding the opposite elbow while the other clutches the V-shaped glass by its stem, that her sister is feeling vulnerable, exposed, but also that she is feeling the need to unload, to free herself of baggage too long carried. She is seeking contrition, and so Gertie decides to hear her confession.

Fidélia, emboldened by Gertie's steady gaze and stillness, continues, "It's not as bad as you think. It's not entirely narcissistic. They do want to be forgiven, but they want the others to recognize them, on their own terms."

"But what good does it do anyone to expose the truth about Father now, and *after* Andrée's passing? We could have done something face-to-face, while Andrée was with us, cleared up all the misunderstandings."

Fidélia scoffs. "You know that's not how we do anything, Gertie."

Gertie nods. She knows, but she wants things to have been different. "This will just blindside her; you know that."

"I know," Fidélia agrees. "But it's not all ill intended. Now everything will be out in the open and we can put Papa to rest, his betrayal of all of us. We can move forward. Those of us who are left."

"By shaming Simone into accepting us when we rejected her—and the others—all this time? We treated Papa's other children like they were no better than dirt. And you're just acknowledging one. What about all the others? Are you going to chase them all down?"

Fidélia looks confused. "Wouldn't they want to be a part of all of this?" She sweeps open her arms toward the gathering behind them. "Besides, we can't let them all in. What would be left for the rest of us?"

Le beau monde. Oh, yes, Gertie thinks. As always, she misread her sister's posture. She was protecting herself from Gertie's judgment, perhaps, but not from that larger thing that Gertie wishes to be rid of—the sisters' ambition, their magnanimity, which hides contempt for anyone who is not an Alcindor or is not part of their inner circle, the upper crust of Haitian and, now, Floridian society.

Gertie glances around at the heavy gold pendants hanging from the women's necks, the large-faced clasped watches of white gold festooned in diamond studs that would have fed a handful of families for several years in Haiti. She thinks of the families contained in the files on her desk at home and how the amassed wealth in the room of the wake could relieve all of them of worry into the next generation, but Fidélia doesn't want to hear about this. All her life, all Fidélia and the sisters have wanted is to preserve their place in this beau monde, to be envied and thought of as beautiful, to lord their position over others as they have over her, their youngest sister. While Sisi might forgive them, she cannot.

"You would be surprised how many people don't want any of this. The money, maybe, but not much else." She sets her glass down on the bar, unfinished. "I'm going to go, Fidélia. I have a stack of papers to get through at home." She taps her sister on the arm in a gesture of goodwill.

Fidélia purses her lips tightly. "They're not going to like your disappearing act."

"Just tell them I had a headache." Gertie smiles, using the excuse that their mother always offered when retiring to her rooms when they were children, and which the sisters use when inconvenienced by their husbands, when they have them. "And that I'll see them at the memorial service."

"You'll be there?" Fidélia asks, surprised.

"Of course, Fidélia," Gertie responds, piqued. "She was my sister, wasn't she?"

Fidélia nods.

Gertie fingers the locket at her throat while Fidélia squints to see what it is she is wearing. When she recognizes the locket, she blanches.

"I didn't know you still had it," Fidélia says, snapping Gertie out of her rêverie.

"Yes," Gertie says, a finger on the silver case of the pendant. "I do."

Gertie remembers the day she was given the locket, at Altagracia's wedding on the other side of the border, when she was lost and thought to be one of the cook's children, brought along to the wedding to help. Her mother called her that name that appeared in so many Dominican love songs, as if a term of endearment. But she knew what it meant in the real world, that she was not quite like them. She shrugged off the hurt and bewilderment when Papa gave her the locket but she was hurt again when Fidélia grasped it for herself. Ever since, she has tried not to wear it around the sisters. Of course, Fidélia would recognize it.

Fidélia straightens up, uneasy under Gertie's gaze. "I guess there are still a lot of things to clear up."

"Many," Gertie says, "but not now. I'm off. Tell the sisters goodbye for me."

Gertie threads through the maze of the assembled. The crowd has thickened since she stepped out on the patio to get some air. She emerges on the front stoop of the condo gasping for breath, the scent of the gathered women's eau de toilette clinging to her skin. All she wants to do is rush back to her hotel room, wash it all off, the perfume, the sting of the sisters' carelessness, their rapacious need to always come out on top, even in death.

In her hotel room, away from the sisters hours later, Gertie lies in the bed after taking a long bath and tries to clear her mind of all things related to them. Andrée's passing has left her, rather than grief-stricken, with a feeling of emptied relief. She thinks about the obituary that will soon appear. It will be printed within the week, sent out within another: the sisters are always efficient when it comes to printed matters. Soon, everyone will know their connection to the Vals, if they didn't know before. Gertie falls into a uneasy sleep with the obituary on her mind, as she is pulled into the deep folds of a dream she hopes might bring her answers.

In the dream, Gertie encounters Andrée, as she was as a young woman, thin, statuesque, her hair coiffed in a chignon, as had been all the rage back in the late thirties, with girls trying to look older than they were, reimagining themselves as Hollywood starlets even if they never got out farther than the Rex to watch their idols on the movie screen. Andrée, unlike others, did not hide herself. She liked being courted and her Sunday afternoons were filled with strolls beneath the cathedral. Gertie sees her surrounded by suited young men, all golden, "sun-kissed," as Andrée might have said, fawning over her. In the distance, Gertie sees another girl, also tall, sitting by a shoreline, with the sea at her feet. It is Sisi, looking like a mermaid ready to leap back into the ocean. Gertie doesn't feel torn between the two. She leaves Andrée behind, and just as she is about to walk into the ocean, to follow the siren's call, a hand grasps hers and she knows without having to look that it is Sisi's hand in hers. But when she turns to look, the girl has turned into a bird and is flying above her, above the crystal blue green of the surface of the water, a blackbird with red wings, disappearing fast from sight.

Gertie awakes the next morning knowing, at last, what she must do. She is tranquil and at peace, as she is with Manuel, who will be there, waiting for her, at the end of the long drive back from Orlando to Miami.

SANTO DOMINGO, 1952

When Gertie meets Manuel, it is not love at first sight.

Their meeting is a case of mistaken identity that should have kept them apart, the fact that it doesn't owing more, perhaps, to Manuel's ability to navigate the preconceptions that are foisted upon him than to Gertie's ability to exercise tact and good judgment. When they meet, she is turning eighteen and Manuel is in his midtwenties.

Before she knows his name, she sees him standing outside the wooden cabana where the snorkeling equipment is kept. The cabana is stationed between the resort's pool and a walkway that leads to an inlet bordered by large stones that have been moved there from the shore so that guests can swim protected from the currents, unworried about being assailed by ocean waves, wind, barracudas, or even errant sharks.

It is early morning and Gertie is shown the way by a hotel clerk who assumes that this is what she is looking for since she came down to the lobby dressed in a one-piece swimsuit and a sheer cover-up that can double as a beach throw. Her Spanish is not strong, despite the high school classes she had at the French international boarding school she attended on this side of the island. The hotel clerk, a light-skinned man with close-cropped hair and a thin mustache, gestures toward the cabana by the pool and tells her to ask "*el Haitiano*" for the snorkeling equipment.

"Does he have a name?" Gertie asks.

"*El Haitiano, el Haitiano,*" the man repeats, gesturing brusquely toward the cabana. By this, Gertie understands, he means that she should look for a dark-skinned man, a darker-skinned man than he, a Black man. She nods but wishes she'd gotten a name.

When she sees Manuel, tanned to a violet-brown color that reminds Gertie of the purple martins that migrate to the islands in winter on their way to warmer climes in South America, he is standing bare-chested by the cabana, wearing thigh-length shorts. Seeing no one else around, Gertie assumes that Manuel is the cabana boy the clerk told her to look for, and at first, it doesn't seem that she has made an error.

"Is this where I get the snorkeling stuff?" she asks him as he swipes sand loose from his bare feet and from the tops of his shoulders. He is running water from a spigot installed at the side of the cabana and spraying his feet.

"What was that?" he asks back, looking at her from over his shoulder.

"The equipment," she repeats, then points to the bay beyond the pool. "For snorkeling."

"Sure," he mumbles. "You can get that here. Somebody will help you."

"Aren't you supposed to help me?"

He continues to spray the water over his feet, the backs of his legs, which she notes are pleasantly muscular, his thighs, then over the rounded back of his shoulders. He closes his eyes and brings the water over his head, lets it pour down. He is breathtaking, Gertie thinks, all sinew and not at all self-conscious. She fails to register that this lack of self-consciousness should tip her off to the fact that he is of a different class than she expected.

Manuel notices Gertie out of the corner of his eye, that she has not budged, and puts the hose down, closing the spigot.

She notices that he has strings of beaded bracelets on both wrists. Several are black and red; one is white. Another string has green beads alternating with red ones.

"Are you talking to me, *mujer*?" he asks her.

Gertie becomes tongue-tied.

"Oh." He smiles wryly. "Oh, I see. You think I work here."

"Well," Gertie says, self-consciously, "don't you?"

Manuel shakes his head, grabs a towel from atop the cabana's counter, and starts to wipe away the water from his glistening body. "You're looking for snorkeling equipment?"

She nods.

"I don't work here, but we can leave a note for the attendant, and I can give you what I just returned." He points to a pile of fins, snorkel, and mask. "I just came in from the bay. Just say that you're returning the equipment for room 32."

"Oh. OK." Gertie, embarrassed, accepts the exchange, writes a note on a pad of paper left on the counter with a pencil, and wonders who, then, is *"el Haitiano."*

"But really, why did you think I was the cabana boy?" he asks, peering at her from beneath the towel he draws over his head to dry his hair by rubbing across loose, pepper-black curls vigorously.

"Just a mistake. The clerk just pointed me down this way and—"

"And you assumed—"

Gertie puts up a hand. "It was just an honest mistake."

"OK, OK." He puts out a hand. "My name's Manuel. You?"

"Gertrude," Gertie says. "Alcindor." She reaches out.

"Good to meet you, Gertrude Alcindor. Last name's Pueyo."

They shake hands and Manuel gathers the equipment he has just returned and hands it to Gertie in one swoop.

"Thanks," Gertie says, "for the equipment."

"Sure." Manuel winks. "Just don't lose it out there. I don't need to be getting more bills added to my room."

"I won't," Gertie responds, seriously. "You can trust me."

"Can I, Gertrude Alcindor?"

Gertie laughs nervously as she walks away with the equipment in hand. She should have asked, first, if he worked there, then asked for the equipment.

Gertie tries to forget about her mistake and about meeting Manuel Pueyo as she takes off her wrap and leaves it on a chaise longue on the beach. She puts on the fins and mask, then wades into the shallow waters of the bay while fitting the breathing tube and mouth guard around her teeth, gripping around it with her mouth.

Beneath the surface of the water, another world awaits her, one that she has been longing for while away, one her sisters promised her would be her gift for finishing school here, on the other side of the island. They told her that if she kept her marks up (she did) and didn't cause problems at school (she didn't), they would take her to one of the resorts where they liked to go with their own families on holiday. Gertie held on to the promise, gripped it fiercely, and did what they told her to do. It is so much easier than fighting them.

Underneath, all is clear, the water translucent, a greenish-blue hue that makes her think of the polished pieces of glass she sometimes finds spat up by the sea onto the shore, which she has collected over the years and keeps on a windowsill in a jar that she likes to look at as the sun reflects through it, helping her to remember Haiti, what things were like before she left. She can now only dimly remember the house in Léogâne, Papa's house in Port-au-Prince, Papa himself, when he went about jovially from place to place like a prince in waiting before he took sick.

Gertie looks out into the vastness before her, the belly of the ocean so far beneath her. The salt of the sea keeps her afloat as she gazes down through the goggles. She spots a couple of rock beauties, their yellow-and-black bodies easily mistaken for butterfly fish, which are the same colors but striped. Then come along aquamarine parrotfish, bodies adorned with a crest that looks like a long head of hair. Their tails swish back and forth, leaving trails of waterways behind them. Something purple and orange darts by, in the distance. Gertie scans the area but it disappears into the blue. Less pretty schools of fish come by, groupers dressed in gray, angelfish, tiny slippery fish called dicks with long streaks of black against white bodies. Far below, farther away, a stingray stirs, sending up plumes of sandy seabed around it as it moves. The ocean is alive. Gertie watches the sea life as well as the coral reef below, filled with green algae, seagrass, and translucent yellow jellyfish. The colors are bright, a stark contrast to the life she has been living above water, first, alone in the family homes, then, away at school. She could stay here forever, down below.

If there is a sound, beneath, she would describe it as emptiness itself, a concave vessel in which she can release all the burdens of her memory while reaching for a possible future, a shape of things as beautiful as the flickering tails of the rainbow of fish crossing her line of vision without a care, without fear of what her body could do as she treads water. She becomes flotsam, starfish, as she extends her arms on either side of herself, wave.

She wants to float away, down, into the sandy belly the ocean bed offers up. For a moment, she thinks it possible, starts to stroke forward and down. A current blankets her, moves her into a downward spiral. She thinks she sees a swirl of black hair moving next to her under the water; then something like song breaks through the deafening sound of her solitude. Is it the Simbi she heard about in childhood stories? But which Simbi? The siren, the snake, the protector? Gertie doesn't have time to find out. As she descends, her breathing tube fills up and she is breathing in salt water rather than air. It takes just a few seconds for her to realize the danger, to stop gasping for breath, work against the draw of the spiraling current, stroke up rather than down and out of the water. Arms flailing, she bursts out of the ocean, bopping up above the surface like a large cork, spits out the mouthpiece, coughs out the salt water filling her mouth, tears off the face mask and wipes at her eyes. Breath returns.

Gertie turns to face the shore, to see if anyone has seen her flailing. She is immediately self-conscious. There is no one there. She turns back around in the ocean, looks out onto the limitless horizon, and remembers. Remembers that morning so long ago when her seven-year-old self sat on an old pier in Port-au-Prince, looking out across the sea, as Sisi's older sister, Margie, told them about the limitless futures before them, about the Simbi. Where are they now, Margie, Sisi? Occasionally, she hears about them from the Lombardos, with whom Gertie's older sisters stay in touch. This is how families of a certain class operate on the island, an unspoken feature of social capital. Apparently, Sisi continues to thrive in school, becoming great friends with Lou, the youngest Lombardo, whom Gertie hasn't kept up with as much since she was sent to finish high school in the DR.

As Gertie bobs afloat on the water, she feels strong pangs of jealousy that she knows, deep down, she has no right to be feeling. The time they were all known to one another is long past, and Gertie should have moved on. She blinks away tears, convinces herself that the sting is occasioned by the salt water as she stirs herself back toward the shore. There, she returns up the beach, dragging the flippers on the sand as if imitating the passage of an errant seal. She wishes that everything could begin again, but life isn't like that. She has lived long enough to know this, deep in her bones.

On the shore, Gertie flops down on the long chair where she left her wrap; she uses the folded towel left on it to dry herself off as she pulls off the flippers and drops them next to the headgear. She pulls on the wrap over her bathing suit and collapses back onto the chair, looking up at the blue above her, as expansive and all-encompassing as the sea has been, horizon all around her. She closes her eyes, overwhelmed by the limitlessness. She falls asleep against the thought that she is returning to the life she knew, before she was exiled by the sisters. It makes her feel that there might be a way back to the beginnings of things, to before Papa died.

What wakes Gertie from her wondering is the feeling that a cloud has moved across the sun, taking away its direct heat and light. She stirs against the chaise, in the humidity of the air surrounding her, wonders if rain is about to come, opens her eyes. Instead of clouds above her, she sees the shape of a person looming, blocking the light. "What is it?" she says spontaneously.

"It's me," the shape says. "Cabana boy."

Gertie sits up, moves into the sunlight so she can see who is there more clearly. She shields her eyes and squints. "Cabana boy?"

"Room 32."

She sees, then, who it is. "Pueyo?"

"*Sí*. Yes. I saw you having trouble out there. *¿Estàs bien?*"

"You saw?"

"Well, yes. I was just hanging out by the pool a bit after we saw each other and I happened to glance out that way"—he sweeps his hand outward, toward the bay—"and you seemed to be having a little trouble, so I just stuck around to see if you were OK. Sometimes, things happen in the water. One sees things or feels things. It can be . . ." He searches for the correct word. "Surprising."

"Yes," Gertie says, embarrassed again. Should she tell him about what she saw beneath the surface of the water, all the wonder, the colorful fish, the teeming life? What about the spirit she sensed there, down below? She tries to read his face. Does he believe in things that can't be named? She isn't about to confess that she thinks she has seen or felt a siren beneath the waters, or a Simbi come from the interior of the land into the ocean. People don't believe in such things on this side of the island, or so the sisters say. Instead of a confession, a phrase of reassurance comes to mind: "*Tout va bien.*"

"So, you're . . ." He hesitates. "Haitian?"

"Yes."

"But you thought *I* was?"

"Well, yes."

"Because the clerk said to look for '*el Haitiano*,'" he muses.

Gertie thinks about lying, but there is no use. She has been found out.

Manuel points toward the cabana by the side of the pool. "That's Rafael," he says. "*El Haitiano* the doorman was referring to."

Gertie looks toward the cabana and at the man standing behind the counter there. He is the same shade of chestnut brown as she is. Manuel gestures at the man. The man waves back. "He's not Haitian, by the way," Manuel says, "and neither am I."

"Ah, no?" Gertie startles.

"We're both Black Dominicans, but not Haitian. Of course, we could be—if we climbed back into the ancestral trees. We all were once."

"We could be related," Gertie replies, picking up on the usual island repartee.

"Well," Manuel says in turn, and winks at her, "let's hope we're not."

Gertie smiles. This is flirting. Grown-up flirting. "I'm OK," she says, finally. "Thanks for checking on me."

"*No pasa nada.*" Manuel adjusts the baseball cap now perched on his head. "I'll really be going now. I've got a long day ahead."

"Of resorting?" Gertie teases.

"Actually, no," Manuel responds. "I have friends to see, but I'll look for you in the dining room at dinner."

"OK," Gertie replies. "I'll be with my family. You won't be able to miss us."

Manuel tips the cap against the strong rays of the sun. "Yes. I know who they are," he says. "See you later."

Gertie feels the first stirrings of butterflies, something she has never felt before, as Manuel walks away, lifting small clouds of sand as he goes.

Dinner is capped with a two-tier *bizcocho* cake topped with a glossy meringue frosting and piped flowers, her name written across the surface in purple, beneath a large *"Felicidades."* The lights dim as the cake is brought out with eighteen lit candles. Gertie feigns delight as everyone in the dining room claps and sings "Happy Birthday" to her. People she doesn't know, singing in a language she has not mastered.

She blows out the candles, the lights are turned back on, the other tables go back to their conversations. The sisters have gone back to their drinks and to ignoring her. Gertie nibbles at her slice of cake, looks around the room, and sees Manuel standing close to the door. He lifts his glass toward her in the gesture of a toast, beckons her to come to him. There is something about him that is trustworthy, worth knowing, familiar even. She follows her instincts, stands up, crosses the room, and goes to him.

"I didn't realize it was your birthday," Manuel says as she stands next to him.

Gertie shrugs. "It didn't seem worth mentioning." She gestures toward her table. "My sisters brought me here as a gift for finishing high school." She reddens. "Just turned eighteen."

"I know your sisters." He nods toward them. The sisters wave back tentatively.

"You do?"

"Our families have been coming here for years. If I remember correctly, I may have met you at a wedding years back. You would have been just a kid. I wasn't that much older myself." He points to Altagracia. "I think it was that sister's wedding. Everybody knows everybody after a certain point. It's a small island."

"Oh." Gertie shrinks a bit. Does she want any further entanglements with her sisters, their friends?

"They're a tough crowd," Manuel says, bringing her back to him. "Your sisters. I've been around their kind long enough to know." He takes a sip from his glass.

"Yes," Gertie says in relief. "Yes, they are."

"Say," Manuel continues, "would you be interested in seeing something outside this place?" He gestures toward the enclosure of the resort.

"Yes," Gertie says, "but I don't know if my sisters will let me."

"Just leave that to me," Manuel says, and walks away toward the sisters' table.

Gertie stays at the door as she watches Manuel talking to her sisters. They all look back at her in unison, curious as they discuss the prospect of Manuel taking her away. Then Manuel straightens himself, gives her a thumbs-up.

Gertie isn't sure what she has agreed to, but she is sure that it is the beginning of something that could change her life, something more than the sisters intend for her. She hears the underwater song from earlier in the day, but she does not fear it. The Simbi are there, as they are at the lip of the ocean, joining sea to land, watching over her, protecting her, making sure she comes back to shore.

ORLANDO TO MIAMI, 1978

AFTER ATTENDING THE MEMORIAL SERVICE, GERTIE IS a bird in flight as she drives south down the I-95, out of Orlando, and away from the remaining sisters, the cousins, their false friends. Away from the tables filled with saccharine-sweet pastries, the tepid coffee in plastic tumblers left absent-mindedly on every side table with a space not covered by a doily or a framed photograph of one of Andrée's husbands, her children, her travel adventures. Andrée, who would have been shocked to see the mess and pleased with it simultaneously: finally, the center of everyone's attention. Now she can torment everyone from beyond the grave.

As she drives, Gertie thinks about the plan that came to her as she dreamed of the red-winged blackbird. She came to know these birds after moving to North America. They are everywhere, it seems, all year round, especially in the Everglades: wetland birds; birds that need water. Gertie likes them because, though they are not so plentiful on the island, they make her think of her connection to water, to flight, of the morning she met Manuel and thought of him as a beautiful bird. They make her think of how Sisi compared her to a tody when they were children, because she loved green and was a noisy child. They make her think of sitting with Margie and Sisi by the docks, the tranquility and safety of it.

Gertie listens to the lyrics emanating from the car's speakers, speaking of buried and forgotten dreams. They quickly fade to an uplifting pop song about a lover bringing the sun into the singer's life. Love can be like that, Gertie muses, all types of love. She has never quite worked out why meeting Sisi at seven made such an impact on her life, except that she knows that it did, knows the hole that was left in her, the desperate loneliness she felt as the sisters insisted that she go back with mother to Léogâne, and then on to a boarding school in the DR, instead of returning to the high school in the heart of Port-au-Prince. With Sisi, unlike with the sisters she grew up with, Gertie felt herself reflected, as if she had found a twin, because nothing had to be explained. Did they fit together so easily because they were sisters, blood returning to blood? Sisterhood always meant heartache for Gertie, pain. For years after Papa's death, when she was in the international school on the other side of the border, she made herself believe that the sisters had saved her from something more painful: finding out that Sisi was just like them. But every time she runs into Margie, since Margie moved to Florida, something of that spark returns, an ease she then realizes she has been missing.

As she speeds down the highway and the lane markings on the asphalt unfurl like a ribbon next to the car, Gertie sees Sisi as a seven-year-old, then as a twentysomething departing emigrant at the consulate where Altagracia worked for a time, then older, in pictures shown to her by Margie, in an act that Gertie took to be boastful, Margie showing the pride she had in her sister when they ran into each other, once, in the neighborhood Publix where they both shop. Margie pulled out the pictures in her wallet to show her, though she knew how Sisi was rejected and cast aside by the Alcindors. Sisi had made something of herself despite them, Margie wanted her to know. Gertie said nothing when shown the pictures. Inside, she, too, was full of pride. Yes, that was her sister. Sisi had made it despite being iced out by the sisters.

Gertie is convinced she needs to talk to Sisi before the obituary makes the rounds. She will find Margie and boldly ask for Sisi's phone number. Margie might be surprised, but Gertie has no doubt that she will give it to her; she loves Sisi too much not to.

Now the car radio is playing the Rolling Stones, Jagger crooning about unrequited love, waiting for a phone call that never comes. Gertie laughs out loud. She can't believe that Jagger has ever been stood up or hung up on a love he could not reach. The lyrics wash over her in waves of benediction. The singer echoes the same words of longing roiling through her mind but she changes their order, their meaning, to a simple "Miss you."

As the miles fly by, Gertie is emboldened by the sight of her sisters' city receding in her rearview and the open road ahead. Maybe the obituary can be an opening rather than an end, a blessing rather than a calamity. She wants Sisi to know she hasn't really changed, despite the sisters' meddling, or, if she has, that she made her way back to that girl she was when they knew each other, who just wanted to be known and to know, who wanted to watch Sisi draw and just be part of the scenery. With a call, Gertie can explain what the sisters meant to do, that it was not meant to harm her, or at least that they didn't think it all through, that she, Gertie, was not part of the plan, that she was not able to stop them.

Linda Ronstadt's "It's So Easy" comes on as Mick Jagger's falsetto fades into the background, and Gertie's thoughts turn to her family back in Miami. She has left fourteen-year-old Ella in Manuel's care despite presenting his excuse of being too busy to attend the funeral proceedings to the remaining sisters. They accept the excuse because they know Manuel is a top litigator who has made a name for himself not just in Miami but through the entire state. The older sisters probably had a good laugh when Gertie decided to go into social work, she muses, shortly after meeting Manuel. They were probably doubly surprised when she *married* him, against all their best advice, asking her why wouldn't she make things easier on herself, on her future children, by marrying not just rich but light? Since the marriage, the sisters have tried to keep themselves from criticizing Manuel because he and his family are so much wealthier than the Alcindors. They tolerate Manuel's left-leaning politics because wealth trumps everything else, in the end. Wealthy background. Wealthy life. Wealthy wife.

The one and only time Manuel came to a family dinner, early in their marriage, Andrée had the temerity to pass her hand through his hair without warning, exclaiming, "*Misye gayan blan nan li?*," surprised at the softness of Manuel's hair. Manuel looked over at Gertie and realized that all the things she had told him about the sisters were not exaggerations. After the hair incident, he no longer fought with Gertie when she asked him to stay home when a family reunion was planned; he agreed that he, and then Ella, were better off kept at arm's length. The sisters were as mean and petty as she had described, superficial, like the stepsisters from fairy tales, except that they were her actual blood relations. As Andrée moved away from him at the table, Manuel smiled, responded, "Aren't we all a little bit of everything, *hermana*?"

Gertie focuses on the knowledge that Manuel will be there when she arrives. He will have lit the candles on the altar they keep to the ancestors, sometimes accompanied by a small glass of dry white wine and dried okras. He made a print of Freda's image, taken from the locket, and framed it for the altar, where it stands next to a framed print of his own grandfather. She arranged for Ella to have a sleepover, so she doesn't have to worry about her when she arrives.

Gertie hums along with the songs playing on the radio, reassured in the knowledge of what she needs to do as soon as she gets home. She feels watched over by gods and ancestors, a feeling she did not know, lonely as she was, as a child. She drives past marshland, acres of trees, what seems to be wide-open, uninhabited space. The divide between her and Sisi is like this, hemmed in by the contours of an open clearing she believes contains all that has been left unsaid. If she can reach Sisi, she could try to stand up to her sisters, even beyond the grave.

Gertie lets herself be carried away by the music, knowing she is headed somewhere she can fall and that she will be gathered up, a safe place in which to make mistakes, be her better self.

SANTO DOMINGO, 1952

It is surprising that the sisters allow Manuel to take Gertie out of the resort the morning after her birthday dinner, without an escort from the family, a man eight years older than her whom she has never met before and doesn't know beyond her family vouching for his. The Alcindors and Pueyos go back generations on the island and though she doesn't remember it, Altagracia confirms Manuel and an older brother attended her wedding long ago, the one at which Papa gave her the locket with Freda's picture inside.

That morning, Gertie follows Manuel out of the resort out of curiosity as well as boredom, thankful to be taken beyond the walls of the enclosure and away from the sisters with their suffocating rules and constant reprimands. She seeks freedom, so she allows herself to be taken, first on a bus, then on the back of a moped, clinging to another sweaty stranger, to end up in a desolate *batey* area far from the capital, an encampment for cane cutters, Manuel explains, but Gertie couldn't have imagined what that meant. She thinks of the cut pieces of cane she ate as a child, sucking on them for their sugar and spitting them out when the juice was all gone. She has never seen cane cut in the field or didn't think about it when she was driven through the countryside, which might amount to the same thing.

She is shocked when, hours later, they arrive—the men and women living in conditions that seem taken from a textbook about cane cutting from long-ago times, the people walking barefoot in the dirt accumulating around their shacks, the children without clothes barreling through the unpaved roads, a few with ballooned bellies, protruding navels sticking out into the wind, full of air. The scene draws her distaste; she realizes, slowly, that she has seen sights like this before, perhaps worse, in the *lakou-foumi* of Port-au-Prince, which one avoids by driving through them without stopping. Manuel senses her discomfort but wants to show her around anyway, this other world in which he finds himself at home, though it is no more his world than hers.

When they reach their final destination, Manuel makes her stand several feet away from a shack with a corrugated roof, taps on the frame of the makeshift door, and then takes a step back, waiting for the owners to appear. He bows almost imperceptibly when a couple appears, sturdy and tanned to coal by their work under the unrelenting sun, but thin, too thin, like the curling palm fronds fallen from the trees that the woman collects to make drawings that speak of their lives, when she has the time and the supplies, to sell to the tourists who sometimes come, as she shows Gertie after the two visitors are invited in, much later into their encounter. Gertie assumes, then, that the couple think Gertie is a tourist.

She is surprised at the warmth with which the couple welcome them both into their modest home, a home without running water, without electricity, the floor made of compacted dirt. The woman—her name is Irís—proceeds to offer them a *cafecito*, with a touch of sugar, just a touch, because their sugar is running low, she says, served in speckled tin cups, chipped at the rims. The cups have seen better days, Gertie thinks, as she considers whether to accept, if the coffee might churn in her intestines later. She sees Manuel register her hesitation as Irís hands her a cup. The corners of her own mouth waver, her hands shake as she reaches out to grasp the cup, thanks Irís. And wonders if she can fake sipping at the coffee without insulting the couple. Minutes later, a child comes in from the alley with change in one hand and a large, yellow-skinned fruit in the other, a *chadek*, a grapefruit, and Irís claps her hands joyfully.

"You shouldn't have," Manuel says.

"*Ou merite'l*," Irís says to them. "You deserve it." Gertie tears up then, a little, because the phrase makes her think of how rarely she hears it in her life, never from her mother, certainly never from her sisters, the weight of the tears pulling down on her, down. She never hears that she deserves anything, except maybe from Papa, the day he gave her the locket. She is submerged once more, as if she is back in the bay being drawn into the deep, the waters swirling about her, the song pulling at her, and then another force, buoying her, carrying her to shore. She feels the sudden need to sleep.

"It's his favorite," Irís says conspiratorially to Gertie. "We knew he was coming, so we reserved it at the market." She thanks the child and gives him back a few of the coins for his trouble, and he runs back out the door toward his own home, gripping the money tightly over his head, crying for his mother to come see. "He has helped us so much," she continues, but Manuel bats the compliment away.

"It's you two who saved me!" Manuel booms.

Davíd, the husband, stays silent, fingering the edge of a frayed shirt.

Gertie watches as Irís peels and quarters the fruit, setting the crescents onto the belly of a cleaned and polished aluminum plate. Everything is spartan but well cared for, she observes. She is shamed, recalling her earlier hesitation, sad that Manuel saw it. She senses among the three the ease of companionship, true friendship. It reminds her of that brief interlude in her child-hood when she befriended Sisi, when Lou joined the circle, then Odette. The pull of her loneliness shrinks, yet she remains guarded, ready to reject everything she receives, as she has been taught to do by the sisters to keep others outside the moat. She sits in retreat, sipping at her coffee. She eats a slice of the grapefruit; she saw it freshly peeled. They sit around a rough-hewn table that serves both for eating and for work. Manuel lays out a stack of paperwork he has brought with him to discuss with the couple.

As she sits and listens, sucking on the fruit and swallowing down its tartness, she learns that Irís came over the mountains at seven years of age, twenty-three years ago, accompanying her parents. She has never gone back to the other side. Despite this, her presence in the DR does not count in the eyes of the law because she is one of those who has come without papers. Gertie is surprised to hear that Davíd, her husband, had papers once, when he started crossing the border as a teenager for the *zafra*, cane-cutting season, even after it was made known that thousands had been cut down in that zone, when the divid-ing line between the two countries was moved to give Haiti somewhat less land and the DR somewhat more, by decree of the tyrant who has now been ruling for longer than Davíd has been permanently in the country. He lost the papers one day when he went to apply for a driver's license, or more precisely, the clerk took his proof of legal existence from him and said that his papers were counterfeit because no Haitian in his right mind would have crossed the border after *el corte*, ripping them to shreds with his bare hands and telling Davíd to go back to where he came from, back over the mountains, to a village that now seemed very far away. He explains he does not want to leave Irís's side, their children. The children are playing with the wind, just then, out in the unpaved street, the dirt they fling up with their feet landing across their sweaty bodies like a fine mist, a golden dusting.

A feeling similar to the one Gertie felt underwater outside the resort overcomes her, a feeling of being in the right place, despite the humidity and heat of the shack. She watches Manuel do his work, listening to the couple retell their story, a story they have certainly told again and again, but this time it is clear from the tenor of their voices that they have hope. Manuel is not just an aid worker or a fly-by-night researcher. Despite all that makes them different, Manuel is truly their friend. Gertie recognizes this from the ease with which they sit together, Manuel's and David's heads nearly touching, recognizes in that familiar posture the way she used to sit with Sisi as she watched Sisi draw or solve a math problem in class that Lou could not decipher. She recognizes it in their collective whispers, the way they all seem not to notice the suffocating heat and draw breath like fish amid coral, slicing through blue-green water as one body, moving in the same direction toward a common goal.

When they are about to leave the home, Irís grasps both of Gertie's hands in hers and says, "Keep us in your heart, sister." She lets go of Gertie's hands and gestures Manuel to the door of the shack. The children are still playing outside.

As Manuel moves toward them, she notices that both he and David wear strings of beads around their necks, almost hidden beneath their undershirts. The beads alternate white and red. David senses her gaze and tucks the beads farther away into the folds of his undershirt. Manuel automatically does the same. Gertie looks away, the shame she felt earlier in the day returning, though she does not know why. She wants to know what the beads mean, how they bind the two men together, what, in fact, has moved her to follow Manuel all this way, a man she hardly knows, as if he might have the answers to the questions she holds about a future she cannot yet imagine.

Manuel reaches the door and Irís holds him back by the elbow and whispers in his ear. Despite the whispers, Gertie can make out some of what she says: "*Yon Simbi*." Discreetly, she points to Gertie. "*Li gayen yon lot Simbi ki ap cheche li*, a twin that is looking for her but does not know it yet." She lets go of Manuel's elbow. To neither of them in particular, she says, "You must not stop the waters from reaching what belongs to you."

Gertie doesn't know what these words might mean, but she knows that there are people who can read into the unseen, who believe in the *lwa* she was never taught to understand. What she knows is that Manuel is disappointed in her. He was from the moment her hand visibly hesitated when she was offered the coffee in the chipped enamel cup. But his touch is gentle as he stirs her away from the door of the couple's home, navigates them back from the dirt roads to the highway, to the station, and lets her sleep on the bus all the way back to Santo Domingo. He wakes her when they reach the gates of the resort. He wants to speak to her, then, but she isn't ready for what he has to say.

"It's been a long day," she says, trying to stall the inevitable.

His disappointment is there, saturating his features, his touch, the way his eyes fall on her, then bounce away, avoiding direct contact. Wait, she wants to say, wait, I was wrong. I've been so wrong about so many things. It's not my fault, she wants to add. I was told to believe so many things that were wrong. Just give me a second chance, like Irís did. "Maybe we can talk in the morning?" she asks hopefully.

"Did you think about why you made the mistake you made when we first met, by the pool?" He indicates the back of the resort.

She shakes her head, no. But she knows. She knows. She reddens. "It was just a mistake," she says.

"There's no such thing, Gertie, no such thing. You're more like your sisters than I thought."

She shrugs, like a teenager, she thinks, which she is, when she wants to say, You've got me all wrong, I'm nothing like them. Or, I can change. I can undo what they've taught me. But she isn't sure if that's true, if such prejudices can be unlearned.

"You have to start thinking about these things. You have to decide who you want to be."

No one has ever spoken to Gertie this way and she wants to implore Manuel to tell her more, to tell her about the red and white beads about his neck, to confess to her their meaning, to reveal how she can prevent herself from becoming the very thing that her sisters have molded her to become: a woman who wears eau de parfum to hide her perspiration, who doesn't walk in the dust of the streets, who prefers to be ensconced in a resort by the ocean rather than to share the shore with those who work the land for a living. A woman she does not want to become, like her mother, like her sisters.

"You've got me all wrong," she says.

"I'm hoping," Manuel says. "Look, Gertie. Your sisters, my brothers, everyone thinks people like Irís and Davíd don't deserve our time, our friendship, only our charity. The truth is the two of them saved my life." His hand flies up to the beads.

"How?"

Manuel sighs. "It would take too long to explain." His hand falls. "I don't think you're ready for the story. I'm just pointing out to you that there's more to people than meets the eye. We could be them, are them, did you ever think about that?"

Gertie thinks about Freda, about how she herself was teased mercilessly as a child by the sisters because of her darker-hued skin, about the ways in which she always felt more comfortable with the servants' children, with Sisi, Odette, people who had far less than she did but accepted her as she did them. Papa tried to make a point about this to her that day with the locket, when he explained to her that color didn't make the person; neither did money.

"You have work to do," Manuel says matter-of-factly.

Gertie's throat is dry. She knows he's right but doesn't want to listen to anything more that he has to say. She turns and walks through the darkened corridors of the resort until she finds her room. She slips into it and then sinks to the floor against the back of the door. Again, the shame rises in her, and she vows to herself that she will make the shame disappear, that she will become a better version of herself, one that deserves the love that strangers showed her that afternoon, that the sea showed her, and, even Manuel, in the hope he holds out for her to step into her better self.

She sees him again at breakfast the next day. He nods in her and the sisters' direction. She thinks they will not speak again before she and the sisters leave the resort, but instead, Manuel takes her aside as they are leaving the dining room. "Here," he says, and he places an envelope in her hand. "It was great meeting you, Gertie. I want you to know that."

She nods, slipping it into a skirt pocket. They embrace under the sisters' watchful eyes. Altagracia tells Manuel to remember them to his older brother. Andrée kisses him on both cheeks, as is the custom.

Back in her room, Gertie opens the letter. In it, there is a single sheet of folded paper on which Manuel has written out an address in Tampa, Florida. Above the address, he has written, "Write me when you want." Below, he has added, "No door ever closes that remains open. Yours, Manuel." Gertie's heart leaps. There is hope. Manuel doesn't dislike her after all. He sees in her a possibility, something that Papa saw too, something that the sisters cannot touch, or own.

She had been thinking all through high school about getting a degree in psychology or in social work that could help her to understand the fractures in her own family, why the sisters are the way they are, why she continues to long, after all this time, for her connection to Sisi. She has already applied to schools in Florida and now, she thinks, she will not be utterly alone. Manuel will be there. She could write to him. They could be friends, perhaps something more. He is throwing her a lifeline and she will hold on to it. She will do with her life something that will make him proud, that will make Irís and Davíd proud, people who live between a corrugated roof and a dirt floor, asking for nothing more than the right to their dignity. One day, she will feel deserving of such unguarded generosity.

In the process of becoming her better self, she might just marry this man who has taken her to the *bateyes* as if this were just the thing to do on a vacation day. She might just give him what is left of her heart.

MIAMI, 1970

Gertie still wonders at the ease with which she followed Manuel out of the resort and into uncharted territories. He assumed she knew who he was, having introduced himself as a Pueyo, but she didn't. What drove her to follow him was a gut feeling, and if Gertie trusts nothing else, she trusts her gut. It is what led her to Sisi, to her friendships with the children of the women who took care of her as a child, who watched over her despite the crudeness of her sisters, and sometimes the cruelties of her mother. It is what led her to question the ways her sisters cast her aside, like the gut-feeling that led her father to give her the locket with Freda's image, a locket she wears daily. She plans to give it someday to Ella, now six years of age, passing down both the object and the story, a story that the path she took out of the resort with Manuel that day led her to discover.

After she enrolled in a university in Miami and started work on her social work degree, she mustered the courage to follow that instinct further, to write Manuel at the address he'd left her, began to let him into her heart. Manuel promptly answered, telling her his story, of how he'd met Davíd about seven years prior, how it was Davíd who found him vomiting into the sea after drinking too much at a bar with friends who had up and left him there, how Davíd had taken him home, sobered him up, introduced him to *las veintiuna divisiones*, and christened him a child of Changó, like himself. He went back to those same waters for a baptism, was given the red and white beaded necklace that he seldom takes off, to begin the long journey back to himself. Manuel, luckily, is from a family in which the mysteries are not denied. He wrote to her about how, in the thirties, his grandfather had financed the combatants gathering from both sides of the islands in the cords of mountains, hiding from the occupiers in the villages along the borders. The leaders of that fight against the Yankees were dead, become gods, and Manuel's father reminded him, always, that a few of them had been from the middle classes, the upper classes, all united against a common enemy. It was not lost on him that to have become a United Statian—as he said, as he believed that the word "American" should belong to all the Americas, not just the people of the US—was to live a contradiction, but he understood that only with the resources he could garner there could he fight the broader wars of color and class on the island, where he tried to put them to use in ways that would not result in his being sidelined or deported. The passport was his *passe-partout*, his key, his way of escaping easy detection, of circumventing politics. He became a lawyer so that he could work on human rights issues and run a free clinic whenever he returned home.

Their correspondence lasted several years until one day Manuel wrote to say that he was on his way to the DR, with a stop in Miami; would she meet him? And she said yes because she had always understood that this chance would return one day and that, when it did, she would grab it with both hands.

Though Gertie had returned to Haiti after the birthday trip, afterward she did so less and less. After Manuel and Gertie were married, they stayed in touch with Irís and Davíd, to whom Gertie became family, Irís a godmother to Ella. Manuel was able to regularize the couple's paperwork and got them visas so they could come visit in Florida. Irís came to help with Ella when she was small, before Manuel and Gertie started going back to the DR.

Gertie's mother had died while she was away at boarding school and she did not relish spending any time with her older siblings, a few of whom lived in Haiti, others in the DR, so she made South Florida home and occasionally returned to the DR with Manuel, to the places he knew best. It was part of her heritage, through Papa, she reasoned, though he was no longer there to indicate to her the things he loved most, the streets he walked; nor was his father before him, to say nothing of the women who might have led her all the way back to Freda. She missed the black sand beaches that could be found an hour's drive or so out from Port-au-Prince, and the gingerbread house where she grew up for a time, but she didn't miss having to go from the home of one sister to another, and sit in living rooms for an eternity to visit with this or that cousin, distant relative or childhood friend, people she rarely remembered—who found her line of work below them and criticized the cut of her hair or the frock she wore to their afternoon coffee parties. As a result, for several years once Manuella was born, they didn't leave the US, but Irís's words from their first meeting, about the Simbi, remained within her. Gertie had thought that Irís was speaking about Manuel, but she knew, deep down, that the sole Simbi she had was Sisi, that, perhaps, this was in fact the meaning of her name, rather than the longer French name from which it was shortened, Simone.

When she was pregnant with Manuella and bought a baby name book, she came across Simone and wasn't surprised when she discovered that the name meant "God has heard." She smiled when she read this because it had seemed to her, even as a child, that this was what Sisi represented for her, an untainted goodness attuned to something greater among the cliques forming in the playground and in contrast to her older sisters, who were playing at measuring up to or surpassing others as their sole pursuit. For their own daughter, they settled on Manuella, feminizing Manuel's name, since he had always wanted a junior, but shortening it to Ella. As a middle name, they gave her Gertie's paternal great-great-grandmother's name, Freda. From the same book, Gertie learned that the combination of these two names meant "peaceful goddess," and this was all she could wish for her own child. Poring over the baby names, she wondered if she would ever reconnect with Sisi, if Ella would ever meet her.

In the early years when they did not return to the island, Gertie was plagued with one recurring dream.

In the dream, she was underwater, swimming with the fishes, as on the day she'd met Manuel, and just as on that day, something pulled her down in a centrifugal force and the long black hair that had swept by her then came to her again, except this time, in the dream, there was a face, then a body, a whole form, swimming with and by her. Gertie didn't know if the form was pulling her down, into the spiral, or trying to keep her from it. She didn't fight the form, or the pull, just tried to keep afloat. But then there were two forms in the water, and it was not clear to Gertie why they were there—for her or for each other—and she began to lose faith in the current, in her ability to keep treading water, and as before, she started to drown.

As she thrashed in the water, the two forms moved past her, around each other, and then back to her, lifting her up, or so it seemed to her, until she was wrapped in the long hair, which was like twisted seaweed, wrapped around her face, chest, legs: she could not move. Then, suddenly, she was on a shore, looking out onto the water, and she could see the two forms in the water, the crests of their heads bobbing on the surface of the ocean like buoys, and she wondered if she had imagined it all, the being underwater and their swimming by her, the force pulling on her and the feeling of drowning.

She was fine there, upon the shore. She looked out onto the water and realized that the two forms in the water were not beings, just markers for the fishermen where they'd left their nets, but she did not remember seeing the netting or a catch, just schools of multicolored fish swimming by until they scattered when the water spiraled and pulled everything down into it.

Gertie turned her back on the ocean, but the force was there. It followed her onto the land and, as she turned, it pulled like a hurricane wind to return her to the ocean. Gertie had heard somewhere that once you turned your back on something, you should never turn toward it again, and she tried to keep walking up onto the shore. The wind returned her scorn with more force, refusing her forward motion. Then, she was there, a woman clad in a multicolored dress, with two scars on her face, a dark-skinned woman just like her, beckoning to her, telling her to turn around, to enter the sea.

Even though she was on dry land, Gertie felt, again, as if she were drowning. Her feet would not move. There was no turning back and no moving forward. Around the woman was a force, just as strong as the wind at Gertie's back, a shield that cocooned her. The woman had a dagger tucked into the waist wrap of her dress, and Gertie wondered what it was for. The woman waved a hand in front of the dagger as if to cut Gertie's gaze, but Gertie could think of nothing else until she was gripped by a fear that immobilized her. There were murmurs in the wind, all around her. Gertie closed her eyes. *Jou ma koule . . . jou ma koule . . .* the day I am cut . . . the day I am bled . . . *map vomi san mwen ba yo . . .* I will spit up my blood and give it to them . . . I will give it to them . . . Gertie opened her eyes to see the dagger cutting into the woman's flesh, cutting it to ribbons. The woman lifted her own weapon against an unseen assailant until she collapsed onto the sand, spent, then vomited blood into her cupped hands. The woman looked up at Gertie with pleading eyes, then brought her cupped hands up and her head down, offered her the blood, which was overflowing onto the sand, staining it with scarlet blooms. No, no, Gertie began to say. She wanted to flee, back into the sea, but her feet would not move her. The wind was keeping her there. She looked over her shoulder and the two forms that she'd thought were net markers were there. They turned away from her, back to the sea. Simbi. She swirled her head forward again, anticipating the cupped hands overflowing with blood, but the woman was gone, and Gertie fell forward onto the sodden ground. The sudden jolt of the fall woke Gertie from her sleep, slick with sweat.

Irís was with them one of the times Gertie had the dream and she made Gertie recount the dream step by step, leaving out no detail.

When Gertie described the woman on the shore, Irís's face took on a look of thoughtful understanding. "I think you were blessed by Ezuli Dantor," she said. "Protectress of pregnant women and of women who go their own way." She thought some more.

Gertie laid a hand on her belly, which was full with Ella at that time.

"The blood," Irís said, "I think it is for the baby: Erzulie is claiming the baby for herself. The Simbi may want her too since you are theirs, but the baby is not for them."

"But what do the slashes of the knife mean?"

Irís thought, consulted the *mistè* behind closed eyes, then opened them to smile at Gertie, though her eyes were sad. "Well, Gertie, she will have many trials, your Ella, because she will be different. You must realize this because you will have to protect her from forces that will not understand her. Next time you have the dream, do not be afraid. Drink the blood as if it is your own, like the baby is doing now inside of you. There is nothing to fear."

"Drink the blood?" Gertie said, aghast.

Irís laughed. "It's just a dream, Gertie. It's not real blood, though the spirits are real, and you are real, and the baby will be real in due time. The dream is a lifeline to the protection you and she are being offered. Take it and do not fear it."

Gertie nodded. She knew very little of such things. She was not steeped in the beliefs the way Manuel was, her siblings had seen to that, but she tried to understand. She had learned what the beads meant, and they had their altar, but she didn't know much more than this.

Gertie had the dream several times before Ella was born, and each time, she struggled to drink the blood the woman on the shore offered. When she was finally able to take it from the woman's hands, it tasted of nothing but warmth and comfort, and in the next moment, the woman's dagger turned into a sunflower that she lit on fire above Gertie's belly as if to burn away any dangers that the child might face in the future. Gertie watched the yellow petals turn orange, then to ash. Then the dream ended. She never had it again.

After the birth, Gertie hung a string of Manuel's beads above the crib, for protection, then forgot about them, forgot the dream—or the nightmare.

MIAMI, 1978

A WEEK AFTER RETURNING FROM ANDRÉE'S FUNERAL, Gertie bumps into Margie at the Publix she knows Margie frequents, usually early on Monday mornings when there are few to no shoppers. She finds Margie in the produce department, scrutinizing plantains. Gertie can tell that she is planning on making a fried plantain dessert by the way Margie returns to the pile the bananas that are too green, too unblemished. Plantains are tricky. Too ripe and they could be spoiled, but not ripe enough and the dessert—the flesh of the plantain cut into oblong pieces and fried in browned butter, then sprinkled with granulated sugar and served with cups of verveine or mint tea—will be an impossible trick to pull off. Gertie watches Margie frown as she pursues her inspection and uses that moment to approach her.

"Margie," she calls out to the older woman.

Margie looks up, squints, adjusts her glasses to focus on the woman before her. "Yes?" she asks. Then her eyes fasten on Gertie's. "Oh, Gertie." She takes a step back as if, Gertie thinks, compelled to reject her. "I haven't seen you in forever! What can I do for you?"

Gertie feels like the child she was when Margie, a young woman, was about to crack open the yolk of life with her stories about the fisherman pretending to be a Simbi about to carry her off to faraway lands. She doesn't know how to ask for Sisi's contact information. How can she explain the sisters' decision, the obituary?

Margie has aged. She is thicker, stouter, shorter than Gertie remembers her. She realizes that she has hung on to the image of a a teenage Margie all these years. How old is she now? Close to sixty? Andrée's age? They have all aged yet Gertie feels as she did when she was younger, helpless, a little lost. All she has left within her grasp is the truth.

"How is your family?" Margie asks into the void between them.

"They're fine. Both Manuel and Ella are fine." Gertie responds too quickly. She remembers that Margie sometimes speaks of a son. "How is your son?"

"Oh," Margie says. "He's fine also. You know how young men are: always out to conquer the world." She flutters a hand over the plantains as if she would have liked to spare him the pain of discovering his lot too ripe or too green. "But what can you do?" She continues, "They have to make their own mistakes, isn't that right?" She takes a step toward Gertie.

"Yes, yes, of course," Gertie agrees. She takes Margie's step forward as a sign to proceed. "Make their own mistakes." The conversation stalls but Gertie finds the nerve to follow through. "There's something specific I want to ask you. About Sisi?" There, she's said it.

"Yes?" Margie muses, looking at Gertie pensively. "Water does always flow back to itself. What is it?"

Gertie takes a deep breath. "I want to ask you for Sisi's phone number. I want to reach out to her. My sisters—" She pauses. "Well, I've just come back from a funeral."

"Oh," Margie says, frowning. "Which of them passed?"

"Andrée."

"Andrée. Andrée," Margie mutters. "The oldest. I only remember her from a fight we had in the middle of the street, about Sisi. She married early, didn't she? She terrorized us younger ones when she was still at the high school."

"Yes. That would be her—a terror." Gertie takes another deep breath. "The point is that Andrée left . . ." She searches for the right word. "Directives. Posthumous instructions, and they include Sisi."

Margie's eyes narrow. "How so?"

Gertie blurts, "She had Sisi's name put in her obituary, as a surviving sister."

"Where was this obituary published?" Margie replies coolly.

Gertie can see Margie's mind trying to understand the scope of the damage. "It will be published everywhere, in all the major papers—here, and there."

"My God," Margie exclaims. "Your sisters never stop, do they?"

Gertie grasps her courage, looks Margie in the eye. "I'd like to warn Sisi myself before it comes out and gets spread about. Maybe talk her through the sisters' thinking." She adds quickly, "I want you to know that I wasn't part of the decision. I couldn't undo it."

"Can I warn her first?" Margie asks. "It might be better coming from me first. Soften the blow a bit? Then she can decide if she wants to be in touch with you or not. You didn't give her a choice back then." Margie pulls out paper and pen, scrawls Sisi's phone number on it, and pushes the piece of paper into Gertie's palm. "Here, here, before I change my mind. Just give me a few days to tell her. Then you can call her."

"What if she doesn't take my call?"

"That's a chance you'll have to take."

Gertie clutches the paper in her fist. She beams at Margie, then turns her attention to the pile of plantains between them. She picks up two that are just the right shade of yellow green. "I think this is what you're looking for."

Margie takes the plantains from Gertie, looks them over. "Quite right, Gertie." She turns her back to Gertie before repeating over her shoulder, "Call her in a few days."

Gertie steps back, sure that her instincts have served her well once more. Whenever she follows them, her life turns onto a better course. In just a few days, she will speak to Sisi, even if the reason that compels the reconnection is as bitter as over-percolated coffee.

It is not Sisi who answers the phone when Gertie calls. It is the voice of a child, a little high, tumbling out like a river coursing over and around smooth rocks polished by its persistence.

"Hello," the girl's voice says.

Gertie did not expect to be speaking to Emma. She wonders if Emma has acquired Sisi's mannerisms, those she can remember, a careful, studied air, if she also draws and is interested in art.

"Hello," Emma repeats, insistent. "Is there anyone there?"

"Who is it?" Gertie hears Sisi in the background, that voice she longs for but hasn't heard in decades.

"I'm a friend of your mother's. Well, not exactly a friend." She laughs softly. "You can say, I'm a childhood friend."

Emma's silence is polite; she is waiting for an identification that makes sense.

"I'm calling for your mother, for Simone," Gertie says. She obviously can't say to the child, "It's your lost aunt calling—the one who hasn't been in touch for ages but cares about you nonetheless." She can't say anything so damning, even if she thinks it true. "You can tell her"—she pauses—"that Gertie is calling."

"Gertie?" Emma asks. "Is that your real name? It sounds like a name you would give to a guppy."

Gertie laughs out loud. "It does sound odd, doesn't it? My full name is Gertrude Alcindor Pueyo. You can tell Sisi that's who's calling."

"Sisi?"

"Your mother."

The child steps up and hands the phone over. Gertie hears her say, "It's for you. A lady calling herself Gertie like she's a fish. She says you used to know her when you were a kid. Her real name is Gertrude something."

"OK. Thank you," Gertie hears Sisi say, followed by, "Don't you have homework to do?" The child's answer is lost in the background as she undoubtedly finds her way to her room, as Ella would have done, forgetting all about her mother. "Yes?"

There she is. Finally. Sisi.

Gertie musters up all her fearlessness to continue. "Hi. Hello. It's me. I'm sorry it's been so long and that, well, I would be contacting you under these circumstances. I'm truly sorry." She waits for an answer, but none comes. "Did Margie speak to you? About Andrée's obituary?"

There is a long silence. Gertie imagines Sisi searching for the right words, as she is, each word coming to mind, then slipping away like quicksand as easily as it rises to the tongue. What comes up at the same time are images of the foot-of-the-bed meeting with their father in the hospital room, the older children hovering about and above them, and then, years later, coming across each other in the French consulate when Sisi was about to leave for Europe and Gertie was there visiting Altagracia, who worked there, the whole country beginning to fall apart under the weight of a regime no one saw coming. The images are fresh, as if they hadn't happened so long ago, but they did, so long ago.

"Yes," Sisi says, and though the voice has aged, Margie can hear in it the singsong of Sisi's childhood voice, its breeziness. "Margie did speak to me, but someone else sent me the obituary." She stops to think. "But I don't understand. Why now? Why me? Why none of the others?"

"Others?"

"Papa's other outside children."

"I don't know." Gertie dithers. "I just wanted to say that the obituary was their idea. Andrée's and my other sisters'. They thought it would be a good idea to—"

"To expose me? Papa?"

"Yes. No. I mean, no. They don't think that way."

"How do they think?"

Sisi isn't going to make things easy, has no reason to.

"They wanted to acknowledge you"—she moves her free hand in the empty air about her—"as an act of contrition, I think, or absolution."

"How very Catholic of them," Sisi says, icily.

"Well, maybe it means nothing," Gertie muses. "I mean, it doesn't have to mean anything, doesn't have to change things." But she wants it to change something, their distance, for instance.

They listen to each other's silence, each other's breathing. This is not nothing. They are both women now, sitting on opposite sides of the telephone line, on opposite sides of everything. Has it always been this way? Gertie has to admit it probably has—upper class and working class, legitimate, illegitimate. But who's to say who had the better bargain of it?

"They really thought I would care?" Sisi asks, her voice lilting as if she is asking Gertie a genuine question.

Gertie feels the opening, like the mouth of a cave, gropes her way around its parameters mentally, to see how far she can dare inch. "I think," she ventures, "they want to be forgiven, a chance at rehabilitation."

"But Andrée is dead. She could have written me a letter, or called, when she was alive."

"This is it, I guess, your letter." She knows this sounds absurd, like a voice calling out in a desert.

"It's not a kindness, you know?" The question is rhetorical, but Gertie understands. She can hear Sisi thinking. "Margie told me you have a daughter?"

"Yes, yes," Gertie enthuses, glad to have another topic of conversation. "I just spoke to yours, briefly. It would be great if they could meet, don't you think? They're cousins, after all."

"I suppose," Sisi says, "of a kind."

"Don't you think we should try to patch things up?" Gertie replies, almost desperately. She wants to keep Sisi talking. "If not for us, for them?"

"I'll talk to Scott and to Emma and see how they feel about it."

"How do *you* feel about it?"

"I can't say."

"You can't say, or won't say?"

"I really can't, Gertie. It's been so long and this, this just came out of the blue. And I have so much going on right now, so much to think through, aside from this. What do you want me to say?"

Sisi's voice is flat. Gertie cannot read it, does not know her well enough any longer to cut through to the heart of the matter. She imagined, somehow, that things would come easily, as easy as that day they met in school, as easy as peering over Sisi's shoulder.

"Do you still draw?"

"Draw? Funny you should ask me that."

"Why?"

"I just started taking classes again, in illustration. The guy I take classes from thinks I have talent. I'm thinking of making a leap."

"You should!"

"You've never seen my work, Gertie. You don't know."

"But I have."

"That was long ago." Sisi gives a little laugh, softening. "I'm better now, actually."

"I don't doubt it."

"It's just that—" Sisi pauses. "I don't leap that easily any longer."

"I see." Gertie falls silent. "Well, I can guarantee that this time, I won't let you fall alone."

"Are we still talking about the illustrating?"

"No. I'm talking about repairing the past—or the future."

"Or the future," Sisi repeats.

"Will you think about it?" she asks.

"Yes, I can do that."

Gertie hangs up the phone, holding her breath in disbelief. They have made a connection. This is all that Gertie can ask for in the present moment. She begins to understand that their memories are hung on different strings, with differing pearls.

Despite this, the two have made a plan to speak again in the New Year, to discuss the possibility of meeting. Both said it would be for their daughters, neither wanting to admit to the other that there is a yearning, deep and unsettling, to see what the years have worn away or left behind, to examine the fine silt left on shore after waves recede.

PART IV

GUANO

GERTIE, MIAMI, 2002

GERTIE OPENS HER EYES AFTER A LONG, DEEP SLEEP—
she takes melatonin almost every night, hoping not to have to
take anything stronger for a time, though she knows she will,
eventually. A younger woman she vaguely recognizes but cannot place sits in the chair where Ella usually sits, with a pad of
paper in hand, sketching with a pencil. The gestures are familiar, remind Gertie of a long-ago time, of childhood, of Sisi, of
an odd-looking bird emerging from beneath the stub of a pencil
held by a small hand, that looked like a squat duck or a pigeon
but that Sisi swore was a rooster. Gertie cackles at the memory
and the young woman sitting in the chair next to her bed looks
up—she had been looking at her but in that way that artists do,
looking without looking, lost in their process—and into Gertie's eyes. The woman brushes away eraser curls from the paper,
puts down her pencil, smiles Sisi's smile. Emma. She is not the
same color as Sisi; she has a chestnut complexion, warmer than
Sisi's olive brown, with wavy, black hair, and freckles across the
bridge of her nose. Gertie marvels at how even adopted children
come to resemble their parents over time.

The girl grins. "Yes. She's here. She just went out with Ella to
get a few things for her stay. She'll be back."

Gertie nods—it took another dying time to bring Sisi back
to her. First, Papa's unexpected goodbye, then Andrée's obituary, now her. "How is your mother?" she asks.

"Fine," Emma says. "Sorry to see you again under these circumstances."

Gertie doesn't respond at first. Would Sisi have come under any other circumstance?

"Do you remember the *morir soñando*, Emma?" Gertie asks, thinking about the trip to the DR when the girls were young.

"Sure I do," Emma says. "I thought it was so great." She adds, "I sometimes make it for friends in California. They can't believe this is a drink somewhere." She laughs.

Gertie smiles. "And you draw now."

"Well, you know, I'm an art teacher," Emma says, reminding Gertie.

"Yes," Gertie says, "I remember now. Your aunt Margie tried to get you and your mother to move to Florida, but you and she moved to California instead to go to college for that."

"Ha! Mother followed me to California is more like it!"

Gertie's eyelids feel heavy. "I thought that was brave of the both of you. I think Ella and I would have killed each other, living in the same space as adults." Gertie starts dozing off.

"Do you want to see what I'm working on?" Emma says, holding up her paper tablet so that Gertie makes the effort to awaken, to open her eyes.

What Gertie sees is the tracing of a face that looks like her own. She vaguely sees the shape of Emma's head behind the paper. Sisi has changed, she thinks. Gertie falls asleep on this thought, hears papers rustle next to the bed, hears the wind move through palm trees.

SANTO DOMINGO, 1979

SISI

If Simone knows joy, it is the moment of flying over the island and seeing its shores buttressed by limpid aquamarine seawater that she can see clear through. If she has one regret, it is that they are flying over the port that once was a stone's throw from her home, over the green brown of the western side of the island to land in the green that lies to the east, the hills there robust with growth and far less populated. How she wishes that they were landing at Louverture Airport, that Margie and Momo and her mother would be there to greet her, to take her home, like a child returning, but nothing is left there but memories.

She also feels joyous because of the presence of Emma at her side, now eleven, barely able to contain her excitement at going on the trip, about to meet a cousin, an aunt and uncle, maybe others that they are related to but that she never heard of until four or five months ago, when she answered the phone and heard a voice not unlike her mother's ask for Sisi. Emma handed her the phone without realizing that the phone call would continue the slow process of change that Sisi had embarked upon the moment that she stepped into the illustration art class, and then the next, when she heard that the starlings had fallen out of the sky, a little more than a year ago, and she too wanted to plummet, headfirst, after them.

Now, all of them—because Scott ultimately came on the voyage—are about to land on the island of her birth, albeit in the nation next door, as guests of Gertie and Manuel, who have invited them to join their family vacation to the DR, to a resort they discovered more recently, that looks out onto the ocean. They will spend time together, Gertie has promised, get reacquainted, despite thirty years of silence, of absence.

Sisi, in the end, agreed, because her life needs upending and if she is not yet ready to end things with Scott, she might as well try to follow the path that Gertie has set before her. For their daughters, it will be a first meeting Sisi hopes might turn into the lifelong friendship she and Gertie were denied.

"Go, go," Scott said enthusiastically, when she told him about Gertie and Manuel's invitation to join them on their yearly vacation in the DR. "You deserve it." He is not completely oblivious. He has noticed the changes in her, or so she thinks, that she takes more initiative, that she serves *riz collé* and stewed chicken almost as often, now, as she makes sloppy joes and hamburgers. The composition of their plates has changed.

"Go, go," he said. "It will be fun for the both of you."

"But what about you?" Emma asked. "Who's going to feed you?"

Scott laughed, reached for Emma, and brought her into a hug. "It might be a surprise for you to know that when I met your mother, she could hardly boil an egg. We just ate chicken from a rotisserie down the street from our apartment and boiled potatoes and green beans to go along with it."

"Every night?"

"Every night!" Scott shouted, then caught Sisi's eye and coughed. "Well, almost every night." He smiled at Sisi.

She couldn't help but smile back. Scott was a good father; this she could admit. She softened, watching Emma nestled in Scott's embrace. "Why don't we all go?"

"Seriously?" Scott asked.

"Yes!" Emma exclaimed. "Yes, Dad. Come with us!"

"I thought you would want your space," Scott said over Emma's head to Sisi. "You haven't seen Gertie in forever."

They'd seldom spoken about Gertie until the call about the obituary. Scott hadn't understood, at first, why it offended her to be named. She explained to him what it meant to be an outside child in island culture, the shame of having "Unknown" typed or written in the space above the line for "Father" on one's birth certificate, the way eyebrows rose every time the document was produced to officials. It was something one kept to oneself, not trumpeted to the world. "But they're accepting you," he said.

"No," she specified, "they're claiming me now that there's something to claim. That's not the same thing."

"Isn't it?" he responded, perplexed.

"It's a form of one-upmanship, like they're saying that now I'm worthy of them or that they're finally giving me what I want, recognition, Papa's name, but I've never wanted, or needed," she asserted, "either."

"You don't have to take it that way."

"There's no other way to take it. It's as if Andrée's reaching out from beyond the grave and robbing me of my right to reject them. I didn't want this. I don't want this. I don't want any part of the Alcindors."

But when she heard Gertie's voice after all that time, after Emma handed her the phone, Sisi's resolve crumbled. She was seven again on Gertie's wraparound porch or eating *jalao* at the kitchen table under Yéyène's supervision, or they were swinging their legs off the end of the port with Margie between them, breathing in the sea air laden with salt, peering over the ledge into the waves, wondering about the spirits below, waiting for their thin ankles to be grasped by them. To recover that joy, that simplicity, was all she wanted, not the Alcindor name, not their benediction. This is why she said yes to Gertie's plan, to meet in a few months' time after she called, late fall, when the girls would be on spring break, on the island, the one thing they yet had in common.

Sisi looked at her husband and daughter and cried out: "Family vacation!"

"OK," Scott said, "I'll call the clinic and get the time off. Done!"

Emma squeezed him harder while Sisi high-fived Scott's upheld hand above her. They were a team again, a unit. Sisi didn't have time to wonder if Scott had changed or could change. He had not stood in her way when she decided to take her illustrations a step further after taking the art classes, decided to write a children's picture book, a story about an owl couple adopting another owl's fledgling, and submitted it to a local press. He'd applauded her when it won a local prize and then went on, earlier this year, to be picked up by a major publisher in New York, who arranged an all-expenses-paid trip for her and Emma. The book will be out soon. She'd taken fewer hours at the university clinic and was almost poised to quit the job. She'd resumed contact with Lou, who remains in Paris in love and living with Samiah, who has become a schoolteacher. The couple decided not to have children and continue to be radicals, albeit more quietly and not out in the streets.

Sisi apologized to Lou for the way she left things after marrying Scott and moving to the US, not explaining that she didn't have the stomach for the kinds of things Lou and Samiah were willing and able to do back then. Not explaining that, in the end, the short of it was that she had been afraid, afraid of the secret police that could be sent so far out of Haiti to hunt down opponents, afraid of the policemen who could so easily toss peaceful protesters, citizens, into the Seine as they might a sack of potatoes. She could not stomach it. She didn't want to think about what might have happened to Odette, could not bear to ponder the tortures, the killings, the way children walked over cadavers on their way to school. She wanted a simple life and Scott offered it: all she had to do was marry him and take a plane and the future decided itself.

Lou invited Sisi to come back to Paris. "It could be like old times," Lou wrote in her letter, but Sisi declined the invitation. She couldn't admit that the touch of Lou's lips upon hers so long ago, at the Expo, continues to linger in her dreams, like an angel's touch. She does not want to admit to this reverie because she knows she loves Lou in a way that she never loved Scott, but also that she could not love her the way that Samiah does, wholly, without reservation. She is too afraid of loss to abandon herself this way to love, too afraid to court it only to lose it. Sisi understands that what Lou sees in Samiah is a quality, a mettle, she does not possess. She loves Lou enough not to begrudge her what she has found with Samiah. She loves her enough to let her go, to nurse the memory of the kiss as a fragment of who she wishes she could have been but will never be. These admissions to herself make her love Lou and Samiah fiercely, in her own quiet, protective way. Sisi keeps up the correspondence with Lou and tells herself that one day, she will make her way back to Paris to see them, perhaps when she is an old lady with fewer regrets and more courage.

It surprised Sisi how easily she and Gertie renewed their childhood sympathies after the phone call about the obituary. It is easier to forgive the dead than the living, and since Gertie had nothing to do with the obituary that Andrée left behind, Sisi decided to keep the channel open. The holiday season came to pass shortly after they first spoke and Gertie, with Manuel, extended the invitation to meet them in the DR. Sisi took it as a sign that there was no longer any reason to stand apart. Just a few months later, she is about to see Gertie in person. Sisi can hardly contain herself. She reaches over Emma to grasp Scott's forearm while Emma leans forward over her lap as the island comes closer and closer into view.

Emma gasps at the color of the water. "It's emerald green," she says, looking out the plane window in wonder. "This is where we're going? Just wow."

Scott smiles over at Sisi and Emma. Sisi senses the possibility of renewal surge.

They land, find their luggage, and hop into a taxi after giving the resort's address to the driver, as instructed by Gertie. They are ready to crash in the hotel room after traveling from Ohio, through Miami, then on to the island; Gertie and Manuel plan to get there a day or so later.

At the resort, Emma leaves Sisi and Scott in the lobby and meanders toward the sea line over which the resort is perched. Sisi watches her go and the word "Simbi" flits through her mind as she thinks of her childhood on the port. Emma's draw to water makes her Sisi's child, through and through. Sisi turns her back on her daughter to attend to checking in to the hotel. Scott stands back, letting her negotiate the reservation, though the man at the counter keeps looking over Sisi's head toward Scott, as if Sisi is of no importance. The man doesn't make eye contact with her when he asks for her passport.

"Simon-ey. Simon-ey" he mutters, pronouncing her French name with a Spanish inflection, as he studies at her, then again at Scott, over his glasses. He examines her passport closely. "It says here you were born in Port-au-Prince?" He puts out a brown arm against hers. "You are lighter than I am, and I am no Haitian." He laughs.

"Well, I was born there. *Soy de aquí*," she says. "Do you want my husband and my daughter's passports?"

"*Aquí* is not Haiti, *señora*. Please don't make this mistake. There are two sides to this island," he corrects her. He wears a name label that says Federico. He places a hand sideways, level with the counter, sweeping to one side, then to the other. "And we have nothing to do with the other."

"Yes, Federico," Simone responds, pronouncing his name in Spanish, hoping that a more intimate address will help the process. "This is my husband." She points to Scott.

"He is Haitian too?" Federico laughs. He gestures to her. "Is there a passport for the child on the reservation? I do not see her. Your daughter?"

"She went out to the beach." Sisi looks over her shoulder to see if she can spot Emma, fears for an improbable moment that a Simbi has caught her, turns back, hands over the other passports. "Don't worry, she'll be fine. We'll go collect her when we're done here."

"But how do you come to have been born over there?" Federico continues, pointing over his shoulder.

"I'm Haitian," Sisi says, aggravated, as if grains of sand are trapped in the sides of her shoes. "Some of us are Haitian."

Federico raises an eyebrow, then taps away at a keyboard connected to a screen next to the counter. "I am sorry to tell you, madam, that we do not have a room for you this evening."

"How is that possible?" Simone says. "My sister made the reservation for us months ago."

"Who is your sister?" the man says, not looking up.

"Gertrude Alcindor?" Sisi has momentarily forgotten Gertie's married name, Manuel's last name. It has slipped out of her mind. How can she have forgotten? She knows that he is from an old Dominican family, his name an unlocking key.

"Alcindor? Alcindor? I do not know this name." Federico taps away at his keyboard. "What we can do," he resumes, "is send you to our sister hotel down the street. It's not on the ocean like here, but you'll be fine there." He smiles quizzically. "Then you can come back tomorrow and check if things have changed."

"This doesn't make any sense," Sisi says. The hotel does not seem full to her.

Scott steps up to stand next to her. "What's the problem?"

"Federico here," Sisi says, gesturing toward the man, "says that they don't have a room for us. I can't remember Manuel's family name. They made the reservation."

"Polito? Pollo?" Scott offers. "Something like that."

Federico regards them over the counter with glazed-over eyes. "You'll be fine at the other hotel. I'll give you directions. Then you come back tomorrow, or the next day, and we can see what we can do."

Sisi looks up at Scott. "I guess we don't have a choice."

He shrugs. "It will get sorted out when your sister gets here, I guess."

"OK," Sisi says to Scott. "Can I have our passports back?" Imagine getting lost on this side of the island without a passport to identify you, she thinks. It would be a nightmare.

"The passports." He collects them and drops them in front of Sisi on the counter instead of placing them in her hand. He pulls up a map from under the counter and shows them the location of the other hotel. It is a few miles inland, toward the city center. "There are taxis outside you can hire. *Hasta mañana*," he says, dismissing them.

They find Emma and leave the resort, clamber back into a taxi, and in a few minutes, they are let out in front of a run-down, motel-looking structure that advertises hourly and half-day rates.

"What kind of a place is this?" Emma says, tumbling out of the taxi, tossing back shoulder-length, black hair.

"Just looks like a run-down place, honey," Scott says, getting their luggage together and leading the way into the hotel. Once in, he lets Sisi handle check-in again and distracts Emma with a display of percussion instruments in a glass case in the front hall.

The man at the registration desk asks the same questions about Sisi's place of birth, also compares his skin tone to hers, shakes his head no against the possibility that since he is darker than she, he might be closer to her heritage than she is. But he gives them keys to a cramped room situated above the kitchen after calling the resort to check out their story. "They say you'll be here a few nights, courtesy of the resort since you're paid up over there, until you sort things out with them," he says to Sisi after hanging up the phone.

"We won't be staying here more than a night or two," Simone responds, frustrated, since she knows that they had been lied to at the resort and that Gertie had, indeed, made the reservation. She takes the keys and signals Scott and Emma over.

The man smirks, holds both his hands with his palms turned out toward her. "It's none of my business."

Bewildered, Sisi leads Scott and Emma down the hallway and up a flight of stairs to the second floor, where they make their way down a dark hallway that reeks of onions and garlic to reach the room. They order food from the kitchen and wait. By the time it arrives, Emma is fast asleep in the middle of the bed. It is too late to dissect what has just happened, the discomfort of it unsettling Sisi such that the excitement of the flight down has died. The smell of burning oil drifts up from the kitchen, saturating everything they've packed as soon as they open their bags. Sisi tries to keep the luggage closed.

"Babe," Scott says, "just leave it alone. We'll sleep here tonight, and everything will get sorted out tomorrow. Look." He points down at Emma, nestled between them the way she used to when she was smaller. "She's fine. We'll all be fine. Let's just try to get some sleep."

Soon, both Scott and Emma are snoring while Sisi remains wide awake. She tries to close her eyes against the dankness of the room, the musty smells, the clanging of the pots and pans being washed up for the next day's service. She hears a headboard banging against a shared wall, a high-pitched squeal, grunting. They are clearly in a day hotel, the kind used by streetwalkers and people having extramarital affairs. She isn't sure what triggered "Federico" to chase them away to this place, like undesirables, but she knows it has everything to do with the place of birth printed in her passport: Port-au-Prince. Yet she longs for home, for Haiti.

GERTIE

"*¿Cómo pasó esto?*" Gertie asks, agitated, yelling over the phone at the manager of the resort after finding out that Sisi and her family are not checked in. "*¿Qué quieres decir con que pensaron que su pasaporte era falso?* She's my sister! *Los dos somos Haitianas.* What? You want to speak to my husband? *Por supuesto. Aquí está.*"

Gertie is beside herself. Why do they need to speak to Manuel when they can very well speak to her? She is indignant. Two degrees in social work later and she is just a woman, just a girl. She is so tired of island ways. She listens to the conversation as Manuel conveys their joint dismay and tries to sort out the situation. He writes down on the pad of paper next to their phone that Sisi has been moved to another hotel, jots down the name and phone. "*No te preocupes,*" he writes. Manuel draws huge exclamation points before and after the phrase in Spanish: Don't worry; we'll get this sorted out. Soon, he hands Gertie back the phone. "It's sorted," he says. "They'll get a room in a couple of days, but now I'm wondering if you shouldn't just go elsewhere. It's a bad feeling, bad vibe. I can find you something else." Gertie nods as she takes the phone from Manuel.

"What are you going to do now?" she says once the manager is back on the line. "Was your conversation with my husband enlightening?" There is dead air on the phone for a moment. "Hello? Hello? Is there someone there?"

"*Sí*," the man says sharply. "It was all just a big misunderstanding. There will be no extra charge from our sister hotel, as I explained to your husband."

"You bet there won't be. We've paid an arm and a leg for the resort. How dare you send them elsewhere?"

"*Lo siento, señora.*"

"*Lo siento. Lo siento*," Gertie laments. "Is that all you can say?" The man hangs up.

"I can't believe it," Gertie says to Manuel. "He hung up on me. I'm going to call him back."

"Just let it go, Gertie. Just call your sister. It's not worth it getting into it further with them."

"Maybe you're right," Gertie replies. She dials the number Manuel wrote on the pad.

"I just don't understand how this happened," she says, as she waits to be connected to the hotel. "We should have been there." When the clerk answers, she asks for Sisi and is connected immediately, as if they were awaiting her call.

"Hello," Gertie hears Sisi's tired voice on the line.

"How are you, *querida*?" she asks. "I'm so sorry this has happened. What a welcome! We would never have let you arrive before us if we knew this would happen! And where they sent you—I have never heard of such a thing! How are you all doing?" Gertie's words come out all in a rush.

"They're fine," Sisi responds. "Emma has no idea what's happening. Scott's taken her out to get fresh air and maybe find a late lunch. I think I understood from the conversation that we're to stay here and they'll have a room for us back at the resort in a day or two?"

"That's what Manuel says, but he thinks that maybe we should all go elsewhere. He's going to make some calls and we'll let you know."

"I really had no idea where they were sending us. I thought they honestly didn't have a room for us when we arrived."

"There's nothing to figure out!" Gertie yells over the phone. "They're just bigots. Racists! Maybe we could join you where you are and go from there?"

"Well, it's not exactly pleasant here. It's a bit creepy, actually," Sisi says, lowering her voice to a whisper. "The whole situation. What else can we do?"

"I'll talk to Manuel. Plans have changed on our end. Nothing to worry about but it looks like Manuel can't come because of a case. One of Ella's friends will take his place and we're getting that sorted out too, so we'll be delayed a little longer. Here I thought you would have an extra day or two by yourselves to relax as a family before we got there, but it's become such a mess. *¡Lo siento!* We'll make them make this right. Manuel will handle it before he goes off to work on his case, OK? Hang in there, Sisi. Don't let this get to you. They're just ignorant bigots. But you'll see, not everyone is like this. It can be a great place. You just can't go around telling people you're Haitian, you know?"

"But I didn't," Sisi interjects. "The place of birth is in the passport!"

"Well, yes. That's true. I don't know what to say." She truly doesn't. Here they were supposed to be enjoying their reunion in the DR, and instead, they're sorting out island diplomacy. "This hasn't happened to me in so long, what with Manuel and his family and all. Well, I'm sorry is all I can say right now. Nothing will happen to you, and Scott is there. Take Emma to the beach or something. We'll get this sorted out and all of this will just be a bad dream, I promise."

"Well, all right. It's definitely not how we wanted to start this vacation." Sisi laughs drily. "But it will all come together."

"That's the spirit," Gertie says brightly. "Now put that joker back on the line and let me deal with him. We'll go somewhere else, all together. Not where you are, not the resort, somewhere else. I'll call you back and let you know where to."

"All right," Sisi says. "If I don't find something else first."

Gertie is frustrated. She and Manuel should have planned things better, thought ahead about the reactions Sisi might receive, a light-skinned Haitian in a world divided by color and nationality, accompanied by a gringo. But she didn't have the foresight, didn't think everything through.

SISI

A few hours after hearing from Gertie, Sisi wakes drowsily in the hotel room. Scott and Emma have not returned. She digs out her guidebook and opens it to the section listing hotels and motels. She reads the descriptions for every hotel, from the most expensive to the least. Some have warnings that they are frequented by grifters and drifters. The hotel to which they have been relocated is among the latter. "Good for a quick overnight stay if one has an early flight out," the guide specifies. Distressingly, many of the hotels have the word "colonial" in their names. She will have to explain the reason for this to Emma, without glossing over the reality of the history shared on both sides of the island, but which seems to not have been condemned in the DR. The colonial era, here, on the surface of things, appears fable-like, without relation to the brutal reality it should invoke. She wonders for a moment what her father would have said about it, whether he wondered about the differences between the two sides as he navigated from one to the other. Sisi scans the one-star, two-star, and three-star hotels until her eyes settle on a listing for a hotel close to the port, in the historic center, that isn't quite a resort, not a motel. "A family place that welcomes children with all the amenities of the best resorts without the price; locally owned; female owned." Sisi reads the description out loud, stars the listing with a pencil, and calls it, determined. She has money from the advance she received for her first picture book in an account with her name on it, attached to her own credit card; her first account without Scott as a cosignatory. "Close to historical sites. Great for all ages." That's the ticket. Sisi reasons that she must make the best of it. If she is trying to be her own woman, this will be one step in attaining more independence. She dials the number of the Colonial Monaco Hotel, wondering if the area will resemble the houses near the docks in Port-au-Prince, if anything will be similar.

The food is different for one thing. As far as she is concerned *sancocho* is not the same as *soup joumou*, though they have the same festive appearance, the kind of dish lovely to have on a cold winter day in the Midwest. *Sancocho* is heartier; some make it with several types of meat. It's flavored with *sofrito*, a blend of fresh herbs and aromatics to season the broth, along with a bouillon cube, while *soup joumou*, though just as filling, focuses on the use of pumpkin. Haitians add avocado to the soup, served on Independence Day, a reminder of what the enslaved labored for, to be free to eat, while Dominicans serve the avocado on the side, with white rice, and trace their dish to travels of indigenous people from as far as the Canary Islands to Colombia, to Ecuador, then to the DR, the ingredients modified from one place to the next until, they say, Dominicans perfected the dish. No, it is not the same. *Pikliz* is not *sofrito* and *pollo guisado* is not the same as stewed chicken, *mai moulu* not *mangú*. Only the fried plantain is the same here, and as far as Cuba, everywhere. This will be no homecoming, Sisi thinks, as she waits on the phone for someone to pick up.

A woman answers, speaking in Spanish. Sisi explains as best she can her need to find new accommodations. She emphasizes that she has an eleven-year-old daughter who has never been to the island before, an American girl on spring break, and that she wants everything to be perfect for her.

"*Señora, entiendo perfectamente.* I understand perfectly. I have a daughter *con nosotras en el hotel.* She stays here with us. *Por favor venga.* Come. Come. *Sé que serás muy feliz aquí.* You'll be happy here. *¡Cuidaremos bien de ti!* We'll take good care of you!"

Sisi is relieved. "*Gracias.* Thank you. Thank you so much. *¿Podemos ir ahora mismo?* Can we come right now? *¿Tiene una habitación disponible ahora?* Do you have an available room?"

"*Sí. Sí. Nosotros tenemos.* Yes, yes, we do. *Ven cuando estés listo.* Come when you are ready. *¡Ven enseguida!* Straight away!"

"*¡Gracias! ¡Gracias!*" Sisi hangs up the phone, pleased with herself, confident that things will change as soon as the move is made, proud of herself that she did not wait for Gertie to call back with new arrangements.

Soon, she hears Scott and Emma returning from their ventures out. The two come noisily down the hall, the lock turns in the door, and Emma bursts forth, holding a greasy bag ahead of her, all smiles.

"We found these," she says. "Try them!"

"What are they?"

Emma shrugs. "Don't know. Beef pastries?"

Sisi opens the bag. The scent of beef and onions drifts out. She peers in. "These smell so good. Were they good?" she asks them both.

"So good!" Emma says.

"Empanadas," Scott says. He looks around the room. "Whoa, what's going on? Did Gertie sort everything? You have everything repacked."

"We're moving," Sisi replies, plunging a hand into the grease-stained bag. "I found us a room with a fold out couch for Emma near the port."

"OK," Scott says. "What happened to Gertie?"

"She says they're going to be a few days, what with Manuel not coming."

"Manuel isn't coming? I was looking forward to meeting him. Am I going to be the only man?"

"Yes. There's going to be one more girl, a friend of Ella's."

"Ella's bringing a friend?" Emma pipes up. "You didn't say I could have brought someone."

"We brought your dad," Sisi answers, biting into the beef pastry. The salty juices of the beef filling burst against her tongue. "Oh my goodness, Emma. You're right. These are so good! It's a little bit like Haitian *pâté*?" Finally, something familiar.

"The stuff they make from ducks? I don't think so, Mom," Emma says, scrunching up her face.

Sisi laughs with a hand up to her mouth. "No, Emma. *Pâté* is our version of this on the other side. I haven't made it for you. We bake ours. This is fried. And the dough is different. Ours is made with a flaky pastry. This is a short crust." Scott and Emma stare at her. They have no idea what she is going on about. She finishes the pastry. "Doesn't matter. It's tasty. As soon as you two are ready, we can leave."

"I'm ready," says Scott.

"When's Ella getting here?" Emma asks.

"Let's move and then we can find out, shall we?"

❈

GERTIE

"*Nou la!*" Gertie shouts out as she reaches the front desk of Sisi's new hotel flanked by two teenage girls, one as plump as the other is tall. The tall girl, her daughter, Manuella, favors her, while the plump girl with straight hair looks out of place, like a piece of sweet plantain on a savory plate.

Gertie is decked out in a green one-piece jumpsuit the color of a blooming banana leaf. She wants Sisi to know it is her on sight. Though they exchanged pictures through the mail over the holidays and each has created a mental picture of the other, Gertie wants to leave nothing more to chance. She has shown up at the hotel Sisi indicated they'd moved to three days after the phone call in which they'd tried to sort things out. Gertie finds it admirable that Sisi took things into her own hands despite not knowing anyone in the DR. She is determined to make a memorable entrance to make up for the bad feeling of the rough beginning. Thus she arrives, breathless, with the two teenage girls trailing behind her like mosquitoes buzzing around a sweetness, clad in the showy green jumpsuit. Gertie swats the girls away, not unkindly, asking for space. "Girls, go, go." She cries after her daughter, "Look for your cousin. You have her picture."

While the girls walk away, hand in hand, giggling, toward the courtyard, Gertie bends over the front desk counter and requests "*la familia Val.*" She cannot for the life of her remember Scott's family name.

"*¿Donde esta mi hermana?*" Gertie asks the woman. As she waits for an answer, she peers around the lobby, up the stairs leading to the rooms, and down the corridor meandering out toward the courtyard at the back of the hotel. They are not on the ocean like the alternate resort to which she and the girls have moved. *Qué verguenza*, she thinks inwardly, what a shame that they are not all together in the same place, by the ocean that has brought them together. "*¿¡Donde esta!?*" she repeats, slapping an open palm against the counter as if swatting a fly, unable to contain her excitement.

The woman points behind Gertie. She turns around to see a woman sitting at the far end of the lobby. The woman has the same golden highlights in her hair that Gertie has, though her hair is thicker than Gertie's and jet-black.

"*Hola, Gertie. Estoy aquí*," Sisi yells out, raising a hand.

Gertie slaps the counter again, squeals, swivels on her heel, both arms outstretched to receive Sisi, and strides through the lobby toward her. "*¡Dios mío!* Oh my goodness: there you are."

Sisi is taller and leaner than Gertie expected. Sisi stands to greet her. She has their father's dimple on her right cheek. Gertie had forgotten this: it doesn't show in photographs. She enfolds Sisi in a warm embrace within seconds.

"Goodness, Sisi," Gertie finally says, once she's eased Sisi out of her arms and holds her by the shoulders. "You're so much taller than I imagined!"

"And you're so much shorter!" Sisi notes, holding Gertie by her girth. At this, they both laugh.

Gertie beckons the two teenage girls over. They have not strayed far. She points out the thin, reed-like girl of the two— "This is my Manuella"—then points to the plumper, shorter girl, who puts out her hand tentatively. "This is her friend Katie, here for the ride." The girls giggle.

Ella steps forward and hugs Sisi fiercely, surprising her. "Hi, Tía. I've been hearing so much about you."

Gertie is elated by Ella's confidence. Sisi seems charmed, hugging Ella back.

"And where is my niece?" Gertie asks. "Where is your Emma?"

"She's here, somewhere." Sisi cranes her neck to look around the reception area. "Teresa," she says to the lady at the counter, "*¿has visto mi hija?*"

"*Sí, sí, señora. Están junto a la piscina, con mi hija.*"

Sisi releases Ella. "She's by the pool with Teresa's daughter." She turns to the teenagers. "You two can go on ahead and find her." The girls follow the arrows leading to the pool area. She turns to Gertie. "And we can start catching up over a *cafecito*, no?"

Gertie squeezes Sisi's arm excitedly. "*¡Porque no!* Yes!"

They sit down and Sisi orders the coffees from Teresa. Soon, a man in a white waiter's jacket trimmed with gold piping and buttons brings them two piping espresso cups and sides of sugar and cream. He smiles at them and, as he pulls back his tray, points to one and then to the other. "*¿Hermanas?*"

Gertie's hand flies up to her mouth. "Sisters? Yes. Well—"

"*¡Caray!* I see the family resemblance. Don't they look like sisters?" he yells over to Teresa. She smiles back, nodding. "Actually, we could all be cousins, isn't that so?" he says. The man's skin is what they call *café con leche* here, a light brown close to Sisi's, his hair cut short but betraying loose curls. He winks at Gertie, then leaves them. "Let me know if you need anything else."

Gertie is startled by their physical difference. Gertie is as short as Sisi is tall and looks more like her older sisters now. Gertie's hair is curlier but a lighter brown while Sisi's is jet-black with sprinkles of brown streaked through by the sun.

"Do you think we look alike?" Sisi asks Gertie.

Gertie laughs. "Not one bit," she says. "This is just something the locals like to say when two women are alone, so they can find out their status."

"Oh!" Sisi says. "I've been married so long that didn't occur to me!"

"Where is your husband, by the way?"

"Scott? Oh. He's in the room sleeping. We had such an ordeal the last days and we haven't acclimated yet. The heat is a bit much for him, though he was raised in the South."

"Ay," Gertie says, "an American." They laugh again, nervously. "I am so glad to see you," she continues. She wants to say: I have missed you so!

Sisi sips at her coffee. "It's been a long time."

"*Una vida.* A lifetime."

"Truly."

"I'm so sorry things started so badly. But this," Gertie says, looking around the lobby, "this is nice. Still," she insists, "it would have been nice to be at the same place."

"I just couldn't stay at that flophouse a minute longer, Gertie, especially with Emma along with us."

"Again, I'm sorry," Gertie replies. "But we can make a new start. The coffee is good, no?"

"Yes." Sisi nods. "This, at least, is the same: good strong coffee."

They sit in silence then, lost in thought.

Sisi changes the subject. "Your daughter is beautiful. She looks just like you."

"Oh." Gertie's eyes sparkle with delight. "She's my every joy. I can't wait to meet Emma!"

"You'll love her." Sisi smiles. "I think it's so great we could get them together like this. They'll make memories for a lifetime."

"Like we did, once upon a time," Gertie muses. "It's so strange that it was Andrée's obituary that brought us back together. It's as if she knew we might reconnect through it."

"I wouldn't give her so much credit."

"I shouldn't," Gertie agrees. "But speaking of serious things: Do you want to join us in the new resort? We're so sorry about what happened at the first place. We didn't know, didn't realize."

"Good God, I thought that stuff stopped happening long ago. Maybe it wasn't such a good idea to meet in the DR."

"Well," Gertie says, "this is where Papa was from. You have to claim your *dominicanidad*."

"Do I?" Sisi questions openly.

"I suppose not," Gertie concedes. "But I have so much to show you, places that Papa used to go, and the rest of the family. You'll be one of us in no time!" she declares. "We have an invitation to visit my brother—our brother—Rico, in Los Cacicazgos. He has a *huge* house! You'll love it! Do you remember him?" She does not give Sisi the chance to respond. She thinks of Freda, Papa's great-grandmother, their common ancestor, who came over the mountains of Haiti so long ago. She is wearing the locket, even now. Should she tell Sisi about it, about Freda? She decides not to in the moment. "If you won't move, you can at least come eat with us back where I'm staying with the girls."

"The food here is pretty good," Sisi says.

"Nonsense." Gertie gesticulates as if shooing away a fly. "I mean," she says, glancing at Teresa, who is staring back, "I'm sure it is *sabrosa*, but this is my treat, for your whole family. We'll thank the Simbi for bringing us back together, two rivers coming together into the ocean—the restaurant at the resort overlooks the sea!"

"You remember the story," Sisi says, surprised.

"Of course," Gertie responds, smiling. "I remember everything." She taps her head. "Like a tortoise."

GERTIE, MIAMI, 2002

GERTIE'S HEAD IS FOGGY WHEN SHE AWAKES IN HER room. She has been dreaming of when she was pregnant with Manuella, when she would dream of mermaids and a tall, stately, robed woman with a dagger at her waist and two scars on her face. She had wanted so much to understand, at first, what these symbols meant, but it has taken her a lifetime to accept, not to turn her back on things that matter, that make life easier to navigate.

Gertie's eyes fall on the chair where someone was sitting, talking to her, showing her a drawing. Had it been Emma, or Sisi? Whoever it was left a paper pad there, with a pencil and white rubber eraser nestled in the depression in the seat where Gertie used to sit to read books before bedtime. Manuel, when he was here, would chuckle to himself, wondering why she didn't avail herself of the coziness of the bed, but she fell asleep with the book in hand if she wasn't sitting up, so she insisted on a reading chair and made it her own. Sometimes, when she was free early from work, Manuel out and Ella long gone, she would retreat to it with a cup of tea on a bookshelf and read in the dimming afternoon light until it was time to get dinner together and see Manuel walk through the door. His shoulders would lift a bit when he saw that she was there and they wouldn't need to get takeout. She misses him dearly, every day.

Gertie squints to make out the drawing that has been left on the chair, facing out toward her. She finds herself looking at herself, as she is now, with all her wrinkles and lines. Age has not been kind, she thinks. Life is a strange journey of milestones and accumulations, inevitable shedding, loss. She, too, is bound to disappear.

Gertie hears muffled voices in the kitchen. She wonders who has come. She thinks she hears Sisi's voice, Ella's, Emma's, but before she can yell out to ask who is there, the door to her bedroom opens, bringing in a shaft of light, and then there she is, the person it seems to Gertie she has been waiting for all her life, not just these last months, holding Zuli purring contentedly in her arms.

It is Sisi, looking as she always has, despite wrinkles and gray hair, with that dimple in her right cheek.

"Hello, my Simbi," Gertie hears herself say. She meant to say "Hello, Sisi," but the Simbi are on her mind from her dream state, and so she repeats rather than corrects herself, "*Bonjou, Simbi. Koman ou ye, Sisi?* Please come in."

SANTO DOMINGO, 1979

SISI

At the Sunday brunch to which Gertie has invited them, Gertie relishes ordering for their table, making sure that Sisi, Scott, and the girls want for nothing. *"Aguacates, yuca con cebolla, locrio de verduras, empanadas de carne, sancocho, chivo guisado, batatas, plátanos maduros y pastelón de plátano maduro,"* she says to the waiter, pointing to the items on the menu.

"¿Ambos plátanos?" the waiter replies quizzically.

"Sí, sí," she insists, *"y morir soñando para las chicas."* She gestures toward her niece, Emma, and the teenage girls. "You are going to love this," she says to them. "You see, Sisi, I've ordered the sweet potatoes and the sweet plantains so you can eat the sweet with the salty like we do at home. And the *bananes pesées,* the pressed fried plantains. Those will come out first."

Home, Sisi repeats in her mind. So near yet so far. But she is pleased when, soon, the waiter brings out the plates of familiar-looking foods to the table. First come the fried plantains, flattened thinly so that they look like pressed sunflowers. Everyone takes a couple on their plate and drizzles a spicy sauce that resembles *pikliz* on top, eating with their hands. Emma smiles at Sisi while Scott helps himself by the handful. Sisi raps his knuckles playfully. Then comes everything else that Gertie ordered: sliced avocados, boiled cassava with sautéed onions, vegetable rice pilaf, beef patties, a beef stew, braised goat pieces, boiled pieces of white sweet potato, and the fried sweet plantains.

"*¿Algo más?*" the waiter inquires of Scott before retreating from the table. Scott's eyebrows jump. He does not understand, and his mouth is full.

"*Nada*," Gertie laughs, dismissing the waiter. "*Y es para mi*," she adds, indicating that the check is for her at the end of the meal. "*Voilà*," she says, "dig in, everyone! *¡Buen provecho!*"

Another waiter comes around with the *morir soñando* for the girls, while Scott opts for a local beer. Gertie orders *santo libre* drinks of white rum mixed with soda for herself and Sisi.

"Well," Sisi says, "to our long-overdue reunion."

Gertie nods, tears coming to her eyes as everyone raises their glass to toast. The girls raise their milky orange drinks.

"Oh wow," Emma exclaims as she tastes it, "this is just like a Creamsicle!"

"Told you," Manuella says, cracking up. "You're never going to want to leave."

Emma hands her drink to Sisi. "Try it. It tastes just like the orange-and-vanilla frozen treats you never want to get for my parties when I ask," she whines.

Sisi tries it. "Delicious." She winks at Gertie. "You've won her heart for life."

Scott is eating heartily. "Sisi, why don't you make more of this stuff at home? It's so good!"

Sisi flushes. "It's another world on this side," she responds, passing a distracted hand up her neck. "It's just not the same."

"But it's the same island, isn't it?" Scott persists.

"Not the same countries," Gertie intervenes, sensing a rising tension. "Not the same histories."

"Oh," Scott says, frowning, "right. I mean it's so close it would seem to me that you'd have more in common than not. You really should try to make more of these at home, Sisi. She's been cooking a lot of island dishes these days," he says to Gertie as if Sisi were not there. "She's a pretty good cook." He extends a hand to Sisi's wrist. Sisi flinches involuntarily under his show of pride.

"Well," Gertie says, "it would take forever to explain all the differences, the history." She glances at Sisi, "Why try? "Let's just enjoy what we can!"

Sisi is about to reply to Scott, but Gertie catches her eye; they exchange a glance and share an understanding that women the world over recognize the moment they are underestimated, pigeonholed. Cook. Mother. She grimaces, wondering why she didn't sever the cord as she had planned to at the beginning of last year. It dawns on her that it has to be for the same reason Gertie puts up with her siblings: it is simpler, and one needs the approval of these relations, of men in particular. It is easier than demanding anything for oneself.

The girls are talking animatedly to one another over the *morir soñando* and Scott exits the conversation with the sisters to serve the girls, taking over parental duties to leave them to talk, unaware of the discomfort he has provoked.

"Sorry about that," Sisi says over her *santo libre*.

Gertie bats her apology away. "Please," she says. "We have other things to talk about."

"It's been so long. Where do we start?"

"I don't know," Gertie says. "I wanted to start by apologizing again, face-to-face, about the obituary. The sisters should never have done that. I truly think they thought that it was a kind of repair, for what they did, for keeping us apart."

"Keeping us apart? We were the best of friends, weren't we?"

"The best of friends," Gertie says, affirmatively, taking a swallow of her *santo libre*.

"Yes. The best of friends," Sisi replies. "But as soon as you found out that we were sisters, you up and left me behind, like I was trash."

Scott looks up.

"Oh, no! Sisi!" Gertie exclaims, a hand coming up to her mouth. "No! I never thought this about you. Never! Don't you remember when I tried to speak to you at the recitation contest?"

"Well, your sisters did. I thought you stopped being friends with me because I was of a different class." She doesn't remember the contest Gertie is talking about.

Gertie's hand falls. "I can't deny that my sisters, and my brother, might have felt that way, Sisi."

"The brother you want us to meet here, in a few days?"

"Yes, Rico. You remember him?"

"I remember," Sisi says wryly, taking another gulp of her drink. "He chased us out of your house that day the girls bullied us at school."

"Make sure you eat," Scott says over Sisi's shoulder as he spoons rice pilaf onto her dish along with goat. "It's all so good."

Sisi starts to eat what Scott is dishing onto her plate.

"They were snobs is all there is to it," Gertie says. "They were. But they controlled every aspect of my life, and they were not kind. They thought that Papa loved me best, because I was the youngest, so they sent me away after his death, like a kind of punishment."

Sisi puts her drink down. "They sent you away?"

"Yes!" Gertie says. "Yes! And I'm pretty sure that they resented you, not just because you were an outside—" She glances up at the table, but no one is listening to their end of the conversation any longer. Scott is telling the girls jokes and they are giggling. "Not just because he had you with another woman," she rephrases, resumes, "but because you favored him."

"Were they really that shallow?"

"Yes, and more!" Gertie says. "You see, when I found out that we were sisters, I didn't know what that meant. And when the sisters forbade me to see you . . ."

"Forbade you?"

"Yes, forbade—and then sent me back to the school in Léogâne, and then out of the country, here to the DR, to finish high school, after the recitation contest. After that, all I could think of was that maybe you would turn out to be just like them, another bitter sister, and I couldn't handle that, not then."

"Thanks, Gertrude. As if I was ever unkind to you."

"No, you never were." Gertie thinks for a moment. "But I was a child, Sisi. I thought like a child. This is why I'm a social worker, because my own family is such a shambles. I don't know what else to say. My sisters really messed with my life." She stabs at a piece of sweet potato with a fork and stuffs it into her mouth.

"Do you still talk to Lou?" Sisi ventures, curious, but also wanting to get away from talking about Gertie's sisters.

"Oh," Gertie says, gesturing. "Once in a blue moon. I saw her a lot after I was sent back to Léogâne, and she talked about you, and Odette, so it felt like I was part of the group a little. That's how I knew you would both be at the recitation contest that year. But we haven't really kept up since she left the country. After we all left."

"Odette," Sisi says. "I haven't heard that name in a long time. It was a shock what happened to her. I think about her."

"Yes." Gertie halts. "I didn't understand how serious the situation was at the time. She came to my family for help, but I didn't understand what was happening."

Sisi stares at Gertie. "What do you mean she came to you? You mean you could have done something?"

"I don't know." Gertie swats a fly away from her plate of food. "She came to talk about the men harassing her family, but I didn't understand that one of them was after her or how it could end."

"What did she ask for?"

"Protection, I suppose, because, you know." She moves her fork above her plate. "The Alcindor name and all that. She thought we could do something, but the sisters didn't do anything. I didn't understand and the next thing I knew, she disappeared."

Sisi chews slowly, taking in the new information. "You could have talked to Lou."

"Maybe." Gertie frowns. "But like I told you, I didn't understand. I always wondered what I could have done differently."

Sisi thinks about the man and woman that she, Lou, and Samiah hid away in Paris those many years ago. Could the Gertie before her be the same little girl she had known who would have done anything to defend her, their friends, or did she grow up to be self-centered like her sisters?

"I'm sure you did the best you could," Sisi says, unconvinced.

Gertie continues, "I feel guilty about so much of what happened back then. Not talking to you before the sisters took me out to Léogâne, not forcing you to listen when I came to the contest, not helping Odette more when she asked for help. There were so many things I wasn't equipped to understand before I met Manuel and started to change my life, for the better, I think." Gertie smiles, seeking reassurance.

Sisi's mind overflows. The sisters prevented their friendship from flourishing. Gertie abandoned Odette. Who are they now, after all these years? She focuses on the food in front of her and slowly the conversation flows back to the table, to the girls exchanging information about their lives in the States, to Scott asking them mundane things like their favorite colors, animals, subjects in school, and Sisi, feeling the effects of the *santo libre*, glides on the flow of the lighter strain of conversation. Gertie follows suit.

After the meal, before they part ways, Gertie takes Sisi aside.

"Leave the girls with Scott one afternoon. Tell them to go to the beach and I'll take you to see someone who can counsel you on which road to follow."

Sisi wonders how Gertie knows, from just one glance at the beginning of the meal, that she stands at a crossroads. Is Gertie, too, seeking answers from the other side of the thin veil that separates the seen world from the unseen?

❄

"No sweetness," the woman says. A woman named Irís.

Gertie explained on the way to the working-class suburb on the edge of town that Manuel introduced them long ago, when they first met.

"No sweetness!" Irís exclaims as she slaps the marked, grooved surface of her wooden kitchen table with so much force that the small cups into which she poured them coffees jump up, then down, clattering in the saucers where each of them has been served a small sweet, *una dulcita*. *"No, no hay dulzura aquí."*

She makes a sweeping gesture toward Sisi. "The Simbi multiply, but you do not listen." The woman starts to weep, but it is a strange tearing. Tears fall from her eyes, but she does not seem to be crying at all. The woman does not wipe the tears away. "The Simbi implore you to get on your path."

Sisi observes that Irís's face is glowing: the tears shine against the dark brown of her skin like a luminescence.

The woman stops talking, takes a deep breath, turns her eyes on Gertie. "These words are for you too. If you do not understand the sweetness in front of you, you will lose it. All will turn to bitterness." She takes another deep breath: "Not all sweetness is sweet at first. You must be willing to dive into the depths, to places you do not understand."

She falls silent for a few long minutes, closes her eyes. Then Irís takes a sip of her coffee, looks at the both of them as if waking from a deep sleep. "Have they spoken? Is it over?" She wipes at her cheeks, surprised by the wetness there. "Why," she says, "must they always weep?"

In Sisi's mind, what happens after that first coffee is a little like the pulling of a loose thread from a knitted sweater, the kind she wears in winter in what she thinks of as the gray country, that place where she lives but has never fully found footing. The kind of loose string that makes everything unravel when you pull on it, leaving a gaping hole. The sort she does not know how to repair because she was not paying attention when her mother tried to teach her how to darn by placing a rubber ball beneath a yawning gap of fabric over which she crisscrossed a threaded needle until the hole disappeared.

GERTIE

Gertie is not paying attention when, having left the girls behind with Scott on another day, they drive into Los Cacicazgos. Rico's house is not just a house but a many-floored thing with land all around so vast that one cannot see the neighbors, a castle-like thing that has probably stood there since time immemorial or, at least, since colonial times. Rico is named for their father, but Sisi keeps forgetting this fact; call it amnesia or a resistance to nostalgia, Gertie doesn't know. They are kept waiting in a sitting room for guests and then brought into a formal room by a maid, wearing a maid's outfit, the kind that is dark gray or black, with a smock sewn in and tied to cinch at the waist. None of this strikes Gertie as unusual since she has been to her brother's house many times.

They are brought to a dining room. A table has been set and ladened with a sumptuous feast. Rico sits at one end and Gertie and Sisi are on either side.

"You didn't have to go to all this trouble," Gertie exclaims upon seeing the banquet.

Rico tut-tuts. "It's nothing," he says. "Simone deserves our best, does she not? We gave her so little! I'm just sorry my family isn't here." He continues, by way of explanation, "My wife and the kids are at the summer house." Gertie flushes despite herself, embarrassed. He turns to Sisi. "Simon-ey!" He booms her name. "We finally meet!"

"Simone," she corrects, and adds, "We've met before."

"Did we?" He frowns. "When would that have been?"

"At the gingerbread house in Port-au-Prince. When we were kids."

Rico searches his memory. "I don't remember this."

"You told us to get out before Andrée found her there," Gertie offers.

"Then the two of you chased us out," Sisi adds.

"Hmmm. I vaguely remember something of the sort." Rico strokes the barely perceptible stubble on his chin. Then his face breaks out in a grin, fissuring with folds the length of his cheeks. He looks uncannily like their father. "Of course. I remember now. Your sister—Margie, was it?—told Andrée off in the middle of the street. It was spectacular! A formidable woman, that sister of yours. Where is she now?"

"Miami."

"Like everyone," Rico says. "They have an enclave called Little Haiti there. You can find everything and everyone you need like you never left home. Where are you in the States?"

"Ohio."

"Ohio? That's nowhere to be! There's no one there—no one from the islands, in any case."

"I'm there with my husband. His job is there, at a university, and we have a daughter."

Rico opens his arms wide, to both sides of the table. "Why aren't they here? There's enough food for an army." He points to the food, indicating that they should serve themselves. "But it could be worse. If you were in Miami, you'd have to deal with the boat people. Sad scourge." Rico wags a finger in Sisi's direction, then gestures toward whichever side of the house points west to accuse Haiti of causing them untold calamities, as they always have.

Gertie looks across the table to Sisi beseechingly. She is so used to Rico's discourse that she has forgotten how distasteful it can be.

Sisi avoids Gertie's gaze. She drinks and eats what is served but will not be able to tell Scott, Emma, or anyone, later, how things tasted.

"Hush," Gertie hisses. "We're all Haitian here." But she speaks up too meekly. Sisi does not recognize her.

Rico stares at Gertie blankly, not used to being silenced. He clears his throat. "Well, *de toute façon*," he says, smiling stiffly, "we all emigrated years ago. Nothing to do with us."

Gertie's mouth is dry. She asks for water. The maid gets her some, but it does nothing to ease her parched throat, which closes up as Rico continues to talk, this time about Ella, asking her if his niece has changed at all since the last time he saw her?

He turns to Sisi. "Have you met our Manuella? A bit of a *garçon manqué*, a tomboy, is she not?" he intones in a voice honeyed with malice. He moves his hand above the table, like the current of a river, to indicate that Ella is a bit wishy-washy, unclear.

Gertie stiffens, stutters in her answer, as she glances at Sisi from the corner of her eye. "Fine," she says, "fine. Ella is absolutely fine. All American girls play baseball and wear their hair short and hang out with other girls all day and night long. It's to be expected, land of the free and all of that." She giggles nervously, makes her own gesture of the wrist into the air, as if to say *Que será, será*, like the popular song they all grew up with, an American import that suggested everything would be better, in the long run, if they lived "*à l'américaine*," and Gertie has done just this. She won't regret it now. But Gertie does regret having brought Sisi to the house, their brother's house. Why had she presumed that Rico might be on his best behavior? Why had she expected an Alcindor not to act like an Alcindor?

Rico blathers on, about his investments, the land he owns on both sides of the island, how business is booming at the bank, and they let him go on, without interruption.

Sisi asks for the bathroom abruptly and goes running to it as soon as the maid points her in the right direction.

Gertie runs after her and, from the hall, can hear Sisi throwing up the drinks, the breads, the beans and rice, the *pollo criollo*, the sauces, everything. Then the retching stops.

"Are you all right?" Gertie says to Sisi, her ear to the door, a hand gently resting on the doorknob. She imagines Sisi, relieved at last, sitting on the floor of the bathroom. It is a sparkling, white-tiled affair with a wide mirror hanging across a two-sink vanity with golden faucets, a claw-foot tub containing a hand-held shower with a golden head, fluffy towels slung over rods as if this were a hotel.

Gertie is afraid that Sisi thinks she brought her to show off, to show Sisi how the Alcindors were able to best the outside families, but it was the furthest thing from her mind.

"I need to go back to the hotel." Sisi's voice comes meekly through the door. "My head is pounding."

Rico arrives at the end of the hall. "She's probably not used to the water," he says matter-of-factly. "I'll have one of my drivers take you back."

He escorts them to the driveway and startles Gertie by embracing Sisi. She sees him slip a wad of 200-peso notes folded together into Sisi's jacket pocket. Gertie is about to protest when Rico catches her eye, chills her into abeyance. She is reduced to being the little sister, as always.

Back at the hotel, Gertie confides to Teresa that Sisi has taken ill. Teresa has them wait at the front counter for a moment as she checks whether she has another room for Sisi separate from Scott and Emma's in case the malaise lasts all night. She does and she helps Gertie take Sisi to the room.

"*No te preocupes,*" she says to Gertie. "We can get her mangoes to ease the stomach pains. I will have bottled water brought to her."

Gertie nods. "*Gracias para todo,* Teresa." To Sisi she says, "Don't worry, I'll be back in the morning and we'll take care of you."

Food poisoning? The water? The conversation? Check. Check. Check, Gertie thinks as she returns to the resort after recovering Ella and Katie from Scott and explaining to him what has happened. She leaves out Rico's comments about Haitians, his slights toward Ella. She apologizes profusely for returning Sisi in such terrible condition and reassures him that she will be there to help in the morning. The trip is making Sisi ill, and it is not over yet. Gertie hopes that Sisi won't find the peso bills or that, when she does, she won't remember how they got there.

No, this has not turned out to be a good idea at all.

SISI AND GERTIE, MIAMI, 2002

AS SOON AS SISI ENTERS GERTIE'S DARKENED ROOM, Zuli, the calico who warmed to her instantly, jumps out of her arms and heads straight to Gertie's bed, where she nestles against Gertie, purring. Gertie puts out a hand to pet the cat as she looks up at Sisi, who is going about the room, opening up the curtains to let light in.

"Do you want me to open the windows?" Sisi asks Gertie. "It's a bit stuffy in here."

"As you like but maybe just a crack," Gertie says. "I get cold quickly." She has lost weight rapidly since the operation of a few months ago, the follow-up treatments. As the pounds shed, Gertie careens closer and closer to the seam between life and death, like the invisible crease between ocean and sky, water and shore. She knows it will be over soon and all she wanted in her final moments was to see Sisi again, in the flesh, to close the one chapter of her life that remained ajar, like a yawning door that resists closure.

Sisi walks around the room, taking care to sidestep any medical equipment, to stay clear of the prescription bottles that crowd on a side table next to the bed. She leans over the waist-high bookcases to heave up the blinds, crack open the windows, and sniff at the fresh air wafting into the room though it is hot, humid. Better than nothing, Sisi thinks.

"You're just like a cat," says Gertie.

"Like a cat?" Sisi inquires, as she inspects the books in the cases.

Gertie laughs weakly. "They always smell the air when I open the windows and like to sit on top of the cases."

"Oh," Sisi says. "I wouldn't know. I don't have cats."

"Well," Gertie continues, "I see you've met Zuli."

Sisi turns around, a book in her hand. "I certainly have. She's beautiful."

Zuli looks up and makes a high-pitched sound as if participating in the conversation. Gertie laughs. "And she likes to talk, as you can see! I don't know where Fredi is, but you'll meet him in due time."

"How many do you have?" Sisi asks, settling into the armchair next to the bed with the book she has taken from the case.

"Just the two," Gertie says. "I got them after Manuel passed away. I needed the company."

"I understand. I'm sorry about Manuel. I should have reached out, called."

Gertie dismisses the apology with the gesture of her hand. "Emma sent your condolences and hers through Ella. We received the card."

Sisi didn't know that Emma sent a card on their behalf, but she nods as if she did. What would she do without Emma? She's raised a daughter with more grace than she has, for which she is thankful. "Still," she says, "I'm sorry. According to what Ella relayed through Emma, he seemed a lovely man and a good father."

"That he was," Gertie responds. "But God gives and God takes away. Isn't that what they say?"

Sisi nods. They are silent for a moment. "Before I forget—I have something for you." She leaves the room and returns with a frame wrapped in butcher paper.

"What is it?"

"You'll have to open it and see." She sets the papered object on the bed between them. "Shall I help you?"

They unfold the paper together to reveal Sisi's painting of a village weaver in all its brilliant color, peering out of a hanging nest of woven leaf strips. She had been working on it when Gertie called her a few months ago, a commission. In the end, prompted by her daughter, she decided to give it to Gertie instead, paint another for the person who had placed the order. "It's not a tody, but I thought you would like it."

"I love it." Gertie smiles. "You've brought me a portrait of Papa."

They break out laughing.

The door to the room opens. Ella's head ducks in. "Everything all right in here? Or do we have to separate you two?"

"We're fine," Gertie replies, her laughter turning into hiccups.

"What's so funny?"

"We were just talking about your grandfather."

Emma appears at the door. "It's a party," she says, smiling when she sees her mother's village weaver.

Sisi nods at Emma. "You were right: she likes it."

"Mama," Ella interjects gently, "I think you both need to get rest. Sisi just arrived and she'll be here all week. There'll be more time to talk." She turns to Sisi. "Emma and I set you up in the guest room. Emma will be in my old room. Let's show you where everything is."

Sisi sets down the painting on the seat behind her. "You're right, girls. We're acting like two little kids."

Gertie indeed looks like the little girl who Sisi met long ago in a first-grade classroom, gazing over her shoulder at her crude drawing. Sisi goes over to Gertie's side, squeezes her hand, and pets Zuli's head. "I'll be back, and we can continue our conversation then." Sisi feels Gertie squeeze her hand back before letting go. She follows Emma out of the room to the hallway as Ella goes back into her mother's room to make sure that Gertie takes her next doses of medicine.

"She's nice, isn't she?" she hears Ella say to Gertie, but she doesn't hear Gertie's answer as she and Emma walk down the hall to the guest room.

Sisi is very, very tired, and she is relieved to find all her things nicely put away, the bed turned down. Emma leaves her and she changes into bed clothes and slips between the bedsheets, taking in their scent of fresh laundry, which reminds her, somehow, of the house near the port where she grew up, of Momo, Mami, Margie. Sheathed in the sensation of being home, she falls into a deep, tranquil sleep.

SISI AND GERTIE, SANTO DOMINGO, 1979

Nothing is as sweet as the first *cafecito*, the first exchange, the first peace.

It takes a few days for Sisi to recover from the visit to Rico's. When she feels better physically, she takes a few days longer for herself in the new room. The past several days swirl in her mind. She attempts to digest all the new information she has received: that it was Gertie's older sisters who kept them apart, whisked Gertie away out of the city, then out of the country, that Gertie could have helped Odette but didn't, that Gertie's family remained the same—Rico is the proof of that, self-involved, haughty fool of prejudice. She discovered folded 200-peso bills in her coat pocket a few days after returning from Los Cacicazgos and surmised they came from him, as if she were a pauper, one of the ghosts that took the used shoes they used to leave outside the door of the Rue Bonne Foi house, free for the taking. The bills made her livid but it was too late to confront Rico about them. Neither can she take them to Gertie and ask her what kind of an imbecile her brother is so she gives the money to Teresa, to cover the charge for the extra room, though the bills are an inadequate expression of her gratitude.

Gertie never brings up the visit to Rico, avoids any mention of the Alcindors. Why did he say all those things, about Haitian boat people, immigrants, her daughter—his niece! He was letting Sisi know, and her too, what he thought of Papa's outside children, where he placed them. Yet Gertie did not stand up to him, meekly rebuffed some of what he said, about her own daughter, but did not rail against him the way Sisi has seen her face other bullies. When it comes to her siblings, Gertie has no fight.

As their stay in the DR nears its end, Emma asks Sisi out of the blue if girls can have other girls as girlfriends the way they have boyfriends, and Sisi doesn't think anything of it. Without missing a beat, she says, "Of course, yes, why not?" Scott raises an eyebrow but doesn't say anything. He is trying to decipher the local paper, which he reads daily, though his Spanish is not strong.

Emma is pleased by the answer. "Carmen, Teresa's daughter, says that Ella and Katie are girlfriends," she says. "I think they are too."

"Well," Sisi says, absent-mindedly, "it's the age." Why did she say that? But by the time they are all dancing merengue on the dance floor of the resort, on the final night of their ten-day stay, swaying along with the crowd, moving to the drumbeats that remind her of her younger self, of home, of the Expo, Sisi wishes she'd paid more attention to things both subtle and large.

She sees Ella and Katie moving closer and closer to each other, until they are just one wave among many. Ella's face edges closer to Katie's and Sisi sees herself, long ago, listening to a similar rhythm, in a crowd not unlike this one. She watches Ella and Katie as if watching herself and Lou. She thinks of how she chose Scott, or let herself be chosen by him, simply because he was the safe alternative. At the time, it all seemed so simple: marry Scott, follow Scott, move to the US to be with Scott, to America, a clean gray slate. She thinks about how Ella and Katie might be able to have any life they desire. She hears the merengue beat and the laughter as the people dance around the girls, whose skirts she loses from view in the throng. This is happiness, or a form of it.

From nowhere, she sees Gertie emerge, cutting through the throng. Gertie reaches for her daughter and her friend, plunging upon them like a bird of prey.

Sisi watches herself following Gertie through the crowd. "*Non,*" Sisi says, slipping absent-mindedly into French. "*Non. Ne fais pas ça.* Don't do that." Her hand falls upon Gertie's forearm, wrenches it free from Ella's shoulder.

Gertie looks at Sisi in surprise. "*Hein,*" she hisses. "*C'est pour leur bien.* It's for their own good," she continues, also speaking to Sisi in French when all this time, they have been speaking English, with smatterings of Spanish, like gringas. She looks around the dance floor. The dancers have resumed their gyrations once they hear French, assume another family drama is playing out on the dance floor: it is none of their business. Arms and legs flow to the beat, to the scraping of the *güira*, closing the passageway that Gertie forged. Gertie and Sisi stand, trapped, in the middle of the floor, surrounded.

"*Je m'en fout.* I don't care," Sisi replies. "*Tout le monde s'en fout.* Nobody cares; they're tourists."

"But I care." Gertie is appalled, pulls her arm back. "What kind of a mother are you? We have to protect them."

But what has such protection ever gotten anyone? thinks Sisi. She slips further into Kreyòl. "*Pwoteksyon?* For what? *Tankou ou te pwoteje Odette?* Like you protected Odette?"

"*Kisa?* What?" Gertie swirls to face Sisi as if struck. "I told you that I didn't know what to do. I was just a kid. This is not the same. That's my daughter, Sisi. Would *you* let . . ."

"Yes, Gertie. Yes, I would." Sisi's mind is whirling. Don't you protect those you love no matter what the situation? Isn't love itself worth protecting? "You'll just drive her away, Gertie," Sisi pleads. "Like your sisters drove me away."

The girls are standing apart, dazed, watching their mothers fighting from the side of the dance floor. Ella holds on to Katie by her pinky. Emma stands a little farther away, off the dance floor, Scott behind her, his hands on his daughter's shoulders.

Gertie looks at all of them. She has ruined everything. Rico's words about her daughter from a few days ago ring in her ears. She is overcome with a desire she cannot place to live up to the Alcindor name when what she should have done was discard the feeling.

"They're just girls. Just girls," Sisi says. "Not all that's sweet looks like sweetness." Sisi reminds Gertie of Irís's words, the tears of the Simbi warning them of what was to come, what is.

"You've got everything mixed up," says Gertie. But Gertie remembers the dreams she used to have before Ella was born, the dream of the goddess whose dagger turned miraculously into a flaming sunflower once she accepted the child for who it was. This is the waking world, she tells herself. Things are different here. Not everything can be accepted.

"*Non*," Sisi says. "It's you who's got everything mixed up. You don't understand how love works. You never have."

"You're wrong," Gertie says. "You're wrong about that."

"So get this right. Your future—her future," Sisi says, gesturing to Ella, "depends on it." She collects her things from the table they sat around before the dance began.

"You can't leave like this," Gertie says, watching her.

"I'm done, Gertie. *Fini*. This was a terrible idea. I don't know who you are. Maybe I never knew, but the girl I used to know wouldn't do what you're doing now, wouldn't allow her brother to speak to her, or to me, the way he did, wouldn't care what other people think."

Sisi turns her back on Gertie, pulling Scott and Emma, who haven't understood a thing of their exchange, along with her. She is tired. Tired of everyone. *No sweetness*. Meeting Gertie all these years later, she thinks, was like being confronted with the Alcindors at the foot of their father's bed, all the worst parts of them.

They leave the island the next day, neither Sisi nor Gertie talking to each other. Sisi wants to leave and never return, to bury the past. Gertie is happy that they aren't staying in the same hotel after all.

Nothing turns out to be as sweet as the first *cafecito*, the two of them alone in the sitting area, away from everyone, without Scott, without the girls. The yarn keeps unraveling, the hole getting wider and wider, a gaping hole that neither wants to look at: it horrifies them, the inevitability of it, its tangibility. They are strangers.

SISI AND GERTIE, MIAMI, 2002

SISI AWAKES IN A ROOM SHE DOES NOT RECOGNIZE. IT takes her a few moments to remember the drive to Gertie's home from the airport. Ella picked them up; Sisi hardly recognized her at first. Ella is now in her late thirties. The last time she saw her in person, Ella was a teenager. The sight of Gertie diminished in her bed, thin and wiry, rather than the flight, exhausted her. Sisi stirs, sits up, and finds that she is not alone: on the edge of the bed lies a black cat. Fredi, she thinks, Gertie's other cat, the one no one could find the night prior.

"Cutie," she says to the cat, as if it were his name.

Fredi squints at her and makes a small, hardly audible chirping sound. Sisi lets him be. She is comforted by his presence as she contemplates the week ahead.

Sisi was compelled to come by Emma and Ella's combined efforts. The two remained in touch after the DR trip. In the years after the trip, Sisi demurred when it came to speaking directly to Gertie. She was tired of the Alcindors then, their lofty ways, as if the air they breathed was somehow purer than what was available to the rest of them. They crossed the Haiti-DR divide easily and didn't think much about politics on either side. Like Scott, they thought everything was interchangeable. But she had not allowed Gertie to fully explain herself or make amends, Ella pointed out. Ella added that the fact that she and her wife were helping Gertie in her final days was proof that Gertie had evolved. If Ella didn't hold anything against her, why should

Sisi? When the girls started talking about how little time Gertie had left, Sisi was suffused with a guilt she didn't know she would feel. She had questions about Papa, whom she never knew the way she thought Gertie did, that lingered. If she didn't go, she surmised, she would forfeit the opportunity to complete the puzzle, to click in the missing pieces of her own life.

Sisi listens to the sounds of younger women moving in the kitchen, to the preparations for breakfast, spoons clinking against the sides of bowls, knives scraping butter onto toast. The scent of percolating coffee drifts into the guest room, awakening memories of long ago when she first arrived at Lou and Samiah's apartment in Paris. She is about to see them soon, also, bought herself a ticket to Paris with Emma's help. She closes her eyes. She will regret nothing about her life. She has Emma, her life in Arizona. Her work, her art, makes life full, and she is surrounded by friends, other artists, with similarly displaced and dislocated lives.

A curly head of hair appears at her door. "Hello," says a young woman with a long, pointed face and high cheekbones, a lilt in her voice that hints at a Spanish inflection. "I'm Reina, Ella's partner? Did you want to join us for breakfast?"

The young woman is chestnut brown, a mixed-race woman like Emma. Sisi graciously accepts. "Of course. Let me just get myself to a presentable state." She clutches the sheets to her chest.

"Take your time," Reina says warmly, and as she starts to close the door, adds, "We're all just family here."

Sisi smiles to herself. All just family. What a phrase. There was never anything simple about being family after the moment of revelation at her father's deathbed. Before that, life was idyllic. She loved her small family. But nothing was ever quite the same, after.

Sisi hurries to get ready for the day, joining the younger women in the kitchen. She finds Emma there, sketching portraits of Ella and Reina from across the table as they eat. Emma sips at her coffee as she sketches. Sisi looks over her daughter's shoulder the way Gertie peered over hers long ago. But she finds nothing wanting in Emma's work. She has become a fine artist. Sisi squints at the details, then places a proud hand on Emma's free shoulder. She looks up at Ella and Reina. "You're going to love these." They nod, agreeing, a cooing brood. "Is your mother up?" she asks Ella.

"She's been up for a while. She wakes early from the effects of the medication."

"Or age," Sisi adds, thinking of her own early mornings.

"She's eager to see you. You can go in if you want and we'll bring your breakfast in."

"I can do that?"

"Of course. You're home here," Ella says.

Home. Sisi has remade home over and over in her life. She thinks of her mother's house, a house to which she has never returned. She nods at Ella. "Thank you."

Gertie is sitting up in her bed. Sisi can see that she has made an effort to dress for the day. Her hair is tidied under a colorful wrap matching her housedress. "I would get up," she says, "but you know . . ." She shows the IV drip going into her arm. "Medication."

Sisi didn't notice the IV yesterday. "Oh," she starts, "I can come back—"

Gertie motions her in. "Come in, Sisi, come in. Do you think I'm going to let this slow me down?" She shows Sisi how the medicine clicks in and out of a plastic port a few inches below her armpit in the fleshy part of the underside of her arm. "Snaps right out when done, like magic. Who would have thought they could invent things like this when we were young?"

Sisi enters the room, closing the door behind her. "I see someone opened your windows today." She goes to the armchair on the other side of the bed.

"The girls are attentive."

"I met your daughter-in-law," Sisi adds.

"Yes, Reina." Gertie smiles, her eyes bright. "She's sweet, isn't she?"

"Dominican?"

"Colombian."

"Ah." Sisi smiles. "Good for Ella."

"Yes." Gertie nods. "I'm happy for her."

"You are?" Sisi asks, cautiously.

"Yes, of course. I never had anything against it, Sisi."

"That's not the impression I had."

"I know. I know. But it was the circumstances. I was just trying to protect her back then. I didn't know what else to do." Gertie coughs. "It wasn't that I didn't want Manuella to be who she was . . . who she is." She pauses. "I wanted to protect her. From people like my brother, from the islanders. From the world, for God's sake. You know how it is! You of all people should know."

Does Gertie know about Sisi and Lou? Does she know everything that Sisi has worked so hard to stifle?

"Of all people?"

"Being an outside child—"

"Come on, Gertie," Sisi says, offended. "After all this time you think in these antiquated ways? I wasn't outside of anything. We had the same father, but I had my own family. I was *in* my own family."

Gertie nods. "Let's not have a disagreement, Sisi. I'm so glad you're here, that you came all this way. It means so much to me."

Sisi shrugs. "I felt strange that whole trip."

"It wasn't what you expected."

"No. I thought the other side of the island would be the same, or similar, but so many things were a shock to my system, the way we were treated at the resort, the food, then the revelations

about the sisters, Odette . . ." Sisi's voice trails off. "The way your
brother talked about Haiti, about Ella," she resumes. "The whole
time was like being in a fun house, in a hall of mirrors. That's
how it felt."

"I wasn't thinking straight. I had a notion that family meant
something. That you could become part of mine."

"Well, I could have."

"You think?"

"Not the way you think. I didn't want to be part of the
Alcindors, but I could have been part of your family, with Manuel and Ella."

"I don't know why I didn't think of that then."

"You were trying to have your family make up for the harm
they caused, but that wasn't your job. We were sisters. We are
sisters. We could have been that to one another."

"I don't know what I was thinking. But look, Sisi." Gertie
points to a row of thin books on a bookshelf next to her.

Sisi follows Gertie's pointing hand and sees all the picture
books she has managed to publish since *Owls' Nest*, all ten of
them.

"You know, I published *Owls' Nest* shortly after the DR trip.
In a way, if things hadn't gone so wrong on that trip, with you,
with Scott, I wouldn't have had the courage to follow through,
to leave Scott, to join Emma in Southern California, and then to
keep finding my way. So I should thank you." Sisi tips an invisible hat in Gertie's direction. "But these books are for kids. You
didn't have to keep buying them."

"And why not?" Gertie chuckles to herself. "You're my sister
even if you don't want to be claimed. That's how I feel. I'm proud
of you. I wanted to support you. I bought them for myself, to
track what you were doing. I bought copies for friends with children over the years, depending on their ages. Emma and Reina
are thinking of having their own now, so they'll get my set, and

the painting you brought." She points to Sisi's village weaver, propped up against the chair where Sisi left it.

Gertie pursues, "*Owls' Nest* helped me to understand that loving someone can be a choice, you know? People like to say that you have no choice in who you love, but when I read your book and thought of your relationship with Emma, I realized that love is not just a matter of family responsibility, or a lightning bolt." She laughs softly. "It's an active decision. I wanted that for myself, for Ella, and though it took me a while to say no to my family, to just sitting there when my brother or someone else in the family says the things they do, I finally stopped going to their gatherings, and if I did, I told them what they could do with their remarks. You should have seen their faces when I started doing that."

"When was this?"

"Oh, maybe a few years after the trip. It took me a while to get the courage. But I got your book, and I thought about all the changes you were making. I had Manuel for an example. Every time someone called him '*el Haitiano*,' he didn't correct them. It's how we met, you know? He was proud to be Black Dominican, and not at all ashamed of having a Haitian wife. Sisi, it took me so long to get rid of the shame, so long. Can you forgive me?"

Sisi deflects the question, returns to the conversation about the trip to the DR. "A fun house. Almost every moment, except when we saw the seer. What was her name again?"

"Irís. She was Ella's godmother."

"Was?"

"She passed away a few years ago."

"Like Margie."

"Yes. I was sorry to hear about Margie. I always envied your having her for your sister. I envied you."

"She's gone but she comes to me."

"Comes to you?"

"Before she passed, I asked her to come to me when she could. She said she'd come in yellow. I saw her the day you called about all this, in my garden. A yellow butterfly."

"Should I come to you too, after?"

"Perhaps."

"What should I come as?"

Sisi shrugs. "Maybe something green?"

Gertie chortles. "That was always my color."

"Indeed." They giggle.

"You know," Sisi chooses her words carefully, returning to Gertie's question earlier. "Is it our father, maybe, that we need to forgive? But if he hadn't done what he did, we wouldn't be here. We might not have created the families we did."

"Time helps things. You helped things," Gertie adds.

"Me?"

Gertie motions to Sisi's books on the shelf. "*Owls' Nest*, for instance."

Sisi blushes. "Small thing."

"No, Sisi. Not for me. Losing you again after the trip to the DR made me think about all the things, the people, the connections I didn't want to lose in the future. You don't know how I've longed for this day."

"And here we are—old ladies."

"Not that old, Sisi. Never too old to make amends. Never too old to understand love better. I had Manuel too."

"Was he your true love?" Sisi finds herself asking.

"Ah," Gertie says, "true love. I don't believe in such things, really. And why should there be just one true love? There was Papa, for me, then Manuel. There's Ella and . . ." She pauses, "There was you."

"Me?" Sisi asks, incredulous. "Why me?"

"I just loved—love—you in a pure, spontaneous way, like a kindred soul. Even when I stopped seeing you every day as we did when we were in school, I thought about you all the time. I wondered how you were and what you were doing, wished for your every happiness. Isn't that what love is, in the end, wanting another's happiness without any thought of our own?" Gertie observes Sisi, wanting to know if Sisi thought about her in the same way all this time. "What about you, Sisi? Who was it for you?"

"Well, certainly not Scott," Sisi blurts out. The two women laugh. Sisi realizes that she remained in Gertie's consciousness, was not altogether forgotten, while Gertie's disappearance had been for her a quicksand, leaving nothing on the surface for her to contemplate. The more time passed, the less Sisi thought about what might be beneath: she allowed Gertie's memory to fade.

Sisi resumes, "I didn't mean it quite that way. I think I married Scott to get away from the past, to get a clean slate, and I was his way of stepping out of his family's expectations, but things withered a few years after Emma's adoption. We had nothing in common." She sits contemplatively for a moment. Gertie waits for her to gather her thoughts; she continues, "I would say Emma, of course, and there was Lou." There, she said it out loud, to someone, finally.

"Lou?" Gertie asks.

"Yes, Lou." Sisi fills in the blank. "She became one of my best friends after you disappeared. I know you two didn't keep up much after leaving Haiti, but we did. It's with her I stayed when I landed in Paris."

"Oh," Gertie says, placing an index finger to her mouth. "Of course, Lou, the Lombardos. They had a shop in the center of the port. I used to see Lou when the Lombardos came to their house in Léogâne."

At that moment, the door to the room opens, and they fall silent. Ella brings in Sisi's breakfast on a tray, all her favorite things, café au lait, a croissant with marmalade. Sisi's eyes sparkle with delight. "How did you . . . ?"

Ella sets the tray down. "We asked Emma. She told us everything we needed to know."

"Not quite everything," Gertie says, as Ella leaves the room. "Lou: You loved her?"

"Yes. And not like you love a sister." They titter.

"Ah," Gertie says. She reaches for a glass on her side table and takes a long draw of water. "But nothing came of it?"

"She left Haiti at the beginning of the regime and when I caught up with her in France, she was married, more or less."

"To?" Gertie asks. "This is something she never shared with me."

Sisi's eyebrows arch; she wasn't the only one to keep to herself, after all. "To a beautiful woman, Samiah. They were happy. I was happy for her. Maybe you're right that wanting another's happiness is the true measure of love."

"And no one since then?"

"No one of importance," Sisi says. "I don't find myself missing anything or anyone. Maybe if I was younger, I would be more daring, but I'm not that brave, Gertie. That was my problem. I did what I could: *Owls' Nest* came out and did well. And then a few years later, Emma and I were watching the departure of the Duvaliers on TV and all I could think of was: Move, Sisi, move. Do something, move forward, leave Scott, work on your illustrations, live where you want to, watch Emma come into herself. I did all that, even if it took me close to a decade to do it. But once I decided to change, my life became full in a way I could not have imagined when I still resided in a place of fear. I've had a full life. I have a full life."

"Well, Sisi," Gertie replies, "that isn't nothing."

"I wonder . . ." Sisi's voice trails off.

"Yes?" Gertie asks eagerly, running her hands over the bedsheets.

"What Papa was like, really like, when he was at home, every day."

"Papa?" Gertie laughs. "Oh, my. You know, Sisi, you think he was with us all the time, but he wasn't. He had as many households as would have him."

"Why do you think he was like that?"

"I don't know. Because men can do as they like, I suppose. Because he was a child of Ochún."

Sisi nods, remembers the green candles they used to light for Papa after his passing. "How did your mother deal with it?"

"She didn't. That was her trouble," Gertie says. "This is hard to say about one's own parents, but I think it was a marriage of convenience. He married her for her money, and she married him to lighten the color of her children." She laughs. "I was the surprise."

"I understand the part about a marriage of convenience. I guess this is what Scott and I did."

They are both lost in thought for a time. Sisi busies herself with her breakfast. Gertie watches her. She has never studied Sisi so closely, and it dawns on her that Sisi has features belonging to a face she has seen before. "Sisi," she says, "would you get something for me?"

"Sure." Sisi nods. "Do you want me to call Ella?"

"No," Gertie replies, "it's right here in this room, if you go over to the dresser." Gertie points to a chest of drawers against the wall, facing the bed. "Top drawer, to the left, you'll find a small jewelry box."

Sisi rises carefully from her chair, setting the tray with her half-eaten breakfast atop one of the bookshelves. She walks over to the dresser, opens the indicated drawer, and rummages around until her hand falls on a box. She starts to take it over to Gertie.

Gertie beckons her back to the side chair. "It's for you."

Sisi opens the box to reveal a silver locket. "What is it?"

"Open it, Sisi, you'll see."

Sisi does as she is told, lifts the locket and its trailing chain out of the box. The locket has been well cared for, the silver polished. The hinge is slightly chipped. She cracks open the locket, then gasps at what she sees. "Who is this, Gertie?"

"I thought you would like to have it."

Sisi stares at the fading image nestled within the locket. She can see her father in the features, Gertie, Ella. Most of all, though, she sees herself.

"Papa gave me this locket around the time we met, when I was having a bad time at one of the older sisters' weddings in the DR. I kept being mistaken for a servant's daughter."

"Really?"

"It was painful. I had forgotten how much so until you went to the resort and something similar happened with you. This is Freda. She's our ancestor. Papa told me she came over the mountains from the DR to Haiti long ago. We all go back to her. He wanted me to know where my color came from. I think I figured out that she was where my tenacity comes from, my desire to be connected to you. I have her color, her smile, Papa's smile. You have her eyes, her forehead, maybe other things I never got to know."

Sisi looks up from the locket to Gertie with tears in her eyes. "Don't you want to give it to Ella?"

"She's seen it all her life. I've talked to her about this, and she wants you to have it. Besides, you'll stay in touch, won't you?" Gertie looks at Sisi anxiously. "You can give it to Emma someday, and the girls will decide who gets it next. We're all family."

"Gertie," Sisi says, moved to silence. She looks at Freda more closely, wonders what this woman might have thought when she sat for the portrait.

Sisi closes the locket on the image, opens the clasp of the chain, and hangs it around her neck. She goes to the mirror to look at the locket hanging on her chest, surveys the lines of age etching the fading brown of her face.

"Freda doesn't look like me, Gertie," she says, "but she does look like someone I see in the mirror every day."

SIMBI SLEEPS

Sisi is wearing the locket when the call comes. It is Ella: Gertie has passed. Sisi feels a sharp pain in her chest as she receives the news that she knew would come since the moment she left Gertie's side to head to the airport after their visit.

She is in her garden when she takes the call. Her hand flies up to the locket and grasps it. *Freda*, she says to herself, silently, closing her eyes, *take care of Gertie as she comes to you. Take care of Papa.* She imagines her loves assembled, somewhere, elsewhere, watching out for one another, and watching over the living. *Margie, look out for Gertie.*

Sisi opens her eyes, and as she does so, a green dragonfly with translucent wings flits by and above her lavender bushes. Then the cats, Fredi and Zuli, saunter by. She took them both after finding out that Gertie wanted her to have them, for company, after. She pets Fredi.

The dragonfly swoops above and away, then back toward Sisi and the cats, then edges away, toward the sky.

"Hello, Gertie." Sisi watches as the dragonfly hovers. Zuli sits up and watches her too.

"Goodbye, love," says Sisi. "Goodbye, sister."

Fredi purrs beneath Sisi's hand.

ACKNOWLEDGEMENTS

WRITING IS SOLITARY BUT IT TAKES A VILLAGE TO GET a book into the world. I want to thank the following for being that village for this book:

My editor, Masie Cochran, for believing in this story from the moment it was mentioned to her as a germ of an idea.

The team at Tin House: Win McCormack, Craig Popelars, Nanci McCloskey, Becky Kraemer, Beth Steidle, Jacqui Teruya, Anne Horowitz, and Rebecca Munro and everyone there working tirelessly to bring words to the world.

My partner in all things, Natália Affonso de Oliveira Assumpção (yes, all the names), first and last reader, for accommodating characters and their lives at all hours of day and night.

Maya, for showing up for the work, and for overseeing animal representation in the work.

My family, those known and unknown.

And, as always, to the ancestors and to the *lwa* for their guidance and blessings.

LOS ANGELES, CA